Fall the Fragile Hearts

All the Fragile Hearts

M.T. Solomon

Fox Poppy press

Copyright © 2023 by M.T. Solomon

All rights reserved. Printed in the United States of America. No part of this book may be used or reproduced in any manner without written permission except in the case of brief quotations embodied in critical articles or reviews.

This book is a work of fiction. Names, characters, businesses, organizations, places, events and incidents either are the product of the author's imagination or are used fictitiously.

ISBN: HB : 979-8-9879420-0-0 ; PB : 979-8-9879420-1-7 ; EBOOK : 979-8-9879420-2-4

Cover design by Etheric Tales

First Edition: May 2023

1

For information contact:

www.themtsolomon.com

To my Champion:
I love you Joseph.

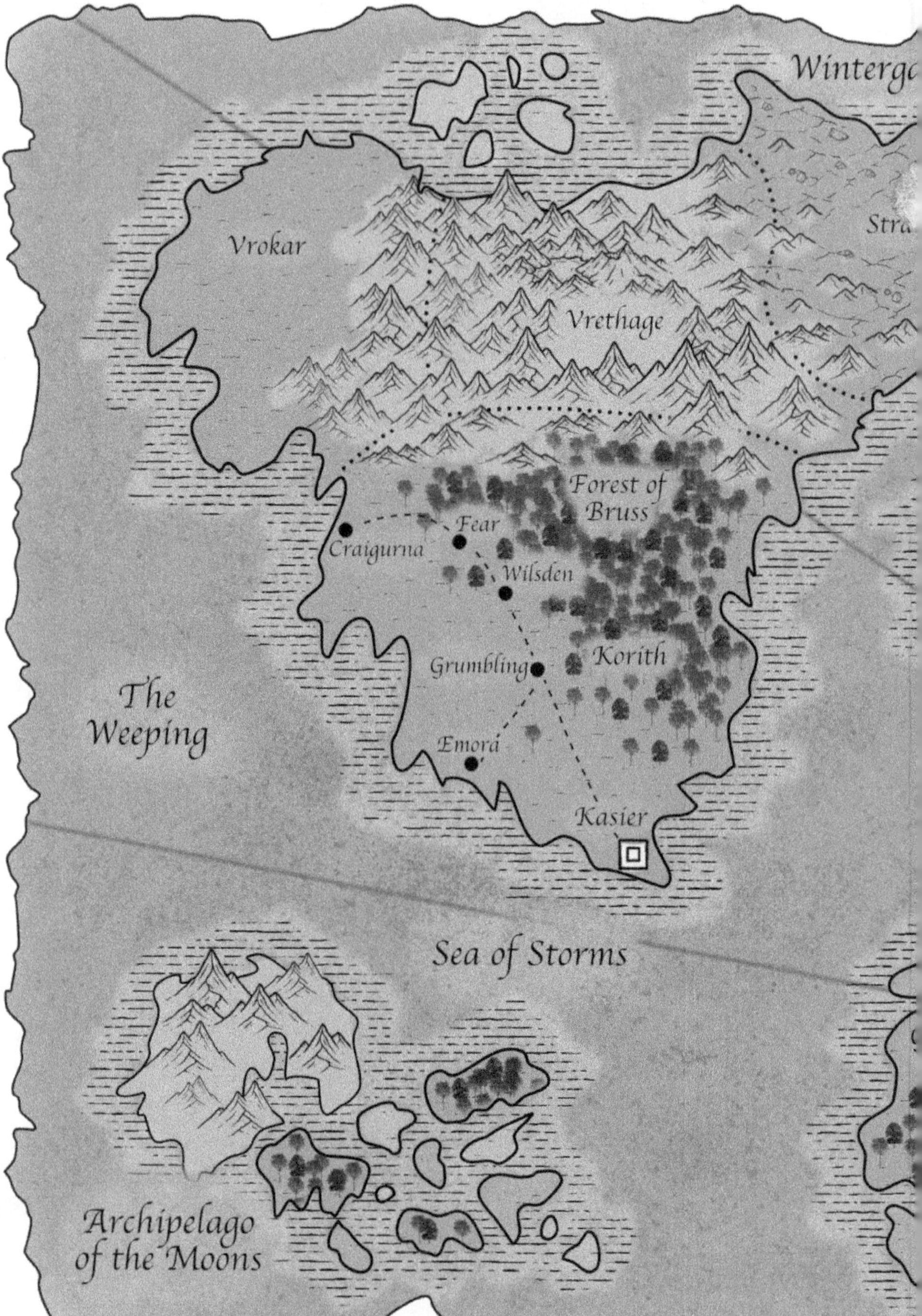
Winterga
Vrokar
Stra
Vrethage
Forest of
Bruss
Fear
Craigurna
Wilsden
Korith
Grumbling
The
Weeping
Emora
Kasier
Sea of Storms
Archipelago
of the Moons

Sea

Phoca

Pyal

Rygon

Rystra

Vocan

Moon Bay

The Weeping

The Crystal Deep

Nubaria

Inush

The Cold Expanse

The people of the Archipelago of the Moons have occupied the islands for over one thousand years. Legend tells of seafarers from the east, in search of a golden temple, sailing into the Sea of Storms only to wash up on the shores of the Lagos' largest island. Since then, the Lagos has remained occupied. The empire expanded over the centuries to include the entire archipelago and some nearby settlements on the eastern lesser continent of Inush. No one knows when the royal family began using the panther as its sigil.

Some say it has always been this way.

Privateer and Explorer Medusa Ramsey
Tides of Adventure

Chapter One

THE MOONS WERE VISIBLE in the bluebird sky, reminding Cecelia that the Mother and Daughter were always watching. She took a deep breath, pulled her eyes from the sky, and centered them on the target before her. Cecelia imagined it to be something worrisome and terrifying. She imagined a hungry mountain cougar or a rabid dog.

Her stepmother.

Inhaling, she pulled the bowstring back and exhaling she let it go. The arrow zipped through the air and hit the target with a thunk. The strike was slightly off center but close enough.

She turned and smiled. "How was that, brother?"

The young man shrugged. His dark curly hair fell just over his eyes and hid his true expression. "Father always says only perfect is perfect, Cece."

Cecelia sighed and walked to the target to retrieve her arrows. Sometimes her brother sounded too much like their father. He was four and twenty, five years younger than her. His voice should be that of youth and merriment, not lessons and hard truths.

"I suppose you'll wish to instruct me on how to improve, then?" she called back while pulling the arrows out with a swift yank.

"I would never imply my lady sister requires improvement," he said with a sly smile.

"*I would never imply,*" she mocked him.

Hair shrouded Danon's view. He blew it out of the way, revealing the laughter lines around his eyes. He was jesting with her, she knew, for her father would be hard pressed to find even one in his household guard that could shoot better than she. But sometimes she wanted a little recognition from her brother.

She looked to Danon to speak just such when a Shadowman emerged from one of the lower arches of the keep. He was focused as he quickly strode across the practice range, his black cape billowing behind him.

"Your royal highnesses," the man called, "King Filip would like a word."

"Oh?" Danon said, "both of us?"

"Yes, your grace."

Danon looked at Cecelia, a puzzled look on his face.

"What?" she said. "I didn't do anything."

"He wished for you and her royal highness to come immediately. He is in his study. I will escort you." The Shadowman turned to lead them back towards the keep.

Danon offered Cecelia one more look before turning to follow. An approaching armsman relieved Cecelia of her bow and arrows, though she yielded them reluctantly. She would much rather remain on the range with her pretend enemies than visit her father. Her talks with him were few, especially since he began sending her away to study warcraft. Especially since her return from the Southern Shores.

Danon waited for her under the archway. "Hurry," he said, "you've grown too slow in your travels."

Cecelia frowned at him. She watched her brother's back sway while they walked up the stairs. His cloak was black linen lined with silk and swished from side to side with each step. He was broad of shoulder and tall of height, nearly half a hand taller than she, and he was handsome. He possessed their father's tawny hazel eyes and arched nose, and his mother's olive skin and dark hair.

Their younger sister, Alaina, was the same. Though she had yet to pass Cecelia in height. And probably never would. It was said she was the beauty of the capital, even the Lagos. Much arbitration was held over who would take her hand in marriage when she was of age.

Even little Lucien, at eight, looked like a miniature of their father. He was quiet, like their father, and stoic, even at such a young age.

Cecelia, on the other hand, was lean, gray of eyes, with long straight hair she often wore plaited. It was the color of sand, and hideous, as Alaina liked to tell her. Though Cecelia thought it pretty in its own way. Her features only stood to show her difference, her otherness, from the rest of the royal family. It marked her as an outsider. Like her mother had been before she died.

When they reached the third floor of the keep, the Shadowman stopped to wait for Cecelia to catch up. He said nothing to her, though his eyes told her he was uncomfortable with her presence. They all were, those that lived within the castle keep, since her return from the far shores of the Archipelago of the Moons.

She wondered what the queen had said to her husband's royal guard, the castle's servants, even some of the lords who came to treat with her father. They'd all shunned her since her recent return from the Southern Shores, but it started before that, when she was briefly home from the Dry Vineyard, when she found Elyeanor snooping in her room.

Cecelia had been in the right. Elyeanor had gone into her room while she napped. The woman claimed to be retrieving a book for the library that she knew was in Cecelia's room. Cecelia, startled awake and disoriented from sleep, drew the dagger kept beneath her pillow. Her stepmother hadn't been hurt. Cecelia showed great control when she finally shook the last of sleep from her eyes to realize it was Elyeanor and not some brigand in her room. But the woman found insult without injury, anyway.

Cecelia's thoughts were too consuming, and she ran into Danon's back.

Danon laughed. "Where are you today, sister?"

The Shadowman grew impatient and gestured with his hands that they should hurry. He ushered them down the hall to the large doors of their father's study. Two panthers were carved into the wood, their teeth bare, snarling at anyone who entered the room.

The panther had been the sigil of the Archipelago of the Moons for hundreds of years. Written records stated that those intrepid sailors who found refuge on the shores of the archipelago had to first befriend the large jungle cats that called the islands home. Befriend them, or find a new place to build a life. The cats proved intelligent, and adept at shifting their habits to live alongside their new companions, and it was for that the people of the Lagos chose the cat as their symbol. Their sigil. Their pride.

"Here, your highnesses," the Shadowman said. He opened the door and stood to one side.

Danon nodded politely at him as he slipped past. Cecelia did the same, though the Shadowman averted his eyes.

Inside, they found their father sitting at his desk. A fire roared high in the large hearth, though it was the middle of summer in the Lagos. He sat with his head in his hands, but looked up quickly when they entered.

"Danon, Cecelia," he did not sound pleased.

His forehead furrowed, leaving many deep-set wrinkles splayed across his receding hairline. It was graying, but a hint of the darkest black remained. He wore it short, though it was said he once wore it long and wavy. Unruly. Cecelia's mother had liked it that way. He wore a short beard–black peppered with silver–and when he stood, he was as tall as Danon. He suggested they sit.

"We came at once, father," Danon said.

Their father looked from Danon to Cecelia, studying their faces.

"Father," Cecelia said, "what is it? Why do you look so ill?"

She said the words, though she already knew the reason.

The rulers of the Lagos were historically Seers. For the last three hundred years most monarchs possessed the sight to see. Some saw in dreams, images so vivid the dreamer could have sworn they were awake. Others saw in flashes, moments interrupting daily thoughts like a battering ram to a besieged castle.

Visions had infected King Filip since the age of ten and nine. These visions were useful, leading Cecelia's father to rule his people deftly and with brilliant success. Though his flashes of visions came at a price. A migraine would shortly ensue and her father would be unable to speak or stand light for over a day. He would become unnaturally cold, which was why a fire already blazed in his hearth. He drank water from a large goblet for soon he wouldn't be able to eat or drink.

"I have had a vision," he said, "one in which involves you both."

Danon glanced at Cecelia before turning back to their father. "The both of us?"

Their father took another drink of water before continuing. "You are to travel, together, to Korith." He sipped some more. "There, you will entertain with King Ramiro."

"Korith?" Cecelia interrupted, "father, that's half a Mother's fortnight's sailing. I just returned home!"

She gripped the edge of her leather seat, her fingers turning white. He was trying to be rid of her again. It was one thing to send her away to fight and train, something she liked to do, but entertaining at court was not something she favored. Or was good at. Her demeanor was too brusque, her brother liked to say.

King Filip waved the outburst away with a hand. "I am aware of your recent return, Cecelia, and I am sorry. But I was shown a vision, and you will obey."

Cecelia thought of ripping the goblet from her father's hand and tossing it in his face. Perhaps he sensed this, for he quickly placed his goblet on the far side of the desk.

"King Ramiro? But why, father?" Danon asked.

"There is something there," their father said. "I cannot say for sure what it is. It is like a creature making noise in the bush. But what creature lies in wait for you, I don't know."

Cecelia rolled her eyes.

"You want us to figure out what it is?" Danon said.

Their father nodded.

"And how shall we do that, father, if we only have your vague vision as a clue?" Cecelia asked.

"Oh, I think you and your brother are smart enough to figure that out," their father said, ignoring Cecelia's impudent tone. He sighed and rubbed his forehead.

"When shall we leave?" Danon asked.

"Soon. Immediately, if possible."

"But father, Korith? Our people have not set foot there since before the rebellion. Perhaps they think grandfather abandoned them in their time of need?" Danon asked.

"Oh please," Cecelia muttered. When Danon glared at her, she offered him a crooked smile and continued. "Norian was insane. Everyone knows it. Grandfather, in the name of their alliance, would have had to help him win the rebellion. His exit paved the way for their victory. If anything, they'll welcome us with flowers and a feast."

"Hmm," their father grumbled. "I don't think feasts and flowers will greet you. But I think the young King Ramiro will accept you in his court, regardless. Out of curiosity."

"Is that it then?" Cecelia stood. "Should we go prepare?"

Their father nodded, but stared at Cecelia. "There is more. But," he pursed his lips, "Danon, leave us a moment. Tend to your mother. She will sup on dinner soon."

Danon stood and nodded. "As you say, father."

He offered Cecelia a bewildered look before he turned to go. She smiled smugly and sank back down into her chair, though truthfully she was just as surprised as he was.

When he opened the door, a physician in their blue robes entered. He held a jar filled with silver liquid.

"No, not yet," King Filip said. "A moment longer. I must speak with my daughter."

The physician nodded silently and backed out the door, bowing. Cecelia picked at the leather of the armchair. Her father rubbed his head again, grimacing.

"Father," Cecelia said. The longer he waited to take the pain-relieving mixture, the worse it would be for him. "Call the physician back."

"No," he barked, "listen." He took a deep breath and set his gaze on her. "There is more to my vision. I am afraid... I am afraid something will keep you in Korith. You will not be returning to the Lagos."

He sat silent while his words settled on Cecelia. Her first thoughts were ambivalent. It was not as if she ever felt a true Panther. Since the age of ten and seven she had spent most of her time away from the capital. Always gone, the people she would one day rule seemed like veritable strangers. Her mother had been foreign, perhaps Korithian herself. Most citizens of the Lagos thought Cecelia foreign too.

But then Cecelia imagined not setting eyes on her father, brothers, or sister again, and her stomach lurched. She brushed some stray hair from her face. When she finally spoke, she attempted to keep her voice calm and even.

"Will I be in danger?"

"The vision did not show you in any danger, no."

Relieved, Cecelia sat a little straighter. "Then I suppose I can manage." She offered him a wry smile.

Her father returned it. "You better than most, I'd say. You are my firstborn. You know what must be done?"

She shook her head yes.

"Good. See that you are successful. And watch out for your brother. He thinks he's smarter than he is."

Cecelia looked down in awkward pleasure. It was rare she received a compliment from her father, even an offhanded one. "When shall I tell him this additional information from your vision?"

"I believe you'll know the time when it comes."

She looked into her father's eyes to assure him of her words. "I will do as you command, father."

"Your travels to the Southern Shore were profitable? You learned something new?" He asked her.

She shook her head. "Yes, father."

Another vision of her father's had sent her south, among the Dancing Swordsmen, to learn their trade and improve her own skill.

"Armsman Brody was an excellent swordsman. I feel I am nearly as good with my steel as I am with my bow."

Not a lie, though Brody had warned her that her willowy body would make her easy to push around for nearly any average sized man. She would need to use her wits and outsmart her foe with a few thoughtful swings and slashes.

You'll never swing a battle-axe like your brother, the old man had told her, *but your swords are just as sharp.*

"Good," her father nodded. "I fear you will have more use of your skills in Korith than I'd like. They do not appreciate a woman's fighting there, mind you, so you will have to be careful."

"I will, father."

Cecelia stood to leave. A bouquet of bleeding hearts sat limp in a glass on her father's desk. She hadn't noticed them before. Her finger trailed across one long, delicate stem.

"Mother's favorite," she mumbled, not really speaking to her father, but to herself. To the child within.

"Yes," her father leaned back in his chair and laced his fingers together. "She loved how exceptionally delicate they were. And how they helped her remember."

"Remember what?"

Her mother was a brief memory of her childhood. Present, but not entirely. Like a specter. Or a ghost. Cecelia's father spoke little of her. But when he did, it was like one small piece to a puzzle for Cecelia. One more detail to add to the portrait she kept in her mind.

"All the fragile hearts." Her father finally answered. He sighed, his words coming out heavy and laden with sadness. "Hearts of those she loved. And hated. Hearts she left behind. That she broke. That she mended."

Her father leaned forward, hands rubbing his temples in circular motions. The pain was growing. It wouldn't be long now.

"I'll fetch the physician." Cecelia rushed to the door.

When she threw the heavy wood open, the blue-robed man waited just outside.

"He's ready," she said.

The physician billowed past her and shut the door. It left Cecelia in the near darkness of the hall. A Shadowman stood guarding the door, his black armor so matte Cecelia could barely make him out. Her father would drink the silver liquid and retire to his room. He would stay there until he felt he could stand without vomiting. It could be a day, maybe two. She'd be gone before then.

But she must obey.

And when his lordship King Antony fled on his ship, King Marian withdrew to his chambers and mourned.

High Steward Robert Ma'Curci
The Trial of the Red Way: A History of Rebellion

Chapter Two

THE SOUND OF A rooster off in the yard woke Viktor. He wondered who had a chicken in the castle keep. He roused himself to a sitting position. If he found it, he'd strangle it. Then he'd eat it.

A bang on the door shattered his head. His body ached all over. He knew he had drunk too much in the mess hall, but it was all for fun. Vincent had been knighted and fought in the king's melee, meant to celebrate the birth of the princess. And then Vincent promptly died. Smashed in the face with a flail.

A flail. How hard is it to see those coming?

He found a tankard of ale, still half full from the night before, and quickly downed it. He'd probably regret it later. The banging on his door continued.

"Alright, alright!" He yelled, stomping towards the door. He opened it to find Kay waiting. "What do you want?"

Kay glared at him. "You're late Viktor. 'Supposed to be your watch for Ramiro, remember?"

How had he forgotten? Oh yes, the drinking.

"Fine, fine," he said, grabbing his cloak. "Where is he? Eating?"

Kay nodded. "On the veranda. He's already asked for you. Seemed a bit turned you weren't there protecting his royalness."

"Oh, I'm sure he was upset," Viktor said, though Viktor knew otherwise.

Viktor liked to think that King Ramiro was more lenient on him than any other Kingsguard because he knew Viktor could - in fact - kill him if he really wanted to. Not that he ever would. But he could. It'd be no trouble.

And there was also the fact that Viktor squired for the king's own father. After leaving his own house–to put space between himself and his rage-filled father–Viktor found a home within Lord Romo's family. And when the rebellion began, Viktor fought beside Romo, saving his life more than once. In return, the newly crowned king gave him a knighthood. Oh, and told him to babysit King Romo's little pip of a son for the rest of his life too, while he's at it.

While Viktor fumed and fussed more than most about the king, everyone knew he was all talk. He was burned out, nearing forty, and only loved one thing: fighting. With the kingdom at peace for nearly two decades, Viktor was bored. And bored Viktor liked to talk. More than he should, but what did he care? He'd protected Ramiro from the beginning, longer than the rest, and in return he expected to be protected, too.

Or so he hoped.

When he emerged into the bailey's yard it surprised him to see so many people bustling about in a hurry. The king's tournament was to be held for two more days, but the activity seemed extravagant, even for that. He grabbed a nearby pageboy roughly by the arm.

"What's happening here?"

When the boy saw who had grabbed him, his eyes grew as large as the moons. Viktor held a bit of a bad reputation in the castle for roughing up the younger boys during drill. The boy shook himself free and scurried off before Viktor could accost him again.

"His abominable brilliance," Viktor swore, staring at the chaos going on around him.

"Ah, Sir Viktor," a voice called from behind.

He turned to find the queen walking with her entourage of ladies and Queensguard.

"Late to your duties guarding my husband as he stuffs his face full of pork pie? Tsk tsk, what shall we do if he chokes?"

Viktor didn't laugh. "His grace is a skilled eater. I doubt it will ever come to that highness."

The queen laughed. Her teeth were too straight and white. Her hair was the color of mud. Some said she was beautiful, which Viktor didn't deny, but something about her made him cringe. Something lurked beneath that fake smile. She always poked fun at her husband's eating habits. He ate voraciously though his waist never expanded past that of a maiden's. And then there was his nose. She liked to call it a beak. Viktor had never truly liked her, though she'd been married to the king for nearly two years.

"Come then," she said, "we'll greet his rage together."

She suggested he fall into step beside her, an honorable position. He accepted, despite not wanting to. She smelled of vanilla and honey. He stopped himself before he fell too deep into her web. That was how she controlled people, and got anything she wanted, by casting her net wide. By enchanting. Bewitching.

They walked to the keep's great arched entrance. As they ascended the stairwell, she stole a look at him, but then continued looking upward. Sunlight streamed onto the landing ahead of them from a large rosette window perched above.

"I trust you've noticed the uproar?" she whispered.

Her ladies followed behind, like birds, their necks bobbing up and down with every step they took. Viktor looked back to see if any of them would answer, but then realized she spoke to him.

"Yes, highness," he said quickly, "but I'm afraid I don't know what for. The tourney?"

She laughed.

"No, not even close. Let my husband tell you. He'll be pleased to see the look on your face."

Viktor wondered how stupid he must be if he didn't know the great news King Ramiro had. The entire castle buzzed with activity like a hive making honey. How did he not know what was going on? There was the tourney, yes, that took up quite a bit of his time and memory. He had enjoyed several days of drinking and fighting. And yet, how could he not know? He eyed the woman suspiciously. It brought her joy to watch him flounder. Viktor thought he should be a fool in her court, not a knight.

As they reached the end of the hall, its barrel ceiling full of morning light, birdsong welcomed them to the veranda. Two of his brothers in arms stood at the door. They looked ahead, though Viktor knew they watched him.

They despised him, or at least most of them did. He was privileged, gaining the trust of the king more than most because of his past with old King Romo. But Viktor didn't care. He had grown up in a home crueler than anything that occurred within the castle keep. He learned early what it felt like to not be liked. To not be adored.

They entered the sunny veranda where a waft of warm air greeted them. It was well into summer in Korith, and the heat was taking over. King Ramiro would take more and more of his meals on the breezy covered porch of the great sea-facing terrace that lined the back of the castle keep.

"Ah Danica, how nice of you to finally join me," Ramiro called to his wife, setting a dainty painted cup on a plate. A servant immediately refilled it.

"Forgive me, my king. I was having a bit of trouble this morning with one of my maids. You understand, I'm sure," she glanced at Viktor, who quickly took his place behind Ramiro, standing as far against the wall as he could.

"Yes," Ramiro replied, his gaze following Viktor, "I suppose I do." He sipped from his cup while his wife settled beside him.

The king's brother sat with them, Lord Rufus. A year younger than Ramiro, he shared his older brother's penchant for eating, yet was not blessed with his slim waistline. The large young man shifted in his chair, sending a creaking of wood through the open-air terrace.

He looked at Viktor. "Awfully insolent to be late for a shift guarding the king," he said.

Viktor had killed many men, older than Lord Rufus, before the boy was even born. But he said nothing to Rufus, instead shifting his gaze to stare out between the tall ivy-covered columns.

It gave an excellent view of the southeast sea. A ship sat there, its large black sails billowing in the wind, waiting for the tide to shift and bring them towards the harbor's shuttering walls.

Black sails. Uncommon. Exceptionally uncommon. The only people who used black sails were those of the Archipelago of the Moons, who called themselves the Panthers.

Viktor looked at the back of King Ramiro's head, wondering when he would notice the ship, or if he already had. At twenty, the king's hair was full and black. He was nearly the spitting image of his father, but Viktor hated that. King Romo had been a good man, a wise man. His son was spoiled and foolish. It was no wonder the general rarely consulted Ramiro when he dealt with outland raiders in the west. The boy was still just that, a boy.

Danica noticed Viktor's gaze. A small smile played across her lips. "My dear husband, something seems to bother Sir Viktor. Perhaps he's noticed our guests." She winked at Viktor. She gently placed a hand on her husband's and smiled devilishly. "Perhaps you should inform him of the news. He's dying to know."

Ramiro turned to look over the back of his chair at Viktor. "Oh?" He too smiled. "Well come, come Viktor, step forward. I shall share the tale with you then."

Ramiro's sudden vigor told Viktor that Danica was right. The tale was extremely pleasing to Ramiro. He stepped forward and stood between Ramiro and Danica, his hand resting habitually on the pommel of his sword.

"Now, it was very early this morn, before the Mother and Daughter had fully set, when a page brought me a message. 'Flown into the castellan's office. A hawk,' the boy said. He hands me the note and I read: *His Majesty*

Filip of House Delacroix, Lord of the Panthers and Keeper of the Archipelago, sends his great regards to his highness King Ramiro of Korith, and asks that he allow his son, Danon of House Delacroix, to land his ship in our harbor. I nearly fell out of bed." Ramiro slammed his hand on the table with glee. "Can you believe it?"

"Positively perfect," Rufus agreed.

Viktor grunted in reply. The Panthers of the Archipelago of the Moons had been absent from Korith for nearly fifty years. They once kept a large chateau on a small island, linked to the capital by a long, arched bridge. King Ludovic would hold court there as a pledged ally with Korith's then king, Marian. But Ludovic must have seen something in Marian's heir, Norian, that others didn't or that others took too long to see. Ludovic abandoned the chateau with no warning, offering Marian an apology on a note.

When Marian died eighteen years later, Norian came into his throne. He cared little for tradition, decorum, or rules. Norian cared for Norian. After ten years of his chaotic rule, the reason for Ludovic's severed ties made sense. No one wanted to support Norian, and so the rebellion began.

"Lord Danon awaits the high tide, and he'll enter the harbor. He brings with him a champion to enter the tourney!" Ramiro beamed at his wife, as if it was all her doing.

She returned his smile.

"And this pleases your highness?" Viktor asked.

"The Panther's presence at the tourney is a great honor," a gruff voice called from the doorway.

General Rees stood large in the door, causing a shadow to spill across the marble floor. He wore black, as was his custom. The army's sigil, a fist holding a dagger, decorated his tunic in silver.

"Yes indeed! I never thought I'd live to see a Panther." Ramiro said.

Viktor nodded, though he didn't share Ramiro's enthusiasm. He had seen his share of Panthers. Their merchant ships entered the harbor from time to time, bringing exotic goods from the archipelago. A tall, dark people, their language was slow and melodious though most knew Korithian well enough. They kept to themselves, and one once told him it was royal decree to do so. Trade and leave, the man had said, take no passengers, thrice check for stowaways. Only a Panther could return to the homeland. Only a Panther knew the way on the dreadful Sea of Storms.

The general took a seat at the far end of the table and accepted a cup of weak tea. He took a sip while staring at Ramiro.

"Your highness, I hold some curiosity as to why the Panther boy is here. I mean, why now?" He said.

"My daughter's birth is not a joyous occasion enough for you, General Rees?" Danica asked, sitting tall as she did so.

Viktor wanted to roll his eyes. He watched Rees' face while he stifled a smile.

"I meant no offense, your highness. And certainly, Princess Jana's birth is an occasion for much joy. But the Panthers care little for the birth of princesses of faraway lands."

"Perhaps they've come to make an alliance. A marriage pact. King Filip has a younger son who could wait for Jana to reach womanhood," Danica said.

"By my understanding, the prince is a boy of eight and his queen mother already aims to marry him to a young lady of their Southern Shore," the general replied.

Viktor knew what it was the general really wanted to say, but wouldn't–or couldn't–in present company.

Perhaps the boy was there because of unrest in the west.

The Universalists murmured for a new king, saying Ramiro shouldn't rule merely because his father deposed King Norian. Danica's words were empty and filled with only hope. An alliance with the Panthers would be good for Ramiro. But General Rees was right. The Panthers cared little about faraway lands.

And yet the boy who would be king was there.

"You seem to know a lot about the Panthers, general," Viktor blurted before he considered whether it was proper. But what did he care for proper?

Rufus moved his lips to speak, perhaps to rebuke Viktor for speaking out of turn or doing some other insolent thing, but the general spoke over him.

"I am the general of the king's army. I protect the kingdom. I must have eyes and ears everywhere. To know where the next threat will come from."

Spies. The general had spies. And why shouldn't he? Rees was right, it was his job to protect the kingdom, but did that involve infiltrating a relatively peaceful people half a world away? Something about it sat wrong in Viktor's stomach. He suddenly felt sick. He did his best to hold his vomit.

He'd never drink again.

"My dear," Danica said, "poor Viktor seems afraid." She'd misread his facial expression. "Are you afraid of the cats, Sir Viktor?"

Rufus chuckled. "Such a large man to be afraid of a little kitty."

Viktor straightened, the sick feeling passing. "I don't like them, doesn't mean I'm afraid of them."

Danica laughed. "Perhaps you better choose another guard to escort the boy from place to place?"

Viktor's neck tensed at the thought of acting like a shepherd. He tried hard not to look at Ramiro too fast, to give away his anger.

"Is it true, highness?" He asked instead, controlling his voice, acting calm.

"Well," said Ramiro, turning back to his breakfast, "I had hoped to give them my best man. The boy will have his own guard, to be sure. I've sent word he's allowed a pair to come on land with him, plus his champion. But he is still in need of an escort." He chomped at his toast.

Viktor bowed his head. "As you wish, highness." He stepped back into the shade of the wall, returning to his act as shadow.

"Oh, come now, Viktor, don't pout," Ramiro said, his mouth full of the honey-soaked bread, "It will be fun!"

"As you say."

"A great honor," Rees added.

"As you say."

The double moons bring strength to our tides, but if man is to tame the sea the tides must, in turn, be tamed. The shuttering wall is a most important tool, allowing vessels of various sizes to remain afloat while the tide goes out, reducing the need for floating ports and allowing the fortification of harbors to protect from pirates.

Logician Mykel Meralko
Oeconomeia

Chapter Three

"Moon Mother, it looks massive." Danon said.

He stood next to Cecelia on the ship's deck. Their father had sent them away on the fast galleon *Sea Maiden*. It had maneuvered deftly between the many hidden reefs around the Archipelago of the Moons and sailed smoothly through the Sea of Storms.

Upon spotting the capital, with the castle keep sitting tall and leering on the cliff's edge, they sent off their messenger hawk. It was only a short time later they received their reply, warmly greeting them and allowing them entrance into the city. They only waited for high tide to bring them to the shuttering wall of the harbor.

Cecelia imagined King Ramiro enjoyed the thought of the Panthers having to sit idly waiting, the entire time faced with the splendor of his capital, Kasier. The great glory of the Korith Empire filled the cliff side with its large white buildings, their roofs gilded in gold and towers that tickled the clouds. A small hill rose in the distance, a golden domed temple sat atop, with large manses scattered across.

The ship still had several thousand rods of rocky shore to wait upon while the tide turned and brought them closer and closer to the harbor wall and the large gate that held the water and ships within afloat.

"I've seen bigger." Cecelia rested her head in her arms and gazed at the buildings.

Danon stood silently. He busied himself admiring the brilliant gold of the temple top. It reflected the light of the sun almost as brightly as the Mother. The ship bobbed up and down with the roll of the sea. Salty waves sprayed into their faces and across the deck. Danon shielded his eyes with his hands and looked up at the sky. It was a cloudless day and was already hot, even with noon several hours away.

"I thought Korith was known for its rain?" he said.

"They have a rainy season that lasts all winter. But it is summer for them as well, though their summer is still young while ours nears its end," Cecelia explained.

"I was only jesting," he said. "I'm not a total idiot."

Cecelia looked at him out of the corner of her eye and smiled. "Perhaps."

"Have you prepared yourself for your introduction?" He asked.

She stood and stretched, arching backwards and throwing out her arms. She yawned. "It will be child's play, brother."

"Pride is the warrior's enemy," he replied, words of their father sounding too serious from his young lips.

She scowled. "And pride is sometimes all that will rouse a man from his bed to fight, when neither love nor honor nor money tempt him."

Danon laughed. "And who taught you that? One of your great armsman of the Southern Shore? Or perhaps the ax hurlers of the Dry Vineyard?"

He turned back to watch the passing cliffs. A sagging gazebo perched on top, in the shadow of the keep itself. Several women stood within, pointing and waving. He waved back.

Cecelia rested her head on her arms again, a fierce heat rising to her cheeks. Danon knew as well as she that it was their father who sent her away, off to the far reaches of the Lagos to train. She was the best, but she could always be better, or so her father seemed to think.

Her father's words, etched in her mind, bubbled to the surface: *A true warrior knows he is never done training.* She looked at her brother, so comely and relaxed. His skin had darkened in the sun during the crossing, making him look even more like his mother. He was a warrior, a fighter, and a good one, too. And yet it was she who got sent away. She wondered if her father regretted it now, knowing she would not return to the Lagos.

"Have *you* prepared yourself?" she finally said. "The Korithians are suspicious people. They cannot know our true reason for being here."

"I'll be fine."

He stared back at the gazebo, smiling. It was when he smiled Cecelia noticed his youth the most. Five years was not much difference in age, but it was five years more for Cecelia to travel, to learn, to experience the world. Their father kept Danon close, always. He didn't sense the danger. She wondered if it was the best time to tell him their father's words. To tell him she wouldn't be coming home.

A large swell stirred the ship, causing Cecelia to fall towards her brother. He caught her and laughed at her tumble. No, it wouldn't do. He was so happy. Cecelia couldn't burden him with the news then.

"I shall retire to my cabin," she said. "Fetch me when we've entered the harbor."

"As you say," Danon replied. He returned to feasting on the scene of the city.

Cecelia's cabin was spacious and overlooked the aft of the ship where several round framed windows collected sea spray and algae. Green tinted sunlight trickled through the windows, giving off the appearance the room was under water. A well-worn featherbed and a writing desk were bolted to the floor. An ancient rug collected dirt and dust. Kicking her boots off on the rug, Cecelia flopped onto the bed. The sheets smelled of must and something sour.

She sighed. Was *she* ready for this adventure?

The cabin door creaked. She raised her head off the pillow enough to see it was the cook, the captain's young daughter, who entered.

"Ada?" Cecelia tried, forgetting the girl's name.

"Anya," she corrected.

"Yes, Anya," Cecelia sat up, "what is it?"

"Forgive me, highness," the girl kneeled before her.

"Rise, Anya," Cecelia said, tired, "you needn't kneel so completely. A small curtsy would do. Or nothing at all. I'm not picky."

"Oh, but, your highness, to do nothing?" The thought seemed to terrify the young girl.

"Fine. A curtsy next time."

Anya nodded in agreement. "M'lady... highness. I... I wanted to ask you something," the girl played with the hem of her ragged skirt. It was wool, and perhaps once dyed the deepest blue, though it had faded and looked the color of stone.

"A request? Speak it then," Cecelia leaned forward, her fingers clasped together on her knees.

"The palace, the king. He keeps men about him. Men that guard him," Anya was having some difficulty with a straggling string. She tugged, and the hem ripped. She looked like she would cry.

"Yes, a king usually has many men guarding him. My father alone keeps four Shadowmen about him at all times."

Cecelia's interest was guttering out. She had spent too many years amongst warriors who were straightforward and quick to reach their point, for if they weren't, their life could be on the line. Cecelia could barely stop herself from barking at the girl to get on with it. Anya had said only four words to them since they boarded, though she cooked a delightful seafood stew. It was clear the girl was not quick to speak, and rushing her wouldn't help.

"No, I mean yes, I know, highness. But... one of them. He's a giant. A mark covers his neck and jaw." Anya looked around before leaning closer and whispering, "I think it's His Brilliance's mark."

Cecelia stood. Marks of the sun god were a superstition, a holdover of the last age when most worshiped His Brilliance over the Mother and Daughter. But there were some who still believed. The Goldenones to the west. Inush. The crescent shaped island of Duwu in the middle of the Crystal Deep, where sacrifices were still made every year on the solstice.

Cecelia herself didn't find strange markings all that mystical, but Anya was getting more and more nervous.

"Anya, has he hurt you? Don't fear telling me if he has."

Anya stared at the floor and refused to look Cecelia in the eye. "He don't scare me none highness. Well, maybe a little. It's only... last time," but she stopped.

"Well, go on!"

"Last time, when we docked at the Kasier port for repairs, he, we... well, I was got with child."

Cecelia was shocked, but only a little. It bothered her more that the girl looked so young. She studied Anya for any signs, but saw none.

"What do you want me to do about it, then?"

Anya looked confused.

"Why did you tell me?" Cecelia asked instead.

"Oh," Anya continued, "It's just the baby, last time... when I left. I did not see him again, but sent word to the palace with a serving girl I saw at the market. She came back with a coin from him, silver. Says it was to help with the baby. Only... only I lost the baby highness." Anya looked about to cry again.

"Oh," Cecelia wished more and more that Anya had not entered her cabin and she had fallen asleep instead. "I'm sorry, Anya."

"Makes no difference, highness. But I was wondering... if you wouldn't mind," she pulled the silver from a hidden pocket and handed it to Cecelia, "I don't feel right taking it, not having the baby anymore."

Cecelia stared at the coin. It was old, prior to the rebellion, with the likeness of King Marian cast on one side. His furrowed brow held up his heavy crown. Slowly, she covered it with her fingers and put it in her doublet pocket.

"I will do as you ask," Cecelia said.

"Oh, thank you, m'lady. Highness," and the girl was gone.

A silver for a baby? Cecelia wondered what sort of lecherous man would do such a thing. Huge and marked by His Brilliance? He shouldn't be too hard to find.

The House of Cerul is rumored to be descended from giants who were gentrified in an attempt to quell fighting between man and colossal, thus their relative size compared to other noble houses. True giants have not been seen on the Great Continent for nearly seven hundred years. The Fair Folk still talk of them, suggesting that the giants aren't gone, just hiding in the mysterious forests and caverns the Fair Folk know best.

High Steward Rodrick Brasden
House Histories and Insignias

Chapter Four

THE PANTHER PRINCE INSISTED on being ushered to his pavilion as soon as his black-sailed ship docked. He, his champion, and two guards. Viktor did not see him himself. A kitchen maid walking back from the serving tent on the tourney grounds saw them while returning to the palace for more food. And then the word spread like wildfire.

Women already whispered in groups how handsome he was. How dark of skin and white of smile. How his gold eyes seemed to glow in a mischievously wicked way, like the moons on the eve of Harvest Day. It made Viktor sick. He half hoped the rumors were false. Fantasies drawn up by the bored serving women. He imagined a round stomached, pock faced man emerging from the tent instead. Then the women would be silenced. Then they'd see Panthers were no better than any other man.

He stood outside the tent, impatiently awaiting the boy's emergence. A *boy*. The thought agitated Viktor. He despised elaborate displays of pomp for someone who didn't even look like he required shaving his face. A white flag with black snarling panther flew high above the entrance. People slowed when they walked by, hoping to glimpse the prince. Viktor wished he was on guard duty, standing beside Ramiro in the shade of the great throne seated in the tourney stands. But since being relegated to escort duty, he had waited outside the tent for nearly an hour in the heat and the sun and the growing swarm of mosquitoes.

One of the prince's guards stood across from him. He wore all black armor. It was light and looked decorative. The man had said nothing to Viktor since he arrived. Viktor liked it that way. Though he was running out of patience. He shifted in his boots, nearly ready to take the first step and then another and walking away. But then the tent flaps opened and the boy emerged.

He was taller than expected. His hair was dark and his skin tanned. He smiled up at Viktor with perfect white teeth and gave a curt nod.

"Sorry to keep you waiting, my lord." His Korithian was good, though his accent was obvious.

"I've been out here an hour," Viktor complained.

"How dare you speak to Prince Danon that way!" one of the Panther guards said. His Korithian was not as good as the prince's.

Danon held up an arm to silence the guard. "Surely an apology is in order. This heat is stifling! I thought it was hotter in the Lagos," Danon said. When Viktor said nothing, Danon smiled again. "I *am* sorry, my lord, for the wait."

Danon waited for no reply but turned to usher his champion out from inside his tent. The champion stepped out, tall and slim. He wore little iron armor, instead preferring the Panther's traditional dress of black laced leather scales. His bracers were iron, but he was ungloved. The leather scales fell into a knight's skirt, covering most of the champion's upper legs. Thick leather pants covered the rest while knee-high boots with iron greaves overlaid the feet. A black leather cap and black woven scarf wrapped neatly around the face, concealing his visage. Viktor noticed the champion studying him with their storm gray eyes.

"Your champion's going to eat dirt if he goes out there like that," Viktor said, suggesting to the skinny man.

The prince laughed. "We will see, my lord. Perhaps you'd like to make a wager?"

Viktor grunted and walked off, the Panther prince following. "I'm no lord, your grace. Only a knight."

"Then Sir, it is. What say you Sir? If my champion beats the crown's champion?"

"Unlikely as His Brilliance. But I'll wager." Viktor shoved his way through a crowd of gawking women.

They pulled away in revulsion to the knight but leaned further in as the prince passed through. Danon's champion shoved him onward when he hesitated near a rather pretty face.

"What does your grace ask if he wins?" Viktor said.

They neared the tourney grounds. The long rectangular area was lightly fenced to keep random spectators from walking across the grounds whilst champions competed. The archery tournament was held on the grounds two days previous and the melee the day before. Jousting was set for the next day. The man already crowned winner of the melee received the honor of fighting again against the Panther champion. A great honor, Ramiro had assured the grouchy man, who was already pleased with his victory and didn't want to try his luck against an unknown combatant.

Viktor would love to enter, but Ramiro forbade it.

"If my champion should win, which they will, I wish for ten gold Marians," Danon said.

Viktor stopped and turned. He studied the young man. His smooth and beardless face looked so childish to Viktor. The eyes were a shocking shade of hazel, nearly gold. The Panther champion stood behind Danon, observing the scene. Viktor thought he spied the champion's eyes upturned in the outer corners, as if he were smiling beneath that face shielding scarf.

"And what makes you think I can pay that?" Viktor said. "Gold Marians are hard enough to come by. You're better off asking for a unicorn. What's a Panther want with old Korithian coins, anyway?"

The boy merely smiled. "I'm a collector, of sorts. I have one gold Marian. Beautiful craftsmanship. I'm rather fond of it. Who could blame me for wanting some more?"

Viktor wasn't amused.

"Besides," Danon added, "gold is gold no matter whose face is stamped on it."

Viktor rolled his eyes and carried on toward the grounds. The boy had a certain tenacity that Viktor couldn't quite decide if he hated or liked. And the silence of the champion was hovering amongst them like a vulture over carrion.

"And you, Sir, what do you request should your king's champion win?" Danon asked.

"Viktor," Viktor grunted, tired of the way Danon's words bounced off his head.

"Excuse me?"

"My name is Viktor, not Sir."

"My apologies then, Sir Viktor." Danon grinned. His eyes seemed to dance with amusement.

Viktor led them through an opening of the fenced grounds and they slowly made their walk across. People pushed against the fence on all sides, all wanting to watch the spectacle of the fighting Panther. Viktor felt their eyes on them. They were like daggers, cool on the skin, ready to break the surface with just a touch more pressure.

"When the king's champion wins," he finally said, "I ask for your champion's sword."

The thin sword sat snugly in its scabbard against the champion's hip. Viktor imagined the blade was sharp, but it appeared rather short for a melee weapon. No good against the king's champion who commanded a double handed monstrosity smelted in the north and meant to kill bears.

"Their sword?"

"Yes. So, I can break it over my knee."

The Panther prince stopped in his tracks. His champion placed a hand on his shoulder and nodded, agreeing to Viktor's terms.

"Your champion has guts. I'll give you that much," Viktor added before they stepped before the king.

Ramiro sat at the top of his royal stands beneath an awning of black and red. Danica sat beside him. She had been absent from most of the tournament, tending to their new daughter, but she was not about to miss the moment. She looked sickeningly beautiful in shades of royal blue. Viktor stepped aside and suggested to Danon.

"Your grace, here is Prince Danon." Perhaps not the right words, or even remotely respectful, but Viktor didn't care. The boy was not his king.

The murmur coming from the crowd died away. The prince prepared to speak.

Danon bowed low and slow. "Your grace, I am pleased to be here today. My champion is honored to fight against your best fighter."

He motioned for the champion to step forward. The champion seemed to have a problem kneeling, but Danon finally shoved the man to his knees. Danon then bowed his head again.

Ramiro stood. He held up both hands as if to hug Danon.

"Your highness, it is an honor. Please, rise, and kneel no more to your friend."

The crowd cheered. Danica clapped. Viktor sighed.

Viktor attempted to guide Danon towards the stairs, but it came off more like a shove. Danon didn't notice. He was too content smiling at all the beautiful Ladies in the stands. He seemed to not notice the scowling Lords. The Panther champion disappeared to the end of the grounds. One of the Panther guards joined him.

A seat was prepared for Danon just to the left of and below the king's own seat. Ramiro was still standing when Danon approached, and they hugged like old friends. Viktor found it strange that though both men were near the same age, Ramiro appeared at least a decade older. Danica did not move, but awaited Danon's attention.

When he finally did turn to the queen, he put on his widest grin yet.

"This could not possibly be your queen, your grace? She is by far too lovely. She is the Daughter herself, transcended to the earth to bless us with her presence." He kneeled and kissed her hand delicately.

This pleased Danica. She returned his smile.

Ramiro laughed. "Indeed, she is a vision. One of my father's better ideas. Lady Danica of House Katvenn."

Danon spoke again, but the crowd erupted with a roar, drowning him out. The champions had taken the field, apparently tired of waiting for the monarch's go ahead.

"Oh, they are ready!" Ramiro said. "Here, a seat, a seat, my lord." He suggested Danon take his seat. "Out of the way, Viktor. A shadow, remember? Make yourself a shadow." He waved Viktor away like a bee.

Viktor felt awkward standing behind the Panther prince instead of his own king but did as ordered.

He watched the Panther champion, tall and slender, approach the Korithian champion, a large man of both height and girth. His biceps were the size of the Panther's waist. He was called Griff of House Cerul, but everyone called him Griff the Giant.

And Viktor knew there was no way the small champion could beat him.

Griff approached with great sword out, heading straight for the Panther. Viktor supposed he wanted to get the fight over with fast. Perhaps when he saw the size of his opponent, he was emboldened. Either way, Griff approached, and the Panther circled with their sword drawn, held behind their body, playing keep away with Griff.

It would be a shame when the Panther warrior, having survived the crossing of the Sea of Storms, died on the melee field.

All to impress some foreign king.

The Panther carried no shield, which Viktor found even more idiotic considering the size of their sword. Suddenly, Griff lunged and swung mightily, but the Panther danced away easily.

"Your champion is agile, your grace." Ramiro said to the Panther prince.

"We Panthers take pride in our agility." Danon replied.

"I hope my husband takes no offense when I say I pray no ill will towards your champion, Danon." Danica said.

Danon's name rolled off her tongue sensuously. He smiled back at her, tipping his head in courtesy, but said nothing in return. Instead, he spun back to the fight.

Griff took several more swings, all missing their target wide, while the Panther easily dodged. This angered Griff, who let out a terrifying roar, much like a bear. He swung again. It was with blind rage and not strategy, and the Panther saw it. They ducked the swing, took one lunging step with their long legs, and jabbed Griff in the armpit where his metal cuirass stopped and his leather arm coverings started. Just as quickly they retreated, sword held behind in keep away again.

Danica squeezed her husband's arm tightly, perhaps surprised by the turn of event, but Ramiro shoved her off. He, too, was surprised by the way the fight was going and leaned forward aginst the banister of the royal box.

Griff stumbled back, perplexed by the pain and sudden movement from the Panther. He reached under his arm and drew out a hand covered in blood. The wound wouldn't stop him though, Viktor knew, and would only anger him more.

Viktor didn't know why he suddenly wanted the Panther to win, but he did, and he felt his stomach lurch every time Griff took a swing at the small champion.

Griff finally connected with the Panther's blade. He pushed with both hands, forcing the Panther to retreat a step while they tried to keep their blade held high. A slip of the Panther's blade and Griff would bring his exceptionally sharp steel down on the Panther's chest or throat, both equally vulnerable in the Panther's leather armor.

The Panther threw their left leg far behind, and then quickly dropped their blade. The result was that Griff's forceful shoving thrust his blade down into the ground while the Panther's back step removed them to safety. And just as quick the Panther swung their blade upward at Griff's head, knocking him backward.

"Ramiro, darling," Danica whispered. She said noting more. A mere raise of her eyebrows was enough.

Ramiro nodded. "Aye, my beloved."

He partially turned toward Viktor and began to speak his name but a deafening roar erupted from the crowd. Apparently, they wanted the Panther to win, too. Danon glanced back at Ramiro. The king sat still, drawn to the fighting before him, his eyes giving away his surprise. Danon then threw a look back at Viktor and smiled before turning back to the fight.

Griff staggered to standing, fighting with his helmet. The Panther's swing had dented it badly, affecting the giant's sight. He finally tugged the metal bucket off and threw it angrily to the side. If Viktor could wager a guess, he'd say the Panther was smiling. Griff looked like a large fool as he huffed and puffed and adjusted his armor, preparing himself for another attack.

"She will finish him now." Danon's guard whispered to the prince. Danon nodded.

She?

"Viktor," Ramiro hissed, "end this. The queen demands no bloodshed."

Viktor obeyed without hesitation. It was what Ramiro demanded of him. He cleared the banister of the royal box in one jump and landed heavily on the packed dirt of the melee ring. Neither Griff nor the Panther seemed to notice him.

Griff roared again and charged. He swung the large blade like it was a practice sword. He swung left, then right, then thrusted. The Panther danced backwards, playing each blow with their own sword. Viktor studied the champion closely, wondering if the guard's words were true. The champion was svelte, indeed, but Viktor had seen thinner champions. The armor gave no hint of breasts, and the scarf shielded the face so well that it was hopeless.

And then Griff swung too high. The Panther ducked once again, taking the butt of their sword and face slamming Griff. He staggered. The small champion waited for nothing this time, kicking the sword from Griff's hands then kicking one leg out from under him. He fell face first in the dirt, eating it.

The Panther lunged, sword swung high to bring down on Griff's exposed neck. But Viktor was there to greet the Panther's steel with his own. He blocked the swing and kicked the Panther. The warrior stumbled backwards, their eyes displaying their confusion. Eyes as gray as the storms that rolled in over the sea. They were cold and angry and not afraid.

The Panther switched their sword to their other hand and answered Viktor's interference with a backswing. A quick step was all Viktor needed to avoid the strike, but the tip of the blade scratched his bracer all the same. The sound tore through the morning air. The crowd had gone silent, watching their king's favorite fight with the Panther warrior.

The Panther lunged before feigning, turning instead into a pirouette. But Viktor expected the trick. He brought his sword down hard on the swinging blade and used his other arm to elbow the Panther in the face. The warrior stumbled. Viktor slipped the Panther's sword from their hand with his own, pressing the tip to the Panther's throat as they heaved for air on the ground.

Griff grunted but did not attempt to stand from where the Panther had left him. He was bleeding and coated in dirt, but he watched Viktor beat the warrior and bowed his head in acquiescence.

Ramiro slowly stood. Danica was beside him attempting to hide the frown that wanted to form on her face. Danon was red faced but offered no remark. He merely waited patiently for Ramiro to speak. Ramiro's gaze unsettled Viktor. There was something there he wasn't accustomed to seeing. Was it envy? Worry?

"I'm afraid I can not allow you to kill my melee champion, your grace." Ramiro said to Danon. He shrugged, "the queen insists. No bloodshed. Not today when we greet old friends."

"As you say, your grace," Danon answered.

With a flick of his hand, Danon motioned to his warrior that their fight was over. The champion stood, ignoring Viktor's offer of assistance up, and ripped their sword from his hand.

Griff reluctantly shook the warrior's hand before stalking off the field and—Viktor imagined—to the nearest tavern.

Danon stood and applauded with the crowd. It was a nervous applause. Most did not know what to think of the performance they had witnessed. Surely some thought the warriors would fight to the death. And that it seemed Griff was going to lose had Ramiro not sent Viktor in to save him.

Viktor, the king's favorite, who never fought in tournaments.

"Your grace, I am pleased to present my champion." Danon gestured towards the Panther, who removed their headscarf and cap.

The crowd grew silent when the woman's long plait of hair fell down her back. Scarlet dribbled down her lip and chin where Viktor's elbow had connected to her face. She wiped it away lazily. Blood smeared across her cheek.

Viktor felt a tight cinch around his chest. Had he hit a woman? Ramiro's mouth hung open as he stood beside Danica whose smile gave away her eerie pleasure.

"Your grace, my champion, Princess Cecelia of house Delacroix. My sister." Danon further explained.

Cecelia bowed, though curtly. She offered another small nod to Danica. "Your graces."

Danon scowled at Viktor. "The wager's off, my lord, for your monstrous interference."

Viktor nodded his head in agreement. *Monstrous*. He looked at Cecelia, whose cheek was smeared with blood, and agreed.

I have sent Myra to the court of the Golden Lord where she will use her womanly talents to gather information. I'm mostly concerned with naval secrets, but I've informed Myra that any information she gleans about the Golden Lord will be useful.

Queen Haigee
Letter to her mother, Lady Lia

With the opening of this academy, I hope to plant seeds among us that will grow and fruit, spreading across the known world, gathering knowledge that will serve the empire for generations to come.

Lady Myra
Speech given on opening day of the
Emissary Academea

I thought she loved me. How foolish I've been.

The Golden Lord
Letter to his close friend, Sir Raiju

Chapter Five

Finely woven tapestries depicted ancient scenes. Some were too old to know what was really taking place. They were indiscernible shapes interacting with other vaguely distinguishable things. Others were newer, woven to portray the victories of the last rebellion. Sharp stitches of contrasting colors, each capturing a moment so vividly it was easy to get drawn in by every detail, told the story of the victories that won Ramiro's father his throne.

Danon had wanted her to clean up in the tent, but Cecelia insisted they meet with Ramiro right away. She wiped her face on a cloth drenched in jasmine oil, offered to her by the queen's own handmaid, and followed the large knight back to the castle.

The knight that had disarmed her.

Cecelia tried to stop her teeth from grinding, but the mere thought of her loss—in front of so many people—aggravated her.

She stopped to study a tapestry, forcing herself to relax her jaw. Relax her face. Let the loss go. It was only a melee. But her pride tugged at the corner of her lips, building a frown. She focused on the tapestry, trying to convince herself there were better things to worry about than being disarmed by a Korithian barbarian.

The tapestry depicted King Romo astride a large, black horse. Bodies, all adorned in the colors of Norian, lay stacked below. The Mother and Daughter, both full, shined down on Romo's newly won crown. A double blessing.

Their knightly escort stopped. He turned to see what the holdup was. Upon seeing Cecelia study the tapestry, he spoke.

"King Romo," he said, "the day of the Great Red Way's victory."

"I know who it is," she said without bothering to look at him.

There was no need to curtsy for him. And how she hated to curtsy. Besides beating her at the melee, she knew he was the man Anya spoke of on the ship. There was no one else it could be. The knight was both tall and broad of shoulder, and his left jaw and neck were painted warmly in scarlet. The mark of His Brilliance. His presence and his face annoyed her already.

"I've studied your history."

"Of course you have," he mumbled to himself, turning to take them further down the hall.

"Cece," Danon growled in their mother tongue, "manners."

Cecelia rolled her eyes, but followed. She was only supposed to butter up Ramiro, not his loathsome guard dog.

"I fought with Romo that day," the knight offered. "You must know why they call it the Red Way, then, champion."

He had taken to calling her that, rather than *highness* or *your grace* as he did Danon. Perhaps he thought it insulted her. Cecelia quite liked it.

"Or did you learn that in your books, too?"

Cecelia laughed. He certainly wasn't your usual knight. There was no grace and little courtesy within him. And yet, he was powerful. Cecelia could see that in his towering height and thick arms. How easily he had disarmed her. He carried himself heavily, though he did not drag his feet like a drunkard or fool would. He was light on his feet, like a warrior.

Like a knight.

And he hadn't let blind rage get in the way of disarming her like the other Korithian had. That man had fallen right into her trap, letting her aggravate him until he could only see red. But this one didn't even let her try. He had read her feint and removed her sword from her hand before she could think of a way out. Before she could outsmart him.

And that bothered her more than anything.

"I've heard you were Romo's squire." She finally said, picking at the leather that frayed at the edge of her bracer.

"Is that all?" The knight scoffed.

"No," Cecelia said. "I heard you saved Romo when he was wounded, and three men surrounded him. You killed them all with naught but a sword and no shield."

"Indeed I did," the knight said proudly.

"A Panther always fights without a shield. It would be no feat for me," she whispered.

Her brother offered her a glare, which she returned with a sweet smile.

The knight ground his teeth, clearly biting back choice words. Rather than offer them to her, he said, "it didn't help you today, did it?"

He turned away from her and carried on down the hall to a pair of large oak doors. The knight pushed the doors open unceremoniously. Ramiro sat behind a desk. A man dressed in black sat opposite him.

"Here they are," the knight said.

Ramiro smiled. "Your graces," he suggested to the man in black. "Might I introduce General Rees."

Rees stood and bowed his head slowly. "Prince Danon, Princess Cecelia," he said.

Danon nodded his head in return. "A pleasure to meet you, my lord."

"You're a great warrior, General Rees. Or so the word across the Stormy Sea says," Cecelia added. She didn't bow.

Rees laughed. "Well, I wouldn't put it that way, but yes, I've done my fighting for Korith, your grace."

"Nonsense. Rees helped win the battle that secured my father the throne!" Ramiro said.

"Is this the same battle that your predecessor died in?" Cecelia asked. "He fought for the rebellion as well. And his death secured your position as general, did it not?"

Danon offered her a calculated stare. She knew what it meant. *Shut up.* But she wouldn't. They would know she did not fear them. Women in the Lagos were hard to scare.

The general stood a little straighter. "General Daws was a good man. His death affected me greatly. I learned much of what I know about warcraft from him."

The large knight glared at Cecelia. She smiled at him. He rolled his eyes. One look from Ramiro and the man backed into the edge of the room, amongst the darkness.

Cecelia smiled at the thought of the knight being one of her father's Shadowmen. Could he pass the tests of subtly all Shadowmen went through? Could he move within the darkness of the shadows, acting as part of it? Could he stand silent and still, for days, starving, not weakening or dropping, always ready to defend the king? She eyed him up and down while he stood in his shroud of blackness.

No, definitely not.

He noticed her stares and shifted further right, further into the shadows. Danon sat in a chair offered by Ramiro. Cecelia remained standing.

"I understand your grace has studied a bit of warcraft yourself?" Rees asked. "You must be an exceptional student. You would have defeated Griff had Viktor not stepped in to stop you." He said it with a slight tilt of his mouth, a snicker hidden in his voice.

"Are you questioning my method, general? Or merely my sex?" Cecelia stared evenly at Rees. "Does it bother you that a woman defeated your man?"

He shrugged. "Griff was not one of mine. Soldiers aren't permitted in the tourneys, only free knights. Viktor seemed to have no trouble, though." He sipped from a glass full of amber liquid.

Cecelia stared Rees down. She was aware Danon begged her to sit without actually speaking. She could feel it, his nervous energy lifting off his skin and reaching for her.

"My father spared no expense with my sister's training," Danon offered, his voice quietly filling the heated silence that crowded the room.

"Well then, a toast to King Filip, Lord of the Panthers, for his ability to see talent where some would not." Rees said.

Ramiro raised his glass obediently. A glass was thrust into Danon's hand, and he did the same.

Cecelia finally sat. She yearned to reach her hand into her boot and retrieve the dagger that nestled there. Her fingers itched for it. Rees' disrespect required punishment. But she squeezed the glass handed to her, reading the warning in Danon's eyes.

Calm down.

"I have to say, your grace, your fight today was spectacular," Ramiro leaned back in his leather chair, the newness of it squeaking beneath him.

"Thank you," Cecelia said. And, after a glance from Danon, "your grace."

"Although I admit, I'd love to see you fight, Danon," Ramiro spoke.

"Yes, I'm curious too," Rees said. "Can the brother outshine the sister?"

A noise from the tall knight drew Cecelia's attention. It sounded like a small choke or stifled laugh.

"Pay no mind to him," Ramiro said when he saw Cecelia looking at Viktor. "He's impudent, but the best Kingsguard a king can find."

"As he demonstrated when he forced me to yield my victory. And yet you have him escorting us around?" Cecelia asked.

"Only the best for my guests," Ramiro smiled.

The knight was a spy. It was obvious. Cecelia smiled at Ramiro, thinking the entire time about how she'd like to skewer him with her sword. It wouldn't take much. The man was no wider than she.

Perhaps thinner.

"While I'm pleased to offer my hospitality, your graces," Ramiro flicked a glance at Rees before looking at Cecelia. "I'm curious to know the cause of your visit. Surely a sail across the Sea of Storms wasn't just for fun."

Cecelia smirked. Now it was their turn to lie.

"The tourney is a great attraction," she said. "No doubt tomorrow's competition will be impressive."

"Will you compete again, your grace?" Rees asked.

She scoffed. "Certainly not. My royal brother forbids me. I shall instead watch and enjoy myself."

She looked at Viktor in his dark shroud and winked. He wiggled further back into the darkness.

"Yes, yes, but that doesn't answer my question." Ramiro's words gave away his agitation.

Cecelia shared a quick look with Danon, hoping he'd keep his wits as he spoke.

Danon cleared his throat. "Your grace, our visit is meant to reconnect with old friends."

The wide charming smile he used on women filled his face. It took everything Cecelia had not to laugh, knowing her brother was performing.

"Trying times are ahead for the Lagos of the Moons. My father merely wants to reestablish old ties, hoping should help be required, Korith could be considered."

Ramiro offered Rees a surprised look, though Cecelia could tell he wished to keep it covered up.

"Allies, then?" Rees leaned forward in his chair. "But from whom? You Panthers are an awfully peaceful lot, commanding loyalty wherever you go." He drank from his glass. "Who would be stupid enough to agitate King Filip?"

It was the moment of truth. Would they take the bait and swallow or fight? Cecelia tried to show little emotion. She looked at Viktor in the corner to distract herself. He had inched his way back, closing in on the group.

"To our east, there is another large island."

Ramiro nodded. "The Goldenones, I've read. A rather angry people. But they stick to themselves, mostly. Surely they haven't encroached on your kingdom?"

In truth, the Goldenones were great trading partners. They offered their mined goods for the Lagos' plentiful food. And when King Filip wished to reduce the cutting of trees on the islands, the Goldenones brokered a trade with Inush and Nubaria further east to bring their lumber. All in exchange for their own goods, of course. But angry? Cecelia wondered where Ramiro could have heard that. He looked young. Younger even than Danon. Perhaps he was just an ignorant fool.

"They've begun taking out a few of our people's fishing sites on our eastern shore, your grace." Danon accepted more amber liquid from a servant. "When my father sent an envoy to confront them about it, they sent him back with no hands. They said the Panthers have stolen fish from them long enough."

Ramiro sipped from his glass, nodding his head. "And your father responded?"

"He captured the small group of raiders and sent words to the Golden Lord, who told my father to release them or die."

Rees raised his eyebrows. "Mighty words to say to the King of Panthers."

"Indeed," Danon said.

"What did your father say to that?" Ramiro asked.

He sat on the edge of his seat, taking Danon's words in like a child hearing their favorite bedtime story. They had them, Cecelia realized, they believed every word.

"There have been small bouts of fighting back and forth for months," Cecelia chimed in. "There seems to be no sight of an agreement. The Golden Lord made one offer at a resolution, but my father turned it down."

"Which was what, your grace?" said Rees.

"My sister's hand in marriage."

Ramiro choked on his drink but recovered. He smoothed out the creases of his jacket, acting like the idea didn't amuse him. "Isn't your sister but a maid, your grace?"

"Alaina is four and ten and impudent," Cecelia shrugged. "But I suppose a royal Panther seemed like a magnificent prize, even to a man as ancient as the Golden Lord."

Rees chuckled. "Spoken like a true older sister."

Cecelia felt a slight blush creeping across her cheeks. She wondered why she felt embarrassed. Danon offered her a flustered smile. She considered that perhaps she should speak less.

Ramiro had joined in with Rees, laughing, but finally settled down. He wiped a happy tear from his eye and poured himself some more drink.

"I must ask, is your father strictly against marrying Alaina to an ally?"

Cecelia wondered if Ramiro really believed he was being subtle with his questioning.

"You haven't any sons to marry *Princess* Alaina too, your grace," Cecelia reminded him.

"It is more my mother's decision," Danon took over.

Cecelia could tell her interjections displeased him. A red blush had bloomed on his neck and his forehead sweated beneath his curls.

"She aims to marry her to a Southern Lord," Danon said.

"So, he isn't against marrying his other children to... allies?"

"No, no, your grace. He isn't."

Ramiro settled his gaze on Cecelia but said nothing. Behind him, Viktor had inched his way back into the light. Cecelia could see his reddened jaw, the one that bore his birthmark. It fought through his peppered beard, a rouge shadow teasing her. She smiled at him, though she didn't know where the urge came from. He averted his eyes.

"Ramiro, Princess Cecelia looks tired. Perhaps they've had enough discussion for one night. It's clear their purpose for being here is peaceful." Rees offered Cecelia a polite nod.

"Yes," Cecelia admitted, "I am quite tired."

"Very well, until tomorrow, your graces," Ramiro stood and gestured for Viktor to do his job.

The large man emerged from the shadows. His size took Cecelia by surprise again. The shadows cloaked his greatness well. She followed him out of the room.

Perhaps he *would* make a good Shadowman.

Every man—and woman through man—has a role to play in the unfolding of history. Primogeniture works directly against this belief because no man can dictate the path of another! The Mother makes it so. The Daughter ensures it is so. Suggesting a father can choose his own son to rule a kingdom is blasphemous and a great insult to the celestial Mother.

Priest Bertrand Epso III
Sermon notes

Chapter Six

WHEN VIKTOR AWOKE THE next day, his thoughts immediately returned to the night before. He left the Panthers in their parlor, where Ramiro had spared no expense. They occupied their own small wing of the castle, complete with separate sleeping chambers, a shared parlor, small library, and a running toilet. Viktor remembered it felt like ages of walking down the long hallway to their parlor door, listening to them bicker.

"You're such an idiot," the boy had mumbled to his sister.

"And you're a coward," she had replied.

On and on it went, neither saying anything but neither shutting up. Something had happened during their discussion with Ramiro that stirred them. The sister seemed the most upset. Though she seemed quick to anger, anyway.

When he left them, he could hear their yelling through the thick oak doors. Halfway down the hallway, he still heard them. Only down the stairs did their voices finally fade.

Even as he dressed himself, he could hear them in his head.

"What I'd do to be rid of the pair," he muttered, tugging on his boots. "Babies won't shut up."

Viktor checked his sword and realized it needed sharpening. *Only a dead man neglects his weapon.* Or so his father was fond of saying. Viktor had no interest in finding out if it were true.

"Now I'm hearing the voices of the dead," Viktor groaned. He let the door slam shut behind him. What type of day did that bode?

Viktor found Cecelia in the parlor, taking her breakfast. She looked up from her plate when he entered, the storminess of her eyes subsided for the moment.

"Where is Prince Danon?" he asked, forgetting all polite customs. "I am to escort you to the tourney grounds."

"He's probably still sleeping," she tossed a glazed roll back onto its platter, not finding it satisfying. "We know where the grounds are, brave knight, no need to mother us."

Viktor stiffened a little. "Ramiro commanded me to be your highness's royal escort, for it is my sworn duty. And so, I shall be."

Though he'd rather be sleeping.

She nodded her head but said nothing more, instead turning her attention back to her breakfast. The table was a display of Korith's generosity. Viktor spied the royal jellies in their golden cups, pressed solely from the castle vineyard's grapes. Poached eggs and fresh bacon snuggled together in silver platters. Steaming piles of mash waited to be sweetened with honey at the eater's discretion. A large plate of fragrant fruit sat the middle of the table, brightly hued citrus overflowing the porcelain bowl. Viktor's mouth watered. But he knew his place. He was still only a guard. A Kingsguard, yes, but a guard, nevertheless.

He decided he should meld into the environment, disappearing from Cecelia's view until Danon arrived. When he passed a divan, he noticed blankets and pillows tumbling off and onto the floor.

Cecelia must have seen his gaze, for she said, "I couldn't sleep in that room. I slept here."

Viktor nodded, though he couldn't say he understood. A divan over a featherbed? It wasn't long before Danon bustled into the room looking disheveled but pleased. He nodded to Viktor and sat next to his sister.

"I trust your night was profitable?" she mumbled to him.

He snatched an apple from the middle of the table and took a crisp bite. He smiled. "Wouldn't you like to know?"

She rolled her eyes. "The monstrosity is here to escort us to the tourney." She suggested to Viktor.

"Must we require an escort? We have our own guards. I'm certain you could go ahead. That way, you won't miss the jousting Sir Viktor." Danon said.

"With all pardons, your grace," Viktor stepped towards the pair, back into the light of the diamond-paned windows.

But before he could speak, Cecelia picked up his words.

"He's compelled to escort us, brother, for it is his *sworn duty*," she mocked. She glared at him before continuing, "I'll grab my cloak. It appears chilly for once in this hideously hot place. I suggest you shove that apple down your throat and grab one to stuff in a pocket. Who knows how long this day will be?"

The door to her room slammed shut behind her as she left the men behind.

Danon gave Viktor a wry smile. "She's lovely, isn't she?"

Viktor scoffed. He'd seen bar wenches act more a lady than Cecelia. Regardless, he offered no further insult to Danon.

"If your grace wishes, I'll wait at the end of the corridor."

"We won't leave you waiting long, like yesterday," Danon said in passing.

Viktor nodded his appreciation. If he never had another day like yesterday, he'd be thankful. All the waiting in the stifling heat had ignited his anger. Being relegated to escorting the Panther prince only added insult. And then Ramiro had forced him to intervene in the melee.

He hadn't meant to strike the princess. Of course, he hadn't known she was the princess at the time. But it still bothered him. It sat heavy in his stomach, sour and aching.

It made him think of his father.

But he shoved these thoughts from his mind and took up his position at the end of the corridor. He waited, one hand on the pommel of his sword, and tried not to stare at the Panther guards on either side of the parlor's doors.

Their meager armor intrigued him. He wondered how light it was. How much pain one felt if hit directly with a sweeping blade. Originally, Viktor would have considered the armor more costume than protection, but after watching Cecelia fight the day before, he wondered what secrets the armor held. What techniques did the blacksmiths of the archipelago know that Korithian smiths didn't?

Cecelia appeared and stalked down the hall. Gone was her armor and in its stead she wore a dress of midnight blue with a black cloak. She had re-plaited her hair, letting it trailed down the left side of her shoulder. When she noticed he watched her, she slowed her pace and softened her face. She had clearly been dwelling on something that made her angry.

Probably her brother.

"Sir Viktor, it appears it will just be you and I this morn." She was trying her best to appear happy, but her smile was fake, and the tempest of her eyes rose again.

"What..." Viktor began.

"My brother... does not feel well. He spent much of the night drinking with the king and is paying for it now. He wishes to keep it discreet, so we will leave, and he will stay." She wasn't looking at him anymore, but down at her dress, adjusting it and resetting it on her bodice.

Viktor couldn't help but follow her gaze, it being only natural, but when she looked up and caught him, she quickly wrapped her cloak tightly around her.

"Come on," she pushed past him. "Nothing I can do to cure him."

Agitation filled her voice again. Viktor made a mental note to stop talking about her brother. If for any reason but to keep her cheerful, and therefore, his task a bit more cheerful.

Together, they marched through the castle. Several servants stopped long enough to bow or curtsy and mumble *your grace* to Cecelia. She nodded politely but appeared tired of the custom.

"Yes, yes, thank you," she hurried them along through a smile of gritted teeth.

When Ramiro's High Steward appeared, Cecelia stopped and showed more respect. She offered her own curt nod to the man, but no words. Her jaw relaxed a little when she smiled, offering a more pleasant appearance than the forced grins she had given the other servants.

When the man finally left them, Cecelia sighed and carried on. A silence settled over them, one that wasn't entirely uncomfortable. Viktor had never been one to fill a void with words. It seemed Cecelia was of the same mind. She snuck a quick glance at him before plowing on down the hall.

"You fought well yesterday, Sir Viktor," she said, still staring off into the distance.

"I shouldn't have hit you, champion." The words flooded from his mouth before he could consider them. It was what he really felt. What he had wanted to say since the moment she revealed her face and he saw the blood drip from her nose. But Viktor knew it best to keep one's true feelings hidden. "Ramiro commanded me to step in, but I didn't consider...I didn't know—"

"That I was a woman?" She looked at him then, eyes stormy, mouth ticked in a smirk. "I daresay no one considered it. And why is that? Why must a skilled warrior be a man?"

"It is uncommon in Korith, your grace."

She crossed her arms as they walked, holding herself tight, almost shrinking herself. Her body felt minuscule next to Viktor's. Again, he cursed himself for not knowing she was a woman. The dried blood might have been wiped from her face, but the cut still leered at him from her lip, reminding him he was no better than his father.

Viktor pushed onward, trying his best to ignore his own thoughts while encouraging her silence. If they made it to the tourney grounds without speaking another word, without stoking the woman's apparent agitation, Viktor would consider it a success.

But Cecelia's silence began to bother him. She was too quiet. Almost meditative. She was a prideful woman and he had — in fact — knocked her in the face. She didn't seem to have a problem opening her mouth most of the time. Viktor wondered if it had to do with Ramiro and their talk the night before.

The king was an idiot for letting them stay.

When they finally reached the arch to the inner bailey yard, Cecelia's mood seemed to lift with the wind. Her smiles at the servants and guards were a bit more sincere. Especially when she smiled at the guardsmen. Viktor tightened his grip on his sword, but for what reason, he didn't know.

Perhaps because they were late.

"Your grace," he began quietly, though he would have rather excluded the pleasantries and get straight to his point, "we should move along at a faster pace. The king hates waiting."

She narrowed her eyes at him but offered no snide remarks. With a final curtsy, she dismissed herself from some ladies of the court. They walked toward the gate of the inner bailey wall, portcullis drawn high to allow the in and out flow of the castle guests and servants. It was only when they drew under the downward points of the portcullis that she spoke.

"An envoy's job is to socialize, you know." The words slipped from her mouth coolly while she nodded at a passing lady.

"Forgive me, champion," he growled, "but I thought socializing with the king would be more important."

"Then you thought wrong," she mumbled to herself.

She said nothing more. Instead, she guided them expertly through the outer bailey and out the large main gate. It seemed she knew the castle already, slinking through crowds like a cat. Guards nodded their heads respectfully at Cecelia and Viktor. Viktor offered them a nod in return. Cecelia offered them nothing.

An uproar of cheers went up from the tourney grounds. The first set of jousters had begun. Viktor picked up the pace, falling in beside Cecelia. She glanced at him, then stared off down the road.

The flags of the tourney participants waved in the wind above their tents. Whipping this way and that, Viktor wondered how the wind would play in the jousting. A favorable wind advantage could lead a newbie to victory, or an old timer to repeat success. Though he never enjoyed jousting himself, it at least promised Viktor an interesting tournament day.

Though he'd still rather be sleeping.

"Are you married, Sir Viktor?" Cecelia asked, her voice breaking through his thoughts so suddenly, Viktor stopped walking.

Cecelia did too, peering back at him with a smile nearly reminiscent of her brother's. Viktor almost laughed.

"I'm a Kingsguard," he grunted before carrying on.

Cecelia was forced to keep his pace then, though she didn't seem bothered by his elongated stride. In fact, she seemed to keep pace with him considerably well.

"Aye, and a knight all the same. Don't knights marry in Korith?" Her voice came softly, Viktor almost missing her words.

She was toying with him, he could tell. He didn't have to look at her face to know she wore a smirk across it. Lovely though it may be.

"Surely some of those ladies I met earlier were married to knights. I think there was one. Or two." She acted like she spoke to herself, but he knew she dug her point in deeper.

"Kingsguards are held to different standards," he spoke.

Truthfully. Ramiro wanted those meant to guard him to think of him and only of him. A woman on a man's mind when it should focus on guarding the king could be lethal. And Viktor liked the simplicity of his life with just this one rule: protect the king.

He had learned long ago, watching his mother and father fight, that marriage was a farce and love a myth. You had to choose to love someone, and not just once, but every single day. How complicated it made things. How messy.

"I see," Cecelia said. And after a moment's pause, "so, no children for you?"

Viktor grunted in reply. What was she getting at?

Before he could ask her, they arrived at the bottom of the cobbled road. Traffic picked up. Large carts pulled by enormous horses, sometimes two or three, rolled by filled with casks of wine. Its musky scent drifted behind to tempt those that followed. Another cart burst with chickens. The acrid smell of the birds mixed heavily with that of wine, creating an unpleasant sensation in Viktor's nose. Several food stalls fed the tournament goers, adding their spices to the market's perfume.

"This way," Viktor yelled over the ruckus of the street.

To their right was a small, cobbled alley, and on the other side, a plaza. A large fountain stood in the center, a seat for young lovers. Children sat idly on the steps, watching their parents peddle their wares to any passerby who would meet their eyes. Some even argued over who saw who first.

Viktor attempted to avoid the children. He shoved Cecelia to the side of the plaza, gently of course, and guided her through the majority of the riffraff. But out of a smaller side street arrived several white-haired priests. Their gray cloaks looked dusty, as if they had been riding and only just arrived.

Viktor recognized them at once as Universalists, heads of the religious sect bent on removing Ramiro from the throne. They didn't think primogeniture was cohesive with a progressive nation such as Korith. They didn't think much of anything was cohesive with a progressive nation such as Korith.

"Will the kind lady share a moment to speak of a dire need in the city?"

"Ah princess! What a moment of your time would mean to the Priesthood!"

"Please, beautiful lady, just a few words."

Cecelia's eyes widened. Her neck tensed as the men closed in on her. The way she slipped her arm within his own, like a lord escorting his lady, startled Viktor. But when the priests continued pushing in, he grabbed her arm tighter within his and pushed through.

"Move," he growled, "or I'll have the king remove your head for you."

The priests finally fell aside, but Cecelia continued holding on until they reached the far side of the plaza. Large arched greeneries marked the entrance to the tourney grounds, and this seemed to relax her. She removed her hand just as quickly as she had placed it.

"My thanks," she said.

"I don't need your thanks. I need you to hurry."

The first match was nearly done. Viktor knew Ramiro had wanted to make a show of seating the prince and princess Panther. It would be hard to do that while people watched the second set of jousters, still talking and yelling and grabbing money won from the first match.

"Of course," Cecelia said.

Viktor looked at her, forgetting that he was speaking to a princess. She did not appear angry. For once, she appeared pleased. Compliant even.

"This way, your grace," he said before leading the way through the worn brick paths.

He must not forget who he spoke to. She was fiery. It was true. And she seemed to have little respect for any man.

But she was a princess, and he was a Kingsguard.

Lord Lystern, I write to apologize for the spectacle I created at the recent jousting tournament at Bluefield. While my intentions were to win the tournament, and thus the honor, I did not mean to do so with such exuberance. I deeply regret the harm I caused your lovely lady wife.

Sir Ylvian
A Letter to Lord Lystern

Sir Erik Ylvian of Bluefield remains the most famous of Korithian jousters, partially for his impressive winning streak but primarily for jousting with such enthusiasm he knocked his opponent's head into the lap of Lady Lystern.

Sir Derrel Baldi
A History of Tournaments

Chapter Seven

THE KNIGHT ESCORTED HER deftly through the winding paths and swarms of people. It seemed like he understood her agitation at having to stop and offer courtesy to people, to make small talk, to smile.

It was Danon who had been bred to entertain at court, not her. A creature of many talents, Cecelia wished she possessed even a minuscule amount of her brother's charisma. But her father saw she was a fighter. So, while she was away training, Danon remained and trained under the tutelage of their father. He sparred with him, learned warcraft with him, and yes, even learned how to make a woman swoon with him.

Just the thought put a nasty taste in Cecelia's mouth. She spied a servant transporting a tray of glass flutes, all filled to the brim with sparkling liquid, towards the king's pavilion.

"I'll take that." She took one off the tray.

The servant rounded, preparing to rebuke the offender, but when he spied Cecelia and her escort, he swiftly turned and continued his trek to the pavilion.

Viktor chuckled at her. She threw back the bubbly as fast as she could. It was tingly and sweet. A buttercream champagne. Not her favorite. But it rinsed her throat of the taste of home and helped raise her spirit.

"How long is the jousting, Sir Viktor?" Cecelia handed the flute to a random passing servant.

The servant looked surprised to find the glass in her hand. By the look of her dress, Cecelia realized she wasn't a kitchenmaid. Most likely a handmaid. The bluebird embroidered on the sleeve of her dress looked like the one on Danica's signet ring. So not just any handmaid. The queen's handmaid. Cecelia winked at the woman before turning back to the large knight.

"Long. Seven upon seven matches, usually." Viktor answered her.

"Seven upon seven?" Cecelia mumbled to herself, "why so many? Aren't all jousting matches the same?"

Viktor laughed, having caught her words. "Not a fan of jousting, champion? More a melee fan?"

They had reached the back steps of the king's stands. She rounded on Viktor and stared down at him from four steps up.

"When the melee is fair." She said.

He looked at her, stunned, but then a hint of a smile teased the corner of his lips. He nodded in agreement and suggested she keep walking up the steps. It wasn't unpleasant, Cecelia thought, his smile.

Viktor cleared his throat to grab Ramiro's attention, but he was engrossed in a conversation with General Rees, half listening to the old man's words, half watching the match. One jouster unseated the other, and he stood with the crowd, cheering wildly. He finally noticed Viktor and then Cecelia.

"Your grace!" He shouted, "I had feared you would not come!"

Rees studied Cecelia closely. She hated the feeling of his eyes on her skin. She inched away from him, stepping into Viktor, throwing herself off balance. The tall man steadied her before turning back to his king.

"The boy, I mean Prince Danon, is running behind. He felt..." the knight glanced down at Cecelia.

"Sick," she finished for him. "Indeed, the drink is so rich here. He is having a time dealing with it."

"I see," Ramiro said, not appearing at all displeased. "I offered him my finest bourbon last night. He seemed to handle it well, but perhaps I was wrong. Ah well, no trouble, your grace. My wife herself has taken ill this morning, though hers may be from the tribulation of childbirth and then the excitement of your arrival. All too much for a woman to handle, I'm afraid." And when he saw Cecelia's scowl, he added, "Certainly a woman such as yourself would have no trouble, but... she is a frail woman."

"Yes," Cecelia said, her eyes steadily focused on the king, "fragility is so common amongst my lot."

Her words sliced through the crisp morning air. She said no more, nor bowed, as she sidled past Viktor and found a seat nearby.

A second chair sat next to the one Danon occupied the day previous. Covered in black silk, the chairs were a nod towards the Panther's house colors. The fabric was cool and smooth. Cecelia sank down into it with a sigh. The morning had just begun, but she wished it were already over.

Viktor stood dutifully behind her seat, watching over the crowd while the next set of jousters prepared themselves. Nestled in a hidden pocket of her cloak was the coin Anya had given her. It would not be a good time to return it, not with Ramiro so close. She watched Viktor shift in his boots, entranced by the jousters.

Viktor's size still surprised her. The top of his head nearly hit on the wooden joists meant to hold up the roof of the king's pavilion. He was at least a hand taller than Danon. Indeed, he towered over everyone. Cecelia had to turn her face upward just to look at him, which she actually found refreshing. Most men in the Lagos never surpassed her. Not she, with her royal blood.

His face was an aged one. It was clear he had seen more years than Cecelia. He would have been nearly a man when she was born.

The birthmark on his jaw trailed down beneath his armor, piquing her curiosity. Where did it end? When his eyes fell on her looking at him, Viktor stepped backwards, out of her line of sight.

They were brown, his eyes, with the smallest hint of green and gold flecks. Like an afterthought. Warm, despite the knight's abrupt nature and seemingly quick temper. When he looked at her, she felt like he was actually looking *at* her, not just her body. Not just what was on the surface.

No, Cecelia realized, it would not be the best time to bring up Anya. But it was still a perfect time to torment the man. She could tease out his misery until a time better suited presented itself. He deserved at least that much for what he did to the poor girl.

"Your grace," Cecelia cooed to Ramiro during a lull in the cheering.

Ramiro turned towards her, offering her a gentle smile, signifying she had his attention.

"I sit all alone," she pouted, suggesting to Danon's empty seat, "and jousting... isn't my strongest competition. I fear we do little of it in the Lago."

She waited, gauging her next words based on Ramiro's reaction. He seemed barely concerned, trying to pay attention to the jousters as they rallied at their end of the track.

"I wonder if I might have someone join me, someone who could help me learn more." She looked at Viktor. "Perhaps my guard. He proved himself a mighty warrior yesterday."

Viktor stepped forward, preparing to repel her request, but Ramiro spoke first.

"Do it," he said, waving Viktor to Danon's seat.

He watched the jousters approach each other at full speed. With a loud crash, one lance connected with the other's shield and shattered. But the rider remained seated.

"Whoa!" Ramiro shouted, rising in his seat to get a better look at the carnage. He looked back to see Viktor still standing. "Sit!" He ordered again.

Viktor begrudgingly moved to Danon's seat. With a thump, he sat down next to Cecelia. She offered him her best smile. Danon would be proud.

"Welcome, my lord," she said sweetly.

"I'm no lord," he fussed.

Cecelia shrugged, leaning back in her chair. The jousters took up their places at the end of the track again. They gave the rider with the shattered lance a new one.

"A Panther man is always styled 'lord.' It is a sign of respect."

Though she did not respect him. But that was part of the game.

"An odd custom. Not every man can be a lord."

"Why not? You sound like your Korithian Universalists."

Viktor frowned. He didn't answer, but focused on the jousters. Now that he sat on her left, she had a better view of his birthmark. It didn't rise nearly as far into his face as she first thought. Merely just to the jawline. It dispersed somewhere in his stubble, wrapping around the back of his neck a little.

"What is it you find so confusing, champion?" Viktor's voice broke the icy silence that settled between them.

Champion again. It didn't bother her nearly as much as he thought it did. Across her lips she painted another sweet smile. "I'm unsure of how a winner is declared if a rider isn't unseated."

She leaned on the arm of her chair, closer to Viktor. He craned backwards, attempting to keep his distance. Her closeness made him uncomfortable. Good.

"It is based on points. Contact is worth one point. A direct blow to the opponent's shield is two. Seven points to win it all. Unseating is an instant victory."

"Points?" she asked. The entire purpose was points, like a children's game? "Ridiculous," she said. "In battle, a rider with a spear does not keep track of how many times he stabs a man. He merely kills him. Done."

There was a reason the melee was her favorite. It made sense. Live or die.

Attempting to hide a grin, Viktor turned back to the riders. "You wish to see more blood, champion?"

"I should wish to see real fighting."

"To the death then?"

She said nothing more. Rees leaned close, his face turned away, but his ear angled toward them, listening in on their conversation.

"Tell me more of the knights," she spoke, wishing to not give any information to Rees he didn't already know. "Why aren't they soldiers in the army? And why don't the soldiers fight in the tourney?"

Viktor sighed. He turned to Cecelia. He smelled of salt and something sweet, perhaps mint. It wasn't entirely unpleasant, so Cecelia leaned in, taunting Viktor with her eyes. Instead of reeling away from her, as he had previously done, he held his ground, prepared to play her game too.

"After the rebellion, a standing army was ordered by King Romo. General Daws was the leader of Romo's vanguard but died before he could be appointed general. So Rees was chosen. Recruited men report to him. And he reports to the king."

"And the knights?"

"Knights are typically landowners or sons of landowners. They have titles. Money. The king requires fealty from the knights, but they have their own responsibilities."

"So, soldiers are typically peasants?"

"Aye, those that aspire to be more," he spoke. "And those that are persuaded to join."

"Criminals," Cecelia gathered his gist.

In the Lago, there were no knights. Every able-bodied boy and girl joined the army on the day they turned six and ten and were only released on their twentieth birthday. Some chose to stay past twenty. Some didn't. It didn't matter though, as newer, younger, Panthers were ready to fill their spots. Ready to die for the kingdom if need be.

"What's so funny, champion?" Viktor asked, having noticed the start of a smile on Cecelia's face.

"Nothing. I was just imagining the horse that would be needed to carry you across the field." Cecelia quietly turned her head just so, away from Viktor, so he could see she was finished with him.

She needn't look at him. She could feel the intensity of his anger from her seat. It emanated off his body like heat from a cook stove. He did not like to be made the joke. To be belittled. Insults did not roll easily off his skin like a man sure of himself. She had found a weak spot. A place to poke. She wanted to smile, but knew she should keep her composure.

After a few moments, she felt him stand and retreat to his hiding spot behind her chair. She fought the urge to turn around and say something else to him, another quip. But she didn't. Danon had finally arrived, his smile suggesting he was feeling better.

"Are you recovered, your grace?" Ramiro stood and greeted the prince.

Danon eyed Cecelia, letting her face tell him what the appropriate response should be. "I am, your grace," he said.

"Come, sit." Cecelia patted the chair next to her. "The company is so dull," she said loud enough for Viktor to hear.

Peeking over her shoulder, she saw Viktor grit his teeth. He glared at her for only a second before moving his gaze across the jousting field.

Brown with flecks of gold and green, she thought. Why did she find she liked them on her skin?

The Fair Folk are traditionally nomadic and have occupied the Great Continent for over two thousand years. They are ethnically and religiously separate from the main citizens of Korith, but have been - by tradition - allowed to remain as part of the populace by the grace of each monarch. Practitioners of common magic, most Fair Folk make their money peddling charms and crafts associated with magic arts. They are roughly organized, choosing to create large family groups when traveling for trade. A Prevailing Mother is chosen every ten years to act as governing ruler over all Fair Folk. When matters are brought before her, her word is final.

Court Historian Alfred Peri
  The Scroll of Children: A Collected History of the Fair Folk

Chapter Eight

With several crushed helms, a lamed horse, and one shredded lance embedded in a knight's armpit, the jousting competition was finally over. The people flooded out of the tourney grounds in jovial moods. Boisterous laughter was everywhere. Music creeped out of taverns and homes. It was as if the mere presence of the Panther prince and princess added to the festivities tenfold.

Back at the castle, Viktor attempted to survive the feast hastily thrown together for the Panthers' benefit. Lords and ladies flitted everywhere. Satin and heavily brocaded linen swished with their every step. Dangling earrings, bejeweled and splendid, tossed the light from the chandelier in multiple directions. Servers darted in and out of guests with trays piled high with food and drink. Sensuous smells of spices filled the air: cinnamon, bergamot, and red pepper.

Viktor wanted to yank an entire flagon of mead from a nearby server, but Danon's laugh cut through the noise, reminding him he had a job to be doing. He turned away from the flagon and went to search for the Panther prince.

He found the boy laughing, leaning in close to the words of Danica. Her wide smile gave him the full force of her beauty and charm. Viktor looked about for his sister. After her initial chattiness, her icy silence later in the tournament irritated him. She seemed handy with a sword and was just as sharp with her words. She was much more interesting than any normal woman.

Danon, on the other hand, was annoying. He said nothing useful and exhibited zero skills Viktor found remotely interesting. Though it seemed the ladies of the court found him interesting enough.

After surviving the princess's abuse during the jousting, Viktor felt the princess owed him for the mistreatment. He wanted nothing more than to interrogate her and ask her where she trained. How had she masterfully controlled her fight against Griff, a man three times her size who carried a monstrous sword meant to kill bears, all while carrying a...skewer? Viktor had disarmed her only because he had had the advantage of watching her fight before stepping into a duel with her.

Had Viktor been in Griff's position, he probably would have lost, too.

Viktor spotted her sneaking off through an open archway to the veranda. He looked around to make sure he was not needed anywhere immediately, checked to see the queen and her ladies thoroughly entertained Danon, and then made his way toward the door.

It was dusk out. The Mother neared half in the sky and the Daughter was three quarters full. Torches in their notches burned along the outer wall. Viktor found the princess far down the walk to his right, dressed in shadows, like she were part of the castle itself.

A cat emerged from the darkness of her feet and meowed. It stretched and purred while she reached down to pet it. She did not hear him approach.

He walked up to stand beside her. "I don't like cats," he said.

She continued to stroke the stray, not looking at him, not acting the least bit startled. "Men dislike strangers. They fear what they don't understand."

He frowned. "I said I didn't like them, not that I feared them."

"What's the difference?" She faced him, firelight and moonlight both falling on her face, illuminating it.

Standing so close to her, alone on the veranda, he could finally study her. To stare and judge, to imprint her features in his mind. He saw she was only a faint shadow of her brother. The same high cheekbones perhaps, the same sharp chin. But freckles fled on ivory skin where her brother's was dark and sun kissed. Her hair, plaited earlier, fell in rivers down her shoulders. She flicked it to the back.

She smelled of pine sap and something woodsy. Cedar. Smells that reminded him of childhood, of days spent climbing trees in the southwest where his family fiefdom sat. It was slightly warmer there, and the heat encouraged monstrous trees to grow just outside the fort.

Her eyes wandered over his face, settling on his birthmark. He twisted his head away, placing his mark in the shadows.

"The difference is my manhood, my lady."

"Oh, I've no doubt of your bravery, Sir Viktor. Or your strength. Or whatever it is men use to qualify themselves as men." She glanced out into the darkness before looking back into his eyes. "No doubt at all."

"My, you have a mouth," he said.

She laughed. "Indeed. In the Lago, women aren't just pretty gems, meant to be seen and not heard. My father taught me to speak. And speak loudly, my lord."

"As I've said, I am no lord," Viktor replied.

She shrugged. "And as I've said, it is a sign of respect in the Lago." She stared back out into the darkened sea.

Viktor looked out as well, but saw nothing. He let the sounds of the waves crashing below rock him into a placid state. When he finally looked back at Cecelia, she no longer stared off into the darkness. Instead, she looked at him. Really seeing him. Before she had appeared annoyed at his presence, but she seemed to target him then, intrigued. He shifted in his boots. She read the worry on his face.

"I needn't call you it if you like." she finally broke her gaze and looked away.

"That would be preferable, my lady," he mumbled.

He had called her champion since her win against Griff. It seemed strange to call her a lady when she seemed so opposite of all the other women he knew.

"I have a word for you, knight," she looked at the moons, their light falling on her, illuminating her in a most beautiful way.

"Viktor, will do," he stopped her.

"Viktor then," she said, turning to face him, her eyes cool and even. "The captain's daughter upon our ship, Anya, wished me to give this back to you."

Reaching her hand forward, he saw the glint of silver. It fell heavy into his palm. Holding it up to the light of many torches, he saw it was a silver coin. The face of Marian appeared on one side, while the other held a single oak tree.

He frowned. "I haven't the slightest idea what this means."

"Oh?" Cecelia asked. "She says she slept with a large man and was got with child." Cecelia pointed to Viktor. "Must we quibble about your size?"

Viktor thrust the coin back at Cecelia. "Take it. Give it back to the girl."

"So, you don't deny it was you?"

"It wasn't me who got her pregnant, but I gave her the silver." When he saw Cecelia had no intention of taking the coin back, Viktor dropped his hand. "I pitied her is all."

"Pitied her?" Cecelia's eyebrows shot upwards.

"Yes. We both drank too much one night in the tavern down by the docks. She was with the crew. My friend Jaz bought her drinks. She barely spoke Korithian, and he thought she was a prize to be won. She fell off her chair, knocked her head, and passed out. I only checked to make sure she was alive before seeking out my own bed. She awoke briefly before passing back out."

"So, she was raped?" Cecelia asked, "by this Jaz of yours?"

"He's no more my friend," Viktor offered her the coin again. "He got in a brawl later that night, stupid boy, and died from his wounds. When the girl told me, and me knowing she'd get no help from a dead man, I gave her the silver."

Cecelia finally took the coin. She stared at it, flipping it over with her fingers.

"That was kind of you, knight. Viktor." She smiled up at him.

"It was a lie," he deflected the compliment.

"A kindness nevertheless."

"A lie is a lie," he placed his hands firmly on the banister and stared out at the tumultuous waves once more.

Stars emerged from behind the clouds, winking at them from their heavenly perches. He counted the seven stars of seven archers, the child queen on her throne, and his favorite — the gorgon and the warrior. Cecelia stood near him, arms crossed, while she leaned against the veranda's posts. She was quiet, but glanced from the stars to Viktor, and back again.

"What are you looking at?" he finally asked.

"I'm wondering why you refuse to admit you have honor." She glanced at him from the corner of her eyes. "An honorable knight who denies his honor is a confused knight indeed."

Viktor shrugged. "And I say a woman who hides her sex to fight a man is scared."

Cecelia laughed. "Scared? Do you think that giant would have fought me had I revealed I was a woman beforehand? That your king would have let me fight at all? He felt the need to send you in, just so no Korithian need suffer the unbearable embarrassment of dying at the hands of a Panther. Imagine the horror at discovering it was by a woman too?"

Viktor was quiet for a moment, remembering Griff. He was a good fighter. Large. Powerful. But not smart. Not like this Panther woman.

He looked at her and nodded in agreement. "Perhaps you're right. And I am sorry about your face."

She waved his words away. "I'm fine. I wasn't born the prettiest, so you did no lasting damage." She studied him a moment longer before adding. "Was he akin to you? You're roughly his size."

"No," Viktor said. "You'll find no brother of mine in the tourneys. The eldest died in the rebellion, no older than seven and twenty. The second rules House Black in his stead and grows old and fat doing so. The third took the prayer beads of the Moon Priests. I haven't seen him in fifteen years."

"And you alone took up the sword?"

"I left home to seek my fortune in a house less volatile than my own. I ended up squiring for Lord Romo. When Ramiro was born, Romo knighted me and told me to guard the boy if he should fall in the rebellion."

"So here you are," Cecelia shook her head, "seems a waste of such a good fighter."

Viktor stared at her. She flicked a piece of stray hair from her face.

"What?" she said when he didn't look away. "You disarmed me in a moment, as if I were a novice. Of course I've spoken to people, asking of you." She gave him a mischievous look, one Viktor couldn't decide if he liked or not. "They all seem so willing to speak of their king's favorite Kingsguard."

"Stories," he replied, "half are made up."

"So half are true?" She smiled to herself. "I wonder which?"

They stood so close together he could feel her body's warmth. With the slightest movement, he could feel her skin on his bare forearm. He looked down at it, marveling.

"Cecelia?" Her name was called from the archway.

Danon smiled lopsided from the archway. "Everything all right?"

"Fine... you?" Cecelia asked.

Viktor saw she held back a grin.

"I was just heading back. Shall we walk together?"

Cecelia smiled at the many ladies that had piled up behind Danon. "You sure? You seem to have plenty of escorts."

The ladies tittered and giggled.

Danon looked back at them, almost surprised to see them there. He looked back at Cecelia and swallowed. "Aye, but I need my sister at this present moment."

The drunkenness was gone from his voice. The Panther's shared a knowing look.

"As you say," Cecelia sighed. She turned back to Viktor. "Apologies, Sir Viktor, for leaving you so soon. I believe we know the path well enough. Good evening."

Her voice had a sense of yearning in it. Viktor found he wanted to follow her, to continue speaking with her, but knew he shouldn't. At least not immediately. They requested space, and space he would give. Cecelia walked away.

Viktor returned to the party, ruminating on the Panther prince's behavior. It was clear Danon had been pretending to be drunk. But why would a man pretend to be drunk when he could really be drunk? It made little sense to Viktor.

Danica stood next to the king, her arm latched around his own. She spied Viktor's gaze and winked at him. Viktor made for the edge of the room, preparing to disappear when Ramiro summoned him.

"Viktor, a word? In my parlor. Ten minutes."

"Aye, your grace." Viktor dipped his head in a curt nod and took his leave.

In the outer hall, the shadows of Cecelia and Danon bob in and out of the arches of the upper parlor. They wound their way down the stairs, but their words floated to him, a mixture of Korithian and their mother tongue.

"No," Cecelia said to Danon, and then words of the Lagos flew from her mouth. Finally, "you can't."

Danon returned her words with a flurry of Lagos speech. He sounded irritated by her worry. But then Viktor turned the dark corner of the back stairwell and their voices were gone.

The inner hall, the secret passageways of the keep where the servants scuttled to and from, was quiet. Unusually far spaced wall sconces lit the dark. They left Viktor in a sea of black before emerging into a wash of fire light only to repeat. A chambermaid approached, but upon seeing

Viktor, she stuck to the side of the wall, startled. She bowed her head before scurrying past.

He climbed the dark steps to the second floor and emerged from the hidden archway into a long hall. At the end were Ramiro's private rooms, his parlor included. The doors were wide open, the firelight's flickering glow spilling out into the hall.

When he entered Ramiro's room, the smell of eucalyptus engulfed him. It drifted in the air and hung there, like rain on a late summer evening. It brought him to a full stop. He wasn't alone in the room. General Rees stood near the veranda door puffing on a pipe.

"General," Viktor greeted him quickly, hoping to hide his surprise.

"I trust you enjoyed the party, Viktor?" Rees blew a smoke ring towards him.

Viktor nodded, realizing General Rees had not been at the party.

"More than you, it would seem," he said.

The old man smiled. "Seems our Panther prince is quite taken with the ladies. But who can blame him?" Rees walked around Ramiro's desk and perched on the corner. "And the princess," the old man studied Viktor's face, his eyes glimmering with what might be glee, "seems rather taken with you."

Viktor scoffed. "I don't know what you're smoking, General, but I'd hope you'd share."

Rees laughed. He puffed a time or two on his pipe again before carrying on. "You don't see it? Of course you don't see it."

Rees stood and approached Viktor. He was a hand shorter, but his bulk lent him authority.

"I'm sure your father taught you that women are trouble. Only useful for getting children."

"My father taught me how long a stick would last during a beating. There was little time for other lessons." Viktor growled.

Rees frowned. He fiddled with his pipe, ignoring Viktor's eyes. "Lord Black was a hard man to please, Viktor. But not Ramiro. Look, see for yourself."

Ramiro escorted Danica down the hall. Their heads inclined towards one another as they whispered and giggled.

"Viktor!" Ramiro called, "Viktor, Viktor."

Danica smiled at Viktor, offering him her hand. He kissed it lightly.

"I trust your day was enjoyable?" she purred.

"Aye, your grace," Viktor forced out the words they wanted to hear. Truthfully, he'd rather have caught up on his sleep.

"Yes, well, who could blame you, what with your blooming friendship with her grace, the princess of Panthers or whatever her proper title is." Ramiro leaned against his desk and yanked the glass topper off his decanter.

He poured himself a drink and offered one to his wife. She politely declined. Ramiro took a quick sip. "Yes, yes Viktor. You've done well."

"Forgive me, your grace, but I am merely doing as you ordered," Viktor responded.

Either Viktor was experiencing a case of mistaken identity, or maybe he was stupider than he thought.

"I saw you speaking with her on the veranda," Danica's cool voice entered the conversation. "I saw the way she looked at you. And you at her."

Viktor said nothing. Cecelia had looked at him, aye, but it was but a moment. And mere moments do not make a friendship. Or did it? His lips tingled, remembering the shape of her mouth when she smiled. The baser part of him, the animal part, wanted to grab her, but he remembered his duty. He remembered the rules.

"Your grace, I..." Viktor began.

Ramiro held up his hand. "No, no Viktor. I'll have none of your squabbling. You were told to escort the Panthers around. You've done your job. This friendliness you've taken with the princess is a surprise and an unexpected delight." Ramiro sipped and nodded his head. "But I think we can use that to our advantage. And that's why I'm so pleased."

"Friendliness?" Viktor finally interjected.

"Please Viktor, if you're not interested in a woman, you're not paying her any mind," Danica said, all queenly composure gone from her voice.

"But not with this one. This one's different." She smiled her wintry smile. "You like this one."

"We want you to continue cultivating this... relationship," Rees added. "We want you to mine it for whatever you can get. We need information. We need to know why they're here."

"You don't believe they're telling the truth?" Viktor asked.

"Do you?" Danica laughed.

Viktor looked away from the queen. The firelight turned her usually beautiful face sinister. Ramiro finished the last drops of his drink and absentmindedly banged the glass on his desk while returning it to the serving tray.

"Your grace?" Viktor yielded to his king.

Ramiro studied him, pursing his lips while he thought. "There are whispers that the Unis have approached the Fair Folk. If they join them, their numbers will nearly double." When Viktor said nothing, Ramiro added, "do as Rees says. Continue to... mine her."

"I don't understand, your grace," Viktor said.

"Do whatever it takes, Viktor," Ramiro said sharply. "Figure it out. We need to know who all the pieces are... where all the pieces go, if we're to play this game with the Unis."

Danica flinched, almost imperceptibly, but Viktor had stared at her face too often not to notice the slight frown forming at the corner of her perfect mouth. The way her eyes hardened at the words of her husband. The way she looked displeased beneath the façade of obedient agreement.

Ramiro flicked his wrists, suggesting Viktor could leave.

With shoulders slumped, he headed for the stairwell. Ramiro's parlor door shut behind him while the trio prepared to scheme some more. But the enveloping darkness comforted Viktor. He walked silently in its depths, never tripping or losing his way, all the way back to his room.

When he finally kicked his boots off and fell into bed, he tried hard not to think about Cecelia. She was a distraction before. A puzzle. Something to look at. Something that annoyed him and fascinated him in equal measures. Yet it was all temporary. She'd be gone, eventually.

But now she was more. She needed to be conquered, as per his king's requests. Viktor shuddered at the thought.

The Nubarians spin a tale most satisfying of an ancient Princess named Ramira. She was said to be a disciplined sorceress whose own father discovered her ability to transform into a swan at the age of seven. She was sent to study at the Golden Dome amidst the Golden Lord's Burned Priestesses, learning incantations, curses, and other transformative spells. King Aabdunos, Ramira's father, married her off to the King of the Archipelago of the Moons where her magic mysteriously disappeared following childbirth.

Privateer and Explorer Medusa Ramsey
   Tides of Adventure

Chapter Nine

A CHAMBERMAID'S ICY FINGERS, her delicate touch gentle on Cecelia's arm, roused her. It was the touch of someone who feared touching. A hand that worried if they woke the sleeping Panther, she might pounce. The maid's words were spoken so softly, Cecelia couldn't hear her.

The frozen memory of the maid's fingers still tingled on Cecelia's skin. She wrapped herself tighter within her blankets. She batted the girl away.

"Away," she growled, "leave me be."

The girl stood, dumbfounded and staring. Cecelia realized she'd spoken in the language of the Lagos.

"Be gone," she barked in Korithian.

"Your grace," the girl's voice wavered, though she stood tall and sure of herself. She struggled with the thick blanket cocooning Cecelia. "You've promised to break your fast with her majesty."

The words struck Cecelia hard. She remembered her promise. And she suddenly felt the weight of that promise. To entertain, first thing in the morning, was the worst act imaginable in Cecelia's mind. The false smiles and interest. The small talk. Cecelia's face formed a frown just thinking about it. She allowed the maid to rip the blankets away, revealing her naked body. The girl seemed surprised. Cecelia smirked.

"It is customary to sleep naked in the Lagos." She stood and stretched, watching the girl blush. "It is hot and humid there."

The maid stalked off into the back hallway, down the servant's hall, her cheeks a growing crimson. Her exit released a flood of several new chambermaids ready with orders to aid Cecelia in dressing.

"I've never required so many to help me cover myself before," Cecelia mumbled in her mother tongue.

"Your grace should learn to pamper yourself more," the Mistress spoke.

A knock from the door cut through the tittering of the maids. One went to see who it was.

"It is Prince Danon, your grace."

"Let him in." Cecelia jumped from her dressing stool.

"But your grace! You're not done dressing!" The Mistress squealed.

Cecelia looked back in the mirror. Her legs were covered and her chest was not bare. She turned to examine her backside, but it, too, was completely covered. Running her fingers through her hair, she tried to tame the wild strands. It was a mess, as it usually was prior to plaiting, but that was normal.

She turned back to the Mistress. "He is my brother," she said. "We swim naked in the palace lagoon until adolescence. He's seen it all before."

The maids whispered to each other, some blushing, but they escorted Danon in anyway.

"Morning, sister." Danon looked around at the giggling women. "Did I miss something?"

"Apparently," Cecelia smirked, "what are your plans this morn?"

"I'm riding out with the king. We're going to do some light hunting before the tourney continues."

"Ah, how manly of you," Cecelia curtsied for him.

"And you? Breaking fast with the queen? How ladylike of you." Danon bowed for her.

He picked up an ivory comb and twirled it amidst his fingers before accidentally dropping it. The Mistress tutted and picked it up. She handed it to another maid, who made it disappear inside a hidden pocket within her dress.

Cecelia began plaiting her hair herself, refusing to allow the chambermaid's to assist her. She ushered them and the Mistress away.

"No, not that!" she said when a maid attempted to approach her with painting pots for her face. "I'll not paint my face. Not today. Not ever."

"Your grace, we do not consider it a vanity to paint your face," the Mistress said, but Cecelia pushed her into the servant's hall and slammed the door.

The siblings shared a long look before bursting into fits of laughter.

"The day you paint your face will be the day I know the Mother descends to reclaim her people." Danon wiped away a tear. "Do you think they know how stupid they are?" Danon took a seat on her bed.

"Steady Danon, overconfidence is easily the death of a siege," Cecelia spoke her father's words so seamlessly she forgot they once came from someone else. And that they referred to warcraft, not intelligence gathering.

Danon chuckled. He leaned back against the pillows. "Perhaps. The queen is certainly overconfident." He fiddled with the tassels that held back Cecelia's bed curtain.

"Oh? Any insights you can offer me? Insights gleaned during a certain conquest?" Cecelia twirled in her dress, stopping herself midway when she realized what she did.

Danon looked at her out of the corner of his eye, an easy smile breaking his lips.

"I'm not interested in such a conquest, you know that. Merely information gathering," Danon ignored Cecelia's insult. "She's frigid despite her pretend warmth. I suspect she's utterly devoted to that fool, Ramiro. But she's vain, Cecelia. Stroke her ego, make her feel non-threatened, the usual. You'll do fine."

"I still don't understand what I might find out that you can't," Cecelia mumbled, accepting Danon's outstretched elbow.

The pair walked arm in arm into the shared parlor. The sun struck low there, casting its orange haze like molten steel across the carpet. The fire, only recently put out, left a trailing scent of smoke behind. Viktor awaited them there, one hand on his sword like a statue, looking oddly cast next to their own guards.

"Good morning, Sir Viktor," Cecelia cooed.

She offered the large man a smile, but he merely tipped his head slightly in her direction.

"Your grace," he barely spoke.

"Will you take the behemoth today, or must he be my burden?" Cecelia asked Danon.

Viktor glared at her as she spoke her mother tongue. By the way he bristled, she knew he realized she spoke about him. She winked at him just to antagonize him some more. He glared but looked away.

"You should take him. Who knows what evil the queen plans," Danon replied, and then in Korithian, "you'll follow my sister today, Sir Viktor. I'll ride with the king. My own guards will suit me. That's plenty, surely."

Viktor nodded but said nothing. He didn't even look at Cecelia.

"I'd rather risk it alone with the queen." Cecelia's eyes rested on Viktor's face.

His birthmark teased her now that he'd shaved. It ran in tantalizing scarlet down his neck, where his heartbeat could be felt were Cecelia to reach for it. She lost sight of it behind the cowled neck of his doublet and chest plate. She wondered how far it went, how much it covered.

"A prosperous day, brother," Cecelia nodded to Danon.

She extended her arm for Viktor to take. "Shall we? The queen surely awaits me."

Viktor took off out the parlor door, leaving Cecelia standing alone. She looked at Danon, who only shrugged.

"Perhaps a smile or two?" Danon said, "without your usual sass?"

"As you say, brother," she huffed and took off after Viktor.

He waited for her in the hall, still avoiding her eyes. When she came within a step of him, he took off again, down the long hall of the wing. Cecelia had to hasten her pace to keep up.

"A beautiful day, I see," Cecelia said when they exited the wing and walked across the upper parlor.

Sunshine poured through in blocky chunks between the archways. The bright light shocked her eyes. It felt like liquid warmth falling across her skin. Laceflower branches splayed across the veranda window, filling her nose with their sultry scent. The soft pink flowers drifted in the morning breeze.

"Today is the last day of the tourney?" she asked, attempting to draw Viktor out of his silence.

"Aye," he turned to lead her down the stairs.

A servant, possibly one of Ramiro's personal pages, climbed the steps towards them. He hailed a greeting to Viktor, who merely grunted in reply and pushed his way past. Cecelia nodded politely and carried on after the knight.

"You know, some nicety would go a long way with your fellow servants," she said, looking out a large window while they wound their way through the lower hallway.

Her body smacked into Viktor's, who stopped to look at her. Her head connected with one of his pauldrons, offering her a ring in her ears.

"I'm not a servant," he growled.

His tone confused her. Had she not started to befriend him yesterday?

"My apologies. I thought all Kingsguard lived to serve. *My lord.*"

She carried on down the hall before him, making him catch up to her instead. It was only a few moments later she heard the hastened pace of his boots on the floor, his hulking body arriving beside her.

"You've got a mouth," he growled at her.

"Aye, as you've said before," she smiled sweetly at him.

He glared before looking away. "It's going to get you in trouble."

They arrived in the hall of Danica's Ladies Parlor.

"I'll take my chances, thank you," Cecelia moved to step past Viktor, but his hand gripped her elbow hard.

"I mean it." His eyes stared deeply into her own. "Watch what you say."

He motioned with his head towards Danica's doors. Down the hall, two guards awaited on either side. They stared straight ahead, motionless. Like corpses. Cecelia and Viktor stared back at them. She caught Viktor's meaning.

"Aye," she said. "I will."

Viktor released her. She rubbed her arm. His grip was monstrous. She wondered if he dared hold his lovers that hard, lest they crumble under the pressure. He followed closely behind while she approached the guards. She greeted them with a nod.

"Her grace awaits me," she said.

The guard on the right immediately moved to open the door. Neither said anything when Cecelia slipped past. Viktor followed. She had not been nervous, but when her feet stepped into Danica's lair, an emptiness gnawed at her stomach.

Arched windows let in a slight sea breeze while gauzy orange curtains danced. Cecelia even smelled oranges the deeper she plunged into the room. Brightly woven carpets covered the aged wooden floor here and there beneath chairs of soft leather. Rainbow light flooded through a stained-glass window high in the wall. It filled the center of the room with reds and blues and yellows. Cecelia thought she heard someone out on the veranda. She glanced at Viktor only briefly before plunging through the orange wall of fabric into the sunshine.

Danica sat, her hair coiled into a crown of brown plaits, studying the shattered light of the sun on the ocean. She swirled a glass of champagne, humming a tune to herself. Cecelia cleared her throat. Danica didn't move. The waves breached the sharp rocks at the base of the cliff, filling the air with its thunderous noise.

Its consistent screams.

Cecelia tried again. This time, Danica turned to peer over her shoulder. She smiled crookedly and motioned Cecelia to enter with the tip of her head. Danica threw back the rest of the bubbly and sat the glass back on the table. A servant appeared from somewhere, Cecelia knew not where, and refilled Danica's glass. They then poured Cecelia her own before disappearing again.

Like magic.

"Thank you for joining me, your grace," Danica said.

"It's my pleasure, your grace," Cecelia returned.

Her throat stiffened around the piece of honey soaked bread she had popped in her mouth. It wasn't a complete lie. Though Cecelia still didn't enjoy entertaining. Playing a part. She'd much rather let her genuine parts show. Naked. Symbolically, but she didn't mind actually either.

She searched for Viktor, wondering where he had posted himself. She found him hidden beneath a nearby pillar, ivy coiling around like a noose. A bee buzzed close by. Viktor eyed the insect without moving.

Danica leaned back in her chair, watching Cecelia. Her eyes were blue, reflecting the clear sky. They startled Cecelia. She wondered how deep they saw.

"You must forgive me," Danica began, still staring at Cecelia, "as a royal guest you're owed much more of me than you've received. I wish to be more present, but the princess keeps me busy." Danica sipped her champagne. "But," she hissed at the bitter aftertaste, "are children not where we are called to pour our energy?"

Cecelia frowned. She popped a grape into her mouth. "Not everyone," she spoke, "not me."

Deep lines set over Danica's forehead as she frowned. "You mean to say you don't want children?"

Cecelia's eyes sought Viktor. Again. She wanted to kick herself, but try as she might, her eyes kept wandering to the giant man. He stared straight ahead, though Cecelia knew he listened to every word.

Cecelia sighed. "The Mother is but one half of the deity, your grace."

"Yes," Danica murmured. She swirled her champagne again, watching the bubbles rise furiously to the top, popping their whispers within the glass. "I once saw it your way. As my father's only child, it afforded me the most illustrious of educations. But all for naught. I was used as a pawn and married off to Ramiro."

"You seem rather in love," Cecelia spoke over her own glass. The smell of the bubbly drink was nauseating, but if she remembered any advice of Danon's, it was always drink what your host drinks.

"I respect him," Danica said. "And, giving my ill-informed ideas up, I've reached the greatest heights available to me, a woman of Korith."

Cecelia raised her glass. "Well done."

Danica stared evenly at Cecelia before she broke her gaze. She glanced at Viktor for a moment, as if seeing him for the first time, before frowning and shoving her plate away. She adjusted her dress and hair, the stirring sending smells of vanilla towards Cecelia. An odd smell, Cecelia thought, for a woman that appeared so cold.

"And you," Danica's smile appeared painful, "the firstborn, but a girl. A strange mother. Your father sent you away to shape you into what? A... warrior? A warlord?"

Cecelia returned Danica's pained smile with a real one. She sipped her champagne, delighted at the way the bubbles tickled her nose, even if the smell still bothered her.

"I passed the Trial of the Thoughtful Warrior at ten and six." She said. "I showed exceptional control. Some said there hadn't been such a taming of the trial since my great-great-grandfather."

"The Trial of the Thoughtful Warrior?" Danica leaned forward in her chair.

The queen seemed interested now.

"A trial, a test, all Panthers participate in when they're of age prior to defending the Lagos. Tea Artists prepare a hallucinogenic tea that is given to those attempting the trial. One by one, we're led into an arena where we must face our imagined demons while defending ourselves from actual attacks."

"To what end?" Danica asked.

"Warriors must display a calm resolve and mastery of their weapon, despite the surrounding influences. Despite terror."

"I see," Danica said, "and the chances of passing this trial?"

Cecelia shrugged. "Most do. Most receive the proper preparation beforehand. To fail would be to bring shame to your family."

"But someone has before?"

"Sure," Cecelia said, "though I couldn't name them."

"And you were... exceptional?"

"I showed great mastery over my fears," Cecelia corrected her.

"So you're not afraid of anything?"

"I wouldn't say that."

"Then what are you afraid of? Motherhood?" Danica laughed. She studied Cecelia over the rim of her glass. Her eyes traced the path of her servants, waiting for them to disappear before speaking.

"Do you miss home?" She asked abruptly.

Cecelia smiled to herself. "Perhaps a little." Though it didn't matter. Her father's words drifted over her thoughts. She'd never see it again. "But Korith is enchanting enough." Another lie that tasted bitter in her mouth.

Danica sensed it though and laughed. "Korith is... strong. A steady place to live and raise a family. But enchanting? No. No, it's not."

They sat silent, eating. Cecelia fought to hear the waves over the noise of servants coming and going. She had found their hole, the door in which they used to enter and exit Danica's room unseen, hidden in the corner. It blended behind a large portrait of a buxom woman breastfeeding a child. The orange curtains billowed in front of it, further hiding it from searching eyes. The servant's constant buzz of activity set Cecelia on edge. The warrior within her didn't know who to pay attention to. What direction the threat–if there were a threat–might come.

But the waves soothed her. She tried to ignore the way the hair on her neck stood on end, sending a warning. Perhaps it was merely Viktor's sour words affecting her. *Beware of Danica.* But the queen seemed contemplative. Sullen, even.

Danica leaned back in her chair in the most unladylike of fashion, toying with the stem of her glass again. The woman was young. Smooth, milk washed skin framed a sharp chin and sharper eyes. Danica had said she was afforded the best education. Cecelia could tell. It was obvious in the way Danica looked at things. At the way you could see her mind toiling through those ice blue pools. At the way she always had an answer, and it wasn't the usual *yes my lord* or *no my lord*.

"Is something bothering you, your grace?" Cecelia asked. She felt as though she danced before a hungry lion. Something, a teasing in the back of her mind, told her she was preparing to take a step down a path she could not return. But what else was she there for, in Korith, but to take risks?

"Hmm? Oh, no, your grace. My mind is just a pool sometimes. So many thoughts swimming, so little time to discern and sort them."

"Perhaps I can help," Cecelia offered. And when Danica stared off into the sea, ignoring her request, Cecelia added, "I'd *love* to help, your grace."

Danica smiled at this. She shifted in her seat, bringing herself closer to Cecelia. They both glanced at Viktor, ever vigilant at his post, before turning their backs to him.

"Your visit seems to have brought with it some... unfelt feelings, your grace."

"Such as?" Cecelia asked.

Danica shook her head, confused. "I built my life as best I could amidst these confines." Danica smirked, "It's funny. As my father's only child, I was afforded everything. Everything a boy might receive. And so I began to think I might... be different. That the typical life of a Korithian woman might not be my path. That I might do more. And yet, here I am. Wife. Mother. Reduced to the same roles and the same duties."

"And what does my arrival have to do with that?" Cecelia asked. She sympathized with Danica. In the Lagos, women were afforded the same rights as men. To be born in a land where this wasn't so? Torture itself.

"You've shown me what I'm missing," Danica said, her words tumbling out in a fit of passion. "I look at you and see a woman of power. Real power. I was fooled, for a time, into thinking I had it. But I know now it is a farce. A distraction to quell any complaints I might have. I see that now."

Cecelia frowned. Danica was a bird. Pretty sure, but imprisoned in a gilded cage. Cecelia combed through her thoughts, trying to find something - anything - that might uplift the downcast queen. Perhaps if she befriended Danica, she'd have a new well to source inside information from.

"You have power, Danica," Cecelia tried the queen's name on her tongue, hoping the familiarity bred confidence. "All women have power."

Danica raised an eyebrow. "How so? Or are you just full of platitudes like my husband?"

Cecelia swigged her champagne, forgetting her manners, gathering her thoughts. If she could leave this meeting having planted the seed of friendship within Danica, she could consider it a victory. With the queen on her side, she'd yield more power in the Korithian court. Then, when Danon finally sailed home, perhaps she wouldn't feel so alone.

So powerless.

But Danica was hard to read. She oscillated between fake friendliness and genuine interest too quickly. Like a viper, Cecelia could never tell when the queen was going to strike.

In the Lagos, the mountain cougars would shrink back and snarl when cornered before leaping to attack. Cecelia couldn't help but see the same look in Danica's eyes. She took a slow breath and prepared, not sure if she'd find fang or claw at the end, but moving forward nevertheless.

"Power is... tricky," Cecelia began.

Danica rolled her eyes.

"No, I mean it. It is hard to define tangibly. It's different for everyone. For every woman. The truly powerful women are simply those that, after assessing their own situation, sought the path to achieve power in their place."

Danica waved a servant away. Which meant she was too busy thinking to eat. Good. Cecelia's words were at least reaching her.

"Your role as queen and mother of the princess does not come without power. You can wield it deftly, should you learn to. Should you try to."

"How so?" Danica leaned forward, taking in every syllable of Cecelia's words.

Cecelia shrugged. Viktor shifted in his boots, further into the shade of the veranda. The bee that plagued him before had moved on. He stared off toward the ocean, though Cecelia knew he was still listening. But he, too, appeared deep in thought. Like Danica, Cecelia could tell Viktor was thinking by the way his eyes looked. Contemplative. Deep.

She turned back to Danica only to find the queen watching her watch Viktor. Danica smirked but tried to hide it behind her champagne flute.

"The Mother knows the multitude of ways a woman can manipulate a man." Cecelia suggested.

"So you're saying I should just manipulate the king using my... gifts? Is that power?"

"Isn't it?" Cecelia couldn't stop the shift of tone in her voice. She hadn't meant to snap at Danica. She simply grew tired of arguing. She suddenly had the powerful urge to return to her room. It was costing her too much energy, too much effort, to juggle Danica's emotional needs with her own. But that is always the cost of socializing. Cecelia wished Danon hadn't gone hunting with Ramiro, but stayed to help her navigate entertaining.

And yet she needed this woman to like her. Cecelia sighed.

"Apologies," she offered the queen.

Danica waved her words away. "Apologies aren't needed amongst friends, dear Cecelia."

The queen didn't mean it - friends. Cecelia could tell Danica had used the word frivolously, but she took it as a sign she was making progress.

"I think I know what you're saying," Danica said. "That, wherever we find ourselves in life, the Mother has meant it to be so. And it is there, where we are planted, we must find a way to grow."

"Yes," Cecelia agreed, though she didn't know if that's what she'd meant.

"And I was planted here, in Korith. The Mother surely has plans for me here. I can feel it. You're right."

Cecelia was pleased, though she wasn't certain she knew what she was right about. Danica pursed her lips in concentration, draining the last of her champagne before calling for more. She directed the serving maid to splash some orange juice in her glass and offered a toast to Cecelia.

"To friendship," Danica said.

"Friendship," Cecelia agreed.

She didn't like the look in Danica's eyes. Cecelia had validated something within the queen, something Cecelia had no way of knowing what unless she asked. And the relationship was too new. Too fragile. She couldn't risk asking intimate questions when she was merely laying the foundation. Not this time, not when she needed to survive in a foreign land.

Viktor shifted his weight. His jaw was held taut and his lips downturned, though truth be told they were usually downturned. He warned her to guard her tongue. Even Danon had told her specifically what to do to keep Danica tamed. But as Cecelia turned back toward the queen, she saw a look of satisfaction on Danica's face, and wondered if she had made a mistake.

As an only child, Danica of House Katvenn received the most privileged of educations. Her father, lacking a son to act as a vessel to pour forth his knowledge, educated Danica in history, politics, and some warcraft. Danica herself favored the history of Korith's ancient houses, particularly the history of House Varga— producer of Queen Vyctoria Varga — Queen Regent some four hundred years earlier. After Vyctoria's husband mysteriously died, she successfully convinced the royal court her adult son was unfit to rule by way of insanity. Prince Vedran disappeared and Vyctoria reigned as queen until her death at eight and sixty. It is unclear what Danica found so enchanting about this history.

High Steward Ustace Loette
Reflections on Kasier:
A High Steward's Time in Servitude

>*Queen Vyctoria, red of hair and sharp of tongue, was a viper hidden within the garden. So effective was her campaign to take the throne for herself that her son Prince Vedran was lost within the kingdom, though her husband's fate proved far worse: his name is forgotten altogether.*

High Steward Rodrick Brasden
House Histories and Insignia

Chapter Ten

Viktor escorted Cecelia back to her wing of the keep. The words she spoke while she broke her fast with the queen muddled his brain. He didn't remember ever seeing the queen enjoy a conversation half as much.

Cecelia gently inched her body closer to his as they walked. She spoke little to him on their trek back across the castle, offering him only a small smile as they exited Danica's rooms. Speaking up only to ask *how was that* before leading the way. He had taken extra-long strides to catch up with her. But once he did, she slowed her pace, allowing him to relax. She pressed against him. Her arm slithered into his.

"Did I heed your words well, my lord?" she asked, her voice a delicate whisper.

Viktor wrested her arm from his. "I think you know the answer to that, champion."

It was a dangerous game. A double-edged sword. Cecelia's words seemed to pacify Danica, but Viktor knew Danica was like a lake. The surface appeared serene, but one could only find out what teemed below the surface if one jumped in.

And then promptly drowned.

"She could have just as easily been insulted by your words. Only the Moon Mother knows what she'll tell the king."

"She'll tell him nothing," Cecelia scoffed. "Doing so would cast judgement on her as well."

"Doesn't matter," Viktor argued, "she has full immunity from Ramiro. She can do and say whatever she likes." He stopped walking and turned towards her. "She has power, remember? You said so yourself."

Cecelia rolled her eyes and crossed her arms, setting her jaw in a hard line to match her eyes. "You sound like my brother."

"Your brother better watch his step, too," Viktor said. "He may come to regret where he lay."

"And what's that supposed to mean?" Anger flushed hot in Cecelia's cheeks. "You dare speak of the prince of Panthers like that?"

"He'll be the prince of nothing should the king find him taking part in any unsavory activities," Viktor took his own step towards her.

She was within reach now. He could feel her breath on his face, tart from the orange juice and champagne she drank at breakfast. Her eyes shifted, no longer angry but somewhat eager.

He hadn't meant to be shrewd, but the Panther prince was in danger of crossing a line he could not retreat from. Everyone knew the queen admired the young prince's youthful disposition and amiable smile. Her loyalty to the king was infamous, but it didn't mean she couldn't get the naïve boy in trouble.

But Cecelia's eyes told him she wasn't angry, at least not entirely. Not at that moment. She pushed her body against Viktor's. Her head inclined upward, and she forced her lips upon his. Without thinking, his hands found the small of her back and pulled her closer. It was what he wanted from the start, when he first saw her take her shroud off at the tourney. A woman, a beautiful woman, that could kill a grown man three times her size?

Yes, yes, please.

Cecelia's hands found their way to his face, where she held both sides gently. She pulled away, her fingers petting his lips and then his jaw. Her hand trailed down his neck, following the trail of his birthmark.

"No," he murmured, moving to stop her hands, "leave it."

She pulled away and stared at him. "What? What is it?" but she tried to push her mouth onto his again.

"Stop," he said again, firmly. He stepped away from her.

Her cheeks reddened, but then her eyes narrowed. "What? What's wrong?" She crossed her arms. "Don't you like me?"

He shook his head. Truth or lie, either way, she'd be angry with him. For the truth meant admitting he did like her, only for her to find out Ramiro had tasked Viktor with liking her. And a lie would be apparent on his face, and a woman like Cecelia couldn't be lied to.

Wouldn't allow herself to be lied to.

"I can't. Rules." He prepared himself for her onslaught.

She sneered. "Scrap the rules, Viktor!"

She waited, but he said nothing more.

"You'd prefer a... a tavern wench? A street maid? His abominable brilliance, you'd probably take any woman. But me? Oh no, she's a princess! Can't do that, there are rules."

Cecelia stalked off. Viktor watched her retreat, her stomping feet echoing off the walls. To follow her would only stoke the fire of her temper even more. It was bound to happen, whether he accepted her or rejected her. Viktor wondered how long her hatred would last. Ramiro gave him a job to do. It would prove difficult should her anger not subside.

But he still couldn't help feeling foolish.

Preferring to give the princess some space, he took the long way around to the Panther pair's private wing. He half expected to hear yelling. They were always yelling at each other. But Viktor remembered Danon was off hunting with Ramiro and instead found Cecelia in the library.

She sat half reclined in a lazy chaise, her clothing changed, opting for her traditional island wear of loose draping muslin. It struck Viktor how less frigid she appeared in it. Her demeanor was relaxed and her face, usually taunt with displeasure, rested in an almost smile.

She glanced up at Viktor only once, offering him no reaction.

With Danon gone, his only chore was to observe and protect the princess, so Viktor took up his post by the door. Minutes passed by with no sound within the library except the distant lashing of waves on the cliffs and the incessant call of the gulls.

Cecelia shifted in her seat but didn't look at Viktor. The heat of the day was peaking, filling the room with stuffy waves of hot air. Viktor sweated beneath his quilted doublet. He looked at Cecelia, noticing her skin glistened with sweat. She toyed with her shoulder. The sash of her dress fell off and down her arm. Her eyes floated across the page she read, hardly noticing the large man by the door.

Viktor tried to distract himself again, looking at anything that wasn't Cecelia. She pulled her hair back, probably to relieve her neck from the hot, sticky air, but Viktor knew it was also to tempt him.

"My lord," she finally called to him, noticing he stared at her, "you must suffer in your armor. Perhaps relieve yourself of some of it. I won't tell." She winked at him.

"A Kingsguard never removes his armor until he enters his bed for the night."

Cecelia looked around and then back at Viktor, a smile spread wide across her face. "Perhaps I'll command you to do it. It is within my power, as royal guest."

She patted the chaise next to her.

It was enough to upend him. He stalked across the floor, pulling her up to him by the back of her neck. She gasped in surprise and delight.

"I knew you'd give in," she whispered.

He kissed her deeply, but only too briefly. The library door flung open and a triumphant and tipsy Danon entered.

"I shot the stag!" He cried, hands held high in victory, "I had had a drink or two with Ramiro. He likes his drink, but I still shot the cursed thing!"

Danon, upon spotting Viktor holding his sister in such a way, slowly lowered his hands. His cheerful buzz of wine was gone.

"What are you doing?" he asked. He stepped towards Cecelia, his hand finding his sword. "What are you doing with my sister?"

Viktor released her, but not before seeing the frown spread across her face.

"Are you alright?" Danon slipped into their native tongue and grabbed Cecelia by the arm, pulling her away from Viktor. "I'll have Ramiro hang him."

"No, it's fine," Cecelia said. "I was teasing him."

"He was choking you."

"No, he wasn't. It's okay. I'm fine."

Viktor watched the exchange, their fluid words moving so quickly, like a running river. He only caught Ramiro's name and nothing else. But the tone. He recognized the tone.

"Touch her again and I'll have you hanged," Danon pointed his finger at Viktor. "I'd prefer you guard from the hallway," he added, suggesting to the door with his head.

Viktor nodded in obedience, dumbfounded by the way things were turning out. Hadn't Cecelia wanted him? Was she explaining that to Danon, or was she telling him Viktor tried to rape her?

Outside, he heard them yelling. They spoke in broken Korithian, using just as many of their native words as words he could understand. But Cecelia was upset. Exceptionally upset.

The door opened and slammed shut so quickly it startled Viktor. He peaked out of the corner of his eyes to see Cecelia standing, wiping a few tears away.

"Your grace," Viktor said but didn't know what else to say.

Cecelia looked at him and offered a weak smile. "It's alright, Viktor. I just need..." she sighed, apparently not knowing what she needed. Finally, she said, "a quiet place. A place to sit and think. Without this," she gestured to the room, the castle, everything, "without anyone. Do you know of a place like that?"

"I do actually," he said, happy to know he could help her.

He suddenly realized the urge he had to see her smile. It was like a heavy meal, sank deep within his stomach. It satisfied him. But scared him, for he did not know what unpleasantness awaited him if he overindulged.

"There is an old sun altar, along the cliff."

"The gazebo? We saw it when we were waiting to make port."

Viktor nodded. "The queen uses it when she strolls, but she has been castle bound since the baby. I doubt you'd find anyone there."

Cecelia smiled and bowed her head. "Thank you, my lord. I can find my own way."

She left out the parlor door, leaving behind a citrus scented wisp in the wind. A Panther guard, having returned with Danon, followed silently in her shadow and she did not rebuke him.

It wasn't long before Danon emerged from the library. He was still worked up, panting, when he walked past Viktor. He paused at the door, turned, and pointed his finger at Viktor again.

Viktor debated on breaking it. He never much enjoyed being threatened, but knew Cecelia wouldn't forgive him if he did.

"You may have fooled my sister, but you don't fool me," Danon growled.

"I don't know what you're talking about," Viktor said. He offered a curt bow to Danon before adding, "your grace."

Danon ran his hand through his hair, frowning. "Whatever... game Ramiro has you playing with her, just stop. Leave her alone."

He turned to leave again, but Viktor wasn't through. The knight didn't take orders from the Panther prince, and he didn't like the boy's tone either.

"Your sister is a big girl your grace, she can take care of herself," Viktor called after Danon.

Danon stopped at the door again. His back was to Viktor, but the knight saw the way the prince squeezed his hands into fists. Danon held his shoulders taunt. A vein pulsed in his neck. The prince looked over his shoulder at Viktor and spoke with a false calm.

"Where has my sister gone, Sir Viktor?"

Viktor shrugged. "She said she wanted to be alone, your grace."

"And where is that?"

Viktor looked away from Danon, taking up his position once again. He stood straight and stared forward. The castle grounds weren't that extensive. If the little prince looked hard enough, he'd find Cecelia.

With a sigh, Danon stomped out the parlor door. Viktor waited, counting the prince's steps down the hall, before leaving his post. He must follow the prince. That was his job, but he didn't have to drift too close. The Panthers could burn him too easily if he did.

Danon searched the upper floor of the keep for nearly an hour. Ramiro and Danica were in their private rooms, indisposed, so he could not ask for their help. The servants were unhelpful, for though the women enjoyed the prince's attention and the men wanted to do whatever was necessary to make him leave them alone, they had not seen the princess.

When he finally had had enough, Danon yelled and stomped off toward his own room. Viktor sensed he'd be better off leaving Danon alone and instead made his way to the walk along the cliff face to check on Cecelia.

The gazebo stood near the edge of the cliff, a lonely silhouette against the vast sky. The relentless wind had shaped the cliff, leaving a surface of smooth stone. The gardeners kept a path of sand for the queen to take her strolls, but everything else was shades of gray.

Once painted a bright white, the gazebo had faded. The weathered wood ribbing of the roof showed through empty tiles. The sun fought its way through, throwing beams on Cecelia's head.

Viktor realized she wasn't alone.

Danica stood next to her, apparently not as indisposed as Viktor thought. Their bodies were so close Viktor could not see the sky between them. They giggled together, and when Cecelia looked up to spy Viktor, an amused smile filled her face.

"Sir Viktor," Danica followed Cecelia's gaze and spied the knight, "shouldn't you be guarding the Panther prince?"

Viktor arrived at the gazebo. On the altar, a round table in the center that once housed a golden sun, was a set of glasses and a decanter of wine.

"The queen thought I could use some wine to calm me," Cecelia said upon seeing Viktor spy the decanter.

He nodded. What else was there to say? She was not his charge, merely his job. Escort her. Protect her if need be.

His eyes trailed across her body to her face. She stared at him.

"Your brother, he looks for you." He shook his head. "Looked for you. He gave up and went back to your rooms."

"You did not tell him where I was?" Cecelia asked.

She accepted the refilled glass Danica handed her. The queen smiled at Viktor while she sipped from her own golden cup.

"You said you wanted to be alone," Viktor answered.

Cecelia bowed her head to Viktor, lifting her glass in a small salute. She sipped her wine. The decanter was nearly empty. Danica drank but avoided looking at Viktor more, instead turning to gaze out at the gray ocean.

Viktor wondered how long Cecelia had been alone. The wine had already stained her pretty lips with a satisfying rouge. He wanted so much to rub his thumb along them. To taste them again.

"Viktor," Danica still stared out at the ocean, "her grace is perfectly protected."

She turned to suggest to the four men that stood back against the castle wall, her Queensguard. A fifth, the Panther guard, stood oddly out at the end. But they all stood solemn, all in an unmoving row, while the wind whipped past them.

"Perhaps you should return to Prince Danon. Soothe his temper before her grace returns. She's had enough dealings with angry men today."

Danica still would not look at him. Cecelia offered him one last smile, small and hidden from Danica, before turning away as well. They started chatting low and quiet, like he wasn't there at all. Viktor had no choice but to turn and retreat to the castle, to return to the bratty Panther prince who was most likely still in a foul mood.

He fought hard against the feeling that settled in his chest. From an early age, he had learned not to care what others thought. He was the one that mattered most to himself. And yet while he walked away, it was like a small wound bled out.

Dismissed.

Lord Ceaszeg, your letter was received in good humor. No kinder words have I ever read. My daughter is very fortunate to have a man such as yourself interested in her hand. Your name is well known amongst the merchants of the Lago. No man possesses a finer fleet or fatter purse than Ceaszeg al Itr. With that in mind, I hate to inform you that I have given my daughter the right to choose her husband. And, in keeping with her stubborn nature, she will not marry a man that can not disarm her. According to my sources, it was she that disarmed you several moons past on the docks of the Whispers. I have several eyewitnesses that can corroborate this story. I will have to decline your offer. May the Mother bless your endeavors.

King Filip
    Letter to Phocan merchant Ceaszeg al Itr

Chapter Eleven

Danon followed her all morning. From the moment she arose and broke her fast in the parlor, to the moment she walked along the castle wall, he was by her side.

At first, she didn't mind. He had spent so much time cavorting with the ladies of the castle. She found she missed his presence.

But that feeling was fleeting.

She'd entertain herself by sneaking glances at Viktor, but after the first few attempts, Danon sent the giant knight to guard from outside the room.

"Ramiro won't take the cursed colossal back," Danon grumbled, sipping tea with her on their veranda. "Says he insists."

"Well," Cecelia sighed, trying to pretend to read. "Ramiro said Viktor was the best."

Danon laughed. "At what? The only thing he's good at I've heard is…"

Cecelia looked at him over the top of her book, waiting to see if he'd finish his sentence, but he caught her eye and thought better of it. He sat his cup down a little too hard. Cecelia jumped.

"Apologies, Cece," Danon said, "I'm just... I guess I'm ready to go home."

Cecelia laughed. "Home? When we've discovered nothing? Who will be the one to tell father we failed? Because I refuse to volunteer for that duty."

Danon frowned. He limped to the veranda's banister. An injury gained while hunting with the king affected his left leg, causing him to list to one side.

Cecelia felt sorry for him. He'd drank with Ramiro despite the bitter drink the king favored having ill effects on his stomach. Danica was a tease, but Danon kept her happy and chatty whenever they chanced to meet, though recently she seemed ill-tempered. Even the servants eagerly opened their mouths when Danon spoke to them. General Rees had been busy with some military matter or another and was the only one Danon had not mined for information.

And what had she done? What had she learned? While Danica seemed eager to earn her affections, Viktor had distracted Cecelia. But she also wondered if knowing she'd never leave Korith slowed her approach. There was time, she knew, for her at least.

There was time for distractions.

As if on cue, Viktor entered the veranda and dipped his head. A new trick. Perhaps to appease Danon. Danon glared at him and turned away.

"What is it?" her brother asked.

"General Rees, your grace, wishes a word. He's in the parlor."

Danon spun on his heels. He did a poor job hiding his surprise. He looked from Viktor to Cecelia, a nervous smile growing on his lips.

"General Rees," Danon said, "I haven't the pleasure of a private conference with him yet."

"He awaits you, your grace," Viktor repeated.

Danon puffed up his chest and marched towards the door. The general's arrival, surprising as it was, distracted Danon from his disapproval of Viktor's presence. He walked past the knight, into the parlor, and left his sister alone with Viktor.

Viktor watched Danon go. Cecelia watched Viktor. When he finally looked at her, she smiled. She slowly closed her book and left it on the table. The breeze brought in a hint of mint, cool across her face. Her skin prickled with the sensation and with the anticipation.

"Are you cold, your grace?" Viktor asked, still not moving from his place by the door.

Cecelia shook her head. She stood.

"I feel like strolling, my lord. Will you escort me?"

Viktor hesitated. He glanced over his shoulder, back into the parlor, and looked back at her. She bit her lip, hoping. Finally, he sighed and shook his head.

"As you say, your grace," he led her towards the steps, and they descended together.

Cecelia said nothing at first. She let his body next to her be enough. His armor was cool when he brushed against her arm, and in addition to the breeze, she shivered.

Viktor paused and looked at her. "Are you sure you aren't cold? We could go back." He looked back from where they came.

She wondered if he thought the same things she did. When would Danon notice they were gone? What would he do? And more importantly, how long did they have alone together?

"This way," she said, taking his arm, "I heard the tourney grounds were being converted to a market."

Viktor allowed her to pull him. He fell into step beside her, not pulling away this time. They walked in silence, their feet crunching the gravel, the breeze rustling the grass, but nothing else. It was enough for her, just touching him. She realized she had yearned for it since Danon exiled him from her presence.

They stopped at the top of the cascading stairs above the tourney grounds. Gone were the tents of the tournament, their lords' banners flying high above in the wind. The wooden fence denoting the jousting arena. The chalk circle marking the melee ring.

Instead, brightly hued canvas tents erupted like blooms. Hammers rang into the wind as stakes went into the ground. The scent of perfumed spices drifted towards them.

Fair Folk milled about, setting up their wares. Cecelia admired their pastel hued hair, wondering if it were natural to have such lavender tresses, deliciously pink fringes, or blue tinted plaits. Their voices echoed across the space, teasing her with their fast pitched way of speaking.

On the fringe were several gray robed figures, their heads bent low, speaking with several elder Fair Folk. Cecelia nudged Viktor.

"It seems our friends from the square have returned," she said.

Viktor nodded. "The Unis don't mingle with the Fair Folk, but Rees says they've been seen together more and more."

"Odd," Cecelia said. "I thought no one mingled with the Fair Folk save for quick excursions for palm readings and love spells."

When Viktor looked down at her, she smiled at him.

"You needn't worry, my lord," she patted his hand, clasped to her arm, "your heart is safe. For now."

They watched the Fair Folk in silence, letting the noise they brought wash over them. Cecelia leaned her head against Viktor's arm, inhaling his scent. It was a strange smell. Sour as much as it was woodsy.

"Why does he let them in?" she broke their silence, sensing the tension in Viktor's body.

While she was certain he enjoyed her body against his, she could tell he had a low threshold for it. Viktor did not seem accustomed to affection.

"Who?" His deep voice rumbled, "the Unis? Or the Fair Folk?"

"Both."

Viktor sighed. With his free hand, he scratched his day old scruff.

"The rebellion was sparked by Norian's incessant desire to rule every aspect of Korithian life. Worship. Trade. Travel." He turned to look at her. "When Romo claimed the throne, he vowed to never push the Fair Folk out again. They've been here longer than us. They're as much a part of the land as the mountains, rivers, forests. Ramiro, I guess, carries the tradition onward."

"And the Unis?" Cecelia asked. "Their entire theology threatens Ramiro's reign."

Viktor looked back at the priests. With their brows furrowed, they moved their hands frantically, like they were attempting to convince the Fair Folk of something. But the old men shook their heads and gestured to a tent further back, a giant blue tent glittering with hanging lights.

"I think he finds them inconsequential," Viktor said. "He thinks they'll never amount to anything more than flat verses spoken in the market square."

"And you?" Cecelia asked, "what do you think?"

He shrugged. "My job isn't to think. It's to protect. And that's what I do."

He wouldn't look at her then, so she watched the Fair Folk some more. A group of children made a circle, tossing coins, attempting to flip the other children's coins over with a smash of their own. A cat, a brilliant white, zig zagged between legs before disappearing into the giant blue tent.

"We should go," Viktor said, "before Danon finds you missing."

"No," Cecelia pulled Viktor back, "stay a little longer."

He rolled his eyes but remained rooted twhere they were. They stood together, huddled against the wind, acting as if they watched the world move around them, but really focused solely on what was happening between them.

Cecelia looked up at Viktor out of the corner of her eye. He watched the Fair Folk building their tents, but there was a stitch of worry in his face. A morsel of sadness in his eyes. She suddenly felt sick over the accusations she made against him that night at the tournament feast. Anya's rapist.

She licked her lips before she spoke, hoping the words would come out right. "I must beg your forgiveness, my lord."

"For what?" He didn't look at her but kept watching the gray robes with the Fair Folk.

They had walked towards the giant blue tent, though the gray robes seemed reluctant the closer they came to it.

"For my accusations. The other night. At the feast."

Viktor sighed and finally tore his eyes from the scene. He looked down at her, studying her. His aged eyes were handsome. She felt exposed beneath their gaze, more so than she ever did in the presence of her father.

"You needn't apologize," he said.

"But I accused you of —" she started before he interrupted her.

"I wasn't guilty of that, it's true, but there are many things I am guilty of, champion."

"Like what?"

He turned back to the Fair Folk. "I drink too much. I like to fight. Also too much."

"And what's too much?" she asked.

When he looked down at her this time, she hoped she didn't seem overeager. It was a childish game she played, but she couldn't stop her mouth from dribbling out the words. A man had never captivated her as much as he did. She had never felt helpless in front of anyone, regardless of station or looks or trade.

Several had tried. Sure. All were revolting in their enthusiasm. None had been her equal in form or station. None, she thought back, could beat her in a duel. Or lift her over their shoulder with one arm.

Or looked at her with that same distant reservation that Viktor observed her with. She did not naturally impress him. She needed to earn it.

She had never yearned for a man as much as she did Viktor.

And to feel his disapproval would be enough to end her. She'd succumb to her anger. She'd melt into a useless, rage-filled woman. Or so she thought. For she'd never experienced what she was experiencing, and to lose it, she didn't know what that'd do.

And she didn't want to know.

He swallowed, clearly not knowing what to say.

"Do I bore you, my lord?" she asked.

He gave a small laugh. "No, champion, you could never bore me."

She smiled. "Good. Then that is enough for me."

"Liar," he said, "you'd have all of me, on a platter, would that you could."

"Would I?" she asked, tugging him backwards, back down the path whence they'd come, "your infatuation with me seems to have impaired your judgment, my lord."

"My infatuation?" He pulled her hard back towards himself, wrapping her tight with his large arms. "It was you who kissed me first."

"Was it?" she teased. "I don't remember."

She stood on her tiptoes, moving to kiss him again, when she heard her name. The syllables bounced off the castle wall, wrapping sharply around the corner. Danon was looking for her. He did not sound pleased.

Viktor immediately released her and stepped away. She watched him, her stomach sinking with the distance. Why was it so difficult for her? She was the Panther princess, heir to the throne. She obtained whatever she reached her hand for. And yet Viktor kept eluding her.

She looked around. The castle walls were nearly pink in the setting sun. Perhaps it was that place, Korith. Her feet were not on the land of the Lagos anymore. Her path was not so easily set out for her.

Her father's words sank in. She wouldn't be returning. Instead, she'd remain in Korith, a place that had yet to yield itself so readily. She'd have to try harder.

Or lacking effort, she'd fail.

Tired of feeling like such a maiden and annoyed at the headache brought on by her own name ringing across the castle wall, she turned to Viktor. Her hands were in fists, and she set her face sober before speaking.

"I will have you, my lord," she said, "one way or another."

The corner of Viktor's mouth ticked upward. He nodded approvingly before bowing his head.

"As you say, your grace."

The worship of the sun, known only as His Brilliance to his heralds, fell out of favor with most of the civilized world over three hundred years ago. Preferring the more motherly visage of the Moon Mother and her demure Daughter Moon, Whisper Wives converted the Great Continent after the fall of viscous King Hallman. The Goldenones and the island nation of Duwu remain the only major civilizations to worship His Brilliance openly, though a few hidden altars can still be found across Korith.

An Unnamed Priest
   Of the Great Moon temple of Mt. Lystra
   The Mother's Testament: A History of Religion

Chapter Twelve

When the Panther prince found Viktor walking with Cecelia, he ripped her from Viktor's arms and stormed away, muttering musically in the language of the Lagos. Viktor knew the words themselves were not so pretty. Something in the prince's eyes warned Viktor. Something told him he'd feel a dagger in his ribs long before he saw it. That if he didn't watch his step, he'd soon find his death.

But the game with the prince was a trifle. Ramiro valued Viktor too much to let the Panther prince play out his dark fantasy of killing him. And for what? All because Cecelia showed an interest in him? That wasn't Viktor's fault.

Or was it?

It's what Ramiro wanted, after all, this friendship as they called it. He was merely doing his king's bidding. Viktor stopped walking. He had made it back into the castle bailey, setting his course for his own room. The Panthers were supping alone that night and had dismissed him. Again.

Servants rushed past, all on their way to some job or another. Kay stood further down the hall, and upon spotting Viktor, called out to him.

"Viktor! You've returned from the dead." Kay laughed. "How goes the Panthers?"

Viktor watched his comrade approach. He had seen little of Kay since taking up babysitting Danon and Cecelia. The man looked hungover, but awake. He slapped Viktor on the shoulder when he neared.

"You've been busy," he said.

Viktor nodded. "Aye, these Panthers are..." but he didn't know what to say.

"Heard they were trouble. The prince has got himself into more rooms than a Unis spy, and the princess is sharp tongued though fine to feast the eye upon, so long as that's all you do."

Viktor tried to laugh but found it wouldn't come. Kay's words were true, but stung Viktor oddly.

"The prince hates me," Viktor confessed.

"So, you must be doing something right!" Kay said. "And the princess?"

"She... tolerates me," Viktor lied.

"Right," Kay smiled, "of course she does. The rumor hags swear up and down she likes you more than that."

Kay waited patiently for Viktor's response with a smug smile.

"Abominable brilliance, can't anyone keep their mouth shut?" Viktor dropped his shoulders. "It's none of their business."

"Is it yours then?" Kay asked, taking on a more serious tone. "Should you be messing about with the princess like that? Seems a dangerous game."

Viktor finally laughed. "You have no idea."

He leaned against a nearby column, suddenly exhausted from the past several days. Truthfully, he had returned to his room every night and immediately fallen asleep. But the sleep was never restful. He never felt ready for the next day. It just piled on top of each other, becoming a heavier and heavier weight for him to carry.

He worried he was making a mistake with Cecelia. Yes, deep down, he wanted her. Any man would be a fool not to. And it seemed she wanted him, Moon Mother's luck, but it was the fact that Ramiro told him to do it. He didn't like being told where to lie, even if it was with a beautiful woman. And he didn't like that Danon hated him for it.

Viktor didn't need jokes or rumors. He needed answers. From Ramiro. He looked at Kay and nodded a goodbye.

"Until later," he said.

"Until later," Kay called after him, "lucky git."

Ramiro would be in his study. He went there every night after supping for a drink and to peruse the mountains of paper delivered to him. Trivial matters mostly. Announcements of births to great houses. Requests for deferred payment of taxes. Requests for deferred arrest for requesting deferred payment of taxes. Letters written by angry mothers who lost sons at some random outpost, harboring ill feelings towards their monarch and his skills of kingship.

He burned most of them. Viktor watched him often enough. Wouldn't even read them, just scan them, toss them in the flames, and sip his wine. He might laugh at the imaginative names made up for his benefit, but usually his face was stoic. Ramiro cared very little for that part of his job.

When Viktor arrived at the parlor door, two Kingsguard stood on either side. They shook their heads at him, cursing beneath their breath.

"King says to leave him be," one, Axel, growled at Viktor. "He's with the general."

"Perfect," said Viktor, trying to push himself through. "I need to speak with him as well."

The pair crossed their arms, barring Viktor's way, and shoved him backwards. Axel pointed his finger at Viktor.

"Don't care if you're the Moon Mother's favorite, you're not getting in there Vic. So run back to your Panther princess and enjoy the evening."

Victor swung at Axel before he could think the action through. The other Kingsguard, Brand, caught Victor's arm before it could meet Axel's head. Axel slammed his fish into Victor's side. Victor inhaled sharply and stumbled backwards.

"Don't want to hurt you, sir," Brand, remembering Victor held a superiority over him, said. "Just following orders. King said no one, not even you."

Victor clung to his side, heaving for breath while staring at Axel. The Kingsguard was young, much younger than Victor. Twenty and three by all accounts, though Victor didn't make a habit of remembering every dirt sack who showed up at the castle.

He prepared for his next onslaught, setting his feet apart and his shoulders square, when a breeze blew in from the parlor door. A breeze meant the veranda doors were open. Open doors meant there were other ways to reach the king.

Victor tipped his head to Axel. "We'll meet again on the training grounds, child, and then we'll see who's the Moon Mother's favorite."

He vanished down the hall, ignoring Axel's retort. It didn't matter. He barely understood the youths' insults. They seemed to change with each passing year, to where they made little sense to anyone else anyway.

Outside the castle, he slipped through an arched doorway, a guard's entrance. But instead of taking it around the bailey wall, he went through, towards the cliff-side of the castle keep. Once outside, the sea breeze hit him. He inhaled sharply, enjoying the smell of salt the wind brought with it. The Daughter and the Mother were both shrouded by clouds. Victor smiled. It would make his sneaking much easier.

There was no path to the veranda of Ramiro's parlor. Instead, Victor climbed through delicate shrubbery and organized flowers. The gardeners would wonder what had happened, but Victor didn't care. He skirted beneath the grand veranda of the hall and hid amongst the shadows of the wall. Slowly, he slid his body along until he was beneath the first window of Ramiro's veranda. Viktor could hear Rees' voice drifting through the window in the evening air.

"Their vitriol must stop, your grace," Rees said.

"It's not their words that bother me Rees. The Unis are full of words."

"Not with the Fair Folk. The Unis have never had time for the Fair Folk."

"Perhaps they've found a new well in which to mine for the redeemed." Ramiro said.

"Or allies," Rees rumbled.

Ramiro was silent. Victor imagined him sipping on his wine, long and slow, contemplating the general's words.

"The Fair Folk take no sides," Ramiro finally said, sounding like the ignorant child he was. "They are neutral in all things."

"Until they're not," Rees warned. "I have reports gray cloaks approached the blue tent of the Prevailing Mother just this afternoon."

More silence. More contemplating.

"The Prevailing Mother?"

"Yes, your grace."

"What would the gray cloaks want with her? And why would she entertain an audience with them?"

"My thoughts exactly, your grace." Rees said.

"This does not bode well for us, Rees," Ramiro sighed.

"No, your grace, it does not. We need to shore up an alliance with the Panthers, sooner than later."

"Yes, I'm aware," Ramiro snapped, "but as you know, I've yet to find a suitable solution to our Panther problem."

There was movement and Rees' voice seemed closer. He had walked towards the window. Victor did his best to fade into the wall, instantly wishing he'd just gone to bed.

"I've given you a solution, your grace," Rees said.

Ramiro sighed again, "I know, Rees. But I'm not sure."

"It's been done before, your grace. It isn't unheard of."

"But her father, what if he disagrees?"

Rees must have turned away, back towards Ramiro, because Victor could not catch the general's words.

"I will speak it over with Danica. I will need her help if the plan is to succeed."

"As you say, your grace."

"And you'll leave tonight?" Ramiro asked.

"Yes, your grace. There are rumblings on the northeastern front. I must quell them now, before we move forward with our plan. Don't want to ruin a wonderful celebration, do we?"

Ramiro choked on a laugh. "No, no, we don't. Do as you must, but return quickly."

"As you say, your grace."

There were footsteps and then silence. Victor heard glass clinking and Ramiro sigh. Papers moved around and then the fire popped, like something had been added to fuel the flames.

Victor sidled away from the veranda windows, enclosed in the darkness of the shadows once again. It seemed Victor and Cecelia were not the only ones watching the Fair Folk that afternoon. But Victor was of the same mind as Ramiro: the Fair Folk don't take sides. They never had. All they wanted was to be left alone to peddle their wares and to pursue life disorganized and in the wilds, like they always had.

It was clear they spoke of Cecelia's father, but what he'd agreed to Victor was more perplexed by. Marriage? Who would Cecelia marry? Ramiro's brother Rufus was younger than the Panther princess herself. Viktor wracked his head, attempting to remember which noble lord was unmarried and warranted an enormous debt to Ramiro.

He decided, uncharacteristically, to loop around toward the Panther's quarters before hitting the rack. While he was exhausted, a deep nagging told him something was wrong. He needed to warn Cecelia. Of what, he still wasn't certain.

Danon was in the parlor, reading. Cecelia was nowhere in sight. Viktor cursed beneath his breath before tipping his head to Danon's displeased face.

"You have stones. I'll give you that, Sir Viktor," Danon frowned. He tossed his reading aside and stood. "I thought I dismissed you."

"You did, your grace," Viktor replied, deciding it best not to toy with the Panther prince's childish emotions, "but I..."

"What's this?" Cecelia emerged from her bedroom, her body barely covered in a silk robe.

"Apparently, the beast just can't stay away," Danon growled. "Can't follow orders either."

Viktor was too captivated by Cecelia to speak. Her robe, barely cinched, displayed her neck and decolletage. A hint of vanilla drifted across the room to him, intensifying the senseless thoughts Viktor had when he looked upon her creamy skin. Seeing where his eyes wandered, Cecelia pulled either side of her robe closed.

"That's enough, Danon," Cecelia finally said. "Let him speak."

"Please," Danon said, "he's clearly here to ogle, nothing more."

"I said enough." Cecelia's voice hit a tone Victor had not heard before. It was a queenly tone, authoritative in its singularity.

Danon frowned, his face turning a shade of pink. He fussed with his sleeves before tipping his head to his sister.

"I'll leave you then," he stammered, "since my presence is obviously not required."

Danon stomped off to his own room and slammed the door. Cecelia stared at Viktor in silence for several moments before finally descending the three steps to the parlor floor.

"What is it?" she asked.

Rather than sitting, she went straight to him. She placed her cool hand on his forearm and looked up at him in the most pleasant of ways. A little too pleasant. Viktor pulled his arm away, forcing himself to not get distracted.

"I need to know when you plan on leaving," he said, "for it would be best if it were soon."

Cecelia furrowed her shapely brows. "I don't understand," she said. "I thought you enjoyed having me here."

Viktor choked back a laugh. "Like having you here? I'm afraid there is more to this game you play than what I like, champion."

"Speak it then," Cecelia dared him, "tell me."

Viktor faltered. What he did could be seen as treason. There was nothing wrong with Ramiro wanting an alliance with the Panthers. Danon himself had said it's what their father, King Filip, wanted too. But he didn't like the way Ramiro and Rees had been talking. There was deception afoot, and Viktor couldn't bear to think it was Cecelia that was to be deceived.

"I just," Viktor stammered.

He couldn't keep eye contact with her. Her eyes were too full of venom.

"I just think you should return home. It would be safer for you to do so," he muttered.

"Safer?" Cecelia said. "I nullified my safety when I stepped foot on this awful continent of yours." And when Viktor still wouldn't look at her, she added, "you needn't worry about my safety, my lord. I can keep pace myself."

He looked at her then. Gone was the anger in her eyes, and what it left was a curiosity of sorts. He smiled at her. She smiled back.

"I know, champion. I know."

The Blessing of the Gracious Giver - the tradition of gifting a gift to one's betrothed - goes back hundreds of years in the Archipelago of the Moons, to the reign of King Agrathys. A historically poor king, Agrathys was left with little to offer his new bride, the princess of a nearby independent isle. But Agrathys' brother, Prince Gregoir the Wild, returned from his worldly travels in time for the nuptials. Seeing his brother worry, Gregoir retrieved from his collected goods several heavy necklaces, each one overwhelmed with gemstones. Gregoir insisted Agrathys select a necklace and bequeathed it to his bride. In this way, Agrathys took his brother's kindness and created what is one of the most sacred of Panther wedding traditions.

Logician Mykel Meralko
    Islands of Fortune: An Examination of Island Nations

Chapter Thirteen

Danon had insisted Cecelia join him for a ride through the countryside surrounding Kasier. Cecelia didn't find riding that enjoyable amidst the blazing sun on such a cloudless day, but she felt sorry for Danon and agreed. He had wilted the night before when she commanded him to leave Viktor alone. She had had little need to command him to do anything since arriving in Korith, but Cecelia had reached her limit. Unfortunately, she embarrassed her brother in the process.

He wore a fake smile while they made small talk with the stable hands. The young men seemed smitten by Cecelia, but she ignored them, deferring to Danon whenever they asked a question directly at her. She knew they saw little of her actual face, just the imaginary crown she always wore, hovering over her head like a dagger at her throat.

They left their Pantheran guards at the city gates, commanding them to keep watch from afar. Outside the walls, Danon relaxed. His shoulders no longer pulled back and his jaw was no longer clenched. Instead, he loosened his grip on the reins and allowed the horse to go where it wished. Cecelia was forced to follow.

"How did you convince Viktor to stay behind?" Cecelia called to him, trying her best to maintain the same speed as they headed towards the kingswood.

"I told him to stay. Like a good dog, he obeyed." Danon steered his gelding towards a vaguely defined path.

Giant oaks filled the kingswood, their branches reaching towards the clouds. Gooseberry bushes weaved in and out beneath the legs of the trees, enriching the air with their spicy scent. Cecelia slowed her horse to enjoy the fragrance. Danon circled back and trotted his horse next to hers.

"You shouldn't call him that," Cecelia stared at her brother.

"What?"

"Viktor. You shouldn't call him a dog. He's a guard. A man with a job. Like father's Shadowmen."

Danon rolled his eyes. "Of course. My apologies, your grace."

Cecelia tightened her grip on her horse's reins. It released the tension she felt in her hand, the tension that made her want to slap her brother.

"Why don't you like him?" She asked, "because he likes me?"

Danon huffed and turned his horse away, heading towards the poorly defined path once again.

"Or is it because I like him?" Cecelia called to Danon's back.

He stopped his horse. It appeared he stared at some gooseberries just ahead, but Cecelia wondered if he were thinking. He turned and looked at her over his shoulder.

"You are my lady sister, and heir to the Panther throne. By right, you can love who you want. I only…" Danon hesitated, glancing away from her momentarily before looking back, "I only want you to be happy."

Cecelia kicked her horse and rode to Danon's side.

"Happiness is overrated, Danon," she sighed. "I'm only… trying to survive here."

Danon nodded. He reached out and held her hand briefly before letting it drop.

"I apologize," he told her. "I should be the last to cast stones."

"No," Cecelia said, "there is more, Danon. More I need to tell you."

Her brother sat quietly while she explained the rest of their father's vision. His jaw gave away his frustration, jutting outward while he tried to stop himself from interrupting. When she finished, she waited, knowing he'd speak when he was ready.

He guided their horses through the trees, weaving in and out of them. When he spoke, Cecelia could hear his anger wrapped around each syllable, though he–impressively–did not yell.

"And you thought to tell me now, after we've been here for how many moonrises?"

"Father insisted I wait."

"Until when?"

Cecelia frowned. "Until I felt the time was right."

He twisted in his saddle to offer her a retort, but a snap beneath a nearby oak startled their horses. The animals froze, whinnying deep grumbles to themselves.

"What was that?" Danon asked, trying to force his gelding to obey his commands and move.

"I'm unsure," Cecelia peered at the tree.

A child emerged, her skin the color of topaz and her hair the palest of pink. She smiled up at Cecelia and spoke.

"Faed'wyn," she said.

It was a Fair Folk. Or more specifically, a Fair Child.

"Oh," Cecelia looked at Danon and then back to the girl, "we don't... we don't understand."

The girl kept smiling. She giggled. It was a musical giggle, like the tinkling of bells.

"It means hello in the ancient tongue."

"I'm afraid we don't know it," Cecelia said. "We are not from Korith, but the Archipelago of the Moons."

"We know," said a second girl, appearing from behind the tree too.

This one was smaller, her hair a shade darker, but the same autumn leaf eyes with upturned corners stared up at them. They sparkled, full of laughter. Cecelia knew the Fair Folk were magic users. They were vessels for it, just like the decanter she shared with Danica was for wine. You could see it if you looked close enough. It glittered in their eyes and in their hair. One could even smell it if one tried. It was sweet, like honey, and emanated off their skin like perfume.

"The Prevailing Mother spoke of the children of the Lagos visiting the king-pretend."

"The king-pretend?" Danon asked.

"Na faed'wyn," a third girl spoke.

She emerged from behind another oak. Her skin was just as topaz as the first two girls, though her hair was the blue green of the ocean. She approached them, her face furrowed in a frown.

"Na faed'wyn," she said again, "aud Kar'yth."

Cecelia realized then the child was no girl, but a boy. His hair was long, like the pink hued girls, but tied back halfway with a leather strap.

The first girl rolled her eyes, "Na Kar'yth, n'as mun d'kith."

"Mun d'kith?" The boy said reverently.

"Uh, hello," Cecelia said, "I'm Cecelia. This is my brother Danon."

"Pawdwyn Cecyl," the boy said.

"Yes, yes, Princess Cecelia," the first girl said. "I apologize, princess. Val does not speak the common tongue, though he hears it well enough and insists on being *precise*."

Val glared at the girl.

"Well, you speak it very well," Danon said.

The girl smiled, puffing up her chest with pride. "My grandmother was the previous Prevailing Mother. She ensured my entire family learned the common tongue well."

"She said it would be useful," the second girl added.

"I'm Kharis." The first girl said, "this is Arnyia."

"Your sister?" Cecelia asked.

"Na's." Kharis said, "yes."

Cecelia smiled down at the children. It was unavoidable, as she felt the air in the forest thicken with their magic. She half wondered if they were bewitching her, forcing her to smile at them benevolently. They wore muted tones of lambskin, cinched, or clasped with precious silver. Even from Arnyia's ears dangled silver teardrops, so finely crafted Cecelia knew to buy them would cost a fortune.

She wanted to ask about the earrings, admiring the way they glittered in the filtered forest light, but was interrupted by the husky voice of someone else.

"Kharis! Arnyia!" The tall figure approached.

The man was pink haired, much like Kharis. His skin was the same shade. His eyes, an earthy brown. He reached for the girls' hands and glanced at Val.

"Cour'se mas, Val'thorn." The man said to the boy.

Val nodded his head obediently and ran off into the woods. The man turned back to Cecelia, his eyes sparkling, much like the children's, though Cecelia could see they were less welcoming.

"The children know not to speak to citizens of Korith," the man said.

Cecelia batted his words away. "They did not bother us, my lord, but were quite charming."

She winked at Kharis, who returned it with a gleeful wink of her own.

The man nodded his head knowingly. "Mun d'kith," he said, "you are the guests of Ramiro."

"Is it that obvious?" Danon asked.

"Only a Panther would style the Fairest Folk 'lord.' It is a charmingly deceitful attribute of your people." The man said.

"I'm Danon," Danon said, "and this is Cecelia."

"Pawd D'non and Pawdwyn Cecyl," Arnyia whispered.

"Na pawd e pawdwyn," the man growled at her. He turned to Cecelia and Danon. "As the Fairest Folk, we do not recognize monarchs of any kingdom."

"A charmingly deceitful attribute of your people," Cecelia smiled.

The man stared at her. His brown eyes were near luminescent in the shadow of the oak branches. There was an arrogance in them, but something else. Was it amusement?

"And your name?" Danon asked the man. "Is it not common practice to exchange names upon meeting? Or is that, too, not something you recognize?"

The man turned his solemn gaze upon Danon. It made Cecelia's stomach sink, though she didn't know why. He looked at Danon like someone looked at a dying creature. A sympathetic look, not kept for long. A look that knew it gazed upon a tragedy, but it didn't matter.

"G'rig." He said, "though the common tongue translates it to Gerrig."

"I'm afraid I hear no difference," Danon said.

"Of course not," G'rig smiled.

"Your grace!" A voice, Viktor's, called from the edge of the kingswood. "Ramiro requests your presence."

Cecelia peered through the trees, spying the large knight on his even larger black beast of a horse. He turned the horse around, attempting to find his way into the kingswood that didn't require his horse tripping over gooseberry bushes.

"Kith d'mas n'yor," Kharis whispered to Arnyia.

"Shhh," G'rig shook the girls' hands.

Viktor, finally finding the poorly tracked path Danon and Cecelia used earlier, rode up. He looked from the Panthers to G'rig, his frown digging deeper as he landed on the Fair Folkman.

"Shouldn't you be prepping your wares to steal decent people out of their coin, G'rig?" Viktor asked the Folkman.

It impressed Cecelia how composed G'rig kept his face. Rather than frowning, the corners of his mouth ticked up nearly imperceptibly.

"Perhaps I could throw your tarot again, Vic, though we both know that won't change the outcome." G'rig smiled before turning away, dragging the girls with him.

"What was that about?" Cecelia asked Viktor.

Viktor watched the man and children fade away through the forest. He only turned his horse back towards the road when they could no longer be seen.

"Don't let them fool you," he said. "The Fair Folk are swindlers. They owe no allegiance to Korith and therefore feel no need to be loyal. Or law abiding. Or kind in any way that doesn't suit them."

Danon scoffed. "The children seemed downright sweet."

Viktor chuckled. "Of course they did, your grace. They were bewitching you."

"I knew it!" Cecelia said. "I felt the magic in the air. Could almost taste it."

"Aye, G'rig's family is very gifted, even amongst the Fair Folk. His mother was the Prevailing Mother previously. She was a well respected Fairwoman, though G'rig goes down bitter."

He glanced at Cecelia, a smile hidden on his lips, but was jostled away when Danon rode his horse between the pair.

"You said Ramiro requested our presence?" Danon asked.

"Aye," Viktor turned and spurred his horse into a gallop.

The Panthers followed.

They were ushered into Ramiro's study, all three, Viktor not even having a choice. Cecelia tried to keep her face composed, though she couldn't stop the worried frown from forming. She hoped Danon's probing with the ladies of the castle hadn't gotten them in trouble. She had warned him to be cautious.

"Ah, your graces. Viktor." Ramiro offered them his biggest smile.

Cecelia's stomach tightened with anxiety. When a powerful man smiled like that, it usually meant his gain and your loss.

"Sit." Ramiro suggested to some chairs.

There was even one for Viktor. Cecelia and Danon sat, but Viktor was reluctant. Ramiro settled his gaze on Viktor, and the large knight finally huffed down in his seat next to Cecelia. She glanced at him and found him looking at her. She wanted to smile or wink or shrug or do anything, something, but all she could do was slowly look back at Ramiro.

"What's the meaning of this Ramiro?" Danon asked, all nicety gone. "Dragging us from a ride like we don't have the right to say no."

His face was all hard angles. At that moment, Cecelia saw so much of her father in him that she took a deep breath and tried to relax.

A side door opened. Danica slunk in. She wore her icy smile, as always. Its whiteness seemed dreadfully opposing to the dim room, and the flickering of hundreds of tiny diamonds hand sewn into the fabric of her bodice was too much for Cecelia. Danica shimmered in the light of the windows. Her dress was nearly translucent in the midday sun.

"You'll forgive me for the abrupt nature of our meeting." Ramiro said.

Danica came to his side and kissed his cheek. She threw a cunning look at Viktor and found a seat to the side of the room. Her eyes settled on Cecelia, trying and failing to hide her concern.

"I realize you were enjoying yourselves," Ramiro added.

"I'll forgive you after you tell us what this is about." Danon said.

"Well, it's about many things. Primarily a wedding." Ramiro poured a drink from a crystal decanter and took a sip.

"A wedding?" Cecelia said, her throat so tight with anxiety her voice moved up an octave.

"Yes, my lady. You see, with the push of war so near, I need allies."

"Seems like you need friends, not more wives." Cecelia mumbled.

Ramiro laughed a dry laugh. He looked at Danica.

"No, no, not more wives for me." He sat his glass down with a thump. "But for you Viktor. Yes, a wife will do for you."

Viktor erupted from his chair. "You can't!"

"Oh? Am I not your king, Viktor? Do you not live to serve me?"

Ramiro's tone ate into Viktor's skin. He sunk back down in his chair, realizing his wrong.

"Forgive me, your grace." He bowed his head and stared at his feet.

Cecelia watched him, trying to urge him without using words to stand, to fight, to do something, but not to give in. She turned back to Ramiro.

"I don't understand. You speak of allies and wars. You plan to marry off your Kingsguard. Why are we here?"

Danica giggled quietly. She smiled at Cecelia. "Forgive me your graces. It is truly a lovely plan."

Ramiro cleared his throat. "You'll have to forgive my wife. A wedding seems like a fun thing for her, though she forgets the importance of its purpose."

"I forget nothing, dear husband. I just find it all that amusing." She replied.

"Well," He batted away her words with his hand. "Anyway."

He looked at Danon and Cecelia. They both stared at him as if they watched a madman.

"I have given Viktor a new title." Ramiro paused, perhaps awaiting some form of excitement from his Kingsguard, but Viktor remained sullen and silent. Ramiro carried on, his mood unaffected by Viktor's. "Viktor will henceforth be known as the Royal Guard Marshal. A title offering him land and immunity from other silly rules other Kingsguard obey."

"Such as?" Danon asked.

"Marriage." Cecelia stared at Ramiro. "Kingsguard can't marry. But as Royal, whatever the abominable brilliance, he can."

"Guard Marshal." Danica interrupted, "Royal Guard Marshal."

She stood, her dress sliding from her seat like sea foam, touching the ground silently.

"It's not uncommon. The title is a mere reinstatement. The post was kept in the courts of Korith over a hundred years ago." Danica reached for her husband's glass and relieved him of it, taking a sip herself. "The land is carved from the kingswood itself, on the eastern side. Beautiful river crossing there." She winked at Viktor.

Ramiro smiled at his wife before carrying on where she left off.

"The title is powerful. Where General Rees commands my army, Marshal Viktor will command my entire household guard. Kingsguard. Queensguard. Men-at-arms." He leaned against his desk, this time his hope for Viktor's approval written across his face.

Ramiro awaited anxiously for Viktor to say something.

"As you say, your grace." Viktor mumbled.

Danon laughed. It startled Cecelia, who jumped in her seat. Danica and Ramiro stared at the Panther prince now, as if he were the one gone mad. Viktor watched him from the corner of his eyes.

"I'm sorry," Danon said between laughter, "it's just... and you assume my sister will marry him? That's it? That's why you've brought us here as well?"

Ramiro retrieved his drink from his wife and tossed the rest back, slamming his glass down onto his desk. The noise momentarily silenced Danon.

"It is an appropriate match. A masculine princess of a second-rate island nation, bastard at that. Half Korithian, as rumors have it. And a high-ranking official in the Korithian court." He looked to Danica for approval.

But Danica stared at Cecelia, studying her face for any twitches or tweaks that gave away Cecelia's displeasure. But Cecelia had played this game before. As a child, she and Danon would often play a similar game, where one would make a statement, whether true or false, and the other had to determine its truthfulness by studying the other's face. They called it Stone Face.

She felt Viktor's eyes on her, too. The heat from him was nauseating. He was nervous, anxious. She knew that much. As was she. But she always won Stone Face as a child, and she didn't plan on losing to Ramiro.

"I assume you've considered my father's reaction to this exploit?" she asked.

Ramiro nodded. "Yes. I'm not the king for nothing, princess." He rubbed his chin, stroking his wispy stubble. "Bastard you are, but you are your father's favorite. He'll want you kept alive. Should he launch ships on us, we shall simply kill you."

Cecelia fought hard not to let the corner of her mouth turn up. Her father's favorite? Ramiro revealed how poor his informants were at spy craft.

"He'll launch ships on you regardless," Cecelia said. "You possess his heir." She gestured to Danon.

Danon watched Cecelia. She could tell he too was playing Stone Face and was intrigued by her words. He didn't know where she was heading, either.

"Prince Danon will be released as soon as you and Viktor wed." Ramiro said, waving his hand at Danon like a pesky fly. "Your father will have no need for hostility. We will keep you here, at the palace. You shall want for nothing. Viktor will, I'm sure, be an attentive husband."

He waited for Viktor to agree. Viktor obediently nodded.

"There, see. You'll be mother to a brood of oversized children before long. We can erect a manor on your new land in a few years, should you behave yourself. There's nothing to fear."

Cecelia stared at Ramiro, testing her skill. She managed getting her mouth in order, a stoic straight line molding her lips. Her eyes wavered for a moment at Ramiro's fresh interest in facial hair before trailing up to his lucid eyes. He was serious. He'd thought it through.

And she had no reason to believe her father would send ships, even for Danon. Korithians did not know how easily Panthers tossed away lost causes, taking up new ones like pretty stones on the beach. He still had Alaina and Lucien. No need to traipse across the Sea of Storms. But Ramiro didn't know that.

"And I assume should Korith go to war, you'd appreciate the assistance of your Royal Guard Marshal's father-in-law. His large fleet of ships filled with well-trained soldiers?"

Ramiro smiled. "That would be expected, yes."

"And if not, then you'd kill me?"

"Well, I doubt it will come to that, don't you?"

Cecelia nodded. Truthfully, it didn't matter how imperfect Ramiro's plan was. She wondered if the young king had even asked Rees to offer his guidance on the issue. But that didn't matter either because her father's vision showed her staying in Korith. Who was she to argue if the way meant marriage?

Viktor refused to make eye contact with her, opting to stare at some object on Ramiro's desk. He stared so intently Cecelia wondered if he'd catch the object on fire. His neck pulsed and he held his head rigid. Cecelia wondered why. Why was he so afraid of a wedding?

"Should you wish my complete obedience, allow the wedding to be performed in the Panther way." She finally said.

Ramiro moved to talk, an objection to her request, but Danica spoke over him.

"Of course, anything you like."

"Good," Cecelia nodded. Viktor's body had come alive next to her, stirring in its seat. She felt his eyes on her then, and that never ending heat.

"Panthers only marry on a double full moon." She said. "And I will require my brother's presence as cleric."

"As you say, princess." Ramiro smirked.

"And a ship prepared for his departure, which will occur as soon as Viktor and I wed."

Danica frowned, but Ramiro clapped his hands with pleasure, moving on.

"Fantastic. A double full moon should be any day now. A ship will be found." He sighed with enthusiasm. "Anything else?"

"Panthers exchange gifts on their wedding day." Danon spoke, reluctantly assisting in the planning of the festivities.

He knew Cecelia, once she made a decision, would be unmoved. She smiled softly at him, offering him her thanks.

"It cannot be something already in possession. It must be new, a gift, given to the person to be gifted to their new partner."

"I see." Ramiro appeared annoyed at the complication the Panther wedding was posing. "Well, I'm sure I can arrange something for Viktor."

He eyed him like a stray dog, annoyed at his presence and the trouble he was causing.

Cecelia smiled at her brother. She already knew what she'd be gifting Viktor.

At the age of ten and six, novice warriors of the Lagos partake in the Trial of the Thoughtful Warrior. A tea is prepared, filled with hallucinogenic herbs collected from the jungles. Only four Tea Artists know which herbs make up the tea. Once drunk, they lead the warrior into an empty arena. An audience of Masters surrounds them, though they watch in complete silence as the warrior battles enemies real and unreal. Training dummies, Adepts, and figments of the mind fight the warrior. Participants are expected to display a calm resolve, despite the hallucinations, and a solid command of their weapon throughout the trial.

Logician Mykel Meralko
   Islands of Fortune: An Examination of Island Nations

Chapter Fourteen

VIKTOR TRIED TO CONVINCE himself that he wasn't looking for her, but it simply wasn't true. He wanted to see her, wanted to speak to her, ever since their meeting with Ramiro the day before. But Cecelia had excused herself to her room and locked herself away for the rest of the day, refusing all guests. Refusing food.

He finally found her the following day, sitting on the edge of a fountain in the pavilion behind the palace, facing the sea. She sat and stared. Her hair, unplaited for once, drifted with the sea breeze. She was so absorbed with her thoughts she didn't notice his approach.

He watched her, following her gaze to the violent sea. The wind cut through the air that day, bringing with it an iciness that reminded it wouldn't be summer forever. On the horizon was nothing but waves and gulls. Viktor moved his mouth to speak, but Cecelia beat him to it.

"A fortnight's journey in that direction," she pointed, "and I'd be at the Lagos."

"You miss home, then?"

She scoffed. "Haven't you heard, knight? Korith is now my home, for I make my marriage vows night after tomorrow."

He said nothing in reply, for what could he say? She turned to look at him, her shoulders wilting when she realized she wounded him.

"I didn't mean," she said, then frowned.

"It's fine, champion." He sat next to her on the fountain's edge.

Cecelia toyed with a piece of dried grass, its yellow blade twirling rapidly in her fingers. She tied it in a bow and slid it along her ring finger.

"I never wanted to be married," she finally said, "but if I must, I am not displeased it is to you."

Viktor stifled a laugh. "An amazing compliment, champion, thank you."

She stared down at her grass ring, fiddling, and frowned. Viktor realized she had meant it in kindness.

"I never wanted to marry either," he told her. "Leave it to my king to command it of me."

Cecelia nudged him with her shoulder. "You thought you were safe as a Kingsguard, didn't you?"

He nodded. They watched the waves come and go together, letting the wind speak for them, filling their ears with eerie whispers. She continued to tie and untie the blade of grass. Viktor watched her, admiring her delicate fingers, and wondered how such hands could so easily clutch a sword and kill a man.

Or how such hands would want to touch him.

"It would have been simpler had you stayed home." Viktor broke their silence.

Cecelia sighed and tossed her grass to the sky. It spun, pulled by the wind, and drifted away over the cliff's edge.

"If I had wanted simple, dearly betrothed," she stood and turned to face him, "I would have stayed home."

With her hands on her hips and the sun at her back, she cast a shadow over him, shielding his eyes from the sun. Her hair blew wildly with a sudden gust of wind, tendrils of it drifting like the blade of grass had. The oils she used to wash it reached him and he inhaled deeply. Pine was there, and mint. He saw the freckles along her cheeks, faded though present, and reached out to stroke them. He stopped his hand short, awkwardly aware of how intimate a touch it was, and let it fall back into his lap.

"Tell me of your home," he asked her, "tell me about the Archipelago of the Moons."

Cecelia smirked, but when she saw he was serious, she rolled her eyes.

"What would you have me tell you, my lord," she said, kicking at a rock, "what Korithian rumor should I dispel first?"

"When you spoke with the queen that day on her veranda, you mentioned a trial."

Cecelia nodded. "The Trial of the Thoughtful Warrior. Yes. What about it?"

"What sort of things did you see after you drank your tea?" He tried not to sound eager, but the trials sounded difficult. What better way to weed out the weak?

But Viktor already knew Cecelia wasn't weak.

"You want to know what I'm afraid of, don't you?" Cecelia smiled. "Is that it? What imagined foes did I fight in the arena?"

Victor shrugged. "Merely curious, champion."

Though she spoke the truth.

"Sure," Cecelia rolled her eyes. She turned to the sea, letting the wind whip through her hair, allowing it to blow across her face. Her fingers tapped out a tune on the edge of the fountain.

"I'll never say, Viktor," she said. "It'd be unbecoming of a lady."

"Hmmm," Viktor said, "Fine. Tell me of your father. Will he send ships to collect you? Ramiro called you his favorite."

Cecelia stopped her finger tapping and let her hand drop. She stared out at the waves, biting her lip, before turning back to him.

"I am not as beloved, back home, as you might think, my lord." She turned to stare back out at the ocean. "Perhaps I remind him too much of her, too much of my mother. Though how would I know, for my memories of her are fleeting. Barely there. I suppose he'll be happy to be permanently rid of me."

Viktor scoffed, "I would think that didn't bother you, champion. You seem pleased with yourself most of the time. Who cares what your father thinks?"

When she didn't reply, he finally allowed himself to reach for her. Her hand was cool and small within his own. He pulled gently, forcing her to look at him. Tears grew in her eyes, though she blinked them back as best she could.

"My father was a dirt sack," he said. It felt good to confess this to her, though he didn't know why. "And my mother... tried, but failed to change him. And in turn she became a shell. A husk of a woman. Not really there."

It was clear that Cecelia's mysterious mother created a sense of shame within her. And while the ways of the Archipelago of the Moons made little sense to him, he desperately wanted to understand Cecelia.

"Ephram was the only good in that house. He protected me. Taught me what my father should have. Von was useless. A jackal. And Arlo was quiet. He had planned to leave us all long before we ever knew about it. Long before he ever left. When he was a child, I suppose. He never felt present."

Cecelia toyed with her lips, pursing them, attempting to keep her face in order and not let the tears part from her lashes. She shook her head, signifying she understood. He squeezed her hand.

"Fragile hearts..." she whispered. She tried to smile, but her face broke for a moment, her lips turning downward into a jagged frown before she managed to reshape her face into something emotionless. "...need tender care. Your loneliness can keep mine company."

She cleared her throat and tried again.

"Because I will spend the rest of my days here with you. Because I choose to." Her face turned, like she tasted something bitter.

Viktor's stomach sank at the thought. Her words made their marriage sound like a sentence, imprisoned in matrimony, despite Cecelia admitting it was her choice. Because it wasn't. Not really. It was then Viktor realized what Ramiro had done. Cecelia would be kept in a cell, walls invisible to the naked eye. And Viktor, already kept on a leash by Ramiro, would be yanked closer, leash pulled shorter.

Essentially, Ramiro had cornered them, punishing them both for his benefit. This is what he got for his years of service?

He watched her stare at the ocean, still trying to keep her face from unfolding. She wiped her nose on her hand and picked some more blades of grass. The wind kept whipping at them, intoxicating him with her smell.

She seemed pleased enough with him. But how long would that last? Viktor was older than her-- by a lifetime, it seemed-- though it was probably only ten and four. He was rough. He was ugly with the large splash of red decorating half his neck and shoulder. And she would miss her home, though she said otherwise.

And Viktor didn't know how to make someone else happy, let alone himself.

After the fall of King Hallyn, King Maurkam and his quiet wife Queen Liosni were crowned. But the battle to remove Hallyn had cost Korith much in infrastructure, money, and lives. The death toll of the war was never officially determined, but scholars estimate some 70,000 men, women and children were killed before Hallyn yielded. To remind herself and her husband the cost of their crowns, Queen Liosni had flowerbeds built and 70,001 delphiniums planted. Until her death, Queen Liosni tended to the plants alongside the royal gardeners. On the eve of her death, she was seen in the garden, speaking to several buds that had yet to bloom. Later that evening she was found in her bed, as if asleep, with a delphinium in her hand.

High Steward Rodrick Brasden
 The Fall of Hallyn

Chapter Fifteen

The smells of cardamom and anise drifted through the stalls, pulling Cecelia along. The queen herself had invited her to stroll amongst the Fair Folk, taking in the sights and sounds and smells, investigating every corner of the makeshift market for trinkets. Danica walked beside her, her Queensguard ever present behind them, scaring the Fair Folk away before they even arrived at a stall.

Danica leaned low over a table, examining a beautiful necklace. Its silver filigree was delicate and its pendant encrusted with rubies.

"Extraordinary," Danica said to Cecelia, "I don't know where they get it."

She stood up and smiled at the Folkwoman behind the table, a short woman with lilac hair.

"The same place we've always gotten it," the woman said proudly. "We know this land better than any so-called Korithian."

Danica smiled at her, though Cecelia shivered at the sight. It was beautiful, true, but it scared her to think about what it really hid beneath.

"Come," Cecelia gently tugged on the queen's arm, "I see some fletchers this way. I'd like to compare them to craftsmen of the Lagos."

Danica allowed herself to be pulled. She slid a cool hand into Cecelia's while they strolled and offered her a genuine smile, one that wasn't so frightening. The ease in which they inhabited the same space, the way in which their friendship was unfolding, perplexed Cecelia. Danica had arrived at Cecelia's room that morning, cheeks flush with the dawn air, enthused to spend the day with her. Genuinely enthused.

And Cecelia needed friends. Ramiro possessed no favoritism towards her. If she were to remain in his court, it'd be good to count on his wife as a supporter.

"Fletchers," Danica scoffed, "when the Fair Folk craft such pretty things? Don't you like pretty things, Cecelia?"

Cecelia smiled at Danica, hoping it seemed more genuine than it felt. She glanced down at the queen, for even though Danica wore heels she was still a hand and a half shorter than Cecelia, to see if her performance was convincing.

Danica amused herself, smiling at the children of the Fair Folk, watching them squeal and hide. Some of the bolder ones, though, glared. One even moved to spit, but his green-haired father covered his mouth before he could. Danica smiled all the same.

How exhausting.

Cecelia couldn't fathom plastering a smile on her face for that long. Her face ached after a single dinner party. But to do it day in and day out? Impossible.

"Pretty things are nice," Cecelia steered Danica towards the fletchers, "but useless when you need steel to pierce."

"To pierce what?" Danica asked, waving at a small, cherub cheeked toddler, "you're in Korith now. Civilized Korith. You'll find no savages in need of stabbing, slicing, or poking here."

She turned to face the table, glancing at the shiny tipped arrows before looking at Cecelia.

"At least, no obvious savages." She smiled.

Cecelia rolled her eyes and picked up the nearest arrow. It was longer than her arm and fletched with several gray goose feathers, each bigger than her hand.

"At least it's shiny," Danica joked, poking at the tip.

"You could hunt with them," Cecelia placed the arrow back and picked up another, examining the tip closely, "they needn't be for savages."

Danica chuckled, "as if my dearest husband would allow me the joy of joining him on a hunt." And when she saw Cecelia peer at her over the arrow, she added, "I'm sure you'll enjoy many hunts with your lordly husband once we construct your new home. Viktor seems a different breed than Ramiro."

"Aye," Cecelia agreed, setting the arrow down and smiling at the merchant.

They walked away, still arm in arm. The sharp scent of anise grew the closer they came to the food stalls. Fire crackled in pits where kabobs cooked.

Danica motioned for a Queensguard to purchase some. The Queensguard stepped forward and bartered with the Fair Folk, offering them two small coins for the kabobs. His mouth was not used to the ancient tongue. His words were stilted, but the man selling the kabobs held his smirk until the Queensguard turned around to offer the kabobs to Danica.

"Your majesty," he said, handing the sizzling sticks of meat to Danica and then one to Cecelia.

Cecelia sniffed it, admiring the pungent aromas. It reminded her of home, sort of. Korithian food was much blander than she was used to. At least the Fair Folk knew how to season.

The first bite filled her mouth with sizzling hot fat. She inhaled sharply. A trail of fat slid out of the corner of her mouth. Danica laughed as she did the same. Cecelia wiped the oil that dribbled down her chin and suggested to Danica.

"Your grace has some as well."

Danica traced the line and grimaced. She extended a hand, and a Queensguard produced a silk handkerchief. She handed it to Cecelia when she finished.

"Perhaps you should serve this at your wedding feast," Danica said before taking another bite.

"Mmmm," Cecelia replied.

She allowed herself a moment to chew and swallow before elaborating.

"There is no feast, your grace," she said.

"I beg your pardon?"

Cecelia laughed. Danica seemed truly appalled at the idea.

"Unfortunately," Cecelia explained, "Panthers wed and then," she motioned with her hand like a bird fluttering away, "off to bed."

"That quickly?" Danica said. She took another bite, thinking about Cecelia's revelations.

"It's better to cut the anticipation," Cecelia said.

"I suppose," Danica replied. "Though it was the many goblets of wine that got me through my wedding night. I was but a girl. Or I felt like one, anyway."

Cecelia feigned offense. "Are you suggesting you find me matronly?"

Danica swatted Cecelia's arm, "absolutely not. The least matronly. But... are you not afraid? Worried?"

Cecelia shrugged. Finished with her kabob, she handed the skewer to a Queensguard's outstretched hand. He expertly flung it into a nearby brazier. A small, blue-haired girl crouched beside it, absently petting a white cat.

"What is there to fear?" she said. "Viktor is not frightening."

Danica chuckled. "Perhaps to some. But to others..." She let her words trail away.

"Worrying is a waste of time. Or so my father says." Cecelia said.

They walked in silence. The Fair Folk parted before them, each trying to stare but avoid them at all costs. Cecelia glanced at stalls filled with baubles and bits, but nothing caught her eye. Danica's hand wrapped around her own. The cool tension made her stomach lurch.

"I am sorry," Danica said quietly, almost a whisper, "it has to be this way."

"Be what way?" Cecelia asked.

Danica was staring at her, watching her face, calculating each movement of each muscle. Cecelia did her best to mask her fear. It was a skill her father insisted she learn when she was younger. A ruler never showed fear, he said, even if they felt it in their bones.

"Your marriage. Your... imprisonment here."

Cecelia raised her eyebrows, "is that what I am, imprisoned?"

Danica smirked and offered her a shrug. "I'm sure my husband would not call it such. No, he'd add some pretty flair to it, make you feel good about it. But we both know that's what it is."

Cecelia frowned and then nodded. "Aye, from the moment he said it, I knew."

Danica sighed. "I have no control. I have no say. Ramiro thought it was a great idea. I... I supported him. Because I had to."

"Because you had to," Cecelia repeated, staring evenly at Danica.

Danica's lip twisted, like she was about to say more, but a voice hailed them from across the heads milling about in the crowd. The mumble of voices around them died out. Cecelia turned to see a white-haired woman approaching. Perched on her shoulder was the white-haired cat. The woman stroked the cat, muttering to it incoherently. When she grew closer, she spoke again.

"Faed'wyn D'ncyea," the woman tipped her head only slightly.

Danica pulled her shoulders back and stood tall. Her face contorted into her most queenly pose.

"Faed'wyn Mother Oora."

Mother Oora looked at Cecelia. While the old woman's hair lacked the typical Fair Folk color, her eyes glittered turquoise. Her skin, though wrinkled, was rosy, and her hands had a youthful strength to them as they reached out to Cecelia's arm and squeezed it gently.

"Faed'wyn Kith d'Mun."

"Faed'wyn," Cecelia whispered.

"I have heard many whispers of the Panther Pawdwyn. How she slayed Gryvlln of Giants. How she speaks intelligently. How her face," Mother Oora extended one finger to Cecelia's cheek and trailed it down the side, "speaks of an ancient beauty not seen on the great continent for many moons."

Cecelia did her best not to flinch, knowing to insult the Prevailing Mother amongst her people would be a terrible mistake. The old woman's finger sparked against her skin, nearly burning. Cecelia wondered if it was her magic contacting through her touch.

"And how," Mother Oora dropped her hand and spoke solemnly, "she tamed Kith d'mas n'yor."

Cecelia remembered Kharis' words. She knew Mother Oora spoke of Viktor.

"I didn't tame Sir Viktor," Cecelia said. "He doesn't require taming."

Mother Oora smiled. She perked up and peered around at her fellow Fair Folk.

"Doesn't he now?" She said, "all men require taming, dearest pawdwyn, whether they know it or not."

Mother Oora winked at Danica, "as this one knows well."

The old woman reached into a hidden pocket amongst her brightly hued skirts and offered a tidbit of something to the cat, who delicately ate the treat, whatever it was.

"Have you come for another palming, dearest D'ncyea?" Mother Oora asked. "I'd be delighted to offer you my visions again. With payment, of course."

Danica smiled her fake smile and turned to Cecelia. "I'm just showing her grace around the market. Letting her see your people for what they are."

"Which would be what, my dear?"

"Merchants," Danica replied, "fantastic merchants."

She gripped Cecelia's arm and pulled her away, tipping her head only slightly to the Prevailing Mother. Mother Oora watched them go, ever stroking her white cat.

They had made their way through the crowd, moving towards the edge of the market. Here the stalls shifted from fine to more common items. Simple leather goods – riding satchels, purses, and shoes — hung from wooden pegs. The smell was horrendous, but Danica showed little care, so long as she was away from Mother Oora.

"She didn't seem so bad," Cecelia said, "but you've met her before?"

"Yes," Danica answered, "before my wedding. There was another market. I had my palm read."

"By Mother Oora?"

Danica shook her head yes.

"And?"

"She said many things. Things I care little to repeat. Things I care little to think about."

Danica looked at Cecelia, daring her to ask another question. But Cecelia knew those eyes and had seen that face before.

Danica was imprisoned too.

They walked with the only sound between them being their shoes grinding into gravel. The low rumble of voices, of the business of the market, faded behind them. Someone had taken up a lute and was playing a frivolous beat somewhere, but Danica pulled Cecelia forward, done with the Fair Folk.

The palace loomed ahead, and Cecelia felt the moment shrinking. Back inside, she feared Danica would withdraw again, put up her walls, and Cecelia would once again be alone. She had only a few more moments, a few more steps, before she would lose her chance to plant a true seed of friendship with Danica. To at least spark a moment that might grow into a fire.

"Had you met Ramiro before?" Cecelia said, her voice cutting through the settled silence between them like a knife.

Danica slowed her steps.

"Before you married," Cecelia clarified, not knowing if the look on Danica's face was one of confusion or subdued annoyance.

"I had met him once before. My father held a party for my mother's birthday. Romo was my father's friend and respected my mother. So, he joined the festivities, bringing Ramiro with him." Danica's hand trailed along the tops of some delphiniums, bending them gently as they walked by. "Rumor at the time was that Romo was looking for a bride for his son."

Cecelia stood next to Danica, plucking at the soft blue petals of the flowers.

"So that's why your father actually invited him?" Cecelia asked, keenly aware of how kings and queens liked to match make for their children.

"Yes," Danica muttered.

Currency. Cecelia looked at Danica, beautiful and strong in her own way, though powerless in the Korithian way.

Cecelia shrugged. "At least it wasn't Lord Rufus he was hoping to find a wife for."

Danica erupted with laughter. She grabbed Cecelia by the arm, and they ran further down the gravel path, weaving between the flowerbeds before stopping at a bench. The Queensguard hurried to keep up, encumbered by their armor. Danica leaned against Cecelia, still laughing at the thought of marrying Lord Rufus.

"I suppose I should thank you," Cecelia said in between catching her breath.

"For what?"

"Well, Ramiro could've wed *me* to Lord Rufus," she turned to gaze down at the now pink cheeked queen, "but I suppose you had more to do with the wedding plans than you admit."

Danica stopped laughing. She sat up and straightened out her wrinkled gown. She cleared her throat.

"I saw the way you looked at him," she said quietly, "and the way he looked at you. Ramiro's been trying to rein Viktor in, anyway. The moment Ramiro uttered Lord Rufus' name, I knew I could not let that happen. I merely planted the seed, and let Ramiro think it was his idea."

Danica wouldn't look at Cecelia directly, instead only glancing at her out of the corner of her eyes. She was trying to gauge whether Cecelia was angry. But how could she be? *She* wasn't marrying Lord Rufus either. A smile teased at the corner of Cecelia's lips.

"You'd make a fine King," she said.

"Wouldn't I?" Danica agreed.

Over Danica's shoulder, Cecelia noticed several bleeding hearts planted amongst the delphiniums, fighting for their own right to grow. They drooped over, dancing in the breeze. Cecelia watched them, her throat tightening uncomfortably as she took them in.

"We should go," she said to Danica.

"In a moment," Danica sighed, grasping Cecelia's arm and leaning against her, "just another moment amongst the flowers. I feel they understand me better than most."

The last Royal Guard Marshal held station during the reign of King Oryian, the ousted King Norian's great grandfather. At the time, the position was rife with nepotistic abuse. Oryian had his younger brother Orrick named Royal Guard Marshal until rumors of Orrick's dalliance with the queen got him beheaded. Oryian then assigned his next youngest brother, Osiron, to the position. Osiron lasted nearly a year before he was caught funneling funds from the royal coffers into his own pocket. Oryian, having had enough, dissolved the title and absorbed the land into the kingswood.

High Steward Rodrick Brasden
House Histories and Insignia

Chapter Sixteen

She came to him in the middle of the night. There was the click of the lock and the heavy door swung open. Turning to search for the source of intrusion, Viktor saw no face. She brought no light. Instead, she was a shadow, drifting through the room. He barely moved his mouth to speak before she shushed him.

She stood in the window, bathed in the glow of the Mother and Daughter, staring out at the night. Lines of worry were etched across her forehead. Her eyes, usually stormy, were far away.

"What's wrong?" He sat up in bed.

"I couldn't sleep," she said, still staring out at the night.

Viktor had had trouble falling asleep, too. Many thoughts fought through his mind, like a storm upon the sea, raging and relentless. He had just fallen into the lightest of slumber when he heard the door open.

"You said your father was a dirt sack," she said next, "but the truth for me is that my father is equally kind and cold. Honorable but distant. And my mother, well," she finally turned to look at him, revealing the wetness on her cheeks where tears had previously fallen. "My father loved her and married her, despite being told not to. And when she died, the people of the Lagos collectively sighed in relief. Their king could marry one of them, a Panther, and all would be right. All that was left to remind them of their king's misstep was..."

But the words locked tight in her throat, and Viktor feared she might choke.

"You," he finished for her.

She shook her head, tears silently falling down her cheeks. The desire to hold her was strong, but when he reached to grasp her she turned away, angrily wiping at her tears.

"I am not a Panther," she growled. "I don't know what I am. But I thought you should know that. That you should know the truth before marrying me, before marrying the *Panther princess.*"

The words sounded vile as she spat them. Viktor felt her anger in the heat of each syllable. He let his arms drop. He let her stand on her own.

"My father beat me," Viktor confessed, "all of us, actually. He was a vile, angry man. Were it not for my eldest brother Ephram, I might not have survived my youth. My mother was useless, though it pains me to say it."

Cecelia watched him with wounded interest. It was her turn to reach for him, to comfort him, and his turn to pull away. They stared at each other for a long time in silence. Viktor watched Cecelia's eyes change, turning from an open heart to a closed one.

"These are wounds not easily tended," she sniffed.

Viktor nodded in agreement. "Aye."

Something in his voice jolted her. She stiffened and stood tall. Wiping the rest of her tears away, she cleared her throat and tried to smile, though the sadness beneath was still visible.

"I should go," she said, turning for the door. "It is an early day for me tomorrow."

"Cecelia?" he groped for her, but she moved too quickly, stepping further from his reach.

She stared at him. Her eyes were sealed up again, a relentless storm bursting behind them.

"Cece," she finally said, "that's what those closest call me."

Viktor shrugged. "I rather like champion."

She smiled, her teeth radiant in the moonlight. And then she was gone.

He laid back down in bed, staring at the dark ceiling, making shapes out of shadows. Eventually, he dozed, though his sleep was fitful. When the cock crowed, he was already sitting on the edge of his bed. Sunbeams fell across his feet. He had but one day to prep for his wedding.

Come moonrise, it would be done.

He broke his fast in the mess hall with the rest of the Kingsguard. They avoided him, opting to leave the table when he sat, feigning they were finished. They shoved what they could in their mouths before returning their trenchers to the serving maids. He ignored them.

He didn't look up from his food until a shadow fell over him. Danon huffed down in the seat opposite him, not even looking at Viktor, but staring appallingly at the food before him.

"You eat this every day?" Danon stirred the oats into the runny yolk of his eggs.

Viktor kept eating.

"For the Moon Mother's sake, this egg is cold!"

"Usually," Viktor cleared his throat with a swig of malty beer, "there's no time for complaining. We all have jobs to do."

Danon rolled his eyes as he forced himself to swallow. "Oh right, I forgot. I'm a useless prince from nowhere. I've plenty of time to complain."

Viktor remained silent, refusing to take Danon's bait.

"You know," Danon pointed his spoon at Viktor, "you're not some commoner anymore, either. You're a lord. That's why none of your brothers in arms want to sit with you."

Danon turned to look at those that had remained. They huddled together at a second table, as far from Viktor as they could get. Hushed words moved between them and stolen glances at Viktor were common.

"So much for brotherhood!" Danon said a little too loudly.

Viktor slammed his fist on the table, ripping Danon's attention back to him. He remembered Cecelia's words from the night before. Her tears at the admission that she was indeed a bastard. A bastard without a home.

"I'll not have your play, Panther prince, not on this day."

If Viktor had wanted to scare Danon, he was sorely mistaken. Danon twisted his lips into an amused grin and carried on eating his food without complaint.

"Ah, yes, today!" Danon said. "Come moonrise, we'll be brothers. You'll have to show me more patience then, my lord."

Viktor stared at Danon. The young prince ate, almost happily, neither gagging nor showing signs of any more disgust at his food. Memories of Cecelia's face in the moonlight came unbidden to Viktor. The way she fought her own sadness. The way she angrily wiped her own tears away. Perhaps she wasn't a Panther, like the boy that sat before him, but she was made of finer stuff than Danon. That much Viktor was certain of.

"Have you a gift for my sister?" Danon asked innocently, avoiding Viktor's eyes, "for I have just the thing should you need one."

Viktor stood, finished with his meal.

"Yes," he said, "I have."

He didn't hear the words Danon spoke next. After dumping his trencher at the nearest serving maid, he exited the hall, leaving Danon to scramble after him.

"Care to share?" Danon's words filled his ear.

"No."

Danon pretended to pout. "You should trust me more. We are to be brothers."

Viktor turned and pinned Danon against the stone wall with his forearm pressed tightly to the prince's throat. Fortunately–or unfortunately, Viktor thought–he had missed ramming Danon's head into the nearest sconce.

"I'll tell you this one more time, Panther prince," Viktor growled, "so listen and listen well: I'll not have your play today. I know she is but half a Panther. I know she is a bastard."

Danon held his composure. He didn't struggle. The only thing that gave away his fear was his dilated pupils, and even those he fought to control. He slowly nodded his head. When Viktor released him, he straightened his doublet. They walked on together in silence.

"She's my sister, Viktor."

They climbed the steps upwards towards the inner bailey.

"Whatever distasteful thing a bastard is in Korith doesn't apply to her. I care about her."

Viktor stopped walking. Family. His own was pockmarked with misfortune and dysfunction. Cecelia's, full of mystery and pain. These were tender wounds, indeed. But how would they fare within a marriage?

"She'll be fine." Viktor heard how flimsy the words were, even as they fell from his mouth. "I'll take care of her."

"But will you make her happy?"

Danon stood a step below. Viktor stared down at him, seeing how young the prince was, as if for the first time. A child. A giant child, playing politics and intrigue like he knew what he was doing.

"Happiness is overrated." Viktor turned and walked out into the sunlight of the bailey yard.

He had no duties for the day. Ramiro graciously, and somewhat forcefully, told him to bathe and prepare to fulfill his destiny. Whatever that meant. So, he headed to the bathhouse and prayed Danon wouldn't follow him there.

Danon didn't.

Afterward he thought about taking his horse for a ride but knew he shouldn't. He'd get hot and sweaty and ruin the purpose of his bath. He sat idle in his bed, wondering what the abominable brilliance was wrong with him and when he started worrying about ruining things like the purpose of a bath.

His eyes stared at the window, remembering Cecelia had stood there just hours earlier. He wanted her. It was certain, but he wondered if he could ever love her.

And what the difference even was.

A knock on his door awoke him. The sun was now falling, dropping behind the castle wall. Sunbeams no longer filled his room, but the promise of the Mother and her Daughter's light.

Danon shoved the door open before Viktor could reach it. He looked down at Viktor, still half in his bed, and frowned.

"Moon Mother, you're not even dressed?"

"I fell asleep," Viktor said. "I... didn't sleep well last night."

"I've heard," Danon muttered, "well get dressed, or would my lord like a valet?"

Viktor grumbled something about not requiring help to get dressed, not since he was a boy of four.

"Well, enjoy your last go at it," Danon said. "Rumor has it Ramiro is gifting you your own set of servants. Valet and steward alike."

"He wouldn't dare," Viktor attempted to figure out what strange garment went where.

Danon smiled coyly and slowly shut the door, leaving Viktor alone once again. He held the dark blue doublet up in the light and sneered.

He tossed it to the side and rummaged over his other garments. He tried to keep himself calm, hating himself for worrying about clothing.

When he finished, he left his room. Danon startled him, emerging from the shadows, exhausted from waiting.

"You say you don't need a valet, but I've seen men of five and ninety dress faster than you."

The prince smelled of fresh air. A pink hue tinged his cheeks, distinguishing itself amidst the flickering flames of the hall sconces, like he had just been outside.

"Is the altar ready?" Viktor asked.

"Yes," Danon said, "all is prepared."

"Then why are you still here?" Viktor turned down the hall, wishing he could walk it alone one last time rather than with Danon. "Shouldn't you be with your sister?"

Danon fell into step beside him, saying nothing.

"If you're afraid I'll take these last few moments to screw up or run, don't worry. I'm not going anywhere."

Danon still said nothing. He offered Viktor a small, amused smile, one a parent reserved for an annoying child. Viktor scowled.

"That's new," he said. "The Panther prince has no words."

"Frankly, I wish you would run," Danon stopped abruptly and faced Viktor. "I think this whole wedding is a trap. A scheme, by Ramiro, and I don't like it."

Viktor studied Danon. He pursed his lips, considering his words. Then he nodded.

"It is a trap, boy," Viktor agreed, "but not for you. For your sister and me. Ramiro practically said as much."

"Did he?"

"Didn't he?" Viktor kept walking, dragging Danon along in the wake of his shadow.

"I'm going to leave my sister here, in this nest of vipers, not knowing if she'll be bit or worse: the whole nest will go up in flames."

"Oh, Moon Mother, what are you talking about?" Viktor slowed his pace, though he never stopped walking.

The moons were rising now, making their ascent past the wall and towards the trail of stars referred to as the Waterfall. There was still time before the ceremony, but Viktor felt suffocated inside the castle. He needed the fresh night air, the rustle of the breeze as it brought the salty taste of the ocean to his lips. But more than that, he needed the weight he felt on his chest to go away.

He wanted to be with her again, alone. It was the only time the feelings left. It was the only time he felt peaceful and like nothing else existed. But that moment in his room had caused ripples, like a stone thrown in a lake. Other feelings returned with the absence of Cecelia, feelings Viktor didn't like.

Danon was beside him again, staring out a window at the moons.

"The Fair Folk are joining the Universalists," Danon said, "Ramiro told me. He bragged he had made this union just in time. I'm to bring a letter home with me, requesting my father send an armada."

Viktor choked out a laugh. "You're serious?" But when he saw Danon didn't smile, he added, "the Fair Folk are always neutral."

"Not anymore."

"The Unis and the Fair Folk will not burn Korith down, if that's what you're so afraid of," Viktor said.

"I'm afraid for my sister," Danon replied, eyes glaringly less childish at that moment, "that I'm leaving her here to die. And the only certainty you've provided me is that you'll take care of her, whatever that means in your thuggish mind."

They turned a corner and began the climb up the stairs, passing a sconce that cast its firelight across their faces. Viktor remembered earlier when he almost knocked the Panther prince out and wished he had.

"Rees won't let that happen," Viktor grunted. "You needn't worry about the Unis. And certainly not the Fair Folk."

"Rees," Danon said amusingly, "a man who enjoys a good opportunity for upward mobility. Of course, he wouldn't see any benefit to a coup. None whatsoever."

Viktor glanced at Danon out of the corner of his eyes. "I'd watch your words, Panther. I hold no ill will towards Rees or you, but someone here might choose favorites. And I doubt you'd be one of them."

Danon stood in the stairwell's archway, still half hidden by shadows. Moonlight spilled across the bailey yard, illuminating every surface it touched in its silvery light. But the darkness made Danon's frown worse. It was almost menacing.

"Something big is coming, Viktor. I need to know that when I return at the head of my father's armada, she'll be here."

"Why? So you can save her?" Viktor felt prickles of heat crawl up his neck. It was hottest where is birthmark traced its path across his shoulder and up to his jaw. Like the sun itself touched him. He stepped towards the prince so his voice wouldn't carry across the bailey yard. "After the ceremony tonight, she's my concern, boy. Do you hear me? Mine."

Viktor turned and left, not looking back at the prince. He didn't know what made him want to say it. The heat of his anger perhaps. Perhaps it was Danon's tone. The way he insisted he knew what was best for her. Or maybe it was because he knew Cecelia didn't really want to go back. Not really. Not anymore. No, it was simply greed on Viktor's part. He had never wanted anything as much as he wanted Cecelia. Her fragile heart called to his, asking to be held.

He stopped walking. In the center of the outer wall, enveloped in darkness, he paused. The feeling he felt when she left, the feeling that sat sour in his stomach, made sense. It was need. A need for her body, yes, but a need to be satisfied. To be seen.

For, if no one else ever loved you, were you ever really there?

The sword worn by the heir apparent of the Archipelago of the Moons was crafted during the time of the Disappearing Heirs. Boasting a line of six sons, King Manul watched in horror as one after the other disappeared, only later to be discovered horrifically murdered. The last heir, Prince Hyrem, took matters into his own hands, forging a weapon to protect himself and throwing himself completely into training with it. Hyrem survived the strange times and ascended the throne at the age of two and twenty. Hyrem passed the sword on to his second son, Prince Grego, when he was ten. And so continues the tradition. Rumors abound that Hyrem had his own brothers murdered in order to claim the throne, but the truth died with Hyrem.

Logician Mykel Meralko
    Islands of Fortune: An Examination of Island Nations

Chapter Seventeen

The Daughter sparkled next to the Mother in the night sky. With her voluptuous, full white surface, the Mother made the night nearly as bright as the day. Or, at least, the poets liked to say.

Cecelia walked slowly towards the cliff. The ancient altar of the sun had been repurposed. With the roof torn off, it was the perfect place to be married. The Mother, full in her strongest phase alongside the Daughter's more modest full phase, watched patiently. But Cecelia still wouldn't compare it to the day.

Shadows fell long across the path and fireflies twinkled in the gardens, reminding her that the Fair Folk liked to call it the most magical hour. She wished some fireflies would drift towards them to distract her, but she knew they favored the protective walls of Queen Liosni's garden over the strong wind of the ocean side cliff.

"I'll ask you one more time," Danon said.

Cecelia held her hand out, stopping him.

"Danon, we've gone as far as we can with your childish questions." She turned to look at Danica, who walked on her other side, "I have to do this."

Danica offered her a polite smile, nodding her head in agreement. "Yes," she said, "let's put childishness aside."

Danon huffed. He eyed Danica behind Cecelia's head and leaned in so his words wouldn't drift towards the queen.

"I spent the day with him, Cece," Danon whispered. "I don't like it."

Cecelia ground her heel into the gravel path. Her hands twisted into fists. It wasn't enough he would return home without her, free to live out his days amidst family and familiarity, but he had to ruin any attempt she made at accepting her fate. Danon took for granted that he belonged somewhere, forgetting Cecelia never felt welcomed in the Lagos. Not really.

"The funny thing is, brother," Cecelia's teeth ground as she spoke. She spoke slowly so he'd hear every word. "You'll ride the waves towards home come morn, regardless if you like it or not. And I'll walk this path towards my betrothed, whether I like it or not. Because the truth is this: neither of us is in control anymore. We're both on a path set in motion by forces outside of ourselves."

She stepped back and smoothed her silken gown. Danica stared at her feet, a slight blush creeping across her cheeks. Cecelia, emboldened by her words, continued.

"Forces," she continued, "father foresaw. And we must obey."

Danon slowly shook his head. "We must obey," he quietly agreed.

They walked in silence then, none wishing to interrupt the solemn calm that fell over them. The waves crashed down below, flicking droplets up and over the edge of the cliff to land on their cheeks. It was high tide, and the water churned in angst. Despite the lack of cloud coverage, it smelled suspiciously like rain.

Up ahead, the altar of the sun stood roofless. Cecelia made out Viktor's large shape and that of Ramiro's. There was no one else. Guests were unnecessary. Danica informed Cecelia that Ramiro wrote to Viktor's brother himself, but there had been little time for his lordship to ride to the capital to watch his baby brother wed.

Or little desire.

Once Danon took his place in front of them, the ceremony began. Viktor barely looked at her. But truthfully, she barely looked at him. Instead, she remembered the night before. The moment stolen in the dark. Her mind wandered over each second multiple times, like a worry stone, until the moment was smooth and rhythmic.

Before long, Danon cleared his throat, bringing Cecelia up through her thoughts like a swimmer cresting the water.

"Cecelia," Danon said, "the gift?"

Cecelia nodded, her heart rate jumping at the intrusion she felt. She wondered if they could annul a marriage based on mere supposition that the person wasn't actually present during the ceremony. At least, not in their mind anyway.

She glanced at Viktor quickly before turning to Danica. The queen smiled sweetly at her, offering the wrapped parcel Cecelia assigned her to hold.

"Your grace," Danica murmured.

Danica bowed her head slightly to her. It was a polite honor Cecelia wasn't owed by anyone of the Korithian royal family. And yet, her new friend beamed with pleasure.

"Thank you," Cecelia said.

Black silk wrapped several times around the object. It had been a nuisance to do, for Cecelia was never one for frivolities. She thrust the gift to Viktor and tried to put on a smile.

"May the gracious giver bless this union," Cecelia said.

Viktor unwrapped the gift as unceremoniously as Cecelia had handed it to him. A sword, black of blade and thin as a razor, rolled in his hand. The handle was polished silver, forged to look like the scaled leg of a dragon.

"It's a sword," Viktor said.

"My brother's," Cecelia explained, "gifted to me."

Cecelia watched as Viktor glanced at Danon's hip, where the small blade had once hung. In its stead was her sword, larger, older, and to Viktor, probably the more ideal blade. But before Danon returned home, an exchange had to be made. Cecelia locked eyes with Danon for only a moment, a fleeting smile on her face.

"And you, Viktor?" Danon asked. "Do you have a gift?"

Viktor grunted an answer. He handed the sword off to Ramiro, who played his part as Viktor's witness joyfully enough, and rummaged in the pocket hidden inside his armor. He held out his fist to Cecelia.

"May the gracious giver bless this union."

He mumbled the words unfamiliar to him, but when he opened his hand, a shimmering emerald ring sat within. It reminded Cecelia of the jewelry she'd seen amidst the Fair Folk's stalls. Delicate, intricate, and clearly ancient. Two silver cat heads, snarling, faced each other and held an oval-shaped emerald between their fangs.

"A beautiful ring," Cecelia whispered.

She was so surprised at his offering she froze, unable to move.

"It was my mother's," Viktor explained, "the only thing she ever gave me."

He grabbed Cecelia's hand and shoved it on her index finger. She admired the glittering emerald in the full light of the Mother. This time, when she looked at Viktor, she genuinely smiled.

"With the gracious gifts exchanged, Viktor, you may now escort your bride to bed in the full witness of the Mother and Daughter, so that they know where your two hearts lie."

Viktor's grip on Cecelia's hand tightened. She assumed he'd find the words odd. Danica had regaled her with the over-the-top productions Korithian weddings were. The days of feasting. The bizarre presence of a Whisper Wife, meant to ensure the prosperous union beneath the Mother's watchful gaze. The ornate clothing. Comparatively, the Archipelago of the Moons treated weddings as they treated nearly every life change: bravely, knowing the moment was fleeting.

They walked in silence towards Cecelia's rooms, now *their* rooms. They would convert the salon and bedrooms to the Royal Guard Marshal's quarters. A benefit of controlling Ramiro's sizeable household guard. A gift, Ramiro had said, for Viktor's continued loyalty and obedience.

Once inside the bedroom, Cecelia felt she needed to offer Viktor her own reward for his loyalty.

The entire truth.

She waited until she felt the moment right. When the early dawn began to creep across the sky and their marital duties were done. Twice.

"Since we are now married, I suppose it best to tell you the truth." She said, peering at him out of the corner of her eyes.

He sat staring out at the sunrise, blankets tossed modestly across him. Cecelia could smell his heat and sweat wafting on the morning breeze towards her. It drew her in. She felt awkward, as if she should fight the urge, but she'd never felt that way about anyone and she couldn't seem to control herself.

"Oh?" He asked, tearing his gold-flecked eyes from the sun to look at her. "There is more to the Panther princess than meets the eye? Who would have thought?" He smiled.

She wanted to reach out and touch his skin. To let her hand trail slowly down his birthmark like a red carriage way, but she knew Viktor would only push her hand away. He was still uncomfortable with the attention she gave it. Still annoyed by its presence, even after living with it all his life.

"I," she began, but faltered. His steady gaze strengthened her resolve. She smiled, carrying on, "My mother was of Korith."

Viktor nodded his head. "Rumors said as much. You told me yourself she wasn't a Panther. Don't bore me, champion, offer me a real tidbit."

Exhaling slowly, she plowed onward, not allowing him time to interrupt with his colorful commentary.

"You realize I am a bastard, born unto my royal father from my common mother."

Viktor stared at her through half-closed eyes. His arm draped across the headboard of the bed, his fingers twitching. The beat of his heart was visible in his neck. Cecelia hoped she hadn't made a mistake.

"Common?"

Cecelia slowly shook her head yes.

"How did she get to the Lagos? I thought your lot thrice checked your ships, or some dirt like that?"

She winced at his language. Not that it bothered her, she was used to it, but that she knew he viewed her as different. Foreign. She wanted so badly to be one, like the wedding ceremony suggested, to use him as an anchor in the strange land of Korith. To finally have a home. Yet she risked alienating him in trying to be honest with him.

Which was worse?

"No one knows," Cecelia said. "Perhaps my father does. Perhaps she told him. They sent him to arrest her that day but couldn't."

"Couldn't?"

A smile tipped the corner of Cecelia's lips. "She proved difficult to arrest. Wild, as some witnesses described."

Viktor nodded, a knowing look in his eyes. "Sounds familiar."

"Their love was nearly instantaneous. And disappointing. To my grandfather."

"Kings are fickle like that," Viktor joked.

"When she died, my grandfather lost little time informing my father it was what he deserved. And with Lady Amara dead, he could right his wrong and marry properly. He could marry Elyeanor, a high-ranking lord's daughter."

"Amara?"

"My mother's name. No surname. No link to any family here in Korith. Trust me, I've checked. Danon helped me some, asking questions of his conquests while here."

"That's what he was doing?"

Cecelia shrugged, "among other things. Espionage, is that not what foreign visitors do?"

She smiled at him, but he didn't smile back. Instead, he stared at her like he was seeing her for the first time.

"What?" she asked.

"Ramiro said I was marrying a princess." He reached for her arms, throwing her onto the bed and pretending to shake her. "But you confirm again I married a bastard?"

Cecelia laughed. She let him kiss her, but couldn't shake the sickness she felt. She had to tell him the truth. The whole truth.

"I *am* a princess," she assured him.

She shoved him away so that she could look up at his face. The glint in his eyes told her he was through talking, but she needed to get it all out, to confess, before the truth consumed her.

"I am *the* princess. The heir. Or... at least I was."

Viktor released her. He stood up, completely uncovered now. Groping for the sheet, he wrapped it hastily around himself.

"What do you mean, you *were* the heir?"

There it was, the tone Cecelia didn't want to hear. He was displeased. Displeasure always came hand in hand with deception. It was expected. But it didn't make it go down any easier.

"I might be a bastard in Korithian eyes, but in the Lagos I am legitimate. As the eldest, it was I who would have inherited the throne."

Viktor stared at the geometric carpet, pondering her words. She wanted to reach for him but knew better. He needed this moment to think. Any stimulation brought on by her would be an unwelcome distraction. And possibly ignite the fuse she did not wish to light.

"Your father will send an armada anyway, to retrieve his heir then."

Viktor wasn't asking, he was stating a fact. But Cecelia shook her head.

"Danon is the heir now."

"How so?"

"I... gave up my birthright. When I gave Danon my sword. It is the symbol of the heir apparent. Worn only by the one to ascend the throne. My father gave it to me when I was ten."

Anger flared in Viktor's eyes, but Cecelia carried on, hoping to speak over his outburst.

"When he returns home wearing it, it will force everyone to recognize him as the heir. Even my father. I gave it to him honestly. He will be accepted. They will all be happier this way, anyway, with me gone. It will be fine."

She wanted to carry on speaking, to fill the room with words hoping to keep out the anger sure to rush in at any moment, but Viktor held out his hand and silenced her.

"I forced you to give up your birthright?"

Cecelia offered him a bitter frown. "You did not force me to do anything. It is Ramiro who is responsible."

"I could have fought him! I could have told him no." Viktor was heaving, his face turning red.

"To what end, Viktor? If not you, then someone like Lord Rufus. At least I like you. I care about you. With you, there is a chance for happiness. A chance for love."

"You would've been the damned queen, Cecelia," Viktor stared defiantly down at her. "I'm not worth that much. I'm not worth anything."

Cecelia stood and forced him to stand still. He wanted to leave, to barge out of the room naked, but she held both his hands tightly and stared up into his golden eyes.

"You are worth it to me," she insisted. "You are worth *so* much more to me."

The Prevailing Mother, elected every ten year, possesses the final say in all decisions of the Fair Folk. Any disagreements are brought before her, and she alone decides the outcome. Notable Prevailing Mothers include Mother Sabat, a prolific healer. Answering a call to the House of Borjet, Sabat healed the newest addition to the Sabat family, Lady Liosni. Liosni would later grow up to become one of Korith's greatest – and most gentlest – queens. Another is Mother Vra'shan. Angry at the treatment of her people, she lead a small group of Fair Folk into the palace and set it ablaze. Vra'shan survived the burning, but not the sword of King Porchi II.

Court Historian Alfred Peri
The Scroll of Children: A Collected History of the Fair Folk

Chapter Eighteen

THE MOONS BOTH WANED, though the Daughter had progressed faster through her cycle than the Mother. She shrank by half while the Mother trailed behind, barely in her gibbous. Viktor stared up at them, alone on the veranda. He had been married for six moonrises and already it felt like a lifetime.

He sighed before sinking down into a chair. It wasn't Cecelia's fault. How was she to know the weight he carried? How could she know that whenever he looked at her, he fought back memories of his own parents fighting. Of his father's sharp tongue and his mother's salty tears? That he saw the crown she was meant to wear still sitting upon her head, and felt to blame for its removal.

Frowning, he pulled his eyes from the moons long enough to find his drink. He sipped it, the amber liquid's bitter sting relieving.

Thoughts of Ephram had also filled his thoughts since his wedding day. Ephram would have been happy for Viktor. He would have joined in the wedding party and offered a gift for the exchange. Ephram was the one that told Viktor he was worthy. Worthy of love. Worthy of happiness. Worthy of life.

But as usual, Ephram's words were drowned out by their father's. Those words were far less pleasant. Like poison, they fought their way into Viktor's heart and he couldn't seem to wash it out. It changed the way he looked at things. It tinted Cecelia's smile as a frown. Her laughter as pity. Her pleasure at his touch as obligation. Usually, he took up drinking in hopes of drowning out the voices — his father's and Ephram's both — but it wasn't working. Not this time.

Viktor stood abruptly, knocking his chair over. He righted it before turning back towards the moons, towards the gardens, towards the sea. He descended the stairs with heavy steps. A walk would clear his mind. A walk would surely make things appear clear.

The gardens were alive with the sounds of night. Fireflies hummed alongside mammoth moths. The waves, ever churning, tore at the cliffside. Gulls squabbled. If he tried hard enough, Viktor thought he could hear the moons themselves. It was his favorite time. A time for things to be simplified. Darkness had a way of doing that, of removing the contours of something until it was worn down to its rudimentary shape. To its essence.

The tourney grounds were still riddled with Fair Folk. Their fires burned large and bright as they huddled around them, laughing loudly. Viktor couldn't wait for them to leave. They left him on edge, these people that looked through him and always found something to frown about. Most were uneasy around him. But not G'rig.

Never G'rig.

Since the day he read Viktor's fortune, the Folkman seemed interested in Viktor. He popped up in the same taverns as Viktor whenever the Fair Folk held their market in the capital. Almost like he was looking for him.

But Viktor didn't want to think about G'rig either. He stood at the top of the stairs, the same stairs he had stood with Cecelia several moonrises earlier, and watched them. They were a nuisance, but they would be leaving soon.

A brilliant white cat darted amongst the feet of several Fair Folk, weaving its way towards the Prevailing Mother's blue tent. Viktor traced its path, admiring its almost luminescent glow. Like the Fair Folk's magic had worn off on the creature. But then a lurking figure caught his eye. Wearing a dark cloak, they floated past the fires, utilizing the dancing shadows to hide. The Fair Folk were too busy socializing to notice. Towards the Prevailing Mother's tent they creeped, disappearing through the entrance.

Something sat wrong in Viktor's stomach. He knew a cloaked figure in the night meant nothing good. And as the Royal Guard Marshall he should be able to utilize the guards to find out what was happening. *Should*. But the Fair Folk lived outside the rules. Any open land they occupied instantly fell outside the jurisdiction of Korithian authority. When they sat their market up on the tournament grounds, the grounds became theirs, if only temporarily. The Prevailing Mother would diffuse any problems.

But what if the Prevailing Mother was the problem?

Viktor bit his lip, considering.

"A bit late, Viktor, to be stargazing." A voice disrupted Viktor's thoughts.

Viktor turned to find the king before him. Ramiro was dressed in his night robe, the silk cinched tightly around him. He seemed more a child without his regalia. More youthful. More frail.

"Your grace," Viktor bowed his head. He gazed past Ramiro to see he trailed no guard. No protection. "Where is your Kingsguard?"

Viktor was still within the fourteen moonrises of his honeymoon. Ramiro required no work from him. No participation in the functioning of the palace of any kind. But Viktor couldn't help but feel like he was failing the king, for it would be his job to assign the men to their duties once he officially took up his office. It would be his job to make sure the king was protected.

Ramiro shrugged. "I am the king, am I not? An evening stroll, alone, seems like a simple wish."

"Simple, yes your grace," Viktor said, "but foolish."

Ramiro studied Viktor, considering his words. He finally nodded in agreement. "Perhaps you're right." He looked past Viktor at the Fair Folk. Their firelight flickered in his eyes, creating an illusion of bewitchment over the king. "Perhaps you'd join me," he said, returning his gaze to Viktor. "And then I'd most certainly be protected."

Viktor forced a smile. "As you wish, your grace."

He moved to fall in behind Ramiro, but Ramiro gripped his arm in passing. "Not behind me, beside me. Like a...friend."

Ramiro's tone was strange. Viktor felt uncomfortable walking beside the king, but agreed with a nod of his head. They walked in silence for several moments, letting the night noise fall between them. He had watched the king grow from a fussy infant to the man beside him. He had watched him learn to ride his first horse, only to promptly ride it into a ravine filled with nettles. He had watched him steal his first jug of wine, only to vomit it all over his bed hours later. He had even watched him marry Lady Katvenn, now the queen.

But they weren't friends. And never would be.

"Rumor has it that the Panther princess is exceptionally pleased with you." Ramiro's voice sliced the darkness, "I must congratulate you, Viktor. Pleasing a wife is no easy thing. I should know."

"Her majesty seems quite content." Viktor said. He had hoped they'd walk on in silence, finishing their walk back at the palace having exchanged no words, only sharing a trek though the garden. But of course he was wrong.

No one had been taught how to appreciate silence like he had.

"Motherhood seems to suit her," he added when Ramiro did not respond.

"Perhaps," Ramiro said. "But I fear its tainted her image of me. She has been...impatient with me as of late. Short tempered. Easily irritated."

"Would you rather she bow down to you?" Viktor teased. He had meant only to think it, but the words spilled forth, his lips loosened by his earlier drink.

Ramiro shrugged. They walked on in silence again, the tall grass now whispering in the wind, adding to the noises surrounding them.

"You know," Ramiro said, "a king was once worshipped like a god himself. Descended from His Brilliance."

"Careful, your grace," Viktor said, "no man can be a god. The men that thought that were ripped from their thrones, proven they weren't as powerful as they thought."

"True," Ramiro sighed, staring up at the Mother and Daughter, "but I do wonder sometimes."

"What's that, your grace?"

"If obedience would be easier if they feared me? Would the Unis cease their grumbling were I to threaten fire and death? Would the Fair Folk?"

There was the truth of it. The weight that fell heavy on the king's chest, preventing him from breathing, from sleeping. The Unis and their dalliance with the Fair Folk.

Viktor ran his hands through is hair. Fear had been his father's game. Fear was how Lord Black ran his household. His landholdings. His children. It might have bred obedience of a sort, but it didn't do anything to breed loyalty. And loyalty was something Ramiro needed more than obedience.

"In the end, fear did nothing for my father," Viktor said.

Ramiro stared at the moons. He was silent and unmoving, to the point that Viktor wondered if the king had heard his words. But finally Ramiro pulled his gaze from the Mother and Daughter, and looked at Viktor.

"Perhaps you're right," he said. He suggested to the Fair Folk. "It will be good when they leave. They seem to set Danica at ill ease. I'm sure she'll return to her pleasant self once they're gone."

"Certainly, your grace."

They walked on, looping back towards the bailey door. Ramiro shared nothing more, to Viktor's relief. A Kingsguard greeted Ramiro just inside. He followed closely behind the king, leaving Viktor alone and in the shadows.

Viktor thought on Ramiro's words all the way back to his room. Ramiro was young and foolish. He was still learning how to be a husband, and now he required learning how to be a father. It wasn't a job suited for everyone. And while it was true the king had not been the most devout as a boy, he had never spoken of His Brilliance in such a way before. Perhaps the stress of a new baby was affecting both the queen *and* the king.

He found Cecelia waiting for him. She sipped on some wine in the parlor, half reading a book.

"Where were you?" She asked innocently.

"I went for a walk," he said. "The king found me."

Cecelia frowned, clearly perplexed by Viktor's words. "Ramiro? Should he not be abed?"

Viktor shrugged. Her staring eyes burned, though he knew she was only thinking. Everything was a puzzle to her, everything held a hidden message. She felt adrift in a strange sea, and was trying hard to steady herself. He attempted to cross the parlor to his bedchamber, but Cecelia's words stopped him.

"What words did he speak?" She asked.

She stared at her book, only glancing up at him when he hesitated.

"He mentioned something about the Unis and the Fair Folk. I think the rumors are starting to bother him."

Cecelia smirked. "I thought the Fair Folk were always neutral?"

"He does too."

"So what's bothering him?"

Viktor sighed. "The queen. The Fair Folk's presence irritates her for some reason. Or so he says. Not my business. Not my problem."

"Will they be gone soon? The Fair Folk?" She asked.

"Yes."

Cecelia looked back down at her book. "Why don't you like them?" She asked.

Viktor huffed. "What's to like?" And when Cecelia frowned at him, he added, "I've never had an encounter with them that was overly joyful, champion."

"Is that what happened with G'rig?" She said. "You two know each other, don't you? You seemed familiar when you saw each other in the forest that day."

Viktor fought the desire to grind his teeth. "I'd rather not discuss it," he said.

"Fine," Cecelia snapped her book shut. "To bed." She stood.

"To bed," he offered her a tired smile.

He asks for blood.
burn them, burn them
Pure and sweet.
burn them, burn them
Praise his fire.
burn them, burn them
Or feel his heat.

Unknown
Worship Song of His Brilliance, performed during Summer Soltice

Chapter Nineteen

"How unfortunate that your honeymoon should end on summer solstice," Danica said, sipping at her orange juice and wine.

It was the fourteenth moonrise since her wedding, and Cecelia had kept little company besides Viktor's, as was expected. As she liked it. But when the bells tolled midnight, Danica sent a servant to knock at their parlor door, demanding Cecelia break her fast with her. Thankfully Cecelia was still awake.

"I'm not afraid of superstitions, your grace," Cecelia said. She nibbled at some bacon that sizzled fresh from the pan.

"Tell that to His Brilliance's Righteous Servant, that hot headed king of Duwu. Today he'll be burning virgins alive. One for each passing chime of the bells."

"Virgins in a far off land pose little influence on my marriage, your grace." Cecelia smiled as she bit the last piece of bacon from her fork.

Danica studied her with her piercing gaze before offering a small smile and a tip of her head. "As you say. Though certainly a queen of Duwu would never burn children alive."

"One would hope she'd convert the entire island to the ways of the Mother and Daughter." Cecelia added.

"Yes," Danica drawled, "or at least be smart enough to see when violence was and wasn't useful."

The words came out in a pleasant enough tone, though Cecelia began to wonder what lay beneath. Viktor had mentioned Ramiro was worried about Danica. She was irritated and short of temper as of late. But she seemed tolerable enough that morning.

"The honeymoon was a success then?" Danica asked, shuffling food about on her plate, ignoring Cecelia's eyes, "can we expect a ginormous baby in nine turns of the Mother?"

Cecelia fought to keep her face from frowning. "I'd rather not speak of such things," Cecelia said, turning back to her food.

Danica chewed slowly, watching her. "Right," she said, gulping down some wine to clear her throat, "I forgot. You don't want to be a mother."

"I'm allowed my own opinions, your grace."

Fresh bread was placed before them, alongside honey and jam. Cecelia helped herself but Danica remained silent. Almost broody.

"I thought the Fair Folk would be gone by now," Cecelia changed the subject.

Danica accidentally dropped her glass, spilling champagne and orange juice across the table. The sticky solution wove between the dishes, stretches its orange fingers towards Cecelia. A servant arrived and immediately remedied the mess.

"Truthfully I'm glad they've lingered," Danica spoke. She stared off toward the market. "Jana has been ill. The Prevailing Mother herself agreed to treat her."

"In the palace? Really?" Cecelia sat up a little straighter. It seemed she had missed much during her fourteen days of seclusion.

"Ramiro was furious," Danica stared down at her hands in her lap, "he didn't care that Jana was dying."

"Dying?"

Danica's face was frigid, though Cecelia wondered if she held it that way to prevent falling apart. "The Specks covered her. Our physicians were useless. I asked Mother Oora, begged her, to help. I didn't ask Ramiro if I should. I just did it."

"Good for you," Cecelia raised her glass to Danica.

Danica smiled. "Thank you. Too bad his grace does not see it your way."

Cecelia swallowed some more wine and shrugged. "Men are stubborn. Kings, more so."

"Aye," Danica agreed. Abruptly she stood, her chair shrieking across the tile of the veranda. "Come. I wish for a ride."

"A ride?" Cecelia frowned. "At this hour?"

Cecelia stared at Danica, hoping she'd change her mind. She often did, mid sentence, change her wants. But this time she seemed certain. Cecelia sighed.

"Fine."

They were waiting outside the stables in mere moments. Cecelia wondered, as she did sometimes, how quickly things changed. How quickly one moment led to the next and suddenly you were in a different place, at a different time, doing something entirely different. She awoke early that morning to watch the sun rise over the ocean, its crimson light bleeding across the bedspread and over Viktor's face. She left him there to break her fast with Danica. The veranda was cool, still hidden from the morning sun, and smelled of pearly jasmine. But these were fleeting moments, for she now smelled horses and manure and hay. The stables were muggy and hot already. Noise approached her from all sides as stable hands jabbered and tossed hay, horses brayed, and flies buzzed. When a mousy haired boy handed her the reigns to a horse, she glanced at Danica who already sat astride her silver stallion, and wondered what sights and smells and moments awaited her next.

"Where shall we ride to?" Cecelia asked her.

Their horses rode shoulder to shoulder. A pair of Queensguard kept their distance behind, as instructed, though they growled at anyone who even looked oddly at the queen. Cecelia imagined they were quite the morning parade as they trundled down the cobblestone thoroughfare toward the main gate. Danica's fur lined cloak fluttered behind her, announcing her station. Her earrings — finely crafted by Fair Folk — shimmered in the delicate light of morning. Cecelia, by contrast, wore black. She preferred it. Black riding boots and pants. Black tunic. Black cloak. Like a shade she rode through Kasier, and the people shuddered and pulled away.

There was a shorter path to the wall. It was meant to be a palace secret though most in the capital knew about the door hidden behind the kitchens that would take a person straight into the kingswood. But Danica wanted to be seen. She wanted a parade, a reason to be looked at. Where Cecelia preferred slinking in the shadows, Danica wanted nothing but the light.

Outside the gate Danica spurred her stallion on, goading Cecelia to race her. Cecelia tried her best, but the horse refused to play. She trailed behind Danica, following the queen around the city towards the edge of the kingswood. Danica guided them toward a stream, which they followed, diving into the forest. Trees erupted around them, as did the gooseberries, and Cecelia inhaled deeply. The pungent perfume delighted her. For some reason it reminded her of her childhood, though gooseberries did not grow in the Lagos. No, this memory was something deeper. A whisper in the dark, telling her she'd smelled this smell before. It was eerie and equally thrilling. She purposefully pushed her horse through them to stir their fragrance.

The last time she entered the forest, she had stumbled upon the Fair Folk children. Cecelia fought to remember their names, but couldn't. But she remembered G'rig. His face and the way he looked at Viktor. At the way he smiled when he offered to read Viktor's fortune again. Viktor hadn't wanted to talk about it, but that only made Cecelia want to know more.

"This way!" Danica's voice called, breaking through Cecelia's thoughts.

She searched for the queen between the trees, barely spotting her cloak amidst the oak. Her horse finally obeyed her spurs, and galloped to catch up.

"We just follow the stream a bit further," Danica said.

She was breathless and clearly excited. Cecelia didn't know what she had followed Danica into. She suddenly felt the hopeless desire to reach for Viktor, but knew she left him asleep hours ago, far away in the castle keep. Moments move on and are left far in the past. It made Cecelia's head spin. She suddenly felt dizzy. Tightening the grip on her reins, she brought her horse close to Danica's.

"Where are we going?" Cecelia asked.

"You'll see, just there, around the bend."

Danica led the way, winding their horses past a small twist in the creek. The forest grew thick with oak and spreading Sun Snares, so they walked their horses through the stream, emerging on the other side into a clearing. To their right, the cliffside of Kasier rose up, the city walls perched high above like a bird upon a nest. To the left, the kingswood grew on, its shades of green a testament to summer. But before them the land rolled away to the sea, and the most beautiful view of the ocean set before them.

The tide was low. The harbor held water and ships alike within, like a mother holding her children. It glittered in the morning sun amidst the barren rocks of the exposed seabed. Further still were the waves, crashing hard onto the beach. Ships sailed past, off to Emora and to harbors further west.

"You'll build your house here," Danica said. "It has the grandest view, does it not?"

Cecelia was speechless. The view was breathtaking. And strange. In the Lagos, the forests were far greener. Warmer. Wetter. The trees grew leaves larger than ones hand, in which fruit would freely fall. The ocean was bluer. More welcoming. And yet Cecelia felt like she could make a place there on that hill in the kingswood. She could create a place that she did not feel a stranger. A freak. Unwelcomed.

She could build a home.

"I love it," Cecelia said.

"I'm glad," Danica smiled. She sauntered her horse closer to Cecelia's. "You will be close. And if the Mother happens to grant you that which you do not wish, it will be a son. And he will marry Jana and be a dutiful husband, helping her rule Korith thoughtfully and deftly."

Cecelia tried to smile. "We will see what the Mother makes of me."

"By my side, you will surely do great things, my dear Cecelia."

"Perhaps," Cecelia winced. "perhaps."

Ephram Black, eldest of the Black brood, was known for his swordplay and knack of out maneuvering his opponents on the field of war. His death during the rebellion was shocking. Pinning Norian's personal division against the backdrop of a cliff, Ephram's army occupied the forest, fearing nothing in their attack. Norian, desperate, filled the snaking Gallenchyl River with tar and lit the water aflame. The fire jumped quickly from river to forest with the help of a brutal wind off the sea, engulfing the trees. Unable to escape their own encampment, Ephram's entire division burned to death amidst the ancient trees of Vealdo Forest.

High Steward Robert Ma'Curci
   The Trial of the Red Way: A History of Rebellion

Chapter Twenty

The office Ramiro assigned to Viktor sat on the east side of the castle and received ample morning light, filling the room with early sunbeams. The brightness aggravated Viktor, though he couldn't particularly decide why. He spent most of the morning pretending to know what to do.

He pored over duty logs, figuring out who worked too much or worked too little. Ledgers from the past several months piled high in one corner of his desk. Lists of names awaiting access to the king sat in another, pending his approval. He glared at this pile, wondering if it was worth the trouble. Perhaps they'd be better off burned in the fireplace. He eyed the white stoned hearth, embers glimmering within, and kept wondering.

When a knock echoed through the room, Viktor thanked the Moon Mother. He tossed the ledger he poured over onto his desk and summoned the guest in.

It was Kay.

The man, once Viktor's equal but now his inferior, sauntered around the room, nodding his approval.

"It seems you've settled right in," Kay teased, "big room for a big man."

Viktor growled, "what do you want Kay?"

"The boys and me have been down to the tavern. Thought we'd see you."

"It's been nary three moonrises since my honeymoon was over, Kay. Why would I be in a tavern when I've a wife to bed?"

Kay shrugged, "so the rumors are true then."

"What rumors?"

"She's a cat in bed as well."

Viktor fought the urge to strike Kay. He wouldn't reach him anyway, not with the distance between them and the giant wooden desk. No, he'd give his friend the benefit of his patience, even if it were short-lived. Instead, he filled his hands with the ledger and stared down at the numbers again.

"It was good you were drinking at the tavern," Viktor said, refusing to take the bait about Cecelia.

"Why's that?"

"With the amount spent on supplying beer to the mess hall these past few moons... I'll have to cut it in half to make up for the bleed Ramiro feels in his royal purse. You should get used to spending your own money on beer from now on."

Kay bristled. He flicked his eyes at the piles of papers on Viktor's desk. "So, you feel mighty powerful behind that desk now, huh?"

Viktor laid the ledger down again and rubbed his forehead. This was precisely why he had never wanted a change. He had been happy in his tiny, dark room, low in a tower of the castle wall. Kay and the others were company enough, and when he tired of them, he could retreat to his own room knowing when he happened upon them again there'd be no strangeness. No awkwardness brought on by power.

He had never wanted real authority, just some semblance of it. Real authority was always what his brother Ephram reached for. And as the eldest, he wielded it deftly. Until he died. Viktor, constantly caught as the object of his father's anger, had merely wanted to disappear.

"What is it you want, Kay?" Viktor asked, slowing his breathing to control his fists.

Kay offered him a crooked smile. "Why do you assume I want anything?"

Viktor rolled his eyes. "We've been friends a long time, Kay." He stared at his friend. "We fought together in the rebellion. Don't."

"Don't what?" Kay asked impudently.

"Don't mistake friendship for favors. Don't think time in familiarity breeds power to persuade. It means nothing, Kay."

"Nothing?"

"Nothing," Viktor repeated.

Kay nodded, a frown forming in the deep-set lines of his face. He was but nine years older than Viktor, still strong and fit, but in that moment he seemed much more akin to Viktor's father. And Viktor didn't like that one bit.

"If that's how you want it, my lord, then that's how it'll be." Kay turned to leave.

"Don't call me that, Kay. I'll always just be Viktor."

Kay stopped short of the door and peered out of the corner of his eyes at Viktor. "Fine." He said and then disappeared out the door.

Viktor stared for a long time at the space Kay had occupied in the doorway. He scratched his scruff, wondering if it was worth it for the hundredth time. His eyes trailed down the stack of papers he had thrown off his desk. Ephram would know what to do. Ephram always knew what to do.

Another knock, this time more delicate, pulled Viktor from his spiraling thoughts of his eldest brother. This time he welcomed the distraction, for Viktor hated dwelling on Ephram and his horrific death during the rebellion.

To Viktor's surprise, General Rees stood at the door.

"Hope I'm not interrupting," Rees said.

He seemed awkward in the doorway, staring around at the room. Rees nodded approvingly.

"Great morning light," he suggested to the sunbeams still falling across the floor, "a great office."

Viktor frowned. "I hope you didn't just come here to compliment me on sunbeams, General."

Rees laughed. His shoulders relaxed, and he entered the room fully. Viktor noticed he still wore his riding boots, which were caked in mud.

"Just returned, General?"

Rees glanced down at his boots, "uh, yes, yes. I apologize Viktor. I heard of your promotion–of the wedding–I'm sorry I missed it."

Viktor scowled. "It was a wedding, General. Your apology is entirely unnecessary."

Viktor remembered the conversation he overheard between Ramiro and Rees. He wondered how much of their plan was fulfilled. Certainly, the shackling of Cecelia to Korith by wedding her to Viktor. Certainly that pleased Rees.

"And the northeastern front," Viktor leaned back in his chair, enjoying the new lack of decorum required of him in Rees presence, "were the Unis quelled."

Rees sank into the chair opposite Viktor. "They were. For now."

"You seem uncertain," Viktor asked. "Rumors are the Fair Folk are joining their ranks."

Rees nodded. "So I've heard. We have the Prevailing Mother and her travelers surrounded in the fairgrounds. They've not been allowed to leave."

Viktor nodded. He had seen the tents remain standing, long after the market was meant to close and move on. It was the only reliable thing about the Fair Folk: they did, eventually, always disappear.

"But enough of me," Rees said, "what about you? What about the Panther princess?"

"What about Cecelia?" Viktor was trying out the taste of his wife's name on his tongue, though he still preferred champion in private.

Rees smirked. He leaned forward, his fingers steepled together while he peered over them at Viktor. "Don't think Ramiro has granted you a favor, Viktor. A life spent bedding a beautiful woman."

Viktor glanced down at the desk covered in paperwork, wondering how Rees thought Viktor saw his new role full of favor. Did Rees enjoy paperwork as much?

"You were meant to marry her and monitor her. Her father sent her and that child of a brother here to spy on us. We need to know why. And we also need to make sure her father plays nice when we need him to."

"Play nice?" Viktor asked.

"Yes. We suspect King Filip might side with the Unis. Perhaps he's already allied with them and sent his children to gather information. But with his daughter securely linked to Korith, he'll have to think twice about assisting the Unis."

Viktor remembered Cecelia's words from their wedding night. Danon was the heir apparent. There was nothing left for King Filip in Korith. Cecelia was practically dead to him. Regardless of why he sent his children to Korith, securing an alliance with him was fruitless. Viktor might hold Cecelia in his hands, but Ramiro held nothing.

Viktor smiled at the thought.

"What?" Rees asked, "what are you smiling at?"

"Espionage." Viktor said. "A difficult duty. But one I'm willing to fulfill."

Rees stood and prepared to go. "I'm sure she'll yield to you," he said. "Just don't forget what your real duty is."

Viktor started to stand, but remembered he no longer had to. Rees frowned slightly as he turned to go.

Duty. Viktor pondered over the word, imagining all the many meanings it had. It perplexed him how it could have more than one.

Duty to Cecelia meant lying in bed most of the day. Sometimes the chaise. And once the tub.

Duty to Ramiro meant opening Cecelia's head and extracting every secret she held. It meant wielding her like a chess piece in a game of actual warfare. It meant using her until there was nothing left to use.

And duty to himself? This was of most concern to Viktor. He didn't want the desk with paperwork. He didn't want land carved from the kingswood or a title. He had just wanted to eat, sleep, fight when necessary and a woman when needed.

He hadn't wanted things to change. Leaving his ancestral home, he sought a place to simply exist. To breathe without feeling afraid an old, angry man would find some offense to it. But as he stared out at the brilliant sun, perched at high noon, he realized things would never be the same. Things were changing. He could feel it in his bones. Like whispers in the dark.

Brightly hued tents were still visible if he peered hard enough from his window. The Fair Folk still milled about, most looking like spirits searching for a body. The Prevailing Mother was probably holed up in her tent, throwing bones or praying or whatever it was she did to lead her people. And surrounding them all was Rees army. The image sank heavy in Viktor's stomach.

The Fair Folk took no sides. So why were they taking sides now?

Viktor pondered over this on the way back to his rooms for the night. He worked it around his mind like the Moon Priests in their Prayer Circles, circling the etched image of the Moon Mother on the floor. He was uncertain why the Fair Folk, traditionally careless in regards to the politics of Korith, would finally decide to care. But there had to be a reason. Hadn't there? But then he'd remember they never took sides before, and the circle would begin again.

A fight broke out in the hallway ahead. Viktor had made his way to the inner bailey and was traversing the grand hall. He was still unuse to this pathway, this new trek his position required of him. For a moment he wondered if he were in the right place. Perhaps he'd taken a wrong turn and ended up near the under hall and its damp pathway towards the barracks. Ahead were several soldiers, their black armor drinking the light from the torches, making them look more menacing than Viktor believed them to be. They jeered at the king's guards, who stood jumbled on the other side of the hallway.

"What's this?" Viktor asked.

"Nothing, Marshal," a soldier, his mustache as black as his armor, muttered. He bowed his head.

"Roaches!" One of Ramiro's guards muttered.

"They've infested the palace, Viktor," another guard said. "Ever since Rees surrounded the tourney grounds and those dirty Fair freaks."

"Not logical to go back and forth to the barracks, Marshal," the same mustachioed soldier said. "The General told us to stay close. Ramiro deigned it allowable. Just these whiney brats who don't seem to want to listen to their superiors. Perhaps you'd help them see the wrong in their ways?"

The soldier wasn't asking Viktor, he was warning him. Viktor straightened his shoulders and offered the soldier a settled gaze, one he learned from his father. It was a specialty of Lord Black, one that always left a young Viktor wondering what creative way his father would find to discipline him. He would squirm in his seat, much like the soldier was as he uneasily looked at Viktor, and impatiently wait for his father to impart on him his punishment. For the worst punishment was having it dragged out, the anticipation nearly as bad as the pain of discipline itself.

"Close does not mean in the grand hall," Viktor growled, "nor the kitchens. Nor anywhere inside the keep. The gatehouse will do for you. Or the outer bailey."

And when the soldier did not move, he barked "out!"

They began to shuffle then, their murmuring dissent barely heard over the king's guards and their snickering.

"And you," Viktor rounded on them. "To your posts!"

This new power he wielded felt raw in his throat. It scraped at him from the inside, a vicious animal wanting out. Viktor didn't know if he liked the feeling. It was overwhelming. A burden. But perhaps all men felt that way at the beginning of their careers. Perhaps Ephram felt it.

Perhaps even his father.

Mother Oora, once a Prevailing Mother of the Fair Folk, was born the only daughter of a family with seven boys. From an early age, she found herself special — unique amongst her siblings merely because of her sex — but as she aged, she found other ways. She'd out-wit them during play and antagonize them relentlessly until they agreed to make wagers with her. So successful was she that by the age of two and ten, she had accumulated a small fortune by swindling her brothers. Outside her family, she struggled to make friends. Other children found her off-putting, blunt, and insufferable. Eventually, she learned to pretend to be what these other children wanted, if only to maintain some image of normalcy, leading to her election as Prevailing Mother in her eight and sixtieth year.

Court Historian Alfred Peri
    The Scroll of Children: A Collected History of the Fair Folk

Chapter Twenty-One

"I HEAR THE MOON temples in the archipelago are all outdoors, their rooftops covered in lattices held up by columns like ancient trees." Danica toyed with her hair, staring off into the distance.

Cecelia nodded, remembering the temples distinctly. She spent many full moons within the palace temple, its walls covered in pearly jasmine.

"Tell me more," Danica said, "I've heard descriptions second hand. But you've been there. Tell me more of these temples that defy the earth."

Cecelia sighed. She always felt a stab of pain when discussing the Lagos. Sometimes, she even felt her throat constrict, a betrayal of her body. It wasn't home, she reminded herself, it never was.

"A small circle of columns sits within a larger one, symbolizing the Mother and the Daughter." Cecelia began. "Columns of differing colors. It depends on where the stone was carved."

"And your temple? The one you worshiped at most?"

"Pink moonstone." Cecelia stared at her hands, her skin dry and still not used to the Korithian climate. "Like the blush of sunrise. Climbing jasmine ropes its way around every surface. Island Roses droop from the lattice ceiling. A reflection pool, full like the Mother, replaces your prayer circles."

Danica sighed. "It sounds beautiful."

"It was," Cecelia agreed, "though I heard rumors my mother would steal herself inside to watch the pool dance when it rained. My father said she always liked the rain best."

"It probably reminded her of home," Danica said, "Amara, wasn't it? Of Korith."

Cecelia twisted her lips, pretending not to be surprised. Indeed, Danica's knowledge of her mother's name proved her friend was better connected than she thought within the castle.

"Don't be angry with me," Danica sipped at her iced wine, "but a queen must survive somehow in this wretched kingdom."

"I am not angry," Cecelia smiled, "your talents and skill impress me."

Danica beamed. Then frowned.

"If I only had good news to give you," she said, "for I inquired about your mother to many, but it seems she was not of the capital."

"That was kind of you," Cecelia said.

"I wish only kindness towards you, Cecelia," Danica said, "for you've awakened something inside me I thought lost."

"And what's that?" Cecelia flexed her fingers and curled them into a fist, a habit she had when she was nervous. Itchy fingers, her father's Master of Arms called it, nervous for the kill shot.

"A need for freedom. I thought marriage would bring it. Then I thought motherhood." Danica bit at the corner of her lip, staring off at the fairgrounds and the Fair Folk tents.

"I'm afraid I don't understand." Cecelia ripped a Wilty Lilac bloom from its branch by the pedicel and tossed it to the breeze.

"Should this rebellion begin, I will fight and claw my way to the throne and rule myself. With your help, we could remake this kingdom."

"A revolution fit for a queen," Cecelia smirked.

"No, dear Cecelia," Danica said, "a king!"

Cecelia settled her gaze on the tents Danica had been so preoccupied with.

"The Fair Folk remain," Cecelia admired the way their brightly hued tents contrasted against the dying grass of the fairgrounds. "Viktor said they'd be leaving."

"Rees has them surrounded," Danica replied, "for they side with the Unis."

"I thought the Fair Folk took no sides," Cecelia said.

She leaned against the giant stone blocks of the veranda's archway. Ants climbed there, crawling hectic paths towards the ceiling. She flicked one away with her fingers. Insects grew much larger in the Lagos, for the warmth year-round benefited them, but she didn't like them regardless of their size.

Danica reached for her glass of wine, the ice clinking inside while she sipped it.

"It would seem they've found a reason to choose," she finally answered Cecelia.

"And what would that be?"

Danica shrugged, her delicate shoulders spreading the thin golden ropes that made up each strap of her dress apart, displaying alabaster skin between threads. They sparkled in the sun. The ropes, from whatever shimmering fiber they were weaved from, but her skin as well. She glistened with sweat amidst the day's heat.

"I imagine the Prevailing Mother, your dear witch, is tired of having nothing to do," Cecelia said.

She slumped into the chair next to Danica and offered her a generous smile. While Cecelia had learned that Danica thought similarly to how she herself thought, she also knew Danica hated the way Cecelia boldly expressed it.

"Besides," she added, "no one ever stayed neutral forever. My father says a bored soldier needs but a dirty excuse to go to war."

Danica tried to hide her laugh. The queen was much more interested in staying in character than Cecelia ever was. Which was probably why

Cecelia liked her so much. She was everything Cecelia should've been, but wasn't.

"You're probably right, your grace," Danica nodded. "War moves many things."

Danica settled low into her seat, feigning sleep.

Cecelia watched the Fair Folk's tents dance slightly amidst the building wind. A pastel head would pass by from time to time, blue or lilac or pink, and disappear. Once, even a child ran by, a miniature of their parent.

"But he can't hold them forever," Cecelia said, startling Danica from a light doze.

Danica glanced over at her, blinking sleep away, trying to understand.

"Rees," Cecelia said, "he'll have to let them go eventually."

Danica yawned and stretched, her roped straps falling completely off one shoulder. She lazily shoved it back up and sighed.

"When it's time to release them," Danica assured her, "and no sooner."

Danica reached and patted Cecelia's hand delicately. The coolness of the queen still left Cecelia feeling strange, like a corpse reached for her. Rumors circled the castle that she suffered from a condition, though Cecelia had yet to discover what this mysterious condition was called. Extra blankets were brought to the queen often, and the fire within her bedchamber was kept roaring all year long.

Death, it seemed to Cecelia, was the only reason someone would be that cold. An undead queen. Cecelia smirked at the thought.

"Don't fret over the children," Danica said, hand still light on Cecelia's.

"I wasn't fretting," Cecelia spat out the word.

Danica smiled at her, but her eyes trailed over Cecelia's shoulder to something behind her. Cecelia turned to find Viktor standing in the doorway. He looked unhappy, but that wasn't unusual. His face held on to anger longer than others, Cecelia found, but it melted away beneath her. Sometimes on top of her.

"My lord," Danica removed her hand from Cecelia's and stood.

"Your grace," Viktor replied, "you needn't call me that."

Danica offered him an affectionate wink. "I trust you enjoyed your day. I selected the office myself for the morning light."

"Yes, the light..." Viktor looked from Danica to Cecelia.

Her body tensed beneath his gaze. After spending days with him following her around as an escort, she found she now missed him. Without him, she was adrift in the sea of the castle, and not even Danica assisted in anchoring her. The queen was her friend, true, but even she still held on to her secrets and strangeness. Viktor was the only thing she knew.

Or at least she thought she knew.

"So, you found it to your liking?" Danica prodded, still not getting the hint to leave.

"It was fine. I stared at paperwork and had more visitors than I cared to entertain." Viktor said.

"Oh?" Danica's eyebrows ticked up.

Viktor sighed. He noticed the decanter of wine on the nearby table and grabbed it. After pouring himself a glass, he sat down in the chair Danica had once occupied.

"An old... friend thought they could persuade me from my new towering position as Royal Guard whatever," he grumbled.

"Marshal," Danica smiled sweetly.

Viktor rolled his eyes.

"And who else?"

Danica danced nervously on her toes. Cecelia watched her wait impatiently for Viktor's response, fidgeting with some loose rattan on the back of Viktor's chair. It irritated Viktor to no end, though Danica didn't notice. Cecelia saw his face reddening at every twitch of the dried grass.

"Rees," Viktor said, "Rees came by."

"He's back," Danica stopped fidgeting.

"Yes, freshly, if the mud he left in my office is any sign and the soldiers allowed to wander in the grand hall."

This news buoyed Danica. She danced towards the door, light on her feet, a smile different from any Cecelia had seen on her face. She stopped and wrapped an arm around Cecelia's shoulders.

"Be with me again, tomorrow," Danica whispered, "break your fast with me. I'll have a surprise on my veranda."

Cecelia raised an eyebrow.

"Surprise?"

Danica held a finger to her lips and turned to Viktor.

"I bid you a lovely evening, my lord," Danica said.

Viktor stood, reluctantly, and tipped his head to her. "Your grace," he muttered.

When she was gone, Cecelia still stared at the doorway. Danica left behind a hint of vanilla and something else. The smell of a cool winter day, when the wind whipped through the mountain of the Lagos, bringing a hint of snow. A scent of cold emptiness. An expanse. But more than that, she left Cecelia feeling sick.

"What do you suppose that means?" Cecelia asked Viktor, settling into the seat next to him.

He held his drink in one hand and stared across the grounds at the tops of the Fair Folk's tents.

"What?" he asked.

He didn't see her when he looked at her, but something else, something he didn't like. His gold eyes were far away, half present but half gone, like a ghost.

"Something's wrong," she said, "let's go to bed. Everything makes sense there."

She stood and went to the doorway. Viktor remained seated. He swirled the wine within his glass and stared at the Fair Folk.

"What do you think?" he asked her. "You've a military mindset. You've been trained. Why are the Fair Folk choosing a side now, after all this time?"

Cecelia's shoulders drooped, disappointed. She had looked forward to returning to the bed all day.

"I don't know," she sighed. She returned to Viktor's side. "Maybe they're bored. That's what I told Danica."

"Danica?" he glanced up at her before returning his gaze to the tents. "Moon Mother, you're on first name basis now?"

She settled on the edge of his chair and wrapped her arm around his shoulder. He didn't fight, but she could feel him tense against her. She took his wine and drank deeply of it herself. When she handed it back to him, he poured her some more.

"I think," she said between gulps, "ambition is sometimes born, sometimes made. Either way, the Prevailing Mother has it. I saw it myself. The way she spoke to Danica. She had little fear."

"So, a lack of fear of queens equals ambition? Well, hurray for me." Viktor took the glass and drained it.

"I think this Prevailing Mother is ambitious. She doesn't need a reason to choose. She's a woman with power. If she wants to do it, she will."

Viktor sat with that thought for a moment, nodding.

"You're right," he said.

"Of course I'm right." She stood and pulled on his arm. "Now, to bed. You must be exhausted."

His eyes smiled up at her, briefly, before he turned away. She dropped his hand. When he looked back, the friendliness was gone. His eyes were closed off to her, and strange.

"Why are you here, champion? What's the real reason your father sent you? Tell me." Viktor said.

Cecelia hesitated, though she didn't know why. Viktor wouldn't care that her father's vision sent her across the sea. That an old man from far away saw something wrong and sent her, never to return. But the words were thick in her throat, for she hated hearing them herself.

"My father," she began, "saw a darkness here. He felt it threatened the Lagos in some way. Danon and I were sent here to seek it out."

"Saw?"

The way the word drawled out from his mouth, the slanted accusation hidden within its spoken syllable tightened around Cecelia's throat. She threw her shoulders back and stood tall, refusing to allow Korithian judgement to diminish the truth of her father's gift. Though she disliked the truth just as much.

"My father possesses the sight. He... he has visions. A blessing from the Mother."

Viktor flicked a flower petal, wilted on the arm of his chair. "And he saw darkness? Here?"

Cecelia nodded.

"What exactly—"

"He did not know. Not clearly. He said it was like knowing an animal hid within the brush, knowing it threatened your life, but not knowing what it was."

Viktor nodded and then went pale. A light breeze rifled through his hair, but it did nothing to lift his sullen mood. Instead, something settled over him. A resolve. A decision. His face was rigid and his frown — his most common feature — was set deeper than usual.

"I'm riding home tomorrow," he said, "to see my brother. I've unfinished business to attend to."

"Then surely I should go with you." Cecelia tried hard to hide the hurt she felt, hating that she felt hurt at all.

She had given him what he wanted, the truth. Why would a man ask for it if he couldn't handle it? It changed nothing between them. Her father had not told her to stay and marry. Cecelia had made that choice herself.

Because she wanted him.

But he shook his head. "No."

"I'm afraid I must insist, my lord."

"No," he said again.

He looked at her, daring her to call him lord again. She wouldn't, not this time.

But his time would come.

The township of Grumbling received its name due to land shakes experienced by those living there. The quakes happen sporadically, though usually before a rainstorm and rarely in the winter. Originally, it was thought a dragon den lay nearby, and the dragon caused the calamity to occur. But hundred of searches were made and no den ever found. More recently, people have considered the Crystal Falls nearby - a eighty rod wide waterfall that plunges into the ground - may be the culprit. Several adventurers have descended into the underground cavern to investigate, but never returned. The Fair Folk, visitors to the falls for hundreds of years, remain quiet on the subject.

Logician Anncept Garoll
Landcraft: The Relationship of Geography and Economy

Chapter Twenty-Two

Viktor left with the sunlight. He didn't tell Ramiro where he was going. He didn't care. He needed away. He needed space between himself and the castle, between Cecelia's body and his own. She was a crashing wave, and he the beach, and he could feel himself eroding with each tide.

Cecelia had been quiet. Which only meant she was angry. He wanted to explain it to her desperately, but he didn't think he had the right words to explain why he needed to leave.

One reason, among many, was to retrieve his father's sword. It was Ephram's, when he was alive, and went to Von when Ephram died. But if a rebellion was starting, if a creature lurked in the darkness for him, Viktor wanted it on his side and not Cecelia's small gift of a blade. He had shoved it in his saddle sack hastily, hoping Von would want to trade it for their father's sword. For, though the Panther blade was useless to Viktor, Von might find its monetary value much more meaningful. Von always looked for a way to earn a quick coin.

But the second reason was the more hurtful reason. The second reason would break Cecelia's heart. For as much as Viktor found he cared for her, he didn't much care for the complexity of relationships. The uneven give and take a marriage nurtured. He had spent most of his life focusing on merely surviving. The simplicity of it was soothing to him. But Cecelia complicated that.

And Viktor wanted easy.

The kingswood grew up to his left, filling the darkness, trees turning black to green with the rising sun. The gooseberries were fragrant with the sprinkle of morning dew, but Viktor kicked his steed on, knowing it'd take him a moonrise more to reach his ancestral home. The kingswood melted away, revealing never ending fields of golden wheat. Farmers stalked silently through the rows, always working the land. Crows circled and swooped overhead, stealing their dinner. Viktor ignored the farmer's hails and the crow's cries, not caring what they called for.

He only cared for the ride.

When the sun was high, he stopped to water and rest his horse. Sitting on the bank of a small stream, he ate the food he stole from the kitchen: an apple, a bread roll, and a hunk of cheese. A jug of beer washed it down. It wasn't enough, not nearly enough for Viktor's appetite, but he'd survive the journey. Once home, he'd demand Von prepare him a feast. He was Marshal Viktor now, with land and a title of his own. Von wouldn't like it, but Viktor would.

For the rest of the day, it was like that. Viktor would ride for hours, growing saddle sore and tired, then he'd stop and rest. Cecelia would often float through his mind at these restful moments. He did his best to push her away, but found it near impossible. She had a way of appearing before his next thought and then his next.

With sunset, a river appeared. It's waters ran sluggish and Viktor vaguely remembered swimming amongst its reeds once when he was a boy. The name escaped his mind, but he knew he'd have to ford it if he wished to rest in the sleepy village occupying the far side. Tentative at first, his horse finally leaped into the water, treading easily. Viktor's riding breeches wicked the water upward towards his knees, reminding him of dark nights spent in wet holes.

His horse reached the far side with little effort. Viktor turned to watch the river flowing behind him, pleased at his progress, only to realize the hilt of his sword - the gift from Cecelia - was gone.

"Curse it." Viktor searched through the saddlebag to no avail.

He watched the river rush, bringing bulky branches along slowly, like lazy rafts. The sword must have knocked loose during the crossing. As valuable as it was, it was gone forever. Some poor peasant would eventually find it and turn their family's plight from desperate to filthy rich.

Viktor couldn't blame them. He hated the sword anyway.

His horse clopped through dusty streets. Viktor kept his eyes out for a tavern. He knew there was one somewhere, though he hadn't passed through the town in years. Lord Black often dragged his sons along when he surveyed his landholdings. *To see their lord is to know their lord*, their father would say. It was one of the only practical lessons Viktor's father ever taught him about lordship. They would be left to follow their father, more like hounds than children, attempting to glean what lessons they could by observing. Ephram paid the most attention. Von just wanted to make trouble. Arlo was always disappearing somewhere quiet to read. And Viktor dragged behind, the smallest and youngest, usually the target of Von's jokes. And their father's wrath.

He finally spied the sign he looked for in the backend of an alley. A red mare with black-robed figure astride it decorated the sign. The old paint peeled and curled away, leaving the mare without a hind leg, but Viktor was sure the tavern was still open. The loud yelling and laughter spilling from the door confirmed it.

He handed his horse off to a stableboy appearing from the shadows. No one noticed Viktor when he entered. He liked that. Whatever amusement each table had found, it was enough to keep them distracted.

Viktor sat at the bar and waved the barkeep down for a tankard of beer.

A voice spoke from behind Viktor. "If it isn't the Guard Marshal himself."

Viktor tried not to act startled. They spoke as if next to his ear, though he knew no one sat there. He turned and looked over his shoulder, spying a pink-haired man. He turned back to his beer.

"What do you want, G'rig?"

Viktor swirled his tankard, watching the foam sizzle and melt away. It was a fine ale, sweetened with local honey. He was sorry he would not be able to enjoy it. He never could enjoy anything with the Fair Folk around.

"Your accents gotten better." G'rig hoisted himself onto the stool next to Viktor.

"I make a quick student when I want to." Viktor glanced at G'rig. "Shouldn't you be in a round-up on the palace tourney grounds?"

G'rig shrugged. "One can find holes anywhere, if they look hard enough."

Viktor choked on a laugh. Perhaps, with another blockade, one could find a hole. But General Rees kept a tight grip on his men. There would be no hole. Not one that wasn't put there intentionally.

"Shouldn't you be with the lovely Panther pawdwyn?"

Viktor chugged the last of his beer and slammed the tankard on the counter. He motioned for the barkeep to fill it up again. He didn't answer G'rig's question. No doubt the Folkman knew enough already. The Fair Folk had the uncanny ability to discern things like that.

G'rig nodded, already reading Viktor's mind, it seemed.

"Let's see, you're on the Red Way, traveling West. No doubt you'll take the turn south at Grumbling onto the Route of Thieves," G'rig tapped his chin, pretending to think, "you're traveling home. And without your pawdwyn?"

Viktor turned to G'rig, waiting for the Folkman to get to the point. But G'rig was having too much fun. He sipped at his beer, smiling in between, before ordering another.

"And one for my friend," G'rig said, "to celebrate his promotion."

"I don't need your charity, G'rig," Viktor growled over his beer, "or your friendship."

G'rig shrugged. "I feel sorry for you, that's all. To be so miserable being married to such a woman."

"It has nothing to do with Cecelia," Viktor said.

"Oh, of course not. It's about you. You're a self-centered dirt sack. I've known it since the day I met you."

G'rig slid the tankard from the barkeep towards Viktor. Foam sloshed over the side onto G'rig's embroidered sleeve. He wiped it off on his pants. Viktor had never liked the Fair Folk style. Everyone was covered in flowers, threaded on to look like gardens or vines or even trees. It was as if the Fair Folk wanted to take the land with them wherever they went. By wearing it brazenly on their clothes like sigils, they were claiming it as theirs.

But Thrash'gar the Destroyer made sure that wasn't true.

"That's why we Fair Folk marry young." G'rig carried on. "Loyalty is a part of our blood. Loyalty above all else."

"You marry young," Viktor said, "because you want to breed early and fill this wretched continent with your thieving spawn."

G'rig grabbed his heart, feigning pain. "You wound me, Viktor."

"What are you really doing here, G'rig?" Viktor asked. "Your kind don't normally haunt places like this. Your taverns are the woods, yours drinks the streams."

"Consider it reconnaissance," G'rig replied.

"Reconnaissance for what?"

"For the future!" G'rig held his tankard aloft, but Viktor didn't lift his to meet it.

G'rig drank the rest of his beer down, wiping his lips on his sleeve, wetting the heads of embroidered pansies. "You'll know soon enough. Surely, you'd know sooner had you stayed at the palace. Now your precious pawdwyn will see before you. But either way, it'll reach you. It'll find you wherever you go."

"Moon Mother, G'rig, what in his abominable brilliance are you saying?"

"Revolution, dear friend." G'rig patted Viktor on the arm. "Revolution leaves no one behind."

Viktor frowned. "The Fair Folk don't take sides, G'rig."

G'rig laughed. "Until they do, Royal Guard Marshal, until they do."

G'rig bid his adieu and disappeared into the crowd. It was then Viktor noticed a table of Folkmen in the corner. How had he missed them when he entered? He was too busy trying to fade himself, trying to hide.

He paid for a room and found it at the top of the stairs. The bed was itchy, filled with ancient straw, but Viktor was tired and soon his eyelids felt heavy. But G'rig's words bounced around in his head, delaying his sleep. It seemed the rumors were true, and the Fair Folk had picked a side. Rees would be right to blockade the Prevailing Mother inside the palace grounds. But it didn't explain what G'rig and his cronies were doing in the tavern.

Reconnaissance. Viktor wondered what type of information the Folkman would search for.

And what, in the name of the Moon Mother, were they fighting for?

Viktor rolled over, his thoughts falling to Cecelia once again. Her body and her warmth, but also her words. Her father had sent her. There was something waiting in the dark. But what Viktor saw was something else — the arrival of the Panthers coincided with the Fair Folk taking sides. Surely that wasn't a coincidence.

So, who was the enemy?

The Fair Folk?

Or Cecelia?

In a village by the river lived a maiden fair and bright
Her beauty shone like silver in the morning's early light
But her father was a Folkman, with power strange and old
He scared away her lovers, with spells so odd and cold.
Her father wove his magic, to keep her love at bay
And the maiden wept in sorrow as her suitors turned away
She prayed to the earth below her to break the spell and see
A man who'd love her deeply and set her spirit free.
The maiden grew so tired of her father's cruel control
She pleaded for her freedom with all her heart and soul
But the Folkman wouldn't listen to his daughter's heartfelt plea
So she left her village home to find her destiny.

Traditional Fair Folk Song

To the sea she fled, she fled, she fled
Leaving behind only hearts that bled.

Tova Whispers, Korithian Bard
Amara's Song

Chapter Twenty-Three

Her frustration at Viktor's absence climaxed when a servant arrived to dress her.

"I'm not a child!" She railed in her mother tongue.

Though her words were not overly harsh, her tone was. The girl sent to dress her bowed low, wiping tears away as best she could, before backing into the hidden door in the corner. Cecelia sat still on the edge of the bed, staring at the hidden door. She tried distracting herself, tried tracing the carved climbing leaf pattern of the woodwork with her eyes. Anything to not think of Viktor.

But it didn't work.

She flung her blanket to the floor and kicked a pillow across the room. Naked and alone, she shivered in the morning breeze. The muggy night air was enough to suffocate Cecelia. She had flung the window open in the dead of night before Viktor had left. If she had known then, she would have stopped him. It had been her hope he'd wait until after breakfast to depart. She'd convince him to take her or force her will upon him. Instead, he left before the sun peered over the horizon. Like a trickster.

Like a thief.

At least he had taken the sword. It usually lay abandoned on the bedroom sidebar, but it wasn't there. Good. Cecelia twirled her emerald ring around her finger. The gem glimmered in the rising sun, receiving constant expressions of admiration from anyone who saw it, but it was the fangs of the creatures she admired the most.

"Her majesty awaits," the Mistress said, arriving from the hidden doorway. "And you've upended your dressing maid."

"I want you to dress me," Cecelia answered her. "I haven't time for weak countenances and childish tears."

The Mistress quietly obeyed, her fingers deftly beginning the process of untangling Cecelia's hair. Cecelia's shoulders relaxed at the touch.

"His lordship left early this morn," the Mistress observed, "a lovely day for a ride."

"His lordship keeps his own council," Cecelia murmured. "I've yet to decide if the day is lovely."

"Surely in the presence of her majesty it will be the finest."

Cecelia raised her chin high and examined herself in the mirror. She insisted on dressing in more traditional clothes and cursed any attempt at putting her in Korithian garb. Her loose muslin dresses suited her figure fine and seemed to keep her much cooler than the layers of frivolity Danica insisted on wearing.

"That will do," Cecelia held up her hands, staying the Mistress and her paint pots.

Cecelia excused the woman and left her room for the salon. She had hoped Viktor would leave her something, a note or a token, but the thought made her equally angry when she realized he had left her nothing.

"I never needed a man," she said to herself, picking up the book she had been reading the evening previous.

It was a history of the Fair Folk, as much fiction as it was fact. The delicate paintings, done in pastel watercolors, attracted her initially. But learning of their history, of their cohabitation with giants and dragons, of their utilization of earth magic, as they called it, left her feeling intrigued.

She had yet to see the Fair Folk practice their magic. Besides the allure generated by their mere presence. At the market, when she walked with Danica, she had seen little of it. Mostly parlor tricks, card games, and the reading of palms.

She wondered if the magic was indeed real, or if the Fair Folk were more tricksters than magicians.

Or perhaps both.

She tossed the book back onto the chaise and left. A guard, assigned by Danica herself, followed her. The path to the queen's private chambers was written in Cecelia's memory. If need be, she could find her way in the darkest night. It no longer seemed like a lair, but another way to see inside her friend's mind. For while Danica was pleasant and called Cecelia a friend, Cecelia couldn't help but feel off balance. She hated knowing less than her opponent, and in Danica's case, she knew nothing.

"Ah, there is my dearest," Danica beamed at Cecelia when she entered the veranda.

The infant Jana sat swaddled in linen on Danica's lap. She slept, though her eyelids wavered with the movement beneath.

"Do they all grow as quickly as she?" Cecelia joked, gently running one finger along the girl's eyebrows and down her nose.

Danica smiled down at her daughter. "No. She is exceptional, is she not?"

"A queen's Queen," Cecelia sank into the chair opposite Danica, swatting at a lemon bee attracted to her citrus juice.

Danica smiled at Cecelia's words before handing her daughter to a nursemaid. Jana remained asleep.

"I should hope I can be an example to my daughter of what a woman can achieve in her lifetime," Danica sipped at her own juice.

"Surely you have done much," Cecelia spoke over the bite of toast in her mouth, "you are far more educated than your Korithian peers."

Danica rolled her eyes. "My father's doing, not mine. But there is time. Time to achieve things others only dream of."

Cecelia slowed her eating. She found the anger over Viktor's absence still resided in her stomach, prompting her to fill it as quickly as possible with food. Slowly, she chewed her honey-soaked toast, forcing herself to experience the full force of the sweetened flavor.

"Meaning what?" Cecelia asked. "Does this have anything to do with the surprise you spoke of?"

Her question renewed Danica's smile.

"The surprise! Yes, of course."

Danica shoved her food and drink away and stood. She reached for Cecelia, her cold hands dragging her up out of her seat and toward the veranda banister.

"I've an excellent view of the tourney grounds from this height," Danica explained.

"So I see," Cecelia agreed.

Danica's apartments were in the upper reaches of the keep. It allowed the choicest breezes to blow, cooling the queen in the summer and the warm air to rise, keeping her cozy in the winter. Logistically, it was the easiest way to keep her safe. It was like a dragon with its hoard, who hides its gems furthest away to keep them safe.

But Danica's words could not be denied. From her veranda, the entire grounds were on display. Cecelia realized that despite Danica's absence during the tournament, the queen could have easily been watching from her private apartments. Everything opened beneath like a stage for players. Only General Rees and his army made up half and the brightly colored haired Fair Folk made up the other.

"It will be but a moment," Danica clung to Cecelia's arm, squeezing it excitedly.

"A moment for what?"

Cecelia didn't have to wait long to find out. The king, followed closely by his brother, walked brazenly up to the line held by General Rees himself. The three spoke together, heads bent low, before General Rees gave the order to open. Ramiro, Rufus, and several Kingsguard entered the encircled Fair Folk and headed straight for the Prevailing Mother's tent. The

Fair Folk slowly backed away, allowing the king and his entourage straight passage to the Prevailing Mother's door.

"What's he doing?" Cecelia asked. Hair stood on the back of her neck and she gripped the banister so hard her knuckles turned white. Cecelia didn't know what Ramiro thought he was doing, but she knew it was not a good idea.

"Danica, what is Ramiro doing?" She asked again.

"He thinks he's going to speak to me," a voice from Danica's bedroom spoke.

Cecelia whipped around to see the Prevailing Mother standing in the doorway, guarded on both sides by tall, blue-haired men.

"Mother Oora," Cecelia whispered.

The old woman bowed her head curtly. It wasn't a sign of obedience, but of respect. She smiled at Danica before approaching.

"The earth nurtures you, D'ncyea." She said to Danica.

"And the Moon Mother smiles on you," Danica replied.

"What will Ramiro find in the tent, then?" Cecelia asked, having no time for fake platitudes of friendliness. "If not you, then what?"

Mother Oora offered her a pitying smile. "Surely a pawdwyn as smart as you can figure it out, Kith d'mun."

Cecelia stared at the tent, willing herself to see through its thick fabric walls. But it was obviously no use. She strained her ears to hear over the birdsong and the crash of waves not far away over the cliff side. There might have been some yelling. Perhaps some steel on steel. The walls of the tent trembled momentarily. Finally, a Fair Folkman exited the tent, sword withdrawn, covered in blood.

"Now you see," Mother Oora cooed, "now you know, pawdwyn."

"Death," Cecelia said breathlessly, "you killed him."

She turned to Danica, who only stared with an eerie smile on her lips.

"Danica," Cecelia whispered, "are you listening? Danica?"

Danica blinked, as if waking from a dream. She glanced at Cecelia, a biting glare on her face. "I did what I had to. For myself. For Jana. For the future of Korith." She glanced back at Mother Oora. "I needed allies."

"You?" Cecelia looked from Danica to Mother Oora. "You're working together? And what of Rees? When he finds out of this deception, he will turn the army on you, Danica, and the Fair Folk. I don't think you've thought this through."

"We have, little pawdwyn," Mother Oora said. "General Rees is with us."

Cecelia found it hard to swallow. Her throat swelled and her face grew hot. Thoughts flooded her mind but not one made sense. Words. All she saw were words, and one of them written boldly: betrayed. Her eyes darted back and forth between her friend and the Prevailing Mother.

"So, the Fair Folk have chosen a side," Cecelia said, "but why?"

Mother Oora sighed. She slid into a nearby chair and helped herself to some toast.

"Why does everyone always insist on knowing the why of things," she said, slathering the bread with butter and then jam.

"Because Mother Oora." Danica returned to her own seat and resumed her meal. "Ambition can never be answer enough, not in a woman's case."

"Surely," Mother Oora laughed with her mouth full, "it must be for a man. For revenge. For something entirely different than the mere will to do it."

"I don't care about your reasoning," Cecelia said, returning to her own chair. "I just want to know if I am safe. If my husband is safe, wherever he is. What moves the Fair Folk to take a side, and if I am included on that side?"

Mother Oora stared at Cecelia, chewing her toast slowly, methodically. She took a large swig of orange juice and sat the glass on the table. Her eyes were unnerving. They glittered turquoise like the water surrounding the Lagos on brilliant summer days. If she stared hard enough, she could almost hear the wind in the palms and the terns surfing the waves. She fell into them, and they transported her back in time and space.

Cecelia shook her head, realizing too late that Mother Oora was alluring her. Mother Oora offered her a demure smile.

"How very like your mother you are," Mother Oora said.

Cecelia forced her heart to stop racing. "What do you know of my mother?"

Mother Oora arched an eyebrow while sipping her juice. "I know a great deal about Amara. We were cousins."

It was hard for Cecelia to not choke on her food. She slowed her chewing and counted, chewing at least ten times before swallowing. Even if Mother Oora's words were off-putting, she wanted to put on a show that she wasn't surprised.

"I don't appreciate liars, Mother Oora," Cecelia finally said, "no matter who they associate with."

Cecelia glanced at Danica.

Danica sat up straight. "I promise you, Cecelia, Mother Oora speaks the truth. I told you I've been inquiring about your mother to everyone. It finally came to me that perhaps no one knew her because she wasn't known."

"That makes no sense," Cecelia frowned.

"It makes perfect sense, little pawdwyn," Mother Oora said, "for the Korithian people do their best to not see the Fair Folk. We are invisible to them in every way lest we are selling something they like. Some shiny bauble that catches their eye or a love spell. Since D'ncyea couldn't find Amara amongst her people, she thought maybe she'd find her amongst mine."

Cecelia crossed her arms. "So you're saying my mother was a Fair Folk? And yet no one ever mentioned she could perform magic. Or had strange colored hair."

Mother Oora shrugged. "I did not say Amara was talented. I said she was my cousin. And she obviously cast a perfect cloaking spell to arrive in the Lagos undetected." Mother Oora allowed her words to sink in before proceeding. "And as for her hair, well, there are many ways to change that." She sharply bit into an apple. "And some don't even require magic."

Lord Von Black's first wife was a minuscule woman of the Ma'Cloud family. The clan traces their roots to the Fair Folk, though the Fair Folk magic and wild hued hair died out long ago. Hana Ma'Cloud respected Von, and the pair were deeply in love. But the pregnancy of their first child was difficult for Hana. She was bedridden the last pair of full moons and used her last breath to thrust a dying child into the world. Von was devastated. He eventually remarried, as was expected of him, but he had no love left for only duty.

High Steward Rodrick Brasden
House Histories and Insignia

Chapter Twenty-Four

THE GRAND ENTRANCE HALL looked as it always had. Antlered creatures hung from every surface, their heads a rack for nearly any object: cloaks, hats, even undergarments. Glass eyes stared at everything and nothing. Forest green carpet led visitors up the stairs, worn away where generations of Black family members walked, their ghostly footsteps guiding the way.

It even smelled the same, like tossed soil and a warm evening breeze, but also spoiled fruit. Viktor turned around, half expecting to find a bowl of rotting food near the door, left for the hounds as usual. But there was nothing.

"This way, my lord," the steward said.

He was an ancient man, having served Viktor's father. Ephram didn't live long enough to replace him, and Von cared little for the intricacies of lordship. He merely wanted the title, the money, the benefit. Actually running the estate bored him. Which explained the many crossbow bolts stuck in some of the animal heads. And the undergarments.

The steward led Viktor to the dining hall. Viktor prepared himself for disappointment, though he hoped Von had received his message. It had been a stroke of genius. In Grumbling Viktor realized he made great time. There was no need to rush toward his home, toward the easily irritated Von, when he could take his leisure. He sent a messenger ahead, a ruddy-cheeked boy who dared call himself a man, to tell Von his brother *the Royal Guard Marshal Viktor* returned.

The boy had the gall to remind Viktor that he was the only brother who'd visit, seeing as Ephram was dead and Arlo was a Moon Priest and sequestered in the temple for the rest of his life. Viktor had fought the urge to strike the boy.

He wondered when he had gone soft.

Viktor's logic was that if he gave Von time to prepare, he'd pull out the stops to impress Viktor. Not for Viktor's sake, but for his own. Von was an egomaniac and enjoyed showing off.

They passed through the many windowed salon, a favorite of his mother's. Viktor's chest tightened with every step. He forced himself to find the door quickly. For while his mother would remember the room as a place to call her sons forward and dote on them, he only remembered his father: dark and broody in the corner, always reading something, constantly mumbling backhanded comments beneath his breath. Sometimes about Viktor or his brothers, sometimes about his mother. Always nasty, always barely audible.

In the dining hall, Von sat at the head of a large oak table. He was balding, and his hair had grayed at a much faster rate than Viktor's. Beside him sat his wife. Or, more precisely, his second wife. The first Lady Black died in childbirth, along with the baby. She had been a rail thin girl, young and naïve. This one seemed little older, though looked stouter than the last.

The steward introduced him. Viktor nodded a greeting to Lady Black first.

"My lady," he said.

He turned to Von. "Brother."

Von chewed his food and stared. He glanced at his wife before suggesting to Viktor with a leg of chicken held in his hand.

"This one sends word ahead to prepare a fine feast because of some promotion or some dirt," Von wiped the chicken fat dribbling down his chin with the sleeve of his tunic, "and then has the audacity to show up late."

"I apologize," Viktor said. "It's been years since I've ridden this way. The road proved nostalgic, and I took longer than I should have."

"Apologize," Von drank heavily from his cup, "what brother is this, that arrives at my door apologizing? Surely not the smallest of us, that bratty little runt, Viktor?"

But he meant it lightheartedly. He stood and clapped Viktor on the back before suggesting to the chair opposite Lady Black.

"Marya, meet Viktor. Viktor, Marya." were all the introductions Von offered.

Viktor tipped his head to Marya again. She smiled girlishly and seemed to wiggle in her seat with some sort of anticipation. Viktor frowned. He never had that effect on women, not even with his own wife. He looked at his brother, who frowned as well.

"She's curious about your wife, Vik. I received Ramiro's letter some days back. Marya was giddy with the thought of a princess as a sister."

"I see." Viktor slid down into his chair.

He turned to Marya and tried to smile, but it just wouldn't play on his lips.

"I've heard she's quite beautiful." Marya stabbed a green bean with her fork.

"Yes," Viktor accepted a horn full of beer from Von, "exceptionally."

He thought back to the many nights of their honeymoon and the joy he missed of seeing her in the moonlight. Her beautiful thighs and the curve of her neck. But then he thought about the enormous weight of having to make someone happy. How it hung around his neck like an anchor, dragging him downward, pulling him toward the earth and perhaps an early grave.

He had something important to do, he reminded himself. Cecelia couldn't always control him with her body. Or her needs.

Von snorted with laughter. "No man admits his wife is ugly."

They ate in silence after that. Viktor had missed the fair of his home. Pheasant stuffed with oatmeal and apples. Lamb braised in brandy. Greens grown in the garden. The smells curated together and reminded him of his childhood, of moments long gone. Of stolen happiness between long stretches of fear and sadness. When he had had his fill, he shoved his plate away and pulled his beer closer.

"So," Von began, grabbing another piece of lamb, "this promotion grants you your own land and title."

"Yes," Viktor said.

"And all you had to do was marry some foreign princess?"

"Yes," Viktor said again.

"And yet, you're here on my doorstep." Von washed his lamb down with some beer. "A place you swore you'd never return to. So, let's cut the dirt and you tell me what's wrong."

"What do you *mean*, what's wrong?" Viktor frowned.

Von shrugged. "You're here for a reason. And without your dear Panther princess."

"Perhaps she's already with child and the journey would tire her so?" Marya suggested, her voice giving away her hope.

Both Von and Viktor disapproved. Viktor imagined Cecelia riding the journey beside him and knew she'd have little to complain about. Instead, she'd have raced him to Grumbling and forced him to lie with her in a field along the way whenever it suited her fancy.

Von threw a hunk of bread at her and told her to shut up.

The thought of Cecelia pregnant made Viktor nauseous, but he drank more beer to settle his stomach. Or at least fill the void he felt there.

"I don't want it. Any of it," Viktor forced himself to speak calmly, evenly, in front of his brother's wife.

Even if Von didn't afford her the same.

Von smacked the table. "Want? For Moon Mother's sake, Vik, you don't have to want it. Just take it."

"Just take it," Viktor mused, "like you did? Just took Ephram's place like you were always meant to be here."

"What are you on about?" Von ripped another bite off the leg of lamb. "Ephram was arrogant and got himself killed."

Viktor stewed in silence, knowing if he opened his mouth he'd lose the calm he had worked so hard to achieve.

"Military genius," Von grumbled through his full mouth, "no military genius gets himself burned up in a forsaken forest."

Viktor held his beer tight. He cracked his neck, hoping to ease the tension he felt building.

"Damned embarrassment," Von muttered.

The syllables of Von's words played in Viktor's ears, an agonizingly annoying song he'd heard too many times. Far too many times. He pushed his horn of beer away and stood.

"What?" Von asked, mouth still full of food, "what are you doing?"

"I had wanted to offer you a trade," Viktor began, "but now I think I'll just take what I want, as you yourself suggested."

"Take? Take what?" And when Von followed Viktor's gaze to the sword, hung in its scabbard from the back of his chair, he laughed. "You think you're going to take that from me? You?"

Marya looked from brother to brother, her cheeks pink with the heat or the drink or perhaps nerves. She pushed herself away from the table slowly and excused herself.

"No," Von commanded, "you won't leave. You'll stay and watch your husband kick his little brother's arse."

Viktor wasted little time. He knew Von liked to talk, liked to make a big show out of things. It was one of his many irritating habits. Where Ephram was a man of action, Von was a man of empty words.

He reached out and knocked Von squarely in the jaw. It was enough to tip Von in his chair, but not enough to disable him. On the contrary, it enraged his older brother, who stood and flung the leg of lamb at Viktor.

Viktor dodged the lamb and dove, tackling Von. Marya screamed. Her screaming seemed to enrage Von even more, but Von was never a good fighter. He easily became distracted and could never use his rage to his advantage. It was why Viktor took the chance and tackled him. It was why, when Von drew back his hand to throw his own punch, Viktor hit him in the side and then beneath the chin.

Von groaned and rolled away, allowing Viktor the time to leap up. He grabbed the sword and ripped it from its scabbard, but by then Von had recovered. Von reached from behind and wrapped his immense arms around Viktor, staying his movements. He squeezed as hard as he could, crushing Viktor's chest like a bear. An immense, angry bear.

It was by accident that Viktor dropped the sword, point end down, onto Von's foot. Due to the occasion and the lateness of the evening, Von wasn't wearing his thick leather shoes, but his house shoes made of fine black felt. Viktor admired the golden embroidery of the family crest until the pointed blade sliced through clean to Von's toes.

His brother screamed. Marya screamed. The steward, having finally entered to see what the commotion was about, screamed as well.

Viktor's body took over. The many years he'd spent fighting played out in his stance and the way his hands formed into fists. He turned and swung at Von again. This time, his brother fell and did not get back up. Blood poured from Von's destroyed slipper. Marya, hair tossed messily over her face, kneeled by Von's side, soothing him.

It wasn't the homecoming Viktor had imagined, though his life had turned into some portrait he'd never envisioned, anyway. There were colors and things present he'd never wanted, but some mighty artist seemed to have added them despite his objections. He wanted to say something to the crying Marya, for after all, they were kin, but the words wouldn't form. He felt helpless again, as he had when Cecelia confessed to giving up her crown for him. When she told him about her father's vision.

It had all been the truth, but the truth tasted bitter. His father spoke the truth when he told Viktor he never wanted another son, before bringing the rod down on his backside. What need did Viktor have for the truth? The truth hurt. The truth just made him angry.

And when he was angry, he made hasty choices.

Instead, he gripped the sword and nodded farewell to Marya, who didn't even notice his departure. The steward flung himself back against the window, begging Viktor not to hurt him.

He crammed the sword into his scabbard and leaned close to the steward. So close he felt the old man's hot breath and smelled the rancid garlic he had eaten for dinner.

"Tell my brother, when he wakes, that the sword is mine. If he sends someone after me, I'll kill them. If he hunts me down himself, I'll kill him too."

He stormed from the front doors of his childhood home for what he knew would be the last time. He'd never see it again, and he didn't want to.

Some things are better left behind.

The exact length of the Age of Queens is highly debated amongst my fellow scholars and myself. Those easily swayed by romantic notions believe it began eighteen years prior to the start of Jana the First Queen's rule, when she was but an infant. Her mother, Queen Danica, ruled the throne momentarily during the tumultuous time known as the Year of Chaos. But those of a realist mindset, such as myself, believe that Danica's rule was short-lived and separates Queen Jana the First Queen's rule by eighteen years and is therefore inconsequential to the Age of Queens.

Court Historian Jepsuth Jeffrees
Age of Queens: A Complete Discussion

Chapter Twenty-Five

CECELIA SPENT FOUR NIGHTS thinking in her salon. She'd break her fast alone, walk through the gardens with Danica after lunch, and immediately be ushered back to her rooms each evening. Danica assured Cecelia she was in no danger. Cecelia was her ally. But Ramiro forged the alliance between Korith and the Lagos of the Moon. And Ramiro was dead.

Cecelia never liked imaginary obligations.

She stared out the door of the veranda. The breeze blew falling petals along the floor. Birds, smaller and less colorful than those of the Lagos, hopped along, enjoying the search for random tidbits. Cecelia sneered. The plainness, the uninspiring brown of the birds, bothered her.

With a sigh, she fell back onto the chaise. Danica wanted her help. She wanted Cecelia by her side while she attempted to rule her volatile land. She also, Cecelia suspected, wanted more from Cecelia. More than she was willing to give.

Rees and his army abandoned their encirclement of the Fair Folk. Instead, they dispersed themselves throughout Kasier, forcing anyone who didn't like the new regime into the dungeons.

There were many.

Cecelia wondered what they'd do with them next. Her father always said prisoners kept alive were only as good as they were useful. Danica would not want her dungeons full. Not with the Unis on the march with their rag-tag army. She'd need the space.

If they won.

And where was Viktor?

Cecelia toyed with her hair, twisting it repeatedly, a bad habit she developed young.

"Your grace will grow a bald spot doing that," a voice filled the surrounding room.

"Baldness is the least of my worries," Cecelia conceded, almost lazily, not even looking at the intruder. "Haven't you heard? I'm half Fair Folk now."

Danica appeared in her line of vision, plopping herself at the foot of Cecelia's chaise, her silk organza skirt sprawling across Cecelia's feet. The skirt was sheer, though she wore enough layers that it hid her figure. Embroidered flowers, all black, spread across the hem. Petunia. Viola. Iris.

"You should be pleased. Now you know where your mother came from. You have family here. Roots."

"Roots." Cecelia said skeptically. "Roots aren't my concern either."

"Then what *is* your worry?" Danica reached for Cecelia's hand, but Cecelia pulled it away, acting as if a stray hair across her eyes bothered her.

"Viktor, mostly," Cecelia admitted.

Danica huffed and tossed her words away with her hand. "I already told you, he was seen leaving his brother's estate. Stole his brother's sword and ran away. You're much better off, you know?"

Cecelia needed to tread carefully with her words. She worried Danica would grow jealous of Viktor, especially if Cecelia conveyed more concern for him than for her. Especially if Danica realized her future conquest would bear no fruit.

"I know," Cecelia sighed, "but he's out there, still sowing seeds of derision. Who knows what he'll do once he hears about Ramiro?"

She distracted herself with her hair again, but glanced at Danica out of the corner of her eye. The young queen traced the sweeping petals of an iris on her dress, her finger shaping and reshaping the petal while her lips sat pursed. It wasn't fair, Cecelia realized, Danica was still young. A girl, really. Thrust into wifedom and motherhood with no other thought.

With no other choice.

"He needs to be found, Danica. He needs to be dealt with." Cecelia sat up, pulling her feet from Danica, folding herself inward for protection.

Danica nodded, still staring at her feet. "You're right."

She looked up at Cecelia and it was clear there was fear in her eyes. But not weakness. It was an angry fear, like the buildup of a cornered animal. It was primordial.

It was survival.

"I'll have Rees send someone right away."

"No," Cecelia picked her moment. She reached for Danica's hand and cradled it, stroking Danica's palm with her thumb. Danica's shoulders relaxed and a serene smile spread across her lips. Danica's youth was her weakness. Cecelia would use it to her advantage.

Just like everyone else did.

"Let me do it," Cecelia said. "Let me do this for you."

Danica scoffed. "And what would I do without you?"

"You have Mother Oora. It is the two of you that sorted this coup, this dawning of a new era."

Danica seemed to like Cecelia's words, for her smile returned. Cecelia took it as a sign to press forward, to make the kill shot, to finish the fight before the fight finished her.

"I will return as quickly as I can," Cecelia assured her, "but he dishonored me, Danica. He ran and left me. He must pay the price."

She squeezed Danica's hand then, not just for emphasis, but she feared the young woman was losing interest in the conversation.

"Yes," Danica agreed, "you're right. The dirt sack. If he should die by anyone's hands, it should be yours."

"I agree," Cecelia nodded.

With the most important part of the conversation out of the way, Cecelia teased out as much information as she could from Danica. It was the only way she'd know what to do next. The more information gathered, the more clairvoyant one seemed. Or so the spies of the Lagos claimed.

"You trust Mother Oora?" Cecelia asked. "You seemed to despise her at the market."

Danica shrugged, "I can play pretend too. It was easier to get our pieces in place if Ramiro suspected I hated having the Fair Folk here."

"So, even then," Cecelia said, "even then, you were both planning on overthrowing Ramiro?"

"Yes," Danica said, "the stupid fool didn't see it coming."

"For how long?" Cecelia asked. "How long did you have this planned?"

Danica smiled wickedly. "Since before my wedding, when she read my palm. She warned me the Unis were grumbling, that they had come to her many times to join them in stopping my husband ascending the throne. But Mother Oora had other ideas. More... interesting ideas."

"She recruited you. Because she needed Rees. And you recruited Rees."

Danica stood and stretched. "When you say it like that, it sounds less romantic."

She straightened her dress and stared off across the room, though Cecelia knew she was seeing some glorious future, some illustrious vision.

"Poets will write about it," Danica sighed, "the Age of Queens. The Age of Acceptance when Fair Folk and Korithians began living side by side."

Cecelia tried, but failed, to mask her laughter. Danica glared at her.

"I'm sorry," Cecelia said, "but is that what Mother Oora wants? Acceptance?"

"Mother Oora wants peace," Danica barked, though her face melted immediately, apologetically. "She wants a way forward that isn't segregation."

"I thought the Fair Folk enjoyed being different," Cecelia said.

"Respecting differences and ostracizing are two separate things." Danica trolled her finger along the back of the chaise, stopping at Cecelia's hair, tousling it.

"Seems to me she wants power," Cecelia mumbled, allowing Danica to toy with the small plait in her hair.

"You don't know her like I do, Cece," Danica snapped, pulling her hands away.

No one had called her that since Danon left. Not even Viktor could bring himself to use the pet name. It sounded wrong in Danica's mouth. Cecelia fought the urge to slap her, encouraging the name to leave her tongue and never return.

She relaxed her eyebrows, which wanted to scowl, and the corner of her lips, which wanted to turn downward. Instead, she smiled, which felt wrong, and reached for this woman she didn't want.

"You're right," Cecelia said, holding Danica's hand, "if you trust her, then that's good enough for me. Now, leave me. I must prepare for my journey. I'll leave in the morn."

"So soon?" Danica didn't want to let go of Cecelia's hand.

"Yes," Cecelia said. "Retribution waits for no one."

Danica was reluctant but finally left. With her gone, Cecelia sat and twisted her hair again. She had fears, of course. Many fears. What if Mother Oora saw her as an enemy, despite their supposed familial relation? What if Rees decided he required more from her? Much more. And what if Danica grew tired of the cat-and-mouse game Cecelia played?

There was hope, too. To be free of the castle walls meant to be free of her chains. She could go where she chose. She needn't even go looking for Viktor. She could instead head straight to the nearest port and find a ship from the Lagos. Or to anywhere.

Why even go home, if home is what she still considered it?

But Viktor pulled at her thoughts. Her mind had a funny way of letting him in, always to the forefront, always embellished over what she should really be focused on. She needed to find him. For more reasons than one, but mostly because he was her husband.

Mostly because, despite his best efforts, she still wanted him.

The Spilled Saucer was established in the village of Wilsden during the reign of King Tallon. It was handed down from generation to generation within the Vral family, a mountainous clan known for their support of King Norian. After his overthrow, the Glades family took the tavern over. A young couple, the pair proved proficient in business and soon the tavern thrived. A cat, known as Kitty, was already a well-known resident of the tavern. Even the oldest of the village remember feeding the cat scraps when they were but children. The Glades know not where she came from or her true age.

Logician Anncept Garoll
    Landcraft: The Relationship of Geography and Economy

Chapter Twenty-Six

Viktor had regrets. Sure. By the fourth night of sleeping in the dirt and using his saddle for a pillow, he began dreaming of Cecelia. The way her body wrapped around his when she slept. The way she smelled of vanilla and pine.

But, of course, then his body would wake him and he'd moan and grumble and roll over, forcing himself to forget her, forget everything.

Nothing mattered except Viktor, his sword, and the ride. It was simple. Easy. And there was less chance of getting hurt if you did all the hurting.

It had happened so suddenly. The assault on Von. Initially, he had no intention of fighting his brother for it. He was going to do his best to manipulate him into giving up the sword. But then Von opened his giant, ugly mouth, and spoke those horrible things about Ephram.

Ephram.

The brother everyone loved. Except for maybe Von. The brother that stood up to their father. The brother that, for all intents and purposes, had been the real man of the house.

Viktor sighed and kicked out his leg, dislodging a stone that dug at his calf.

"Curse you, Von," he grumbled.

He fled Kasier, not knowing if he'd return. Deep down, he didn't want to. It was too complicated. Viktor hated complicated. But there was a conflicting side, a side that fought with the part of him that enjoyed routine and the ease that came with simple obligations.

And Cecelia was no simple obligation. She came with many strings. Chains, even.

She didn't want him, anyway. Not really. He was territory to her. A place to stake her flag. An anchor in the sea that was Korith. And what does one do with anchors when they're done with them? Pull them up. Cease their use. Ignore them.

Or so his thoughts ran on, tangling themselves, knotting up into a web so dark even he couldn't make heads or tails of it. So he shoved himself up off the ground and prepared for the day's ride.

Twilight pierced the horizon, flooding the night sky with inky blue, then cobalt. He didn't pay attention to the sunrise, didn't see the red bleed into orange so quickly it was like the red was never there. A Bloodletting the Fair Folk called it. A sign of loss to come.

It wouldn't matter if he had. The Fair Folk's beliefs in the suspicious aspects of nature annoyed him. A people, magic filling their blood, afraid of signs given them by a sunrise? Or the dregs of one's tea? Or a leaf that just happened to fall to the ground before you?

G'rig was tolerated because it was a necessity. When Ramiro wished for a message to reach the Prevailing Mother, tidings of some dirt or another, Viktor and his fellow Kingsguard were entrusted with it. No one else. And G'rig was always their contact man. No one else.

Though Viktor often wished it weren't the arrogant pink haired man. The first time they met, G'rig forced Viktor to take part in his card trick, efficiently stealing every coin on Viktor at the same time. When Viktor, on his way back to the palace, realized the wrong, he confronted G'rig. The Fair Folkman only laughed in his face and sent Viktor to sleep. He woke up, neck kinked, slumped in an alley between two taverns. Viktor did not know how G'rig had done it.

Ramiro had been furious. At Viktor.

He avoided G'rig after that. When they did meet again, Viktor obeyed Ramiro's commands and played no games with the Fair Folkman. Instead, he watched him throw tarot cards through the air. The corners pierced a nearby wall. G'rig plucked them from the wood and whistled with concern.

"It doesn't look good, Viktor," he'd say.

Viktor rolled his eyes at the memory. He mounted his horse and wondered if there'd be any way to continue his journey without thinking at all. Just mindless wandering. A complacent, yet simple life.

He sighed. Ahead lay the road. It was still wide, compact dirt. Small forests or fields encroached on either side before receding and allowing a river to flow past. A wooden bridge, built long ago by Fair Folk magic, crossed the rushing water. Giant beams, clearly formed from ancient oaks, looked freshly cut, though Viktor knew that was part of their magic.

On the other side was a town, its name forgotten but to those that called it home. It didn't matter. They all were the same. But on the other side, he could see the mountains. Their long arms extending into the plains, billowing, creating rolling hills before jutting upward sharply. Grassland gave way to scrub brush, scrub brush to forest, forest to stone. Ultimately, stone to snow.

He'd be safer in the mountains. No one would look for him there. He was almost sure. And if he got antsy, in need of an adventure, he could always wander down the other side to the coast. There'd be ships there.

Perhaps even a ship of the Lagos.

But he forced that thought from his mind. His horse's hooves echoed across the giant beams, making Viktor feel small against the backdrop of the Fair Folk's monstrosity. Four wagons could cross in unison if they wanted. An entire regiment. But Viktor knew it was not for Korith's benefit, but Fair Folk's own. Their caravans often looked more like parades than long chains of wagons. The more extravagant, the bigger, the better.

The scent of roasted meat met him on the other side. He was pleased to be off the giant bridge, the hairs on his neck finally relaxing with a shiver. Fresh grub would warm him and fuel him. If he pushed his horse a little harder, he'd make the gradual ascent of the mountains before nightfall.

He moved to turn his horse down the road when the horse whinnied and shuffled sideways. Viktor growled and yanked the reins, attempting to make the horse obey. It whinnied again and made to buck him, but he forced her to stand down.

"It's there, sir," a dirty urchin pointed his black nailed finger at something below the horse.

Viktor, frowning, leaned over and peered around, only to find a large gray tabby cat. It seemed to ignore them, admiring its own fluffy tail, but remained steadfast in front of the horse.

"Cursed cat," Viktor growled.

He yanked the reins again and tried to steer the horse around, but the cat ambled in front of the horse again and again.

"What's going on?" Another urchin appeared, this one older, possibly the first's brother.

"Kitty took a liking to this traveler," the first urchin said.

"Kitty is a dirthole," Viktor grumbled, still attempting to outmaneuver the feline.

The second boy shook his head. "Kitty is smart. She finds things."

"Yeah, like what?" Viktor said through gritted teeth. "Her untimely demise beneath my horse's feet?"

The horse, completely indifferent to Viktor's control, jerked the rein from his hands. It was no use. He would have to wait for the annoying creature to move on.

"She found our sister once," the older boy said, "when she got lost up the glen."

"Aye, she did!" The younger boy said. "And she found our uncle's glasses in the cemetery."

"And when old Lucie got clobbered, she found the man who did it," said the older.

"Alright," Viktor rolled his eyes, "Kitty is good at finding things. The question is, can she find me an ale and a meal?"

The boys shared a look before turning to Viktor and smiling.

"Our ma runs the tavern," said the younger boy.

"If Kitty likes you, then ma is sure to like you." The older added.

Viktor nodded. "Will Kitty lead the way?" He wasn't hopeful.

The cat, as if understanding, turned and waltzed down the middle of the street. The boys danced around her and then raced each other ahead towards the tavern. A large wooden sign swung from an iron stake.

Painted upon it was a cat tipping a saucer of milk.

The inside of the tavern was dark and far more humid than it should have been. Viktor ducked his head to enter the door. Once inside, a buxom — albeit old — lady greeted him.

"I see Kitty made a new friend," the woman smiled, petting the cat that made itself at home on the bar top.

"Kitty almost made an enemy." Viktor plopped down on the seat next to the cat. "But your boys assured me she was friendly. Said she was good at finding things."

"Yeah," the woman sized Viktor up, her smile dissolving and her words growing frosty, "depends on what you're looking for."

"Information, mostly," Viktor said. "I need the safest path to the mountains. Wonder if the road is any good."

"Why wouldn't it be?" The woman poured Viktor a malty beer.

He shrugged, sipping at the fizzy head of the drink. "You tell me?"

The woman studied Viktor for a moment. Kitty mewed before settling down on the counter. The woman hurried to slide a saucer of milk in front of the cat, who noisily lapped it up.

Since speaking with G'rig, Viktor worried. He worried he was missing something, and he worried he had left Cecelia in a viper's nest.

Danon would skewer him alive.

Despite not being able to do anything about it, he still felt he needed to know. He needed to know what he left her to. He needed to know how large his treachery was. What he traded for his freedom.

"Word reached us after they killed the king," the woman finally sighed, "apparently Queen Danica rules in his stead."

"Ramiro is dead?" Viktor nearly choked on his beer, but knew better than to waste it.

The woman studied him closely again, but decided it was best to carry on. "And the Fair Folk grow reckless, wandering into town and demanding they pay less for drinks and less for beds. Less for everything now that they're accepted."

"Accepted?"

"Aye, this is the Age of Acceptance, or some dung such as that. Kept chanting it while they drank my supply away."

It seemed Viktor missed a great deal after he left.

"And the Panther princess, any word of her?" Viktor tried to speak calmly, but the words tumbled out all the same.

The woman shrugged while she wiped up the cat's milk mess. "All I know is what I've heard. And what I've heard is that three women rule us now. Queen Danica, alongside the Prevailing Mother and some third thing. Perhaps this Panther princess."

Yes, Viktor thought, Danica would rope her slimy tentacles around Cecelia. But at least, on Danica's good side, she'd be safe. Surely.

"And Rees? The General," Viktor sputtered, "what of him?"

He hoped he was dead. Though he knew better.

The old woman laughed. "Doing what a man like that does best."

"And what's that?"

"Following orders."

The Dule of Whisper Wives was founded during the dark reign of King Hallyn. Hallyn claimed to be directly descended from His Brilliance, excusing his cruel behavior for the will of the sun god. To motivate Korithians to overthrow the horrible king, the Unnamed Priest sent his wife to spread the good news of the Moons. The Mother and Daughter promised balance, something Korithians desperately needed, and peace, something Korithians desperately wanted. The woman proved adept at her task, and soon thousands of converted Whispers Wives flew across the kingdom, bringing with them the end of sun worship and Hallyn's reign.

An Unnamed Priest
    Of the Royal Temple of Kasier
    The Mother's Testament: A History of Religion

Chapter Twenty-Seven

THE STABLE WAS QUIET, save for the horses. Some snorted in their sleep. Several stomped on the ground, thinking Cecelia's presence meant it was nearly breakfast time. The mixed smell of warmth and compost irritated Cecelia, and she fought to keep from sneezing.

She hushed a black gelding that Danica had said was Ramiro's. It was in need of a new owner. The young creature seemed docile enough, though her approach in the darkness put it on edge.

"There, there," she cooed in the tongue of the Lagos. "I will be a better rider than Ramiro."

She sat the small lantern on the wooden floor and began brushing the creature, hoping to gain his trust. When she thought he was ready, she slowly removed his tack from the stall wall. It took longer than she had hoped; it being a long time since she saddled a horse herself. But the sounds of the stable were soothing, reminding her of memories long ago in a place far away.

Perhaps she was too deep in thought, for she didn't hear the footsteps on the stable floor behind her.

"Off to chase the Guard Marshal?"

Cecelia froze, swallowed hard, and continued to buckle the saddle. Her hands shook slightly, but she forced them to be still.

"In my opinion, your grace, he isn't worth the follow."

Cecelia smirked. "I don't recall asking for your opinion, general."

She turned to face him. He looked older and tired in the shroud of shadows the stables offered. A shoulder hunched forward, and he grimaced as he put his weight on his right leg.

"You look like dirt," Cecelia said.

It was Rees' turn to smirk. "I've always admired your ladylike way with words."

Cecelia turned to finish gearing her gelding. "What do you want, Rees? Danica knows I'm leaving. I have the queen's blessing."

Rees arrived at her side, petting the horse. Up close, she saw the etched lines on his face from years of worry. He smelled of iron and blood and sweat. Cecelia knew that smell. She knew what it meant.

"The Unis haven't given up, I see," Cecelia sighed, climbing into the saddle.

Rees habitually grabbed the reins, steadying the horse. His eyes harden. "They'll yield, eventually," he said.

Cecelia nodded. "I'm sure Mother Oora uttered those words to Danica about you."

Rees released the reins like they were white hot. He wiped the sweat from his forehead, the beads glimmering in the light of the double moons, and sighed.

"Leave Mother Oora to me," he growled.

"Fine," Cecelia said, "she's all yours. I've no interest in their coup. Or their war."

"Danica will be sorry to hear that."

Cecelia cocked her head to the side, intrigued by the way the queen's name came from Rees' mouth so easily. So familiar.

"Careful, general," Cecelia said, "familiarity breeds disdain."

"Words of your father?" He asked, the tone of his voice shifting.

"No," she said, "mine."

She yanked the reins and her gelding neighed in reply, excited for a run. A journey. A new path.

"You're a fool to follow him," he said, "a damned fool. Stay. Rule beside Danica. Bring this country into a golden era."

Cecelia laughed. "You sound just like her. Did she send you? Did she put you up to this, to lure me back?"

Rees looked away. He was embarrassed to be Danica's errand boy. A great general, reduced to the queen's new dog.

"I yield to no one, Rees," Cecelia broke the silence of the night, "run and tell her that. No one, do you understand?"

He bowed his head, but spoke into the darkness, "so you will not yield when you find him? You'll kill him for your dishonor?"

Cecelia bit her lip, debating. "I will do as I please with him," she whispered.

They shared a long look. Rees shook his head. He understood.

"Will you protect her?" Cecelia said.

"With my life."

"Oora can't be trusted, general."

Half of Rees' mouth turned up in a crooked smile. "She's not nearly as smart as you give her credit for."

He appeared certain. Though his shoulder drooped, his posture was tall and proud. Or as tall and proud as it could be. The Unis would not give up easily. There would be more fighting. More deaths.

"A word of advice, general," Cecelia turned the gelding around in a circle. It was extremely giddy. It was ready for the ride. "The ones who appear the stupidest often aren't."

She kicked the gelding into motion. Rees remained standing in the darkness of the stables, silent, as she left into the night.

Outside, the air was cool. The humidity of the outdoors was nothing compared to that of the stables. Cecelia took a deep breath and glanced up at the moons. The Mother was waning half while the Daughter already waned crescent. Soon the Daughter would be new, if only for a night. The perfect night for making children, the Whisper Wives would say, when the Daughter hid from the Mother.

She pulled her cloak tighter around her shoulders and let the gelding find its way down the street. It seemed to know where it was going. Danica had said it was his hunting horse, and that Ramiro boasted of the animal's sure footedness after every ride.

Victory was the horse's name. Cecelia had found the name absurd before, and she certainly found it absurd after Ramiro's death. She considered renaming it, but had never named a horse before. The horses she rode in the Lagos were already named, those of her father or the Dancing Swordsmen. The axe hurlers of the Dry Vineyard preferred giant rams, bred especially for traversing the steep mountains of their island.

Cecelia sighed and stared down at the horse's flowing, black mane. It was a complete black, with no sign of white. True black. And handsome.

She instantly considered Blackie but knew that was too infantile. Something Lucian might call the horse. Then she thought of Journey, for that was what she was on, or Vengeance, for that is what she yearned for. But both names didn't sit right. Alaina would have hated them, for her sister preferred fashionable names such as Starlight or Saffron.

The horse wedged itself between a small hidden door of the castle walls. One Danica told her would be open and waiting for her. With the castle finally falling away behind her, she kicked the horse into a trot and then a run down the winding street. She realized then how strange it was that her thoughts drifted back to her siblings. She hadn't thought of Lucian or Alaina at all since arriving in Korith. Perhaps for the better. She doubted they missed her.

But she realized she missed them. And as she glanced down at the horse, finally reaching its full stride, she knew what she'd call him. Where she really wanted him to take her, if she were to belong anywhere.

Home.

She rode into the darkness of night for what seemed like days, but was probably one one or two chimes of the bell. The Mother's light was strong, even at half strength, and Cecelia had little trouble finding her way. The rhythmic stamping of Home's hooves lulled her into a light sleep.

She dreamed of her mother, faceless and fearsome. Of her father, afraid. She dreamed of Viktor, smiling and calling her champion. And something else. An aching she didn't remember feeling before. A pain in her abdomen. Fear filled her throat and she couldn't breath. Her hands reached for her chest but the panic of suffocating was too much. Too great. Too heavy.

A sudden jolt stirred her. She awoke to find she still rode Home, but the horse seemed spooked. He slowed his run until he eventually stopped. He whinnied and tossed his head.

"What?" Cecelia said, "what is it?"

She leaned forward and peered into the darkness. Instead of the usually night song of birds and insects, there was nothing. Only silence, eerie and out of place.

A rock skittered across the road. Gravel crunched beneath feet. Cecelia had no time to think. It wasn't a time for thinking. Moments like that were meant for instinct and action. Leave the thoughts for after. She kicked Home hard, forcing the gelding to sprint. Whatever spooked him before now motivated him to run. She yelled into the night, hoping to confuse whatever lay in wait for her.

It worked. Hands reached for her and then recoiled temporarily, perplexed as to why she screamed already. A sword simmered through the darkness but she saw it in time to kick it away. A rock grazed the side of her temple. Warm blood trickled down her face and onto the edge of her lips. It tasted metallic and bitter.

Another sword appeared. Cecelia caught the blade on her bracer, tangling herself up with it though she managed to stay seated on Home. The horse turned in terror, dancing amongst enemies. Cecelia grappled with the swordsman before finally relieving him of his weapon. She kicked him hard in the face before turning the sword over in her hand and throwing it end over end like an axe hurler, settling the tip deep in an approaching attackers chest.

Home ran. Cecelia yelled. The attackers fell behind.

His Brilliance took many forms when depicted by his worshippers. A sun with sevens rays. A seven-sided star. A bush on fire. A torch lighting the darkness. Personified versions of His Brilliance did not appear until the reign of Queen Lyana, who mourned the death of the Prince Consort, Georgo. Lyana was a devoted worshipper of His Brilliance, so when she claimed the sun god himself came to her in a dream and told her to shape his face in stone, no one questioned her. That His Brilliance looked very similar to Georgo was coincidence, most said, and the few that publicly voiced their concern disappeared in the night. Generations later, King Hallyn would take after his Great-great Grandmother Lyana, and shape the image of His Brilliance after himself.

High Steward Rodrick Brasden
The Fall of Hallyn

Chapter Twenty-Eight

KITTY WAS STUBBORN. DESPITE Viktor's many attempts at persuading the cat to remain at the *Spilled Saucer* and to leave him alone, she followed him through the packed dirt streets past the edge of the village. She ignored him when he tried to reason with her, and she purred when he cursed at himself for speaking to a cat.

The aging woman of the *Spilled Saucer* assured him Kitty knew what she was doing. She came and went just like the phases of the moons. No one in the village could remember a time when Kitty wasn't at the Spilled Saucer, but all things must end, the woman had said, and who was she to deny Kitty an adventure if she wanted one?

Viktor tried to lose her outside of the village, where the forest grew thick and tall. Ancient spruce and giant birch stood watch there. Birch brush thrust from the base of the trees and filled any gap it could fill, offloading its pungent scent to the breeze.

The horse proved more willing to obey him that morning and rushed down a small footpath before Viktor yanked the reins and doubled back down a dried creek bed. A birch branch walloped Viktor in the face, leaving its sticky residue across his cheek, but he rode on. He rode through the thick old growth forest for a while, not daring to return to the road until he was well and sure Kitty had been left far behind. No common cat could follow so closely in such thickly grown trees.

Kitty sat patiently waiting when he finally returned to the road. She cleaned her paw, meowing at him innocently when he huffed at the sight of her.

"What kind of cat," he began but stopped.

He wouldn't stoop to speaking to the cat. Not again.

Instead, he rode on, only resting when the sun was high in the sky. The road had been a steady incline for several hours. The birch trees, so wide canopied with their vibrant green leaves, gave way to black spruce. These trees towered over everything, leaving the road in shadows. Thick, globular sap oozed from many where beetles consumed them from within. More than one appeared dead. Viktor guided his horse around several fallen trees, their insides rotten and pockmarked from the beetles.

Kitty followed.

Viktor sat on one of the fallen trees and ate some cheese. The old woman of the *Spilled Saucer* had given it to him. He offered some to Kitty, reluctantly, who took it and nibbled loudly.

"I hate cats," he muttered beneath his breath.

Kitty hacked a hairball and continued eating.

Viktor, finished with his food, stretched out across the tree and stared up at the sky. The sun danced behind clouds, but the trees were so tall it didn't matter. Clouds or no clouds, the forest was dark. He glanced at Kitty, who had finished eating too. She sat and stared at him before ambling off into the dense undergrowth.

"Good riddance." Viktor shut his eyes and hoped to drift off to sleep.

But his nap was short-lived. Gentle steps padded across his stomach and chest, and something fell just below his chin. He opened his eyes to see Kitty sitting on him. Her tail flitted back and forth, pleased with herself.

"What is it, beast?" He picked up whatever prize she had dropped on his chest.

He studied it closely. It was a finger, ancient and petrified, though the more he stared at it the more he thought it made of stone. A ring sat on one end, giant and metal. It was too eroded to make out the markings clearly. Viktor had been through war and seen many disgusting appendages leave their owner. The finger didn't perturb him, though he wondered if that had been the feline's plan.

He looked over at Kitty. "Why did you bring me this?"

She stood and leaped off, landing a few feet away on the ground. Looking over her shoulder, she meowed at him. She wanted him to follow.

Viktor turned the finger over in his hand. He was certain it was stone, though he'd seen mummified remains once before as a child and recalled how stonelike the remains appeared. Kitty meowed again. Viktor sighed.

He sat up and threw both legs over to sit on the fallen tree. "I'll follow you, witchy cat, but whatever it is, better be good."

Kitty hissed and walked away. Viktor checked to make sure his horse was secure before stepping into the undergrowth after her. She guided him past thickly growing spruce and several Poorman's Berries until he nearly tripped. The forest floor descended sharply into a hollow. Viktor peered through the brush to see Kitty waiting for him below.

The fall was steep and coated in built up forest litter. Viktor slid all the way down. At the bottom, he wiped the debris from his pants and looked around.

"Well," he said, "what is it?"

He tried to forget he was talking to the cat again, and that he followed her deeper into the forest away from the road. He tried to forget he didn't know what he was doing or where he was going, only that he was on the move. There were many things he tried to forget, and in that instant, he was rewarded. For deeper into the hollow, crumbled and forgotten, was a stone statue.

Viktor approached the ruined relic slowly, pulling away old growth to better see.

Years of rain erosion produced a misshapen face. Only an eye and half a nose remained. The bottom half of the face was gone completely. A crown, once perhaps polished bronze but now green with age, sat lopsided on the curly hair. It was His Brilliance, the sun god, or at least a thoughtful personification of him.

Viktor's eyes dropped to His Brilliance's hands. The statue held an algae infused bowl that still held water. Worshippers once loaded the bowl with parts of their harvest. Fruits of the earth and of work with their hands. In famine and in feast. Willingly and sometimes unwillingly. Temples in the cities were known to demand gold that mysteriously disappeared after dark.

Taking the retrieved finger from his pocket, Viktor attempted to return it to its rightful place. It barely clung to the hand, its hold tentative. Viktor watched and waited.

"The sun god," Viktor said, staring at the hole meant to be an eye. "This is what you wanted to show me?"

The island of Duwu still sacrificed to the sun god. Viktor had heard as much from some sailors taking port in Kasier. Every year on the solstice, when the Mother and Daughter were at their weakest, a queen was chosen. Wined and feasted, the woman would experience a day like none other while watching virgins burn with every chime of the bell before walking to her own death in a giant fire set atop a golden temple.

Viktor looked at Kitty, who busied herself cleaning her tail. He sighed.

"Dirty cats."

A snap sliced through the muffled forest air. It came from behind the statue. Viktor glanced at Kitty, who stared intently at the sound.

"Very well, Kitty," Viktor said on the exhale, loosening his sword from its scabbard but keeping it hidden at his side. "Let's see who you've found this time."

A small man appeared. A Fair Folkman. He was short for his race and possessed the darkest green hair. A good choice for a scout in the forest, for he camouflaged well. The man peered around before settling his gaze on Viktor.

"The word?" The man said.

Viktor frowned. "The what?"

"The password," the man said again, "what's the password? So I know you've been sent."

"I don't know no password," Viktor growled.

"Then why the abominable brilliance you here?"

The Fair Folkman pulled a dagger from his boot. It shimmered, even in the dark forest, filled with light itself. A Fair Folk blade, razor sharp and enchanted so any wound it made wouldn't heal. Not without the right healer. Not without the healing only the Fair Folk offered.

Viktor suggested to Kitty. "The cat brought me."

The Fair Folkman glared at Viktor and then the cat. He tipped his head to Kitty.

"An enchanted cat. Old." He said.

"Aye, and a witch, I reckon. Look, I was just following her through the thicket. She brought me a finger from that statue there." Viktor suggested to His Brilliance, and as if on cue, the finger lost its hold and fell off the statue once more. "But I'd really like to get back to my horse and my journey."

The Fair Folkman stared at His Brilliance for some time, blowing a fallen strand of hair from his eyes. The shade of the forest was cooler than in the direct sun, but the trees had a way of trapping the heat. Sweat beaded up on the Fair Folkman's upper lip. He wiped it away and shook his head no.

"Sorry," he said, "orders are if you don't know the password, then I have to kill you."

Viktor nodded knowingly. He glanced at Kitty once, who seemed to enjoy the exchange, before turning back to the Fair Folkman.

"I was hoping you'd say that," Viktor said, unsheathing his sword.

Father, you'll be pleased to know that I and the baby are well. Mother was right, it was another boy. I've taken the liberty of naming him after you in hopes that he'll carry on your easy smile and jovial manner, the Moon Mother willing.

Lady Alisa Black
    Letter to her father, Lord Viktor LeBrand

Korgi, another boy. I need another one of those like we need another moon. Lissy named him after her father of all people. Viktor LeBrand, lord of swamps, will be pleased no doubt. We'll see what time makes of him.

Lord Ephrates Black
    Letter to his friend, Korginathian Di'Walt

Chapter Twenty-Nine

Trees receded and buildings grew. The town of Grumbling sprung up around her. Before Cecelia realized it, she was in the town's central square. Home the gelding was indeed surefooted, as Ramiro concluded, and loved the run.

There had been a part of Cecelia, a small part, that wanted to enjoy the journey. She wanted to gaze at the forest moving with the rolling hills, another form of an ocean, only made of oak instead. She wanted to stop and watch the farmers, wondering what they grew and how their harvest fared.

But the attack on her the night before haunted her. She saw their faces, still leering in the moonlight, the shimmer of their knives meant for her throat. They were Unis mercenaries. It was evident in their armor. Their lack of color. No Fair Folk would cover their natural hair. None would think twice about their brilliantly embroidered clothes. Most would have used magic to subdue her, but there had been none. No tingle, no tickle beneath the skin telling her someone nearby possessed the ability to pull from the earth. Only steel to pierce. Only angry faces.

Her mission hung heavy in front of her, like a carrot for a horse, and she focused solely on that. On finding Viktor.

She had followed the Red Way toward Grumbling, knowing it was the same path Viktor would take on his ride home. Yet once there she realized there'd be no need to go further. Arriving at the tavern, she asked after her husband, and was informed of the happening at the House of Black.

"Heard Master Vik done beat his brother silly," one man informed her.

"No, no," said his friend, "Lord Von is twice the size of Master Vik, 'member? Viktor was the sickly, runty one."

The runty one? Cecelia wondered just how large Viktor's brothers were.

The first man shook his head adamantly. "No, I know what I heard. The little one beat the big one."

The second man gestured with his hands that his friend was crazy and moved his mouth to speak just so, but Cecelia interrupted him.

"What did he do?" She asked the first man. "How did he beat his brother?"

The first man looked smugly at his friend. He leaned in close to Cecelia, a bit too close, but she allowed it on account that his information was what she needed.

"Supposedly," he began, his breath thick with the local beer and fish, "he knocked Lord Black out and took his sword."

"His sword?"

The man nodded. "Aye. Was Lord Ephram's before that. And then, of course, the mighty Lord Black before that."

"On and on," his friend added, wanting to join the conversation with the lady, "as those of high birth tend to do with their nicer things."

Cecelia frowned. She slid the first man a golden coin, pulled from a hidden pocket in the cuff of her cloak. The man took it with a too-wide smile. "And where is Master Vik now?" She asked.

The men looked at each other and shrugged. Cecelia rolled her eyes and removed another coin from her hidden pocket and slid it across the table. The man reached for this coin but it was snatched by the second man.

"Headed toward the mountains he was," the man said. "Toward Wilsden."

"Wilsden?"

"Fair Folk country. Or, at least it once was."

Cecelia bid the men a good evening and found a seat at the corner of the bar. Cobwebs decorated the large timber beams holding up the roof. A giant hearth, formed from large red stones, played host to a slew of antlered creatures. A warthog stood most prominent among them, his tusks decorated with golden rings.

There were many tables scattered about the great room and many alcoves for those that wished to remain hidden to do so. But Cecelia didn't. She sat prominently in the roaring light of the fire, her black riding pants and tall black boots still clean and crisp from her journey. Her cloak was the deepest green, embroidered with golden thread, and demonstrated her station. It was even clasped shut with a brooch of Danica's: moonstones in the form of tulips on golden stems.

Everyone knew who she was. She needed no introduction. Whispers, even those formed in the palace at Kasier, moved fast. Much faster than a gelding could run.

"Kith d'Mun," a man's voice said.

She turned to see a pink-haired man grinning at her, offering a glass of wine.

"G'rig," she said.

The Fair Folkman handed her the wine, which she happily accepted. "Imagine the coincidence. I saw Viktor but several moons ago in a tavern much like this one, and now I'm seeing you."

Cecelia sipped her wine, staring evenly at G'rig. "I don't believe in coincidences."

The corner of G'rig's mouth ticked up handsomely. "Oh, I don't either, pawdwyn. I don't either."

"Why don't you tell me what you talked about?" Cecelia sat her wine on the bar top. "When you just so happened to see my husband."

"Well, firstly I told him he was crazy to leave you, alone, at the palace. What kind of man I wonder."

"Mmm," Cecelia agreed, "I as well. But you know that's not what I meant, G'rig."

G'rig fiddled with his stein, spinning it in its own condensation sloughed off on the bar top.

"Little else, pawdwyn. Only," but he trailed off, staring down into his beer.

"Only what?" Cecelia asked.

She squeezed her hand and released it as it sat in her lap. Itchy fingers. Violence would do her no good, she knew that. Diplomacy would suit her better. And yet she couldn't quite shake the feeling in her hand. She shoved it beneath her leg, sitting on it, to stop the urge from acting.

"Perhaps I should just show you?" He watched her, gauging her reaction to his innocuous question.

She smiled politely. "Do you think I'm that stupid, G'rig?"

He shrugged and took a drink of his beer. "Never, pawdwyn," he said. "But if you're looking for Viktor, and I know you are, then you'll want my help."

It was harder to keep her face still and emotionless the second time. Her desire to find her husband pulled at her eyebrows, making her want to scowl at G'rig's knowledge of her need. She bit her tongue, pretending to purse her lips in thought.

"Fine," she finally said.

G'rig paid for their drinks and led Cecelia back to the stables. He tipped the stableboy when he brought Cecelia's gelding around to her.

"I'm no pauper, G'rig," Cecelia said, waiting for the boy to bring G'rig's horse.

G'rig tipped his head, "I assure you, it is out of respect and nothing else pawdwyn. No doubt your husband has filled your head with many lies about us Fair Folk. How we are thieves. Tricksters. Cheap."

Viktor had said all of those things in much more colorful language, but Cecelia did not let on that he had. Despite his abandonment of her, Cecelia still felt some loyalty to Viktor. She felt him beneath her skin. Her desire to see him again fought her desire to teach him a lesson. A Panther wouldn't allow themselves to be embarrassed. To be abandoned. To be unloved.

G'rig's horse was a thickset mare. Brown in color, she looked of the earth and from the earth. A horse fit for a Fair Folkman.

He led her out of town and into the forest. The sun was setting and everything bled with red. The Mother — in her crescent — and the Daughter — nearing new — glowed in the distance, momentarily amplified by their proximity to the horizon. But soon they were hid amongst dark branches and bushes.

"Perhaps it's too late to ask, but where are we going?" Cecelia kept checking her peripherals and over her shoulder.

"Don't worry, pawdwyn, you are safe with me," G'rig stopped his mare on what seemed like a game trail.

Cecelia brought Home close to G'rig and stared at the Folkman's face in the shadows of the forest. His eyes filled with light and transfixed her. They were warm and inviting. Eyes she could trust.

Or perhaps that was G'rig's enchantment working on her.

"The Prevailing Mother says to leave you be. So leave you be I shall," he smiled.

Cecelia scowled. "Is this what you think leaving me be means? Bringing me into a dark forest?"

"Relax pawdwyn." G'rig kicked his mare into action, cantering down the trail. As G'rig moved away, the inviting warmth Cecelia felt dissipated. "We're nearly there. Can't you hear it?"

Cecelia sat back in her saddle and stilled her breathing. Besides the gentle swishing Home's flanks made through the tall grass hemming in both sides of the trail, she heard nothing. She felt something, though. A rumbling. It sat deep in her chest. The further Home walked, following the slow pace of G'rig's mare, the higher the rumbling climbed. It moved up her spine and soon into the back of her skull.

G'rig took a corner and pulled some birch branches down, displaying the scene before them. Cecelia gasped at the beauty.

Rings shaped as His Brilliance were fashionable during the peak of his worship. Artisans would shape and sculpt razor sharp sunbursts and set a fiery stone within the prongs. Stones were usually Blazing Opal or White Tanzs. Gold was preferred, as it was thought to glimmer with the light of His Brilliance itself. Silver was second-rate but allowed if it was the only thing available. Rarely were the rings made of iron. Since the practice of decorating statues and altars of His Brilliance with jewelry was common, most of these rings appeared on the fingers of stone hands. A few, however, were kept and adorned by devout followers of His Brilliance as a sign of their piousness and their usefulness for self-protection.

An Unnamed Priest
  The Mother's Testament: A History of Religion

Chapter Thirty

THE NOTE FOUND ON the Fair Folkman's dead body told Viktor everything he needed to know. And some he didn't. Or wished he didn't. The password had been "the Tower," and the man the Fair Folkman had been waiting for was a Unis contact. A gray robed priest with dark secrets to deal.

Apparently, the Prevailing Mother enjoyed playing both sides. Viktor didn't know what it meant for the queen, but he knew what it meant for Cecelia: another viper to contend with.

He debated on turning his horse around and returning to Kasier. But playing the hero never suited him well. That was always Ephram's job.

Viktor didn't want to return, either. Kasier was a death trap, only you didn't know where the dagger was coming from. Viktor preferred knowing.

His horse took to the trail, Kitty in tow. She had mewled at him when he searched the Fair Folkman's body, but he hissed back, and she disappeared into the undergrowth. Now that he continued his journey, she sulked in the shadows, present and absent at the same time.

"What did you expect me to do?" He asked her, aware he sounded crazy for speaking to the feline.

She sniffed a Poorman's Berry before biting it. Viktor grimaced. The berries were called such for a reason. Only a man, poor with his luck and starving, would eat such sour orange fruit. But it didn't seem to bother Kitty, who ate two more before carrying on down the trail.

He watched her go, hesitating once again. For a moment, he thought of Cecelia. He faltered. She said she could take care of herself. She seemed capable. Sighing, he kicked his horse into a trot and followed Kitty.

Dusk settled over the trees by the time Viktor arrived in a small village. It snuggled next to the growing mountain, protected on both sides by the distant edge of the high valley. The trees rippled upwards with the breeze, funneled toward the peak of the mountains. The sharp scent of mountain berries cut through the crisp air. Viktor pulled his cloak tighter. It felt more like fall. There, the seasons moved onward at a faster pace, several steps ahead of the rest of the country.

An aging man digging in his garden hailed him when he neared.

"Hallo, sir," the man called, "bit late for riders."

Viktor cleared his throat, wondering where Kitty had gotten off to. "Yes, well, I met with some misfortune in the forest. It detained me some."

"Misfortune?"

"Fair Folkman," Viktor replied.

The man nodded his head knowingly. "They grow bold, what with word their Prevailing Mother rules side by side with the queen."

"So I've heard," Viktor noted the man did not mention a third woman. "And the Unis, have you had trouble with them?"

Kitty appeared at the man's garden post. She sat with tail dangling, swinging back and forth, interested in their conversation.

The man squinted at the creature. "That your cat?" He asked.

Viktor glared at Kitty before answering. "If I say yes, would it matter?"

"Enchanted cat," the man said, "bad luck."

"You've no idea," Viktor muttered.

The man licked his lips and spat. He looked from Kitty to Viktor. "You'll have to head on, sir," he said. "Our modest inn don't have room."

"Really?" Viktor frowned. "Your modest inn is just bustling with travelers, is it?"

The man eyed Viktor and spat again. He picked dirt from beneath his fingernails, avoiding Viktor's eyes. "Didn't say that. Said it doesn't have room for *you*."

He turned and pointed at Kitty. "Enchanted cats are bad luck. Gummer won't let it in his establishment. And you," the old man pointed at Viktor, but thought better of it and let his hand drop. "Well, you're marked by His Brilliance. We don't allow your kind here."

"For the Moon Mother's sake, what are you on about?"

Viktor's horse sensed his irritation and danced on its feet sideways. He reined her in and looked around. The town was indeed modest. There was a principal street, with barely two or three smaller ones running off it. The inn took up the most space, occupying a well-appointed place in the center of town.

The road continued upward with the mountain, but Viktor knew there'd be no other village. Not until he reached the other side of the pass, which could take days, depending on weather. The village was his last option.

Or sleep in the woods.

Viktor peered past the tops of the buildings at the darkening forest. It was full of spruce and prickly aspen roses and home to loud Robber Ravens that cawed endlessly through the night. And something else. Not a physical thing, not yet anyway, but a feeling. Whispers that pulled at his thoughts. Discomfort would be the least of his worries. He turned back to the old man.

"I don't know what you mean, old man, but I won't be deprived of a bed because of suspicions and superstitions."

The man raised his eyebrows but said nothing. He pulled out a small pipe and began stuffing it with something from his other pocket. He used the pipe to point at Viktor's hand.

"Seems my suspicions are true, what with you wearing that. Only the most devout display tokens of His Brilliance."

Viktor looked down at his hand, forgetting he had shoved the giant ring from the broken finger on before leaving the dead Fair Folkman. It had been custom to dress statues of His Brilliance in real jewelry. When the ring turned out to be genuine silver, Viktor took it with the thought of trading it later, should he need the coin. It was a bulky piece, in the shape of a brilliant sun, with small radiating spikes of exceptional sharpness. A giant stone once sat center, but was missing.

"I stole this from an eroded altar, back in the forest." Viktor suggested back down the path. "The Fair Folkman attacked me there."

The old man studied Viktor's neck. He had exposed it when he turned to point down the trail. Viktor cursed beneath his breath and pulled the collar of his doublet up further. But the old man said nothing. He seemed to consider Viktor's words. He tapped his pipe against his leg, then held it to his mouth to light. After taking several puffs, he held it to his mouth, still staring at Viktor.

Viktor prepared to unleash his anger on the old man, but a howl cut across the muffled silence of the valley. There was something else, too. Something different from an animal, like the raking of chain mail. The old man lurched, spinning to peer across his garden at the field beyond. Dark shapes, unknowable except for the relentless noise they made, moved back and forth along the tree line: wolves.

"Tell you what, big man," the old man stared across the field, "you do us all a favor, and I'll see to it myself Gummer gives you a room and a hot meal."

Viktor stared across the field, too. The wolves danced back and forth along the trees, preparing themselves for their hunt. The people of the valley kept sheep in the hundreds and corralled them close to the village at night. Viktor assumed a pack that large could reduce the sheep's numbers quickly, depriving the people of their livelihood.

But there was something else there. A larger specter. It moved amongst the wolves as if one of them, but Viktor wondered if it was something else entirely.

"Three nights," Viktor said, "and meals to go with it. And supplies for my continued journey through the pass."

The old man bit down hard on his pipe and frowned. "Three?"

"There's got to be five wolves, and something more there, something you don't want to tell me about. If it were easy, you'd already have them strung up."

With his pipe dangling from his lip, the old man gripped the fence. He stared at his feet and took a deep breath. Then he shook his head yes.

"Alright, fine," the old man said, "three nights."

"And the cat too," Viktor said.

The old man stood straight, preparing to argue, but the wolves' howls pierced through their words again.

"Fine," the old man relented.

"Good." Viktor reined his horse around to the garden fence and edged her around toward the field. "Kitty, to work."

The cat leaped from the fence and stalked into the field ahead of Viktor. He didn't know what good the cat would do, but he had grown accustomed to her presence.

Perhaps she'd find him some victory.

One for the ear, one for the heart.

Traditional Fair Folk Proverb about secrets

Chapter Thirty-One

CRYSTAL FALLS WAS DEAFENING. The falls thundered through her ears and down her neck. It filled her chest, and she could hear nothing. G'rig spoke to her, leading her down a hidden trail, but the words dissipated into the roar of the water.

Spanning forty rods, it was bigger than most waterfalls decorating the jungles of the Lagos. G'rig's mare expertly led them down a small path which grew rockier and steeper the further they went. They finally reached the ledge, where the water collapsed into a dark recess in the earth, but instead of stopping, G'rig plunged his mare through the falling sheet of water. Cecelia hesitated for only a moment before holding her breath and ushering Home through the water after the Fair Folkman.

Cecelia gasped. The frigid water sank down her neck and back. Some even filled her boots. G'rig chuckled at her before tossing his hand into the air. The motion was all he needed to dry her clothes instantly. Magically. The residual effect was a tickle across her skin. It stung where she was most wet, but the feeling passed quickly, like an afterthought.

"Thank you," Cecelia nodded her head curtly.

She brought Home up beside G'rig's horse. Once past the freezing falls, the path widened. It wound and hugged against the cliff face, meeting the ferns that tangled with overhead roots. It smelled heavily of earth. Of the most basic of scents. Of life itself. Further ahead, carved into the jagged rock, was an arched doorway.

"Where are we, G'rig?" Cecelia asked.

G'rig smirked before kicking his mare onward. He held out his hand to the falls, letting it slice through the wall of water like a knife.

"The Fair Folk know this land better than anyone," he said. "If Korith is the heart, we are the blood."

Small purple flowers fought to grow within the cracks of the rock next to the dark green foliage of the ferns. Together they wove a delicate tapestry, one Cecelia gently rubbed her hands along, tracing the leaves and petals. Cecelia admired their beauty and resilience but frowned all the same.

"Spare me your lecture, G'rig. I'm an islander. I don't know nor care about your people's ancient grievances. Save them for your Prevailing Mother. I hear she has the ear of the queen now."

G'rig stopped his horse and looked at her over his shoulder.

"Spoken like a true Korithian. Viktor would be proud."

Cecelia's shoulders slumped.

"Should you see your husband again, what will you do?" G'rig asked. "Forgive him? Kill him?"

Cecelia shook the weight she felt from her shoulders and sat a little taller. She stared at G'rig, not allowing his illuminated eyes to unnerve her. Besides their light, they were like any other eyes, an organ in which to see. She noticed he bore several scratches along his forearms and a dusky purple bruise.

"Have you been in a fight?" She asked, suggesting with her head to his wounds. "What's the use of your magic if you can't heal yourself?"

G'rig glanced down at his arm before pulling down his sleeve.

"Again, spoken like a true Korithian," he said. "Magic can't cure everything. But, then again, humans know very little about magic."

"And again, I don't care."

She shoved Home past G'rig and led the way, despite not knowing where they headed. But there was only one way to go: down. The path descended slowly, ever driving them towards the archway. Cecelia thought she saw a flicker of light, a change in the shadows just beyond the arch, but she wasn't sure.

"You show very little thanks for someone with the favor of the Prevailing Mother," G'rig said.

"I didn't ask for her favor," Cecelia said.

She didn't ask for any of it.

She kept Home steady on the path. G'rig didn't need to know of her father and his visions. Of her lack of place, especially now that she was no longer heir to the Pantheran throne. He didn't need to know that she asked for nothing and only obeyed. And how tired she was of receiving nothing in return. Her hands gripped tighter on Home's reins as the difficulty of her journey sank in. It would have been better had she gone with Danon, like Viktor told her too.

Viktor.

"The men I spoke with in Grumbling, they say Viktor fought with his brother and stole his sword before fleeing towards Wilsden. How true are their words?"

The thought that G'rig would lie to her didn't cross her mind. She knew he wouldn't.

"True enough."

"Why would he do that?" Cecelia asked.

She knew her husband enjoyed fighting. But there was a distinct purpose in his fight with his brother. Viktor left the palace with something in mind, some goal. Cecelia needed to know what it was.

G'rig, though, only laughed. "I thought you knew our man better than that. He's always down for a good fight. Especially one with Von. Vik has probably been dreaming about decking his brother for years."

"Von," Cecelia said his name slowly. "Do you know the family well, G'rig?"

G'rig shrugged. "As well as a Fair Folkman cares to know a Korithian family. The House of Black is great in name. Perhaps once in character too when Ephram was alive."

"The brother that died during the rebellion?"

"The same," G'rig said. "Viktor worshiped him. Von, as second born, was a dirtsack. Arlo was the third brother and, therefore, inconsequential. And Viktor, well, he was born early and marked by that red. Whispers abounded about it being a mark of His Brilliance."

Cecelia scoffed. "But it's untrue. It's just a birthmark. My great grandfather possessed such a mark."

G'rig shrugged. They had arrived at the archway and halted their horses. The darkness within seemed to grow, reaching for them, but Cecelia knew it was merely a trick of her eyes in the dark. She shut them tight and opened them again, willing them to adjust.

"Humans are superstitious and stupid," G'rig concluded. "My family traveled through the Black's lands often enough to learn that Viktor was an unhappy child. Many things contributed to that unhappiness. People, mostly. Lord Black and Von the most."

G'rig dismounted and suggested Cecelia do the same. With her feet planted firmly on the rocky path, she could feel the power of the falls beneath her feet. Power like that, unbridled and raw, made her feel sick. She grabbed her stomach and took several deep breaths, begging the nausea to leave her.

"Are you alright?" G'rig asked.

"Fine," she spoke into Home's neck, "fine."

She peered ahead and examined the archway. Runes covered the arch, each one beautifully finished. Cecelia dragged her hand along them, feeling the etchings, knowing they were carved hundreds of years earlier.

"So why would Viktor want Von's sword?"

"Ephram's sword," G'rig said, "he wants Ephram's sword. Ephram was a hero to him. No doubt the sword represents some sort of romantic notion inside your husband's head."

Cecelia considered whether Viktor was capable of having a romantic notion.

"Your husband was a broken child, pawdwyn. Lord Black made sure of that." G'rig said.

He hesitated, preparing to say more, before changing his mind. He turned and pushed past Cecelia and stepped through the archway, disappearing into the darkness.

"This way," he called. "The darkness will swallow you once you step through but is lighted on this side."

Cecelia did not hesitate. She stepped through the darkness, not knowing what to expect, but refusing to be afraid. After the icy shower of the falls, it surprised her to find something colder. The darkness ran across her skin and froze her, cutting through to the bone. Her cheeks burned and her lips felt like they would burst. But then she was through, standing beside G'rig, and the pain dissipated.

"You did well," G'rig said, "most humans find magic exceptionally painful. Must be that half-blood of your mother."

Cecelia glared at G'rig. "I hate liars, G'rig." She growled.

G'rig shrugged. "I only speak what the Prevailing Mother speaks. She is truthful. She knows no other way."

"Aye, and the Fair Folk take no sides," Cecelia drawled.

She pushed past him and stepped closer to the rocky ledge. Before her, a great cavern unfolded. A giant barreled ceiling played host to thousands of soft glowing worms. Far below, a river flowed, its noise echoing up the chamber in eerie song.

"An underground river," Cecelia said.

"The Hidden Way," G'rig answered. "Korithians have no knowledge of how extensive it is. The Fair Folk usually use it for fast travel across the kingdom. But lately," he suggested to the many Fair Folk sitting around, preparing weapons and gear.

Cecelia knew what they were doing. She'd done it countless times herself.

"You're mobilizing an army."

Wilyna of Wilsden was a half-blood. Her father, whom she never met, was a Folkman and her mother was Korithian. Because relationships with Fair Folk were frowned upon, Wilyna's mother kept her daughter's magical aptitude a secret, making the young sorceress promise to tell no one about her powers. The girl proved to be rather adept at channeling the spirit of the forests around their home, allowing her to find and source the ingredients her mother used for poultices, ointments, and medicines that she sold at market. After her mother's death, Wilyna capitalized on her power, selling her services to local villagers. It was while working in the forest she stumbled upon the Crown Prince Jepsuth II, lost from his hunting party, and sealed her fate.

Didymus Hargrove
Walking Trees and Other Fables

> *She loved him well, the prince so fine*
> *But she could never call him*
> *'mine.'*

Tova Whispers, Korithian Bard
The Witch's Woe

Chapter Thirty-Two

It didn't take Viktor long to figure out what the other creature was. Wolves have a very low tolerance for other animals. Monsters, even less. But the barghest had ingratiated itself with the wolves somehow and ran among them like it was one of them.

Its black body was sinewy and thin, with fangs that dripped saliva. Viktor scowled. It was an ugly creature.

"Well, Kitty," Viktor said, only realizing too late that Kitty was nowhere to be seen.

"I hate cats," he growled to himself.

He had dismounted and let his horse go while still traversing the field. The horse would be a distraction for the animals, sure, but Viktor rather liked the horse and hoped he'd survive the barghest encounter to recover his ride. Approaching on foot, the wolves retreated to the wood line, leaving the barghest to confront the large man.

"They'll make you do the work," Viktor said to the creature, "and then they'll feast on my body when you're done with it. Is that it?"

The creature growled and dug its long claws into the moss-covered earth. Black, reflectionless eyes stared back at him. They reminded Viktor of holes. Deep, dark holes dug into the earth, their depth so unforgiving that sunlight couldn't even make it to the bottom.

Like the pit Von had left Viktor in when he was but a boy of eight.

He tightened his grip on his sword and gritted his teeth. Thinking of Von made him angry, but perhaps anger was what he needed. The beast snarled and lunged. Viktor barely had time to sidestep, bringing the sword slashing downward. Too late. The beast was nowhere beneath the blade. Instead, it crawled in a circle around him, taking its time, figuring him out.

"Take all the time you need," Viktor breathed heavily already. "I've got all night."

The creature roared again and ran at Viktor once more. Only this time it feigned left. Viktor sidestepped the wrong way, and the beast barreled into his knees. The force was immense. The pain that followed unimaginable. Viktor crumpled, his breath catching in his chest. His palms bit into the ground.

He searched frantically for the barghest, only to eye it turning around on its run and barreling back toward him. With mere seconds to spare, he rolled onto his back and avoided getting knocked over again. The animal's claws dug into Viktor's armor, grating against the plate, searing the sound into Viktor's ears.

It jumped onto Viktor's chest, giant forepaws searching for any crevice it could find. Saliva from its snarling mouth dripped onto Viktor's face.

Sharp rocks strewn amongst the moss dug into the back of Viktor's head, and his knee bloomed with pain. It was the moment he knew would one day come, though he had never imagined it'd end with a barghest on his chest.

But suddenly the beast ceased its snarling. It peered past the top of Viktor's head, its eyes tracking something. It growled, though less in rage and more in fear, the sound rumbling from dep within its chest. Viktor couldn't move, couldn't see what the barghest gazed at, but he could hear something moving amongst the trodden grass at the edge of the field.

A hiss came, followed by a deep mewl. The barghest trembled. Before he lost his chance, Viktor pried his dagger from his belt and carefully prepared to stab the beast. The barghest lurched, attempting its retreat, so Viktor thrust upward into the chest.

A piercing howl erupted from its mouth. It jumped off Viktor and stumbled toward the tree line, drops of scarlet left behind. But it didn't make it far. It collapsed beneath an ancient oak, its body convulsing once and then nothing.

Viktor turned to find Kitty sitting in the grass. She cleaned her paw, but meowed at him when he looked at her.

"Cat," Viktor muttered.

He stood and wiped forest debris from his pants. Viktor approached the barghest slowly and kicked it once, but he needn't worry. The beast was dead. He eyed the wolves pacing in the forest. They seemed just as frightened of Kitty as the barghest had. He sighed before going to work, relieving the barghest of its head. When he walked back towards the field, his shoulders heavy and his knee screaming with pain, he tipped his head to Kitty.

It surprised the farmer to find Viktor returned, and so soon. He stared at the barghest's head and scuttled backwards when Viktor tossed it at his feet.

"You... you did it," the farmer squatted down to examine the creature's fangs.

"Yes. Now, about that room. And a meal."

Kitty encircled herself around Viktor's legs. The farmer's eyebrows pulled down and he frowned.

"Yes, right. This way then." The farmer picked up the beast's head.

The modest inn wasn't as modest as Viktor imagined. Inside, there was ample room for several traveling parties. A few groups already filled the cavernous drinking hall, but moved aside when the farmer pushed through with the barghest head held out in front of him like a talisman.

"This here traveler killed the beast that's terrorized our village for some time!" He crowed, frightening a woman with the lurch of the head.

"A barghest," someone muttered, "hasn't been one of those around in ages."

The farmer slammed the head on the bar top. The barmaid, a burly woman who possessed her own long sword mounted behind her on the wall, seemed unamused.

"What am I supposed to do with that?" She said.

"Mount it, throw it in a pot for stew," the old farmer said. "I don't care. But this man is a hero, and a hero deserves vittles."

"And a bed," Viktor muttered.

"And a bed!" the farmer added.

Viktor thought it impossible, but the barmaid frowned deeper.

"You paying for it, Argus?"

The farmer, Argus, hesitated. He eyed Viktor and then the barghest before nodding his head.

"Yes, Helyna, I am. And you can tell that to Gummer."

"You know as well as anyone, Argus, Gummer takes orders from me." Helyna finished drying a glass before turning her attention to the barghest on her bar top.

"Three days," Viktor spoke over Argus' head. "Three days' food and shelter. Me and the cat."

Viktor suggested to Kitty, who had found her way along the many legs of patrons and onto the chair nearest the barmaid.

Helyna glared at Kitty. She stared at her, taking her in, her frown remaining on her face.

"I don't serve her kind here." Helyna removed the barghest and wiped down the counter.

Blood spilled over the edge and dripped onto the packed dirt floor. Kitty leaped to the ground and lapped it up.

Viktor, attempting to hide his disgust, leaned into the bar. "People keep saying that, but I just see a cat. If it weren't for the damned thing, I'd be dead and your barghest would still be terrorizing your flocks."

"Not my flocks," Helyna sneered. "Do I look like a shepherd?"

"Your patrons do," Viktor said, "and if that beast killed their livelihood, there goes your modest inn."

Helyna gazed at Viktor over the stein she cleaned. Her dimpled chin moved with her lips and her oak-colored eyes hinted at amusement. She finally nodded her head, agreeing to Viktor's terms.

"You're a mighty big man to have such a companion," Helyna poured Viktor a drink and suggested with her head to Kitty.

Viktor, relieved he'd be allowed to stay, slumped down on the nearest stool. He glanced down at Kitty, still drinking the pooled blood, and nodded.

"She followed me from Wilsden," he said. "Whole village said she'd been there forever. Never seen her leave."

Helyna stopped pouring. "Wilsden? You should have said so."

She leaned over the bar, her ample bosom impeding her progress some, to peer down at the cat.

"Wilyna the Witch, most likely," she said.

Kitty mewed at her and continued drinking.

Argus laughed and spat in the dirt next to Kitty. "Wilyna's been dead for over two hundred years," he said.

"Wilyna?" Viktor asked.

Helyna glared at Argus as she began her tale, daring him to interrupt. "An enchantress that lived in Wilsden. A diviner. Good at finding things."

"Yeah, they said Kitty was good at finding things," Viktor said, but upon the look from Helyna, he took a large swig of beer and remained silent.

"She was good. So good, until she found herself in love."

"With who?" Viktor, impatient, forgot how sharp Helyna's glare was.

"The Crown Prince," Helyna said matter-of-factly. "He refused her, and she fell into a deep sadness. Useless after that. Rumor was she killed herself, but no one really knows, only that she disappeared into the misty moors down by Wilsden."

"Disappeared?" Viktor muttered.

He glanced down at Kitty, curled up beneath his feet, asleep.

"Or maybe she found a better way."

Salyana Suu'thani was a General of the Fair Folk army, commanding its ranks from the beginning of the Year of Chaos to nearly the end. She met her demise at the hands of Grand Marshal Viktor Black in the waters of the Gallenchyl. She underestimated the Grand Marshal's ability to strategize, not knowing he had the river prepped prior to battle to be lit on fire. A lesson he learned from his brother Ephram's death.

Logician Yesmin Croany
　Chronicles of Chaos: People and Events Held Responsible

Chapter Thirty-Three

The Fair Folk were, if nothing else, efficient. They kept their gear and weapons within a black pack, the weight of which Cecelia could only imagine. The fabric itself was woven with expert hands. Black flowers trimmed the edges: iris, pansy, viola. Cecelia remembered Danica's dress and started to wonder.

Each Fair Folk, whether woman or man, could disassemble and assemble their gear back into the pack. Weapons of scythes and stilettos were lashed to the bags while swords and bows were kept on the body. The children sharpened. Anything and everything. Fair Folk would approach a child, pale hued hair kneeled at a whetstone, and watch the miniature being go to work. The weapon always came back gleaming. Swords that could slice a hair. Arrows that could punch through the toughest of armor.

"This is well organized," Cecelia said.

G'rig led her through the maze of soldiers. "A little unknown trait of the Fair Folk: we enjoy organization. Within our homes, within our caravans, and within our armies."

G'rig smiled pleasantly at her, but Cecelia refused to return it.

"It means you've been preparing for this coup for a while," Cecelia stopped and faced the Folkman. "Danica told me Mother Oora approached her before her marriage to Ramiro, but this looks much more complicated, G'rig. This looks like it's been mapped out for years."

G'rig shrugged.

"There is more to this than you're letting on." She stared out across the gaping floor at the rushing water beneath. "There's more you're not telling me. Does Danica know?"

"And what do you care if she doesn't?" A voice cut across the cavern.

Cecelia turned toward the voice to find a stocky, purple-haired Folkwoman approaching. She wore a blackwood bow across her back and had painted her eyes black to match.

"Salyana," G'rig tipped his head curtly at the woman, "I've retrieved the Prevailing Mother's prize."

"I'm nobody's prize," Cecelia sneered.

Salyana smirked. "No, I wouldn't call you a prize either. But Mother Oora has got it in her head you are her blood, and blood does not abandon blood."

Salyana studied Cecelia, her eyes settling on the ring she wore from Viktor.

"So it is true," Salyana said, "you are wed to Kith d'noir."

"Yes," Cecelia said, "though I don't see why that matters."

Salyana shrugged. "It doesn't. The House of Black has left its poisonous stain upon this land for generations. I pity you."

"I don't need your pity."

"No, you don't," Salyana seemed pleased. "Call me Sal, for Salyana was my grandmother's name, and I prefer not to feel an old woman. Yet."

Sal crossed her arms and squared off toward Cecelia. The Fair Folkwoman, though short in stature, was clearly not one to mess with. Cecelia compared her to the axe hurlers in the Dry Vineyard, their stature being much shorter than the rest of the Lagos.

Though still just as deadly.

A vibrant red peeked out beneath the shortened sleeves of Sal's tunic, ink embedded in the skin of her arm. A tattoo. It swirled in patterns only the Fair Folk knew. Patterns that told of days long gone. Sal noticed Cecelia's stares and turned away, toward the shadows.

"You'll not last long looking at us like that," Sal said.

"Like what?"

"Like creatures in some king's menagerie. We are not animals, pawdwyn. We are the land itself."

"The pawdwyn cares little for our... what did you call it?" G'rig spoke. "Grievances? She is an islander and feels she is exempt from caring."

Sal snorted, a quick burst of laughter filling the cavernous room. "Exempt?" She said. She tilted her head to the side, her lips curling in a unpleasant smile. "No one is exempt. Our story is the story of the many before us. Of the many after us. Its the story of your mother, fleeing a continent that hated her, only to find a patch of islands that hated her just as much."

Cecelia felt the heat beneath her skin before she realized how angry she was. It flooded across her cheeks and chest. Her hands clenched and unclenched, itching for a fight. She estimated how hard she'd have to hit Sal to make her fly backwards into the echoing cavern below. But sensing her thoughts, Sal stepped backward, away from the danger, still smiling.

"No wonder you make a good match, you and Kith d'noir. I'm surprised your aura is not as black as his," she said.

G'rig's face twitched as Sal's words. He fidgeting with the sleeves of his tunic, smoothing and resmoothing the edges. The sudden change in his countenance perplexed Cecelia, who looked from the Folkman to Sal and back again.

"Why am I here?" She asked.

"As G'rig said," Sal spoke but turned toward the rushing waters below, "Mother Oora wanted you retrieved. She wants you kept safe."

"From what?"

Sal smiled up at the glow worms. The green light fell oddly upon her hair, shifting the color, making it putrid and less beautiful.

"From the war to come," Sal finally looked back at Cecelia, "from the wreckage we are to bring upon all of Korith."

Her anger subsided, a chill fled across Cecelia's flesh as her father's words came to life. Goosebumps rose along her arms where it was only recently burning. She shivered. A darkness that brewed over Korith. What could be darker than an army of Fair Folk, organized, angry, and empowered by their Prevailing Mother? Her stomach ached deep within itself. She clutched it and forced herself to fight through the nausea she felt.

Sal watched Cecelia, nodding knowingly, but said nothing. She distracted herself with observing her troops. There was an ease about the general. It was a worn feeling, and Cecelia felt she was meant to be there.

But that didn't mean she liked it.

"What will you do with me?" Cecelia asked. "Keep me trapped beneath the ground in this giant sarcophagus?"

Sal frowned. "The Hidden Way is sacred. Consider yourself blessed, human, to have seen in." She kicked a rock over the edge, sending it hurtling down to the river. "You aren't a prisoner. You may go where you like. With protection."

G'rig nodded his head. "The Prevailing Mother commanded me to find you. I will keep you safe."

Cecelia considered her options. She could go home. Mother Oora would surely not deny her that request. But as soon as the thought entered her head, she knew it couldn't be so. She still yearned for Viktor. She still yearned to know where he was and know that he was safe.

For even though he abandoned her, it may not have been his fault. Perhaps Viktor never learned how to love.

Or how to grow.

"I want to find my husband," Cecelia said, "Kith d'Noir. Some in Grumbling say he headed towards Wilsden, probably towards the mountain pass and then,"

"The sea," Sal finished for her. "He's running."

"Pfft," G'rig spat, "Vic doesn't know how to run from a fight. He usually starts them."

"Not from a fight," Sal suggested to Cecelia. "From her."

Cecelia's hands clenched into fists. This time Sal stood staunchly, prepared for a fight.

"We'll find him," G'rig interjected, stopping their fight before it could begin, "I know the way well enough."

"Fine," Sal said, "take two more. Ansa and Tra'lo. Both are good. Both will keep you alive."

G'rig bowed his head quickly and backed away, calling to his sister and brother in arms. They were not far away, discussing shooting techniques with their bows in an alcove decorated in luminescent moss. Sal and Cecelia watched him go.

"Will you kill her?" Cecelia asked, still watching G'rig approach the short archers with their bows.

"Who?" Sal drawled.

"Danica," Cecelia turned to face her, "with this war. Will you kill her?"

Sal shrugged. "That is for Mother Oora to decide. The queen seems docile enough. Perhaps Mother Oora will show pity."

"She is nearly a child," Cecelia spoke, "barely of age."

"She's nearly one and twenty," Sal said, "not a baby, Kith d'Mun."

Cecelia grabbed Sal by the wrist and squeezed. "Leave her be," she said. "She is ambitious, true. No woman should be punished for ambition. Leave her be."

Sal glared at Cecelia, but the longer Cecelia squeezed, the more relaxed Sal's face grew. Finally, she nodded her head.

"I will speak to Mother Oora when the time comes."

Cecelia released Sal. "Thank you."

"I won't do it for you. I'll do it for her. For as you say, no woman should be punished for her ambition."

A witch or wizard is a Halfling. One parent descends from the magic baring Fair Folk while the other is human. The child's power is usually less potent than their Fair Folk ancestors, though anomalies do occur. The greatest, and most corrupt, Halfling was Lady Rusalia. She terrorized the continent during the reign of King Vroshun, enchanting men into loving her only to eat their heart when she was finished. The great lords begged Vroshun to do something, so the king mounted an attack against Lady Rusalia. Cornered between the king's army and the tumultuous sea, Rusalia cast a most powerful spell and walked across the water, away from the continent, forever.

Court Historian Alfred Peri
   The Scroll of Children: A Collected History of the Fair Folk

Chapter Thirty-Four

Fear. That was the name of the village Viktor saved. It hadn't always been so, but the locals had lived with the monster long enough to forget the real name. So they made up a new one.

Some locals, the older generation, often called it Fearing. Either way, Viktor soon learned how great a favor he did for the village.

That first night, Helyna found her way to his room. She assured him she just wanted to thank him for what he had done. He assured her it wasn't necessary. He watched her descend the stairs, each footfall announcing his rejection of her, and found himself missing Cecelia. He'd forgotten her, for a time, and felt lighter for that moment. But it came crashing back, like the dip in his adrenaline after the fight with the monster, reminding him quick fixes didn't exist. He'd carry this weight with him forever. He'd carry the thought of her to the grave.

Like a tattoo upon his skin, she was a part of him.

Argus appeared at his side in the morning. A new companion he didn't need. He slapped Viktor on the back, or as close as he could get, and ordered breakfast. A small girl approached, bearing a ribbon tied into a flower.

"For the cat," she said, her voice barely audible behind her scarlet cheeks, "she... she helped, didn't she?"

Viktor took the ribbon and nodded.

"She's a witch, ain't she?" Another smaller, though clearly less afraid, girl asked.

"Course she is," said a third, "see her eyes. Only witches have eyes like that."

Viktor turned to study Kitty as finely as the children did. Her eyes didn't seem out of the ordinary. At that moment, almond-shaped pupils sat inside apple green eyes and stared back at the children. Her tail twitched back and forth while she watched them, head tilted slightly to the side.

"I think she's just a cat." Viktor turned back to them.

The smaller girl shook her head. "No, lord knight. My ma says barghests are afraid of witches because they can use their power to bring the beasts back to the darkness."

"And *my* ma says cats are keepers of the darkness, and that's why the barghest was afeared!" The third girl argued.

Argus chuckled behind Viktor. He sat on the stool next to him, enjoying the dry bread Helyna had brought to dip in their eggs.

"Whatever she is," Argus said with a mouth full, "it changes not your chores. Ladies, good day."

The girls all frowned three identical frowns, nodded their heads respectfully at Viktor, and sulked away.

Viktor turned to the old farmer. "I don't see it," he suggested to Kitty.

The cat made herself comfortable wherever she went. She snuggled into a pot Helyna had left to dry and stared at patrons. Some giggled. Some ignored her completely. But try as he might, Viktor couldn't see how Kitty was anything but a cat. A stupid cat, but a cat.

Argus shrugged. "The cat is strange, that is sure. But, Wilyna is dead."

Viktor nodded in agreement and tore into another hunk of dry bread. He chewed and stared at Kitty, watching her doze.

"And if she were," he spoke with mouth full, "why would she leave Wilsden with me?"

Argus sighed and took the last piece of bread. "Who knows why women do anything, lord knight?"

With breakfast finished, the pair stood to leave. Viktor didn't know what he planned on doing, but it seemed Argus planned on doing it with him. Suddenly, the door slammed open and shut and someone stepped into the inn.

Their regal looking cloak was soaked and their boots dripped mud. The rain had begun early in the dawn, tap tapping on the roof above Viktor's room. It was not a day for riding, unless important business was at hand. The traveler removed their hood. Sandy hair fell to her shoulders and Viktor felt his stomach lurch. But it was for nothing. The woman smiled at someone behind him and passed with all but a nod of her head. Her eyes weren't even gray, but brown.

"You alright?" Argus asked.

"Fine. Why?" Viktor growled, shoving past patrons on his way back to his room.

"You look like you've seen a ghost."

Later that night, while he lay in bed, he considered what he would have done had the woman been Cecelia. Would he run to her and grasp her? Would he kiss her so hard he'd inhale her? Or would he back away, searching for an escape?

Again.

Water dripped in the room's corner. The drip-drip-dripping ate through Viktor's mind, clouding his thoughts. He grew hot. Angry. He couldn't think. Every time he thought of her, he grew afraid. Afraid of what, he didn't know. It was like she was a ceramic bowl, and he didn't want to drop her. But he was a clumsy child, or so his father always said, and he knew he'd drop her, eventually.

And he couldn't bear the fallout.

She deserved much better. She deserved a choice. Viktor remembered what she'd told him that first night as husband and wife. He remembered what she gave up.

She deserved to be queen.

He slammed his fist into the wall. Blood crept from his knuckle where it nicked the wood. The scarlet on his skin gave him pause for thought. He was always wrecking things. People, mostly, but he had done his share of vandalism. Von, most recently. Cecelia, eventually.

Viktor swung his legs over the edge of the bed and sat up. He squeezed his hands together so tightly the knuckles turned white and blood poured from the wound on his hand. A spike of His Brilliance's ring stabbed Viktor's opposite hand, causing more blood to pour.

"Damn." He ripped the ring from his finger and threw it across the room.

The pain was instantaneous. A white hot that he was unaccustomed to. He'd taken enough punches to grow numb towards the blunt force of someone else's fist. And at last count, he'd taken nine stab wounds in his life. Those, while painful, did not rip through his body like the ring had. It caught fire in his hand but quickly crept up his arm, his back, and his neck.

"There has to be a better way," he said to himself.

Blood dripped onto the wood slatted floor and seeped between the cracks. He'd do it differently this time. He had to.

He limped to the door, a trail of blood drops left behind. He'd need paper and ink. If he wrote Cecelia a letter to let her know where he was going and to meet him there, she'd come. She'd have to come.

Surely she'd come?

He stopped at the top of the stairs. He remembered the way her body reached for his and the way she looked at him with those stormy, gray eyes.

She'd come.

The Fair Folk possess no creation story. For as long as their history tells, they have always been on the great continent, occupying the same land as what would later be Korith. There are certain caves, hidden amongst the mountains and unknown to Korithians, that the Fair Folk maintain as their temples. Within them, ancient wall writings depict the Fair Folk sprouting from trees. Archaic runes, once written in mud but transformed to stone, tell of a people in love with a power gifted them by an unknowable, earthly entity.

Court Historian Alfred Peri
   The Scroll of Children: A Collected History of the Fair Folk

Chapter Thirty-Five

"How do they work?" Cecelia gazed up at the glowing worms on the ceiling.

Their haze settled over them, tricking the brain, making one think the light was warmer than it was. She sat in the middle of a small wooden raft, manned on either side by Ansa and Tra'lo, who she learned were twins. The pair were short and stocky, but strong, much stronger than Cecelia. Perhaps even Viktor. They rowed the boat effortlessly, maneuvering it from one side of the river to the other around obstacles Cecelia had yet to see.

"Haven't the slightest," G'rig grinned at her, "but they've been doing it for centuries."

"Is there anything else living in these caves?" She peered at the water over the side of the boat.

Once they had left the large, barreled ceiling cavern with its torches and braziers, the only thing left to light their way were the worms. The water transformed from blue to icy green. The temperature dropped substantially. Cecelia wrapped her arms around herself but forced her body not to shiver.

"Ic'i pawdwyn," Tra'lo laughed.

The Fair Folk wore their traditional garb. Cotton pants adorned with embellished hems. Long-sleeved tunics beneath leather vests. They were less dressed like soldiers than market goers. Cecelia imagined they were used to the chill but frowned at Tra'lo anyway. She didn't need to speak their tongue to know he poked fun at her.

"He says you're cold," G'rig explained.

"So I gathered," Cecelia growled. "Na ic'i." She lied.

Tra'lo nodded his head, impressed. "Pawdwyn pral'a Earthwen?"

G'rig shook his head no at Tra'lo.

"Na pral'a. Brant'o." He said.

Cecelia waited patiently for G'rig to translate. He had performed this duty diligently enough since boarding the boat. It neither seemed to annoy him nor please him to do it. He simply did.

"He asked if you spoke the ancient tongue. I told him you're just smart."

"Earthwen," Cecelia said, "is that what you call it? What does it mean?"

"It is hard to explain in Korithian," G'rig leaned lazily back on the rudder, allowing Ansa and Tra'lo to do most of the work, "even harder in the tongue of the Lagos."

"Ah, but I am brant'o, remember?" She smiled. "Try me."

G'rig smiled back. "Earthwen means... of the earth. Not child, not Kith. But... a part of. We are the earth. The ground. This... place."

Cecelia nodded. Viktor told her they were a people of the continent, having claimed the land for thousands of years, long before Korith existed. Practiced travelers, they stayed nowhere longer than necessary. Cecelia wondered why they never thought to leave Korith, the continent, behind them. Especially when they were turned into outcasts. Especially when the world grew strange but dared to call them stranger.

Her mother had left. Or so they kept telling her. She peered at G'rig through the darkness, trying to remember any detail of her mother's face that could prove she was a Fair Folk. G'rig's eyes glowed as they did in the forest. Like a lantern in a window, they seemed to call to her, comforting her just as much as they disoriented her. But her mother's eyes never glowed. They had been gray, like Cecelia's, and just as stormy her father liked to say.

"Why does Mother Oora think I'm her blood?" Cecelia interrupted the cool darkness, her words slicing over the sound of the oars cutting through rapids.

G'rig stared at her as if he didn't hear.

Cecelia tried again. "Sal didn't seem convinced. But Mother Oora... she seems certain. Did you know my mother? Did you know Amara?"

The Fair Folkman ran his fingers through his hair. Even beneath the glow of the worms it shimmered, perhaps more so than in the sunlight. Cecelia fought the sensations the Fair Folk brought with them, the sense of enchantment and their magic, with every breath she took. But she could not deny their beauty.

Ansa and Tra'lo had made it obvious his steering skills weren't needed. G'rig shuffled forward and sat next to her on the bench. Her body instantly warmed with his closeness, another effect of G'rig's magic. He leaned back on his hands and stared up at the worms.

"I knew Amara."

"And?"

G'rig sighed. "I don't know. Amara is a Fair Folk name, true enough, but there are many names the Korithians have adopted. The ancient Queen Bressa was named after the Prevailing Mother who predicted her birth to the barren Korithian queen."

"You're not convinced either," Cecelia said. "That makes two of us."

"I didn't say that." G'rig said. "I knew Amara. She was smart. And powerful. If anyone could escape Korith and make it to the Lagos, it would be her."

"I have no power," Cecelia argued, "wouldn't I have inherited some of that Fair Folk magic you're all showing off?"

G'rig glared at Cecelia. He watched her a moment before peering back up at the worms.

"Halflings don't always have magic. It depends."

"On what?"

"Many things. Strength of power in the family line. What you're breeding with. Sometimes it's just random."

"Random," Cecelia repeated.

Nothing was ever random. Her father taught her that.

"So, what I gather from you," Cecelia said, "is that regardless if it's true or not, I should just enjoy Mother Oora's gracious favoritism?"

G'rig shook his head. "Sounds good to me."

"But that doesn't answer *my* question," she argued. "Pretending my mother was Fair Folk born does not actually mean she was. It makes me no closer to knowing the truth of my mother's origins."

"Origins are simple," G'rig said. "From the earth we come and to the earth we go. We are simultaneously everyone before us and after us at once. It matters not where your mother hailed from. She is within you. You are present. *You* are all that matters."

Cecelia shook her head. "No. I do not make purchase of your earth worship. There is a purpose. The Mother makes it so. I just have to figure it out."

"I will not argue religion with you," G'rig said, "it is like arguing with children, and it bores me."

Cecelia's scathing retort caught in her throat. The boat rocked a little too hard. Until that moment, the rapids had moved the boat through the water, shifting it either way. But never violently. The boat thudded again, this time rocked even harder. G'rig spoke rapidly to Ansa and Tra'lo, who threw down their oars and took out their bows.

"What's going on?" Cecelia asked.

G'rig squatted close to Cecelia, gazing into the darkness of the cavern, dagger in hand.

"Earlier you asked if other things lived in these caves," G'rig said.

The boat shook violently again. Ansa pointed behind Tra'lo and yelled, the ancient tongue too quick for Cecelia to follow. It was noise. All of it was noise.

"You're about to find out."

And the Mother, her hands the tides that shape our land, thusly influences us. Let us happily give our thanks within our holy founts, praying that the Mother–and the Daughter in her turn–continue to help shape and mold us into beings worthy of their love.

An Unnamed Priest
   Sermon Notes

Chapter Thirty-Six

On Viktor's third day in Fear, Argus told him he'd better prepare himself to leave.

"But I like it here," Viktor leaned into the bar top, sipping his ale, "perhaps I'll stay."

Argus glanced at Helyna. The woman busied herself with cleaning. He fiddled with his hat, taking great pains to avoid Viktor's eyes.

"Argus," Viktor finally said, "spit it out, for Moon Mother's sake. You're making me nervous."

"Well, Viktor," Argus finally said, "truth is, word arrived from the capital last night."

"Word? What word?" Viktor sipped loudly.

"Well, there's a warrant out for the arrest of the Royal Guard Marshal. And that's... well that's,"

"Me, yes I get it Argus, no need to trip on the words."

Viktor said nothing more. He drank his beer, allowing Argus to stand awkwardly and watch him. Kitty slept in a breadbasket nearby, courtesy of the local baker's daughter. When he finished, he slid the glass to Helyna and motioned that he'd have another.

"I saved you all from a barghest." Viktor clasped his hands together and stared at them, admiring how his knuckle healed, but the stab wound from the ring did not.

"Yes, but," Argus stuttered.

"But what?" Viktor didn't mean to raise his voice so much, but he was heated. Perhaps he had drunk too much too. Either way.

Argus dropped his hands and sighed. "You're trouble. You're running and we don't want what you're running from to find you here."

Viktor smiled. Then he laughed. Argus imagined he ran from the queen, but the truth was much more complicated. But Argus didn't need to know that. Viktor nodded and shoved the freshly poured beer back to Helyna. He couldn't stay anyway, not after the letter he wrote to Cecelia the night before.

"If that's how you feel, Argus," he stood and turned to the inn full of villagers, "if that's how you all feel, I'll go."

He made a grand show of mounting the stairs and heading to his room. The sleepy town on the mountain had been a needed rest, but truthfully, it bored him. He needed to know what went on in the capital.

Helyna met him at the top of the stairs, eyes moist from tears, though none fell. "Thank you again," she said, "for the barghest."

Viktor nodded his head and tried to shimmy past her onto the landing. She leaned toward him, pinning him against the railing. In her hand she held a small letter, intricately folded in only a way the Fair Folk knew how.

"This arrived for you," she said, "thought you'd like to have it discreetly. What with the problems the Fair Folk seem to stir nowadays."

Viktor took the letter and thanked her. She continued to press him, enjoying the proximity, until he forced his way down the steps. In the main hall, he glanced down to see G'rig's cramped handwriting spell out his name. In Korithian no less. He flipped the note in his hand, but stopped. Last he saw G'rig, the Folkman spoke of revolution. Viktor remembered how smug he had been. How sure of victory.

As he walked past the fire, Viktor tossed the letter in amidst the flames. It popped and sizzled, the magic within dying against the heat. Kitty mewled at him from the hearth. She sat and watched the flames momentarily before following Viktor.

"To the trail," he said to her when she caught up.

She kept her eyes trained ahead, like she could see everything at once. Like most cats naturally could. Like most witches.

A few of the village children waved to him and called to Kitty, but both travelers ignored them. They had eyes only for the road and on what lay ahead. Though Viktor did not know what that would be.

They neared the saddle of the mountain where it kissed the peak next to it. From there, it would be downhill travel to the coast. If Cecelia received his letter, she'd hopefully find her way. If she took a ship, like he suggested, she might even beat him there.

His horse waited for him at the stables on the edge of the village. Kitty led the way and the horse followed without Viktor's need to press her. He sat back in the saddle, allowing the creatures to guide him.

He only tugged on the reins when they were just outside the village. They had rounded a bend in the road and a copse of birch erupted from the typical pine. The stark white trees surrounded the village's Moon Temple, coating the rounded roof in leaves and moss.

The temple was small, though the village did not require a large one. He dismounted, despite Kitty meowing at him from up the road.

"Easy," he called to her. "I just want a look."

But it wasn't the temple itself he wanted to look at. It was the flowers that grew at the archway, a fading pink against the dappled gray of the walls. He extended his hand and stroked the petals. Kitty arrived at his side, sniffing at the plant.

"Bleeding hearts," Viktor said. "My mother liked them. She'd pick them and bring them to the temple for the altar."

Kitty meowed.

"Moon Mother knows why." He stared through the archway at the run-down temple.

Within, the floor sagged where rainwater dripped from the ceiling. Vines broke through the walls and grew along the crown of the room. Nettles pushed up through the soddened floorboards. The altar, a pillar centered inside the prayer circle, was water stained. On top was a bronze bowl, aged and lichen coated, full to the brim with dirty water.

Viktor glanced at Kitty before entering. The floor squelched beneath his feet, but he didn't stop. It smelled of mildew and raspberries, which Viktor noticed grew in the corner. The bleeding heart he had plucked felt soft within his palm. Softer than any flower.

Softer than any heart.

He strode to the altar and looked down at the water within. Others had left their own offerings. Other flowers floated. Small, brilliant-colored pebbles lay in the depths. A golden chain. A pair of pearl earrings.

All for nothing.

Viktor placed the heart on top of the water. It floated there, next to a daisy, like a ship upon the sea. He remembered how often his mother would go to the temple. How often she'd bring the flowers, begging for the Moon Mother to intercede with her husband. To cure his heart of what ailed him. To make him happy. To make him kind.

But you can't cure dirtsacks.

Outside the temple, Kitty waited patiently. She stretched and rubbed up against his legs while he prepared his saddle.

"Enough." He bent down and pet her, realizing he never had before. "Let's get on with it."

The surface tension broke across the bronze bowl, and the bleeding heart sank. Viktor never saw his mother's prayers answered, and he didn't expect to see his own.

*Like the ebb and flow of tides, the river's dangers thus do hide.
Beware the current's undertow, for her creatures lurk below.*

Traditional Fair Folk Song

The Riversnare is thought to be extinct, having been hunted for its scales, which were used for housing shingles. The meat is only semi-edible, needing to be soaked in a salty brine for several nights before cooking. Generally docile, the Riversnare males grow exceptionally violent during mating season. All documented deaths attributed to Riversnares occurred during this time. Rumors abound that the creatures still exist, surviving in the recesses of the earth, where only the Fair Folk dare to go.

Lord Nikolas Farmsmythe
Compendium of Korithian Creatures

Chapter Thirty-Seven

Cecelia's throat burned. There was a weight on her chest, but she couldn't remove it. Then suddenly, she could breathe again. She inhaled quickly and sharply. It was short-lived. She plunged beneath the icy water again, dragged to the shallow river floor and raked along the stones.

When she was brought back up, she felt lightheaded. She prepared herself to die, for if she were slammed beneath the surface again, she knew she wouldn't make it.

Someone called her name. She was certain they were yelling, though it barely sounded like a whisper in her ear. Her body flew and landed on hard ground. Disoriented and with a raging headache, Cecelia attempted to clear her vision and see.

See, Armsman Brody's voice rang through her head, *see what is before you, Cecelia. What is there and what isn't.*

She squeezed her eyes hard and opened them again. It burned to breathe, but she forced herself to inhale and exhale slowly, making herself calm. She had been ten and six when submitted to the Trial of the Thoughtful

Warrior. Only ten and six when she was force-fed hallucinogenic herbs and told to fight.

This was nothing. This was fatigue and darkness. What was there was real. Whatever was there can be killed.

She groped for her sword, thankfully still firmly stuck in its scabbard. As her eyes adjusted, she could see movement. Ansa and Tra'lo stood on the capsized boat, firing arrow after arrow. G'rig was nowhere to be seen, but Cecelia could hear him. Her eyes trailed over the cavernous river, following the sounds of his voice.

Finally, she saw it. A monstrous creature, three times the size of the boat, lumbering back and forth in the water fighting G'rig. The Fair Folkman stabbed with his dagger, fighting off the creature's many arms. Arrows landed all around him, hitting their target but bouncing off.

The beast bellowed when an arrow of Ansa's struck one of its many giant eyes. It thrashed its arms angrily, threatening to send G'rig beneath the water's surface. Cecelia took a deep breath and screamed.

"Here!" she yelled at the beast. "Here, you ugly river trash!"

Several eyes turned towards her. They were as large as wagon wheels, and luminous, casting an oddly moonlike glow over the river.

"Cecelia!" G'rig called to her. He fought to free himself from the many legs but got tripped up. "Cecelia no!"

The animal reached for her. She swung at the sharp suckered arm, severing it and sending it sinking to the bottom of the river. It screeched again, shaking the cave, sending rocks and worms tumbling to the water below. A large stone struck Cecelia in the face, scratching her cheek.

"You'll only make it angry!" G'rig yelled.

He had fought his way across the river and climbed the small embankment next to her. He was bleeding from the forehead and his clothes were soaked through.

"What is it?" Cecelia said between heavy breaths.

"A riversnare," G'rig said, "there's only one way to kill it. Beneath the belly there, its body is weakest and thin. If one can strike hard enough, one can penetrate all the way to its heart."

The riversnare sat in the water, its many arms protecting its gray and rubbery scaled body, attempting to keep anyone who dared to find its weakness from reaching it. The arrows Ansa and Tra'lo shot at it did little damage. It was mostly to distract it.

"You'll never get to it by approaching from the front," Cecelia said.

She ran her hands through her wet hair, shoving it out of her face, thinking. If the weakest part was below, there would only be one way.

Cecelia grabbed G'rig by the arm. "Keep distracting it."

"What are you going to do?" He asked her.

She shoved her sword back in its scabbard and pulled a dagger from her boot.

"Cecelia, what are you going to do?" G'rig asked again.

"Distract it, G'rig," she barked at him, "Do as I say!"

She ran towards the edge of the river, and with one final breath, dove. The river was murky thanks to the rock and dirt stirred up by the riversnare's thrashing. Cecelia relied mostly on where she thought the creature was. A heavy leg swept beneath but didn't stop to grab her. She kept swimming, diving deeper toward the bottom of the riverbed. Finally, the glow of the worms disappeared. Something above her blocked out the light.

Nearly out of breath, she swam upward. Her head struck something soft. She reached up to feel with her hands a fleshy underside. Beneath the skin, she felt a heavy beating. Her chest burned and felt like bursting. She couldn't wait any longer. She thrust the dagger upward toward the beating heart, using her other hand to help shove the dagger deeper.

A monstrous scream echoed above the surface. The entire river shook. Cecelia's chest throbbed. It heaved. She felt weak. She released the dagger and sank, letting the river tow her under.

When her eyes fluttered open, it was G'rig's face she saw. He seemed surprised and happy she was awake, but then he seemed angry.

"Stupid, stupid girl," he growled. "You could have gotten yourself killed!"

Cecelia enjoyed the sweet inhalation of air. She closed her eyes again, reveling in the feeling of breathing.

"It was the only thing to do, G'rig," she said with eyes still closed.

"I could've handled it," he said.

"Yes, you seemed to have been doing quite well." Cecelia opened her eyes.

The Fair Folkman stared down at her. His brown eyes twinkled in the cave's darkness. They weren't angry, not entirely. Cecelia thought she saw something there. Something like amusement.

He reached down and helped her sit up, then he sat next to her. The riversnare was upriver. Cecelia realized she must have gone under and floated quite a way before G'rig could retrieve her. Ansa and Tra'lo were righting the boat and bringing it towards them.

"So, glow worms to riversnares. Does it get any worse?" Cecelia asked.

G'rig glanced at her. He seemed unamused, but then a smile broke his face and he started laughing. Cecelia laughed too.

"They are usually not that volatile. Slow, even. But it is mating season and the males are often quite unruly."

He wiped his pink hair away from his face and used his sleeves to dry his eyes.

"You saved us," he said, "and for that we are indebted to you."

Cecelia nodded her head, too tired to argue.

"But I cannot allow you to risk your life for us like that again."

She turned from the river to the Fair Folkman. He wouldn't look at her. Instead, he watched the river flowing past. She could see its reflection in his eyes, blue on brown, a ghostly river.

"Why?" she asked, "because Mother Oora demands it? Would she kill you if something happened to me?"

G'rig shook his head. "No." He pulled his gaze from the river and settled it on Cecelia. "But Viktor would."

Emora sits at the end of the Route of Thieves. The road itself received such a name because an infamous bandit, Dread Rocko, and his gang of riffraff patrolled the road from Emora northward. They seized control of the town, creating a hideout and safe place for those who wished to partake in the darker deeds of life. A city of unimportance, most kings and queens left Emora to its devices. It was King Maurkam who finally had enough, dispatching his army to rid the continent of Dread Rocko. Once dead, the city cleared out most of the hardened criminals. Now, officials are bribed to allow Emora to live on as a city with little control and even less concern for obedience to the law.

Logician Anncept Garoll
   Landcraft: The Relationship of Geography and Economy

Chapter Thirty-Eight

The mountain's downhill trek was arduous. The shale seemed thicker on the other side of the saddle. Viktor feared his horse would slip. He ended up walking her several times. Kitty pranced ahead, afraid of nothing, fearless. She'd stop and prowl the tall grass beneath the trees, returning with an afternoon snack.

"No thanks," Viktor muttered when Kitty offered him a fat vole.

Kitty gulped it down in three bites.

The road followed a small river. Sounds of gurgling water overlay with birdsong and the wind. It wasn't long before Viktor found himself lost in thought. In memories. In dreams.

If he were to do it again, he'd still have left. He squeezed the handle of Ephram's sword. It was too precious a thing to leave in Von's care. But perhaps he would have brought Cecelia with him. Or at least explained himself.

Words. How he hated them. Danica used them superfluously. Ramiro too. General Rees was calculated. G'rig, like most Fair Folk, favored riddles that confused. But his hatred for too much talk started before them. It started when he was a child and his father spoke too loudly, too harshly, too much. When he told Viktor he could be a quiet boy or a dead boy.

Viktor cracked his neck, the tension from the mere thought of his father manifesting itself physically. It wasn't enough that he was dead. Viktor wanted the memories of the man buried, forgotten. But how do you forget someone who is a part of you?

The horse whinnied, pulling Viktor from the hole he thought himself into. Ahead lay a ravine. The stream pooled up there, creating a lake. Beside it was a wagon and an aged man sitting around an empty firepit.

"Aha," the man stood when he saw Viktor. "I prayed to the Moon Mother to send me a savior, and the Moon Mother provided!"

Viktor frowned. "I'm no savior," he said when he arrived before the man. "Just a traveler on his way to Craigburna."

He peered past the man at his wagon. It was covered, akin to the ones the Fair Folk pulled around, though this one was smaller. It relied on only one horse, which was meandering nearby in the weeds. The man seemed alone, so Viktor relaxed a bit.

"Craigburna? Well, wherever you're off to, the Moon Mother sent you this way."

"It's the only road down the mountain," Viktor said.

The man smiled dumbly, undeterred by Viktor's mood. Viktor waited for him to continue, but the old man seemed pleased enough with standing and staring.

"And why," Viktor asked, "do you need a savior?"

"Ah!" The man emerged from his stupor. "For this."

He ran to the firepit and pointed to it. Logs stacked strategically awaited their fiery penance. Watery eyes stared up at Viktor, expecting him to understand.

"That's a mighty fine stack you have there," Viktor said slowly, "but what does it have to do with me?"

"Fire!" the man growled. "I can't make it. Never been good at it."

The old man stood and wiped his hands on his pants, smearing ash down his legs. He marched back to Viktor with his finger pointed.

"You've the mark of a man who'd know how to do that."

Viktor turned the side of his face that bore his birthmark away from the man. "And why do you say that?"

The man pointed to Viktor's sword and then gestured to Viktor in entirety. "Did you not say you were a traveler? A sword carrying traveler. Man like that must have seen some lonely nights on the trail. Reckon he'd have to know how to make a fire. Now do you, or don't you? Otherwise, I have little to offer you but some hard ground to sleep on near my wagon. Reckon you can find that just about anywhere, though."

With hands on hips, the man stared at Viktor, waiting for his answer. Viktor, as per custom, frowned. He glanced at Kitty, who sat on a rock nearby, watching the conversation.

The man followed Viktor's gaze. "Fancy cat," he said.

Viktor grunted in reply.

"Reckon it knows how to make fire?"

"I'll make it," Viktor finally said, "for some food."

The man's smile filled his face. He slapped his hands together and rubbed them thoughtfully.

"Vittles is exactly what I had in mind," he said.

It did not take long for Viktor to get a fire going. The man had all the supplies, just not the know-how. Lucky for Viktor, Ephram taught him how when he was a boy of seven. Their father had taken to blindfolding Viktor, riding him into the middle of the forest, and leaving him to find his own way home. The first time, Ephram found him before he froze to death. He taught Viktor what he needed to know. How to make a fire. How to hunt small animals. How to avoid bigger ones.

The second time, Viktor wandered home in three days. The third, he stayed in the forest for a week before coming home. His mother had been distraught, but Viktor had stopped caring.

"Thank you, sir knight." The old man sat on an upturned log and warmed his hands.

"Viktor," Viktor grumbled, "call me Viktor."

Viktor sat back and leaned against another log. Kitty came to his side and sat, rubbing her head on his knee.

"Zeb," the old man suggested to himself, "old Zeb they call me."

"And who is they?"

It was clear the man was a drifter. Merchants preferred hard-sided wagons to move their goods. Land ferries used open roofed. Zeb's wagon was specifically used by people who expected to always be on the move, to never settle down, to drift endlessly.

Zeb shrugged. "Haven't been home in many moons."

And when Viktor stared, still awaiting an answer to his question, Zeb sighed. "Emora, to the south."

"Emora," Viktor said.

"Now I know what you're thinking. Ain't nothing nice ever came out of Emora."

Viktor smirked. "That's exactly what I was thinking, Zeb."

Zeb picked up a stick and jabbed at the fire. "Well, I could have lied. I could have said I was from Zinco or Trillig or Boast. But I didn't. I told you the truth."

Viktor shrugged. "Even thieves know how to tell the truth when it suits them, Zeb."

Zeb stared at Viktor, stick aloft like a sword. He slowly nodded in agreement.

"You're right, of course," he tossed the stick aside. "But I'm no thief. I was run out."

An impressive feat, considering Emora was a town of low morality and even lower standards.

"You must have been a monster," Viktor joked.

Zeb lost his smile. "Worse. I was in love with a Folkwoman."

It was Viktor's turn to nod in agreement. "I see."

He said nothing more. He returned to his horse and unsaddled her. She meandered over toward Zeb's horse and the pair whinnied at each other. Viktor returned to the fire and sat his saddle down.

Zeb fidgeted with his hands. He twiddled his thumbs, stealing glances at Viktor every now and again.

"What, Zeb?" Viktor finally asked.

"Nothing, Vik, can I call you Vik?" Zeb said, "it's just, when I tell people that part, they usually want nothing to do with me either."

"Do you often tell people that part?"

Zeb thought a moment before shaking his head no. He stared at the fire, thinking. A pained looked filled his face, reliving some past heartbreak. Viktor sighed.

"Look, the only things I care about right now are where my next meal is coming from and making it to Craigburna," Viktor said.

Zeb sat up straighter. His darkening mood lifted. "Well, I said I'd help you with one of those things!"

The Fair Folk favor Tansy wine for its complicated preparation and complex taste. The wine comes and goes out of style with Korithians, though the last surge of popularity stemmed from a fictional story written anonymously. The story told of two lovers, destined to be apart. The lady, rather than live a life heartbroken, drank improperly prepared Tansy wine. The lord, devastated, kissed the last drops from the lady's lips and joined her in death.

Lady Lillyana Fenstock
Herbarium

As he tasted the wine on her lips, he knew that time was fleeting. The Tansy was sweet and tasted of high summer. It reminded him of moments past and moments never to come.

Anonymous Author
Tansy Kiss

Chapter Thirty-Nine

Caves were everywhere amongst the land of Korith. They emerged from the dense, old-growth forests like pockmarks on a man's face. Cecelia was relieved when G'rig finally made them leave the boat and ascend a wooden stairway upward, into the light of day, through one of these caves.

"Where are we?" Cecelia asked.

She bent backwards and peered up at the tall pine before her. It was a giant among giants, clearing the heights of the nearby trees by ten rods, or perhaps twenty.

"Generally or specifically?" G'rig asked. "Generally, just east of Wilsden. Specifically, at the base of Tall Tree, an ancient site of congregation amongst Fair Folk."

"Ingenious name," Cecelia mocked, "never would have guessed."

The pine swayed in its uppermost branches, dancing with the wind. Cecelia tripped over a bare root, thicker than her leg, as she attempted to walk around the tree to get a better look. A hand reached from the dark undergrowth and grabbed her by the wrist.

"The word?" The voice growled.

Cecelia wasted little time. Her other hand snaked its way to her sword and had it halfway withdrawn before G'rig grabbed her, staying her hand.

"En t'ire," G'rig said.

He shoved Cecelia's hand down, forcing her to sheath her weapon. She glared at him, but the voice from the darkness spoke again.

"Ah, faed'wyn G'rig."

"Faed'wyn, Padric'a."

A Folkwoman stepped from the shadows. Her pink hair, the longest Cecelia had seen, was plaited and wrapped around her waist with drops of pearls hanging from each strand. Her golden eyes stared Cecelia up and down, a mischievous smirk ticking up the corner of her mouth.

"En Mun d'Kith," Padric'a said, "tay litto'o."

G'rig smiled amusedly at Padric'a's words. He glanced at Cecelia and then nodded confirmation.

"Na's. Litto'o."

Cecelia thought she saw G'rig's cheeks turn slightly pink, but the shade of the tree obscured what she saw. She looked at Padric'a again. There was something about her that seemed familiar.

"You're family," she finally said.

G'rig nodded his head. "Yes. My younger sister."

Padric'a smiled and patted G'rig on the head. It was choice words that made G'rig call Padric'a younger, for she was not smaller than G'rig. She beat him in height by a hand.

"Come," Padric'a said in a thick Fair Folk accent, "the Prevailing Mother waits."

Cecelia's heart jumped to her throat. She suddenly felt she had walked into a trap.

Beside her, G'rig frowned. "Mother Oora is here?"

Padric'a nodded her head. "And she hates waiting, G'rig."

G'rig sighed and ran his hands through his messy hair. He glanced back at Ansa and Tra'lo before turning back to Cecelia. He awaited her response. She smiled back at him, admiring the way his eyes glimmered, even in the shade. It had taken all her focus to fight the magic the Fair Folk sloughed off like a common person exhales. But she was tired, and a convenient side effect of the magic was feeling rested even when you weren't.

"Shall we?" She smiled.

They followed Padric'a further into the woods. The trees grew thick before vanishing. A clearing was made, cut from the center of the forest by Fair Folk. A large fire burned in the center, and near it, on a tree-branch chair, sat Mother Oora.

G'rig tipped his head to the Prevailing Mother.

"Faed'wyn Mother," G'rig said.

But Mother Oora only had eyes for Cecelia.

"I'm glad you are well, pawdwyn," she said to Cecelia.

Her eyes twinkled with amusement. Cecelia couldn't help but feel like a creature the panthers of the Lagos caught and played with prior to killing them.

"Your people have taken great care of me," Cecelia replied.

"They are your people as much as mine," Mother Oora said.

Cecelia cocked her head. "That I am still uncertain of."

"I'm not," Mother Oora said, "or else I wouldn't be here."

Mother Oora signaled for a Fair Folkwoman to bring them wine. The girl, stout and purple-haired, offered Cecelia a leather wineskin. Cecelia sniffed it. It smelled sharp but pleasant. Mother Oora smiled.

"Why would I kill you now?" She said. "Blood does not abandon blood."

"So I've heard," Cecelia drawled before taking a deep drink of the wine.

It was bitter at first swallow, but then sweetened considerably. Cecelia sucked in her cheeks at the tang of it but went for a second swig. It was unlike any wine she had ever had.

"Do you like it?" Mother Oora asked, accepting the wineskin from Cecelia.

"Delightful," Cecelia wiped her lips on her sleeve, "though I doubt you came here merely to share wine."

Mother Oora swirled the wineskin, smiling to herself. "Tansy wine," she said. "Only the Fair Folk know how to make it. Tansy is highly poisonous otherwise."

Cecelia swallowed hard and tried to smile. Everywhere she went, something was trying to kill her. Mother Oora drank from the wineskin. A droplet escaped from the corner of her mouth and cascaded down her chin. She wiped it away before thrusting the wine to G'rig, who took the offering greedily.

"You are right, of course, dear pawdwyn," Mother Oora said. "I didn't come here to share wine."

She seemed in little hurry to speak on. Cecelia twisted her foot into the soft earth, irritated.

"I seek my husband, Mother Oora, and you detain me. Speak your purpose and let's hope to the Moon Mother it isn't to stop me."

Mother Oora barked a laugh. "I wouldn't dare, pawdwyn. Danica, on the other hand, seems to have regrets."

Mother Oora settled her eyes on Cecelia, their sparkle hinting at her amusement and her magic. Cecelia clenched her teeth. Danica.

"Is she well?" Cecelia asked. "I heard it's hard to survive a stabbing in the back."

Mother Oora shook her head. "You understand little of the continent, pawdwyn. There are things happening, things that have been in motion for years. Since the beginning of our cohabitation with Korithians."

Cecelia rolled her eyes. "Grandiose words for something so simple: betrayal."

G'rig shifted next to her, uncomfortable with the way she spoke to Mother Oora. He glared at her sideways, but she only smiled in return.

"Oh, I'm just getting started, pawdwyn," Mother Oora said. "Once the Unis help secure our victory over Danica and Rees' army, I will share some Tansy wine with them."

She gestured for the wineskin back, which G'rig quickly returned.

"And who is to blame if the wine were prepared improperly? Certainly not I."

She sipped the wineskin. Cecelia felt the heat rising in her throat, but she forced herself to speak.

"You're going to kill them all," Cecelia said quietly, "and take the throne for yourself."

"Not for me, little pawdwyn," Mother Oora snapped, "for us!"

She gestured to the clearing and the multitude of Fair Folk that had emerged from the wisps of mist. Their eyes glowed in the setting sun, creating an awful illusion of predators surrounding their prey. Cecelia shook her head to clear her thoughts.

"I only want to find Viktor," she said. "I'll have no part in your war."

Mother Oora nodded. "That's why I've come. Danica would have retrieved you herself, but I assured her I could convince you to return to Kasier. Though I have no intention of doing so. You'll carry on with G'rig. He'll keep you safe. And out of the way."

G'rig shifted on his feet next to her. Cecelia thought he meant to argue, but he remained mute. He nodded his head dutifully at the Prevailing Mother. Cecelia turned back to Mother Oora.

"You won't even know I'm here."

"Oh, I don't want that," Mother Oora smiled. "I just want you... kept safe until needed."

"Needed?" Of course Mother Oora would have a use for her besides an ornament amongst her family tree. Cecelia knew better.

"I'm waging a war, little pawdwyn. Wars require an army. And ships, if you have them."

Cecelia inhaled deeply. Mother Oora's words did not come as a shock. Ramiro wanted the same from her, too.

"My father will not send them," Cecelia said. "Danon is the heir. He has no need to retrieve his bastard from a far off land."

Mother Oora laughed. It was sharp and ugly and cut through the night air like a knife. "You are a foolish child, pawdwyn, if you think your father does not wish you safe. Does not wish his first grandchild to be safe."

Cecelia pulled her cloak tight around her, protecting her from the gaze of Mother Oora. She was uncertain, but knew deep down that Mother

Oora's words were true. The truth climbed up her throat, filling it, choking her. Cecelia found the nasty words she wanted to speak to the old woman wouldn't form.

G'rig stiffened beside her, stealing his own glance, though there was nothing there for him to see.

"Take her," Mother Oora signaled for G'rig to do something besides stare at Cecelia, "get her out of here. I'll contact your father for you, dear pawdwyn, and share the good news."

G'rig's hand on Cecelia's arm was tight and cold, like a blacksmith's vice. Cecelia tugged away once, ready to argue with Mother Oora, but G'rig yanked her around toward him and shook his head no.

"It isn't worth it," he whispered to her, "not here. Not now."

Cecelia nodded, admitting her defeat, and allowed G'rig to guide her back into the darkness of the forest.

Craigburna is a port town known for its discretion as much as it is for its mermaid sightings. A bronze mermaid fountain, bare-breasted and smiling, sits amidst the town square. Sailors toss coins into the water in hopes of calm seas on their travels. They will also visit Sally's Champagne Palace, rumored to employ several mermaids, before departing in case the seas prove petulant and their breath their last.

Logician Anncept Garoll
   Landcraft: The Relationship of Geography and Economy

Chapter Forty

Viktor walked in the shade of the trees down the mud filled road. He was thankful Zeb had left his boots on when he stole Viktor's things in the middle of the night. But that is where his thanks ended. The old man took Viktor's bags and sword. The sword itself was insult enough, but Zeb also took his horse and saddle. Viktor was left with nothing but what he wore.

Kitty weaved in and out of the Poor Man bushes, enjoying the morning. Viktor scowled at her. She had offered him nary a sound in the middle of the night. No warning. Nothing.

"You better help me find it," he growled at her, "stupid cat."

Kitty meowed and took off into the underbrush. After a mouse, perhaps. Viktor carried on in the shade for some time, delaying his inevitable entry into the sun and heat of the day. He only stopped when he reached a small creek.

Bent low to bring the mountain cooled water to his lips, he startled when Kitty leaped onto his shoulders.

"Get off!" He shoved her aside.

She hissed at him and scurried back toward the tree line. She sat and waited. Viktor glared at her before continuing to drink. When he finished, he took several more handfuls and tossed them on his head. He wetted down his hair and face, enjoying the sweet smell of fresh water. It never smelled like that in Kasier.

The city had experienced an influx of villagers since Ramiro's coronation. The young king, convinced he needed to demonstrate his greatness, dumped money into the pockets of any artisan willing to capture his likeness in their chosen form. Sculptors, painters, and bards filled the city. They outnumbered practitioners of medicine and blacksmiths. And every night the taverns were full of bards, all wailing to be heard over the other.

It was good for Ramiro. It was even good for most businesses. But it wasn't good for the city's sewage system. Viktor took another splash of cool water to the face, agreeing to never return to Kasier again.

Kitty meowed. She still waited for him by the tree line.

"What?" Viktor said, continuing to wash.

She let out a low mewl, almost a growl. He peered at her from the corner of his eyes, his anger already heating his skin, his face.

"I suppose you expect me to follow you?"

Kitty stood. Her tail waved slowly, interested in his words.

Viktor shook his head. "Moon Mother. It's just a dirty cat," he muttered to himself.

He stood and dried his hands on his pants. A light breeze ran across his skin, and he shivered. There was something strange in the breeze. Some strange scent.

"Fine," he said, "fine."

He took off after Kitty, his boots squelching in the mud. She immediately turned and dove into the underbrush. Viktor cursed beneath his breath, pushing branches aside to follow the cat. A pine whipped him in the face, and he stopped to collect himself.

"I'll kill her," he muttered. "I'll kill her and eat her."

Kitty meowed up ahead. Viktor took off in the direction he thought he heard her. She sat on a log, waiting. Next to her was an eroded column, built of stone ancient in appearance. Viktor's eyes traveled up the column and fixated on what was there: a rusted, smashed in sphere. Originally, it would have been metal, dipped in something to appear gold, though it looked like nothing coherent anymore.

"Damn," Victor said, "another sun temple. What is..." but Victor clamped his mouth shut.

In the distance was the crackle of a fire. Smoke rose and curled into the treetops, pushing forth into the cloudy sky. Beyond the fire was the temple, eroded like the column, but still standing.

Victor crouched behind the log with Kitty. Along with the fire, he heard voices. He looked at Kitty. He grew tired of being dragged into the midst of ancient sun temples infested with Fair Folk. Though the words drifting through the trees weren't foreign to him. They were Korithian. He held his breath to better hear them.

"I heard it was over before the sun was high," one voice said. "Stupid general didn't see it coming."

"You think he would have realized when the Prevailing Mother went missing." Said another voice.

"He couldn't care less about that fraud. It was the missing queen that distracted him. That got him panicked."

"And then killed," laughed the second voice.

"The great and mighty general, reduced to grave soil."

"Not so mighty now."

Viktor glanced at Kitty again, who stared at him eerily. The voices continued.

"The mercs' general must be enjoying that throne."

"Just until the fraud mother returns."

The second voice made a sound like they were vomiting. It was a disgusted sound and the first man laughed.

"Aye, she'll throw a party to celebrate. She'll thank us Unis and our mercs for our help. And then she'll kick us out."

"Some thanks we get," the second voice said.

"Don't worry. The Patriarchs have got a plan."

"A plan?"

"Not so loud. Lean in here and I'll tell you."

The voices disappeared into the wind, rustling through the trees. Viktor backed away, crawling through the underbrush until he thought he was far enough to run. When he reached the creek, he stopped to rest. The smoke from the Unis' fire still drifted into the sky. His heart pounded. He was too close.

Across the creek, he entered the trees. He'd stick to the tree line parallel to the road until he felt he was safe. Until he was far enough away to breathe.

The Unis hadn't mentioned Cecelia. Hopefully, that meant she received his letter and had left already.

Hope, that's all Viktor could do. And he was unaccustomed to it. It was hard to cling to and felt like drifting away. Dark thoughts blossomed in its stead. Thoughts that made him angry.

What if she was dead? It would be his fault for leaving her there. A viper nest Danon had called it. And a viper nest it had become.

The road turned around the mountain's arm, and before him was a great valley descending towards the coast. The sharp blue of the ocean glittered with what little sun could fight through the clouds. A brown road snaked its way across the green of the valley, crossing through forest and field alike. He could reach Craigburna by sundown if he tried. Zeb's wagon tracks led in that direction. He could find the old man and take back his things and begin his search for Cecelia.

If he tried. It was all he had left. One foot in front of the other, head pointed towards the port. Mentally, he prepared himself for a fight. He'd scrap and scratch if required to retrieve Ephram's sword.

Hope might elude him but fighting never did.

The Brotherhood of the Moons enjoys near celebrity status in Stratosgar and Vrethage, while Vrokar and Korith pretend they don't exist, which works in both kingdoms' favors until a need for paid killers arises. And while their base of operation remains on the great continent, they have been seen as far south as the crescent island of Duwu amid the Crystal Deep. Made up mostly of orphans and criminals, the mercenaries go through a rigorous training that lasts two years. Once complete, the soldiers join the ranks of the Brotherhood, and may never leave.

Court Historian Ludwig Ma'Hanlen
   Rebels, Robbers, and Thieves: Paying for Violence

   Loyalty follows payment.

Brotherhood of the Moons Maxim

Chapter Forty-One

THE RIVERBOAT'S WHEEL ROTATED around and around, picking up water and dropping it just as easily. The boat propelled forward at a constant, smooth speed. It entranced Cecelia.

G'rig explained the Fair Folk magic kept the wheel turning. No need for anything else. She sat with her hand on her arms, watching the wheel spin. Mother Oora insisted it was the only way to travel topside, above the Hidden Way. They'd reach Wilsden before nightfall.

Cecelia's fingers itched for something. She flexed them and stretched them, begging for them to cease their complaints. She didn't know what it was she wanted. Be it Viktor, or merely an opportunity to use her sword again. It had felt good to fight the riversnare. Too good.

G'rig arrived at her side and produced a plate of pastries. Cecelia resisted smiling.

"I don't recall saying I was hungry," she said.

"You don't have to. I can see it. You might not practice magic, but all living things reflect it. Like an aura. I can read yours, and yours says you're hungry."

Cecelia tilted her head and peered at G'rig. She fought the desire to glare at him and instead snatched a roll from the plate.

"Thank you," she said with a full mouth.

G'rig selected his own treat and sat the rest on a nearby bench. They stared at the wheel, eating in silence, both stealing glances at the other.

"I feel a fool for not noticing," G'rig said, gesturing with his roll to Cecelia's abdomen.

"Don't," Cecelia cut in.

"Mother Oora's sight is far greater than mine. Or any other Fair Folk for that matter."

They continued to eat in silence. Cecelia suddenly wasn't hungry anymore, but she chewed on the bread over and over again until it turned to paste in her mouth. She swallowed hard, tossing the rest of the roll into the river.

"Does Viktor know?" G'rig's voice cut through the slicing of the waterwheel.

Cecelia laughed but stopped. She cleared her throat, feeling as if about to choke, and shook her head. "How could he," she said, "I barely knew myself."

"So you're looking for him... so you can tell him?"

G'rig leaned against the banister, his roll forgotten in his hand. He picked it apart, flinging pieces into the water, a disappearing trail.

Cecelia stared at the Folkman. His pink hued hair fell down his shoulders, reminding Cecelia of the blossoming Moss Apple trees of the Lagos.

G'rig stood rigid, his smile gone and replaced by a frigid scowl. "I threw his fortune once."

By the way he stared so intensely at the water below, one might wonder if he were speaking to it instead.

"I shouldn't have. It's frowned upon to read someone's fortune when they haven't asked to know."

"Then why did you?" Cecelia asked.

G'rig's posture wilted. His shoulders sagged. His face, full of anger at one moment, dissolved to sadness.

"I had to know. His aura was so dark, so black. What could possibly cause that, I wondered."

Cecelia sighed. She stared at the water wheel, allowing its rhythmic turning to distract her eyes. She couldn't stand G'rig's face and the sadness written across it.

"You knew who he was, G'rig. You knew what he came from."

G'rig nodded in agreement. "Aye, but auras are mixtures of our past and our future. Where we've been and where we're bound to go." G'rig tossed the last remnants of his roll into the water and faced Cecelia. "The dead lined the path of his future, Cecelia. None could I see clearly. None except one. And I thought for certain I was wrong. Certain I misread the cards because—"

"Because it was his child," Cecelia spoke slowly, her throat thick with tears swallowed. "And you wondered who could ever love him? Who could ever give him a child?"

G'rig could not look her in the eyes. Instead, he shook his head and wiped his hands of bread crumbs. Cecelia watched him, impressed with his clean nails and fine hands. Hands meant to perform magic. To throw fortunes.

Cecelia didn't believe in fortunes. She believed the Mother set one on a path and it was that person's job to follow it as best they could. That the Daughter offered protection for those that lost their way.

And a baby, Cecelia thought as she reached her hands down to her stomach where the warmth of life had just begun, might have been what she wanted all along. Who was she to argue otherwise?

Fortunes, as far as she was concerned, were lies. Deceptions and nothing more.

G'rig's hand gently brushed her cheek, startling her from her thoughts. He pulled his hand away, offering an apology with his eyes. Cecelia wiped roughly at her face.

She hadn't known she was crying.

When she was certain every tear was wiped away, Cecelia spoke. "Do you think it will work?"

"What?"

"The rebellion. Mother Oora's plan to take the capital and then dispose of the Unis. Do you think she'll succeed?"

G'rig smiled, amused. "I know she will."

"How can you be so certain?" Cecelia asked. "I've seen armies, on the brink of victory, fall. Generals, once renowned for their warcraft, lose their minds and fail."

G'rig leaned against the banister. "Yes, sounds an awful lot like General Rees. He's fallen, you know. Kasier. It's under the control of the Unis mercenaries. Mother Oora travels there now."

"Kasier... fell?" Cecelia couldn't believe it.

She had spoken to Mother Oora just a sunrise earlier. The old woman had spoken as if the battle had yet to begin. But it seemed it was already fought. And won.

"General Rees would not have fallen so easily," Cecelia argued. "Surely you lie."

G'rig shrugged. "The Fair Folk distracted him and his army within the palace. The Unis and their mercenaries attacked the unmanned city walls. I heard half snuck in through a hidden door behind the palace kitchens."

Cecelia frowned. "The doorway was a secret. Danica told me as much."

"Ah, but you don't know the mercenaries. The Brotherhood of the Moons leave no stone unturned when it comes to their sieges. They will find a way. They always do."

"Brotherhood of the Moons," Cecelia mumbled, "sounds childish."

G'rig said nothing more. He reached for another roll and ate in silence. Cecelia's cheeks grew hot. How could the capital have fallen? How could Rees be so foolish? Her thoughts fell on Danica. The queen distracted him, like she distracted everyone else.

"So, Mother Oora will... she'll betray the Unis now. At the party she'll throw."

G'rig sighed and nodded. "Yes, pawdwyn."

"What happened to Danica?" Cecelia knew better than to ask, to reveal too much of herself, but the words tumbled forth anyway.

G'rig side-eyed her. "Gone. Disappeared. No one has seen her or the princess for several days."

Cecelia stared at the water wheel, thinking. Danica must have left after Mother Oora. Cecelia peered over the bank of the river, half expecting to see the queen there. Perhaps Danica hadn't distracted Rees. Something else did.

"Viktor was seen descending the far side of the mountain. Headed that way after dispatching a barghest in Fearing."

"A barghest?" Cecelia's thoughts of Danica and Rees slipped away.

"A monstrous dog-like creature. Rare it was thought, though it's confirmed he killed one."

"Interesting." Cecelia watched the water ripple away on the surface of the river.

"He has a cat with him, my informants say. An enchanted cat. Most likely a witch." G'rig watched Cecelia closely, gauging her reaction.

Cecelia continued to stare at the river. It was a game she played with herself, a game she'd played since she was little. Watch the ripple, see where it leads. Watch it until it disappears, or your eyes grow so tired they tear up and shut of their own.

"Why would he travel with a witch, pawdwyn?" G'rig asked.

Cecelia turned to answer, her mouth half open, when the boat shook mightily. Cecelia's stomach lurched, a body memory of the riversnare and its attack in the Hidden Way. There was shouting somewhere within the riverboat and Tra'lo ran upon them.

"Unis!" He shrieked.

He stared at the riverbank, where several soldiers stood, flamed arrows nocked and ready to let loose.

"Unis," G'rig repeated in a growl.

He shoved Cecelia aside just as one shot past her head. With his hand uplifted, he raised the river, cresting a wave that washed over the archers. But it didn't matter. More archers arrived from the forests. A ballista emerged through the tree line. A man, his armor gleaming black in the setting sun, raised his fist.

"There's too many," Cecelia yelled.

The boat rocked again. The ballista ripped through the side of the hull.

"Stay down," G'rig commanded. "They must have learned of Mother Oora's deceit."

"You should have stayed neutral," Cecelia yelled back, but her words got lost in the roar of flames erupting along the deck of the boat.

The boat shifted sharply. Cecelia rolled along the deck, smashing into the railing. A hunk of bread rolled past her and over the edge. She craned her neck, searching for G'rig or Tra'lo, but she could see neither. Closing her eyes, she took two quick breaths, and forced herself to calm. The Fair Folk shouted in the ancient tongue around her, and the Unis screamed in Korithian from the banks. The fire added its sharp dialect to the mix, and somewhere water rushed and sizzled the flames.

"It's going down!" someone, somewhere, yelled.

A hand reached for her and pulled her up roughly. Cecelia opened her eyes and saw the emerald green of Ansa. The Folkwoman growled in the ancient tongue at Cecelia, shoving her towards the listing railing.

"All'a," Ansa yelled, shoving Cecelia, "all'a!"

Cecelia could not control her fear of the rushing river, reaching angrily for the sides of the sinking boat. It raged, white caps splashing on her cheeks, its voice bellowing in her ears.

"Jump?" Cecelia asked. "You want me to jump?"

Ansa shook her head and shoved some more.

"I... I can't!" Cecelia cried.

Her hands gripped the railing's edge. They turned ice cold. The ship turned in the water some more, like a giant creature enjoying a bath. Like a riversnare. Ansa lost her footing and slid away. Cecelia reached for her but couldn't grab her hand. A large wooden freight box slid along the decking, smashing into Ansa before the Folkwoman hurtled over the far edge.

"No!" Cecelia screamed, turning back to the nearing water.

The boat tipped so sharply she had to climb over the railing and sit before preparing her jump. A few more deep breaths, she told herself, and then she'd do it. But a hot pain shot through her shoulder, and she nearly tumbled backwards. An arrow from the banks skimmed her skin, leaving a gash that poured scarlet.

Without another thought, Cecelia plunged into the raging river, unsure of the outcome, unsure if she'd survive.

Her body collided with a large rock on the bottom of the river before fighting upward for air. When her head finally crested the waves, she caught sight of the boat, completely dressed in flames and sideways in the water.

As she drifted beneath the surface once again, she could still hear the screams.

Regi, I will keep this letter short, as I know that's how you like your correspondence. I've opened my own entertainment hall, using local lore to add a sense of mystique to my business. Since you plucked me from the streets as a child and taught me everything I know, I've enclosed my first gold piece for you. Take it, it's yours. Without you, I'd be dead.

Salmora Li'Adamou
    Letter to her mentor Reginalus Vull Athros

> *Her voice so sweet and her beauty fair,*
> *The mermaid's magic fills the air.*
> *And as we dance and as we drink,*
> *With every glass our troubles sink.*

Tova Whispers, Korithian Bard
The Palace

Chapter Forty-Two

CRAIGBURNA WAS KNOWN FOR two things: mermaids and Sally's Champagne Palace. The latter wouldn't exist without the former, though rumor had it otherwise. Some said Sally wove such a tale of mermaids employed in her establishment that it began a decade's long lie. A lie that offered benefit to the entire town in pilgrimages and business ventures, but a lie nevertheless. And yet no one visiting Sally's Champagne Palace left with doubts. So, there must be some truth somewhere.

Viktor had no interest in Sally's. He steered clear of the giant whitewashed building. But it was difficult. The ocean front town centered itself around the monstrosity. Its double stories, filled with windows, reflected the ocean at high tide and the glistening seaweed on the exposed sea bed at low. Its brick steps descended onto a boardwalk. Flowers trailed out of manicured beds. The scents of jasmine and ginger drifted from open windows.

Every road Viktor took led back to the place. Every person he asked suggested Sally's was the best for information. Viktor stood in the main square, a bare-breasted mermaid bronze enjoying the middle of the fountain before him, and stared at the building. He heard music. And laughter. Lots of laughter.

With his choices dwindling, he finally relented. There was no place else to look. Zeb's wagon led to the town. Like a fool, Zeb ran straight to the place Viktor had intended to go. Like a fool, he probably sequestered himself inside Sally's, knowing her ironclad privacy rules would protect him.

Viktor squeezed his hands into fists until his knuckles popped. Little did Zeb know it would take more than that to protect him from Viktor. He strode to the front of the building with heavy steps. Once, he would have enjoyed a visit to Sally's. But something had changed. He'd lost too much of himself. He felt like parchment, easily torn.

At the large rosewood doors, mermaid shaped handles gleamed gold. Viktor grabbed a tail and pulled, only to have the door shoved open against him. A beautiful woman, minuscule in stature and round in shape, stared up at him.

"Welcome to Sally's Champagne Palace, good sir." Her smile was youthful.

Viktor's stomach churned at the thought of her age.

"I just seek information," He said. "I'm looking for someone."

"Everyone who visits Sally is looking for someone," the girl winked. "I'm Theolania, won't you come in?"

Her small bow unnerved him. He squeezed by her, but Kitty darted off down the boardwalk. Something spooked her. Viktor hesitated for another moment, but then pushed on without her. He had a job to do, he reminded himself. He needed Zeb. And his sword. And then he needed to find Cecelia.

"Care for a treat, good sir?" Theolania held a silver plate before him, edges scrolled like seashells.

Small, sugar dusted hard candies sat nestled inside tissue paper. She smiled pleasantly at him, taking one for herself to demonstrate the candy's harmlessness. But Viktor knew better.

"Alcohol is my fault, girl," He assured her, "not laced candy."

Theolania shrugged and handed the plate back to another woman. This one was slightly taller, her skin iridescent with pearl powder. The woman disappeared into the shadows behind a silk curtain.

"Your loss, good sir. The leaves used to lace the candy hails from Duwu. The most delicate of flavors and the most heavenly of lifts."

Viktor raised his eyebrows. "How old are you?"

Theolania smiled, displaying her dimples. "Old enough."

Viktor grew tired of games. He felt the heat rising at his neck but tried to distract himself by looking for Zeb. They were in a large hall. Ceilings drifted high, taking up both stories. Within the arched intersections were paintings of mermaids in various stages of undress.

At the far end was a wide staircase, carpeted in the most regal of purple, leading to an upstairs gallery where guests disappeared on either wing of the building. There was also a bar, where a tall, muscular looking woman served drinks to visitors. Scattered around the main hall amidst potted plants were groups of chairs and tables, couches, and a few chaises. All occupied by someone. All entertained by one of Sally's girls.

"I'm looking for an old man," Viktor spoke, still searching the room for the thief's face.

"We cater to all, good sir."

Viktor glared at Theolania. "He stole from me, girl, that's all. I want my things back. Goes by the name Zeb."

Theolania straightened up. She smoothed her silk chemise and repositioned the large, raven black bun on top of her head. "I'm afraid I'm not allowed to tell you if someone by that name is or is not here. Nor can I permit you to harm him if he were here. Not that he is. For any reason."

Viktor leaned in close to Theolania, so close he could smell the mixture of body oil and body odor drifting off her skin. It was the scent of salt and chamomile. He disliked it.

"I don't give a care for your rules, girl," he growled. "The man stole from me, and the law of this land is that if something is stolen, I have a right to take it back."

Theolania did not wince. She didn't even look scared. She smiled wickedly and nodded her head. "The law of the land, good sir, aye. But this place is of the sea."

She moved her mouth to continue, and Viktor opened his to argue, when they were both interrupted by another. A woman as white-blonde as moonlight and rounder still than Theolania, floated toward them, or at least it looked that way. The woman wore layers of green silk, all soundlessly gliding across each other and dragging behind her, masking her feet, making it appear as if she floated like seaweed upon the waves.

"Theolania, is that any way to speak to our guest?" The woman purred.

Theolania stood rigid and stared at the floor. "No, madam Sally, but the good sir insisted on finding a man–" but then Viktor picked up the words.

"Who stole from me. A man I have a right to retrieve said things from, no matter the way and no matter where he hides."

Sally, her eyes outlined in sea-foam green, suggested to the silk curtain with her head.

"Away with you, Theo," she said, "I'll tend to this good sir myself."

Theolania retreated, head still downcast. Sally smiled at Victor. It made him feel uneasy. Unsettled. He shifted in his boots and looked around the hall again. "His name is Zeb," the words spilled out, "took my pack. My brother's sword."

"I thought you said he stole your things, not your brother's."

Viktor twisted to look at Sally, whose smile contorted her brilliant pink lips.

"*Was* my brother's," he clarified, "until it became mine."

"I see," Sally fluttered a layer of silk, "well, despite Theolania's lack of tact, she is correct. I can't permit you to fight him here. If he is here. Which I'm uncertain if I can verify since patrons are not required to give their real name. Or any name, really. It's our code. Our pledge of discretion for anyone who wishes to enter the Champagne Palace."

"Well, nothing is stopping you from letting me look for him then, is there?"

Sally shrugged. "I don't see why not. So long as you pay."

Again, her smile unsettled his stomach.

"I don't think you heard me, woman," Viktor said. "My things have been stolen. *All* my things. I haven't a coin to spare you."

Sally batted his words away, her strange smile still pasted on her gilded face. "Don't worry. It seems you've come just in time. I have a need for a man of your," she eyed him up and down, "stature."

Viktor swallowed his retort. Whatever it was the woman wanted him to do, he'd have to do it. He needed Zeb.

"Fine," he snapped, "what is it?"

"Oh," Sally slipped her thick arm into Viktor's and petted his chest with her finger, "don't pout. I think you'll like it. It's right up your alley."

The Forest of Bruss is the largest uninterrupted forest within the boundaries of Korith. Unofficially named the Liosni's Forest, the Queen made it her mission to preserve as much woodland as possible for future generations to enjoy. Bisected by the river Rochele, several smaller arms break off and spread throughout the forest, invigorating the life within. Wildlife abound and magic is said to lay dormant deep within the roots of the ancient Redwall trees. Bruss is said to welcome all that enter with good intentions, and many a person - or family - wishing to disappear have gone within its trees never to be seen again.

Lady Lillyana Fenstock
   Herbarium

Chapter Forty-Three

CECELIA OPENED HER EYES and then immediately closed them. Intense pain ached along her temples and sliced deep within her ears. Every inhale earned her a sharp stab at her side. Every exhale bore a long burn in her throat. Her stomach ached deeply. She caught her breath, knowing what had happened.

There was a movement near her. Though her eyes were closed, she knew someone stood above her. Their hand reached out and gently petted her forearm, shushing her.

"Easy, strange girl," the woman whispered. "You've been through much. Rest easy. You are safe."

Cecelia tried to form words with her lips, but they felt dry and weak. The woman, still merely a shadow in Cecelia's vision, disappeared and returned. A sponge soaked in spring water sweetened with honey was placed on her lips.

"There," she said, "that should help."

Cecelia licked her lips and slowly tried to form words. At first, only her native tongue would come to mind. She racked her brain for the memory of Korith and its language, but it wouldn't come. So, she spoke in the language of her father.

The woman's face was cloudy, but Cecelia thought she saw her smile.

"As I thought," the woman sighed, "you are the Panther pawdwyn." The woman slumped down in a chair next to Cecelia. "I'm afraid I don't understand you. We'll have to wait until you can remember some words of Korith."

She busied her hands with something. Cecelia attempted to turn her head to see, but her eyes were immediately rewarded with a deep ache. She squeezed them shut and kept her head from turning.

"The pain will pass," the woman said. "Take your time. We are in no hurry here."

Here. Cecelia wondered exactly where. The last thing she remembered was the inferno on the water and the screaming. So much screaming.

"Where?" she forced out, the word appearing in her brain like a flower fresh in bloom.

"The forest of Bruss. My husband and I make our home here where it is safe for our children."

She stopped whatever she was doing with her hands. Even though Cecelia couldn't see the woman's face yet, she could feel her sadness. She tried to reach out to the woman, but only her fingers moved in uncoordinated twitches.

"No, don't do that." The woman settled a calloused hand on Cecelia's own. "While it is time for you to wake, your body still needs rest."

Cecelia sighed. She sensed the woman smiling again.

"Who?" Cecelia forced out, eyes closed.

"My name is Meira," Meira said. "My husband is Respen. He's the one that found you on the outer banks of the quag."

"When?"

"Two moonrises ago."

Cecelia sighed again. She shifted on the bed. Her back was full of pinpricks. Meira, sensing her need, adjusted the pillows surrounding her. There was a clatter across the room and the indistinguishable words of multiple children's voices. Meira left Cecelia's side quickly, muttering in the Fair Folk tongue. The noise ceased. The room was silent. Cecelia thought she was alone, but heard Meira clear her throat from across the room.

"I apologize," she said. "The children are curious. They've rarely seen outsiders. And never someone from off continent. Never a Panther."

"You are Fair Folk," Cecelia said.

"Respen is. I am Korithian. Our children are halflings, not welcomed anywhere." Meira slouched back down in the chair next to Cecelia. "So we've made them a place here, in the forest of Bruss."

Cecelia swallowed hard, finding the motion painful.

When she spoke, her voice was hoarse and raspy. "Honorable," she said, "though my father always said there is no honor in hiding."

Meira touched Cecelia's dry lips with the sponge again. "I never much bothered with kings. Or queens. Let them speak all they want of honor while kept high in their palaces. Give me the earth. The needles of the pine. Nightdrop Berries. My children and their laughter."

Meira dabbed at Cecelia's forehead. The coolness soothed her. The smell of lavender surrounded her. She relaxed.

"The boat," Cecelia said, struggling to swallow again. "What happened? Others were onboard."

Meira shook her head. "We heard of a riverboat attacked by Unis mercenaries. But that was far upriver, on the main arm. If you were on that boat, you're lucky to be alive."

"You've no idea," Cecelia sighed.

G'rig had disappeared on the boat, into the inferno. Despite his magical ability, nothing could protect him from the flames. It was the cost of magic. The elements, while easily bent, did not yield.

"Respen will be home tonight," Meira said. "He can tell you more. He's hiked to the nearest village for more supplies. You... you've lost quite a bit of blood."

"What wounds have I?" Cecelia croaked. "I feel nearly dead."

"A broken rib. Severe scrapes. All evidence of your trip down the river. But also," Meira hesitated.

Cecelia opened one eye and stared at Meira. Her vision was clearing up. Before her sat a young woman, raven black hair braided in many braids. Freckles splashed across her face and warm brown eyes stared down into nervous hands.

"What else?" Cecelia asked, though she already knew.

"An early miscarriage." Something hardened in Meira's eyes, and she stared back at Cecelia. "I doubt you would have known."

"I knew," Cecelia said.

"I'm sorry," Meira said, "it was very early. There was... nothing to save."

Cecelia cleared her throat and looked away. She stared at the wall of the small house, birch bark wrapped on wooden posts, and told herself to breathe.

"There's nothing to apologize for," Cecelia spoke to the wall. "I never wanted children."

"But the father," Meira said.

"Gone," Cecelia interrupted her, "I was on my way to find him when the Unis attacked."

Though she couldn't see her, Cecelia felt Meira's eyes. She wondered how long the woman would stare, but someone busting through the door interrupted the moment. A child, whimpering and crying, spilled out words of the Fair Folk, describing some wrong done to them by their siblings. Meira moved away from Cecelia, picking up and soothing the child.

She began singing a song before transitioning to humming it. The child quieted down, her sniffles interrupting the song intermittently.

Cecelia still stared at the wall, tears silently falling down her cheeks. She possessed flitting memories of her mother, a presence more than a face, wrapped around her and singing.

It was the same song.

Vrokar, one of three northern kingdoms of the Great Continent, is walled in by the Slumbering Mountains to the east and sweeping cliffs of basalt to the north. The Weeping Ocean, colloquially dubbed the Weeping, girds in the rest of the kingdom's shoreline. Secluded from much of the rest of the Great Continent, Vrokar enjoys independent development. With little influence from Korith or neighboring Vrethage, Vrokar discovered the kingdom's penchant for art. Some of the world's most famous, and infamous, artists hail from the small, cloistered kingdom. Most notably is Ellyich de'Briev, known for her masterful adaptation of watercolors on dried human skin.

Court Historian Aron Dyuman
Ethnographica

Chapter Forty-Four

Viktor was relieved when Sally began describing the task she wished for him to complete. She was right. It was right up his alley, but there were many streets to a man and he had been worried she yearned to stroll down one in particular. One he was less inclined to share, especially since marrying Cecelia. But he needn't worry. It was his fighting she required of him.

"I pay my girls well, good sir," Sally began while she poured herself a glass of amber liquid from her private selection in her office. "Everyone comes to Sally's of their own will and accord. I assure you."

Viktor nodded his head, accepting a glass offered to him. It was bitter but smoothed itself out on the swallow. Vocan cognac had the distinct pleasure of burning the eyes of one unaccustomed to it. Viktor wiped away a tear.

"There are those, though, that find me a liar. Can you imagine?" Sally sipped at her drink.

"It's unimaginable," Viktor finished his cognac in one swig.

Sally smiled before sipping some more. "Well," she continued, "the so-called Children of the Forest, protectors of all things alive as long as it's not a human, think otherwise."

Viktor shrugged.

"I see you aren't following," Sally sat her glass down on her desk a little too hard.

"I'm waiting for you to get to the point."

Viktor cracked his neck and glanced out the window. Sally's office had a beautiful view of the harbor. One could watch the ships floating in the shuttered harbor all day. Gulls dove for crumbs tossed by children. Pirate Seals climbed onto the docks, barking at fishermen, arguing for their share of fish. Women with tightly woven baskets scampered along the revealed rocks of low tide in search of muscles and rock crab. Combined, the odd noises created a cacophony in his ear, though he imagined one would get used to it with time. When he finally looked back at Sally, she smiled at him.

"You make a striking Royal Guard Marshal," she said. "Even with that mark of His Brilliance."

Viktor rolled his eyes and turned his birthmark away from Sally. He hated superstitions. He sank into the leather seat nearby, thrusting his glass at Sally. "Then pour the Royal Guard Marshal another drink."

Sally obliged. When she handed him back his glass, her hand lingered on his a bit too long. She stared down at him, fluttering her silk layers again.

"The Children of the Forest attack my ships."

"A merchant as well as a purveyor of fantasies? Look how far you've come from Vocan, Sally." Viktor downed his second glass of cognac.

"Yes," Sally mused, "and I'd like to keep it that way. The ships are for moving my girls. For retrieving them. The Children have been attacking them, thinking they are freeing the ladies. When, in actuality, they are only getting in their way."

"You mean *your* way?"

"As I said," Sally sighed, "everyone comes of their own accord. Whose matter is it how I persuade them?"

"Not mine matter," Viktor said. "When do you suspect the next attack?"

"I have a ship anchored safely off the Vrokarian port of Rabes, just north of the mountains. The Children of the Forest don't dare cross kingdom lines to commit their crimes. The Vrokarians would flay them, happily trailing their bodies as flags on their mastheads."

"Naturally," Viktor agreed, "but what would you have *me* do about them?"

Sally took a deep breath, apparently preparing herself for the explanation. "Word is the Forest Freaks plan to descend upon the ship when it nears the Spit of Scree. The water there is shallow, and with little skill the insects can traverse the spit, skim the waves and scale the ship."

"How good is your word?" Viktor gazed into the bottom of his empty glass.

"The best money can buy," Sally said.

"And I'm to stop them?"

Sally pursed her lips in a fake frown. "Hmmm, persuade them." She purred. "For the spit is narrow and you are big and strong."

She winked at Viktor, which only made him want to leave the room faster than before. He stood and walked to the window. Outside, he thought he spied Kitty, but the creature disappeared behind the corner before he could be sure.

"How many?"

"Nine. Ten at most."

Viktor eyed Sally over his shoulder. "You flatter me," he said, "to think I can handle ten men at a time."

Sally smirked. "You handled a barghest."

And when Viktor felt the heat rush to his cheeks, Sally's smile broadened.

"Yes, word travels fast this side of Korith." She said.

Viktor turned away. The creature still took up space in his nightmares, though the image grew blurrier with each passing night. It would be many moons before he could forget the creature's face. The fear it showed at Kitty. The pain it showed at death.

Sally sighed. "I don't intend for you to go it alone. I'm sending you with two of my best."

"Best what?" Viktor asked.

"Why, my personal swords, Royal Guard Marshal." Sally fluttered her lashes demurely. "To assist you in any way you see fit."

"If you have your own personal swords, then why do you need me, Sally?" Viktor asked.

He didn't like the way she looked at him. He didn't like Sally, period. But he needed Zeb and his sword. Suddenly, her warm face melted to stone. She poured another cognac and threw it back, much like Viktor had done.

"Frankly," she began, "I don't like losing money on investments. I pay my swords well. The thought of sending them off to possibly die wounds me."

"Wounds your purse," Viktor corrected.

"Either way," Sally batted Viktor's words away. "I can offset those costs by sending you. What you ask for isn't coin, just a man."

"Much less valuable than money," Viktor said.

Sally shrugged. "Such is the way of the world, Royal Guard Marshal."

Viktor said nothing more. He stared out the window, willing the creature he thought was Kitty to return, but it never did.

"I'm afraid it's your only way out, sir Marshal." Sally's voice came from behind him. "I'll keep Zeb here until you return so you can exact your revenge on him as you see fit. You have my word."

She leaned back in her chair, as beautiful as she was intimidating. A mountainous woman filling the scene that bore her, demanding obeisance. Viktor frowned.

"There are orders to turn you in, you know," Sally produced a cigar and flourished it like a wand. "You must have pissed off someone important."

"You have no idea."

Lisi Ne'vander was a pink-haired sorceress who joined Princess Jana in her war to reclaim the Korithian throne. Though slight in stature, the woman commanded a pack of animals that obeyed her every command. The appointed leader of these animals, a red fox, accompanied Lisi wherever she went. Said to be undead, or a ghost, little is known of Lisi's childhood save that she came from the Forest of Bruss. She would not speak of her childhood to anyone save for speaking of the lesson she learned as a small girl: there is no honor in hiding.

Court Historian Jepsuth Jeffrees
 Age of Queens: A Complete Discussion

Chapter Forty-Five

Respen challenged everything Cecelia knew of Fair Folk. His voice was soft, though it resonated, and he wouldn't raise it even when his listener asked him to repeat himself. The only exception Cecelia found was when the children made too much of a ruckus. Only then would he raise his voice, and only to be heard, not to scold.

"They are lively," he smiled at Cecelia over a bowl of Goliath pea soup.

Cecelia nodded. "Indeed."

Meira and Respen's four children were always moving. The eldest boy and girl, twins, were Meira's helpers. Aron and Nora. For a while, the only words Cecelia heard them speak were *n'as mera*. Yes, mother.

Black of hair, like their mother, Aron and Nora offered no hints they were halflings save for one. Their eyes. A startling lavender, the color was made even more beautiful against the midnight of their hair.

Their third son, Rosta, was a miniature of their mother too. His hair was the same black. Even the way he walked seemed reminiscent of Meira. His eyes, too, though lilac in shade, leaned more gold, more akin to his mother. Halfling, for sure, but passable.

And then there was Lisi, the youngest. She burst through the cottage door, hair aflutter in the afternoon sun, screaming in delight, weaving between her siblings as Rosta chased her.

Hers was hair the color of blushed apples. Of delicate pink roses. Odd compared to a Korithian child's. Beautiful compared to the Fair Folk. Identical to Respen's. He pulled the running child onto his lap and smothered her in kisses. She squealed in delight, smiling at Cecelia through her father's arms. Cecelia couldn't help but smile back. Across from her, identical dimpled smiles beneath identical purple eyes.

Meira brought them tea. Lisi wiggled away and out the door, Rosta on the chase again. Aron and Nora went to the garden to continue harvesting the Goliath peas.

"Do your children do magic?" Cecelia asked.

She inhaled the sweet steam from her cup. Honey, harvested from Respen's own bees, sweetened the rose tea. It danced on her tongue, sweeter than anything she'd tasted before.

"Some," Respen stirred his tea, bewitching the steam to twirl into shape-shifting dragons, wyverns, and birds. "The girls dabble with magic. Neither boy seems to carry it. Lisi possesses the most. It finds her."

"What do you mean?" Cecelia asked.

Respen glanced at her through his enchanted steam. As if he finally came to some conclusion, he blew the steam creatures away and sipped his tea. When he sat his mug down, he leaned his chair back, running his calloused hands over his face.

"The Fair Folk are of the land." Respen sat his chair back down. "And I don't mean merely born here. I mean here," and he leaned down and patted the hard packed dirt floor. "We were made here. Born here. We are *in* this place."

Cecelia nodded, though she'd heard it all before and still felt she held little understanding of the notion. Even she, a daughter of the Lagos, knew that her people once hailed from somewhere else. That it was travelers, voyagers, adventurers on ships seeking new worlds that planted the seed to her people.

"Because we are of this land, and the magic is in the land, the Fair Folk act as funnels. Channels for it. We can use it if we try. Some better than others."

"Could a Korithian learn to channel it?" Cecelia asked.

"Some have tried," Respen sighed, "to little avail. Magic is... unruly at the best of times. Humans possess little insulation against something going wrong."

"But Lisi, a halfling, wields it well?"

Respen smiled then and shook his head. "Perhaps in time," he laughed, "she'll learn to. She shows some giftedness."

"And Nora?"

Respen's smile faltered, but only for a moment. "Nora's power is a quiet power. Almost unnoticeable, unless you are aware of it." He pointed to Cecelia. "You've benefited from it."

Cecelia thought hard, but couldn't remember witnessing the girl perform anything in her presence. No tricks. No charms. Not even a sleight of hand. She stared down at her bruised body and wondered if Nora had assisted Meira in her healing.

"She's an empath," Respen smiled, "her powers leave no mark upon you, no mention in your memory."

"And how did I benefit from her power?" Cecelia asked.

Meira joined the conversation then, sliding in to sit next to her husband. Dark where he glimmered with light, Meira didn't diminish beside Respen. In fact, she shined.

"When you were... delivering. Blood was everywhere. You were afraid. You were... uncontrollable. I hesitated on bringing her into the room. The girl is but ten and five but I needed her help. *You* needed her help."

Cecelia's throat tightened at the thought of her weakness. She forced herself to sip her tea and swallow. She inhaled deeply of the rose petal scent, forcing herself to remember the moment, remember the fear. But it wouldn't come.

"You won't remember," Meira said. "She soothed you. She stood there in the corner and worked her power. You were quiet and calm within moments."

Cecelia sipped her tea once more. "And did she suffer any side effects?"

Meira glanced at Respen then, deferring to her husband. His purple eyes gazed over Cecelia. She suspected he was looking deeper than just her own eyes, past the clouds she used to hide, to her soul. But she couldn't be sure. It was only a feeling, fleeting in the moment, like fingers gently brushing the skin.

"I'm familiar enough with magic to know there is always a price. There must be balance."

"She grew sick," Respen said matter-of-factly, "and vomited after. But otherwise she's fine. A life lesson, at ten and five, which few receive."

"I see," Cecelia frowned.

"I am sorry," Respen said then, "for your loss."

Cecelia tried to smile, but couldn't. "I never wanted to be a mother," she said frankly. "I am only sorry your daughter had to witness it."

"She'll be fine," Respen assured her. "The question is: will you?"

Cecelia fidgeted with the handle of her mug, avoiding Respen's penetrating stare. She cleared her throat, finding it tightening again, like hands wrapped around her throat.

"I'll be fine," she echoed Respen. "Consider it a life lesson, at twenty and eight."

Her smile turned Respen's into a frown.

"What leads a man to abandon his wife when she is with child?" Respen then asked. "If you don't mind me asking."

Cecelia slouched back in her chair and sighed.

"He didn't know," Meira answered for her. "He couldn't have known. It was too early. The pawdwyn barely knew."

"So then what?"

The pair looked at Cecelia, who leaned back in her chair and stared at the ceiling. She traced the shapes she saw within the great ceiling beams' grain, following swirls and reaching dead ends.

"Fear," she finally answered them, not even caring to look, "of one thing or another, as all men have."

"So, in other words, you don't know why he left." Respen said.

Cecelia slumped forward, her fists banging on the table a little too hard. Meira jumped in surprise. It was Cecelia's turn to peer into Respen's eyes. To see what was beyond the surface. She saw a proud man. Quiet, but proud. He thought they were safe in the forest of Bruss. He thought he had beaten the system that sought to punish Meira and himself for daring to love each other. For daring to have children.

He thought he had won.

Cecelia abruptly pushed herself away from the table, hiding the pain it shot through her ribs, spilling tea as she went. Meira jumped up and started cleaning immediately.

"Its fine," Meira murmured, wiping up the tea quickly and efficiently.

Cecelia looked first to Meira but then settled her gaze on Respen. His words were ugly. But the truth often was. It didn't make it hurt any less. She hated how little control she seemed to have over her eyes, the tears already welling up in the corners again like they did on the boat with G'rig. The pain of G'rig's truths combined with that of Respen's was too heavy.

But she pushed back her shoulders and wiped fiercely at her face before heading outside.

"There is no honor in hiding." Cecelia stopped at the door and repeated the words of her father over her shoulder. "My husband will learn that soon enough. The question is: will you?"

While Scree appears destitute, and the people hungry, many a visitor claims to have seen untold treasures hidden within the Scree people's homes. Small statues of gold sit on lopsided mantels. Necklaces of the blackest stone hide behind old women's layers of rags. Bottles of the rarest vintages tucked away beneath a loose floorboard. No one knows where they get them. No person of Scree will tell. Though the rumor remains that when ships fall foul on the Spit of Scree, the ship — and its crew — disappears.

Logician Anncept Garoll
 Landcraft: The Relationship of Geography and Economy

Chapter Forty-Six

Two of Sally's best personal swords ended up being Lara One-Eye, a Korithian privateer once famous for sailing the Weeping and sinking many a ship, and a Statsogarian named Ullazor ult Vrash Neagor who communicated by hand gestures and grunts. When Viktor was introduced, he side-eyed Sally.

"Don't worry," she assured him, "they really are the best."

"If you really thought that, we wouldn't need him," Lara One-Eye scowled.

The eye patch over her left eye moved and shifted with her brow. Rumor had it she lost it in a fight with a kraken. But the truth was muddied beneath many more such rumors. There was one that suggested Sally herself took as payment for the powerful protection she offered her employees. Another that Lara slipped and fell, the dagger she keeps hidden in the toe of her boot misfiring, resulting in the loss of her own eye.

However she lost it, the woman still possessed a mean scowl. Viktor wasn't afraid, though, and shoved past her on his way down the steps. Ulla, on the other hand, stood taller than Viktor and twice as wide. The leather of her bracers could have been greaves for any normal man, Viktor included. Geometric tattoos patterned her shaved head. The guttural grunts she issued were off-putting at first, but Viktor soon realized she wasn't stupid. She had simply never bothered learning Korithian.

Viktor grew uneasy on the ride to the Spit of Scree. Lara, who spoke often, was volatile and quarrelsome. Sally assured him prior to leaving that this was Lara on a good day. He didn't want to think about what Lara One-Eye was like on a bad day.

Ulla remained silent, though she led the party through the winding track along the coast. After following the shoreline for several leagues, the track rose with the dunes. The spine of the Slumbering Mountains surged in the distance. The spit stuck from the shore just south of the first mountain's foot. Scree was nothing but a fishing village made up of huts and shambles. Viktor watched the smoke rise from their fires, writing unknown messages into the sky long before he even saw the village.

They stopped their horses at the top of the hill, staring down at the spit. It stuck out into the Weeping like a giant thumb, flat and rocky. Children were known to skitter across the rocks in search of mussels, but nothing occupied the spit as they watched and waited, save for the common gulls that favored its shelter.

"Hope you're as good with a sword as Sally seems to think," Lara said, watching the gulls sweep across the sky, crying their irritating song.

"I am," Viktor said.

"Hmph," Ulla grunted before guiding her large horse down the steep incline.

"You could wait for us here," Lara said. "We won't tell Sally. You'll be out of our way. The job will get done. Everyone will be happy."

Viktor said nothing. He followed Ulla, his horse kicking rocks down the hill ahead of him.

"And let you have all the fun?" He called back to her.

He still didn't look, but heard her horse make its way down the path behind him. Rocks tumbled by, telling him Lara was hot on his heels. They rode in silence for several moments, descending the rocky trail steadily. When they reached the bottom, Viktor turned his horse towards Lara.

"You'll not sway me to step aside, One-Eye," Viktor growled at her. "Sally has something I need, therefore I'll do what Sally requests. The sooner you realize that, and fall into step, the smoother this job will go."

Lara smirked. She sidled her horse up against Viktor's and leaned towards him, offering him a sultry wink. "As you wish, my lord."

He watched her ride ahead with Ulla, who neither waited for them nor cared that they chatted without her. Something in the way Lara spoke sat oddly with Viktor. Beneath the surface, he felt something was wrong.

"Coming, my lord?" Lara called back to him.

He kicked his horse into a quick trot and caught up with them. Ulla glanced at Viktor once but remained focused on the path towards the spit. Viktor followed her gaze and stared out at the ocean.

"I don't see a ship," he said.

"It will be there," Lara pointed to the rocky cliff past Scree, "hidden behind the rocks. The wind whips terribly around the spit. Ships do better following tightly to the coast before emerging out alongside it."

Viktor nodded. He had no knowledge of the land there. He had no reason to doubt Lara. Though he found he did, anyway. Ulla continued to lead them, a steady constant, whereas Lara seemed distracting. She pointed to the huts and shambles and mocked the people that lived there. She whistled at children and hissed when they came near. Lara constantly called Viktor's name, drawing his attention to some dirty child or odd aspect of the inhabitants of Scree.

"Does mocking them make you feel better?" he asked her when they turned away from the small village and made their way onto the spit.

Lara choked on her own laugh. "Self righteous man," she said, "you think ignoring them is better than seeing them? In witnessing their destitution?"

"Your witnessing sounded a lot like mocking," Viktor said.

Ulla held up her fist, signaling for them to halt. She dismounted, and Viktor and Lara followed.

"Tis the same thing, my lord," Lara hissed in his ear. "For I see them as they are. You and your kind, you don't even lower yourself to look."

"My kind?"

"The kind that fancies castles and titles."

She pushed past him and caught up with Ulla. The two bent their heads low and exchanged a few words, or rather syllables, on Ulla's part. Viktor glared at them, but then shifted his thoughts to their surroundings. The spit was desolate. He wondered how often a ship washed ashore there, caught in the current, drawn perilously close by the wind. The people of Scree looked hungry, their greedy eyes peering out at them beneath filthy hoods and hats. Perhaps a beached ship provided them with more than entertainment.

Ahead, Lara and Ulla scrambled past a large boulder. They disappeared behind the rock's mass. Viktor heard a whoop and a scream, though they sounded joyful and not afraid. He tried to calm his rushing heart, following the narrow path amidst wave-worn pebbles around the boulder.

Lara stood staring out at a ship, its bowsprit barely visible behind the cliff. Viktor approached her, his eyes sweeping left and right for Ulla, but not seeing her. He found it surprising that the large woman could disappear so quickly.

"Where is Ulla?" he asked, though he stared out at the ship, slowly moving into view.

Lara didn't answer. Instead, she watched the ship fight the ocean waves. The elongated bowsprit gave way to the figurehead, though it was too far away for Viktor to make out. The forecastle emerged and the masts carrying billowing sails. Viktor squinted, thinking the sun played tricks on him. The cliff cast a shadow across the ship, obscuring the fabric. Surely, he thought. Surely they weren't black.

He turned to speak such words to Lara, but found her smiling at him in wicked delight.

"Don't worry," she smiled at him, "we're just doing as Sally requests."

The blunt pain across the back of his head blinded him. It was so intense and so extreme his knees buckled. He fell to his hands where his palms scraped against sharp stones. Blood seeped into the bubbling waves, turning the foam a sickly shade of pink. He rocked back and forth, attempting to overcome the nausea, to overcome this battle of mights. But a fresh surge hit him, and with it, a boot to the side. He fell into an oncoming wave and salt rushed his nose. Lara's laughter filled his ears over the sound of the water.

Ulla's bulk appeared above him. He fought to keep his eyes open, but the water stung and Lara's one-eyed face stung more. Deceived, he realized, the word blooming in his mind like the ugliest of flowers. Why had he believed he could trust someone like Sally?

Ulla reached down and grabbed Viktor by the front of his armor. She withdrew his face from the water and he took one final breath before she drew her other arm back and planted a punch firmly on his face.

Viktor thought no more about the deception. He tasted iron and salt and then he tasted nothing.

The magic gift a Fairchild possesses is thought to be favor passed on by an unknown entity of the earth. The earth in which the Fair Folk tend in return tends the Fair Folk. It is unknown how long the Fair Folk have wielded their magic. Oral histories surpass ancient records, reciting the tales of magic using Fair Folk. It is said that when Thrash'gar the Destroyer first set foot on the Great Continent, he was turned away by a large tribe of magic wielding people, all with brightly hued hair and glittering eyes. Nothing of their like exists anywhere else in the known world. No other being possesses the power of the earth, save the Fair Folk alone.

Court Historian Alfred Peri
   The Scroll of Children: A Collected History of the Fair Folk

Chapter Forty-Seven

THE FOREST OF BRUSS grew up around Cecelia. Trees swallowed up the sky. The forest floor grew cool. Cecelia pulled her cloak — lent to her by Meira — tighter around her shoulders and pushed onward. Respen had explained the path clearly, precisely, and told her she'd make it to the great forest's edge by nightfall.

A crisp snap from behind startled Cecelia. She turned on her heel to find Meira.

"Apologies," Meira smiled weakly, "I only felt it fair I help you find your way."

Cecelia frowned, though inside she felt relief. "Your husband was clear enough. I can find my way."

"I'm sure you could," Meira agreed, arriving beside her.

The woman's cheeks were flush, and her breath emitted small wisps of frost. She carried with her a sack heavy with provisions.

"But I couldn't forgive myself should I not help you," Meira said.

"Why?" Cecelia studied Meira.

Meira struggled with finding the right words, her lips twisting together as she thought. Finally, her shoulders drooped, and she sighed.

"You have been through much," Meira spoke slowly, shyly, "I only wanted… to ease your burdens. If only through the trees of Bruss."

Cecelia tapped her foot on the forest floor, considering Meira's words. "Like Nora did?" She asked.

Meira averted her eyes, turning back towards the cottage.

"Come along." Cecelia reached for her wrist, staying Meira's retreat. "You can walk me, but you must explain more of Nora's power. I should know, for it was me she used it on."

Meira slowly nodded in agreement and fell into step beside Cecelia. They walked amongst the roots, stepping high over the feet of the trees, ducking beneath thick conifer branches. Meira aided Cecelia in climbing over a fallen tree, one as tall as Respen's cottage. Cecelia only grimaced once, when a branch bent backwards and whipped her ribs. The rest of her pain she buried deep, reliving it only in her mind when she felt a moment of quiet.

When they reached a small stream, one Respen said to follow west, Meira slowed her pace and brought forth a chunk of cheese from her pack. She offered half to Cecelia, who took it with a bow of her head. They sat on a nearby rock, basking in the dappled sun which fought through the treetops, allowing the sound of the creek to wash over them.

"The magic," Cecelia asked, forgoing all manners and speaking over the food in her mouth, "when did you first know Nora possessed it?"

Meira swallowed a bite of cheese and pursed her lips, thinking. "She was but four. She and Aron were inseparable, as twins usually are. He fell over the stoop and skinned his knee. He cried. He was always crying. A very tender boy. Anyway, Nora stood nearby, wouldn't come near him, just stared intently at him. His crying ceased but Nora sank to the ground and cried of stomach pains."

"And Lisi?"

Meira dropped her eyes and stared down at her hands, a piece of cheese still sitting there, asking to be eaten. "She threw a tantrum one day," Meira said, "made a bowl fly against the wall and explode."

"I see," Cecelia took another bite of cheese, "which is why you seemed little interested in demonstrating Lisi's power to me."

"She's not a Fair Folk freak, bred to entertain ladies of the highborn like yourself," Meira said, still staring at her hands.

She squeezed the cheese into crumbles that scattered to the ground. When she looked up at Cecelia, her eyes were glassy and held back tears.

"Apologies," Meira whispered halfheartedly.

Cecelia chewed her food slowly, staring at Meira. Cecelia's questions agitated the woman, though she offered answers freely enough. It pricked Meira, the inquiries into her halfling children. It was something she perhaps expected to avoid, living isolated within the forest of Bruss. Cecelia cared little for the aims of others, though.

She shrugged and finished her cheese before standing. "I care little for apologies," she said, "from lowborn or high. I only want answers."

"Answers to what?" Meira wiped a trailing tear from her face.

"The song you sang, the other day when Lisi came crying and I lay recovering, where did you learn it?"

Cecelia stared so intently at Meira that the woman stood and stepped back, situating the bag between the pair as protection.

"Twas sung to me by my mother. And her mother before that."

"So it is a familial song?"

Meira shook her head no. "I suppose not. Many in the village I was born in sang it. It is known well across the kingdom."

Cecelia bit her lip, but finally nodded. "As you say," she stared out at the moving creek, "as you say."

She was so engrossed with the tiny rapids, the rupture of the smooth surface against random stones, that she did not notice Meira approach and place a hand upon her shoulder.

"What is this about?" Meira asked her.

Cecelia stared a moment longer, admiring the way a leaf bravely traversed the rapids before finally succumbing to the violence and sinking beneath the surface. She cleared her throat before answering Meira.

"My mother died when I was young, younger than Lisi, when I was not quite a baby and not quite a child."

"I'm sorry," Meira responded.

Cecelia shook her head, fighting away the false apology. "She was a stranger to me. Memories flit about sometimes, smokey and dreamlike, but her face still eludes me. Only her eyes do I remember, gray, and warm."

Cecelia sighed and glanced at Meira. "My father refuses to speak of her. Rumors abound she was of Korith. Some that she was Fair Folk. The Prevailing Mother herself seems certain she was some cousin."

Meira choked on a laugh. "The Prevailing Mother is a position of great power. And great manipulation."

"So I've experienced," Cecelia said.

"Respen always says a good Prevailing Mother is no Prevailing Mother."

Cecelia fought a smile. She turned and pushed past Meira, starting herself down the path by the stream. Meira hesitated only momentarily before hurrying after her.

"I came here hoping in doing what my father asked, I might finally figure out where my mother came from." Cecelia said when Meira fell into step beside her.

"So the song and the questions about the girls' powers... you were trying to find your mother. And yourself." Cecelia avoided Meira's gaze then. "I am sorry I have been of little help. If your mother fled the continent, I can't say I blame her. The Fair Folk aren't free, not really." Meira added.

Cecelia ceased her walking and stared back at Meira. "I've failed, Meira. I've failed at finding the truth. I've failed at my marriage."

She felt torn in two. Equal halves occupied her, one wishing to sink to the forest floor and weep and the other wanting to seethe with anger until the sadness burned away. Tears fought their way out of the corner of her eyes and she wiped them away angrily.

"I will leave this damned forest and travel to the ocean and seek the first ship home." She was nearly screaming then, though not out of anger at Meira, merely the intensity with which she found her feelings leaping forth from her heart to her throat. "I want to go home," she said. "I want nothing more than to go home, but I haven't the slightest idea where that is anymore." Her voice cracked and her throat screamed in pain. She allowed one shudder of grief to work its way along her spine and into her ribcage before she forcefully exhaled and shoved the pain away. "Worse than it all: I have failed my father and the promise I made him."

The spasm of grief teased her abdomen again. Another sharp exhale forced it back, but it was Meira's arm wrapped around Cecelia's waist that finally stopped the fear of its return. The woman squeezed Cecelia firmly in her grasp, an embrace Cecelia had not expected though did not despise.

"Sometimes, little girls grow up and flee, leaving behind broken hearts." Meira spoke into Cecelia's ear in a whisper reserved for the closest of friends, "Sometimes, a woman must choose to do something just for herself."

Princess Iliana of Sunstone is the youngest child of the Golden Lord. According to the Sun Priests of the Golden Dome—who prophesied her birth—a child of moonlight would be born to his Goldenness and bring forth an alliance with the moon worshippers of the archipelago. Despite initial doubt, the Golden Lord acknowledged the validity of the prophecy upon cradling his daughter for the first time. With her lavender eyes and moonlit complexion, Princess Iliana was raised intending to please the monarch of the Archipelago of the Moons, hoping to secure a marriage alliance with his eldest son.

Logician Mykel Meralko
   Islands of Fortune: An Examination of Island Nations

Chapter Forty-Eight

VIKTOR IMAGINED STRANGE THINGS: his mother crying while he himself was small again. Ephram, alive and laughing, teaching Viktor to ride a horse. He even imagined his father, in full armor, angry and cursing. This last image incited Viktor to move. He wouldn't stand the man's abuse any longer, and swung out hard to hit Lord Black.

The movement startled Viktor, and his eyes finally opened. Above him was a white wooden ceiling. Intricate paintings detailing a forest full of large leafed trees that Viktor had never seen filled the planks. A rolling motion brought forth a storm in his stomach, so he rolled over to vomit.

Miraculously, a woman appeared, ethereal, nearly luminescent, to catch the seawater rushing forth from his mouth. She cooed at him, dabbing at his forehead with a silk cloth so soft Viktor couldn't help but close his eyes.

"Your grace is weak,"

Her voice, thickly accented, took him by surprise. She was so celestial, Viktor half imagined her to be the Daughter herself, and who knows with what words a goddess speaks? He ripped his eyes open and stared at her.

"Who are you?" He growled.

He attempted to push himself up, but the nausea struck again, and he sank down in the soft bed.

"Your sister," she bowed her head elegantly and offered him a polite smile, "for we both claim a Panther as our prize."

"A Panther?" Viktor stuttered.

A door behind the woman burst open. Sunlight flooded the room momentarily, blinding Viktor's tired eyes. He closed them and opened them again, forcing them to focus, forcing himself to see what needed to be seen. When his eyes finally found the newcomer, he frowned.

"Danon," he said.

Danon offered him his own frown. "Brother," he tipped his head only ever so slightly.

"What are you doing here?" Viktor tried to sit up again, this time slowly and with more patience.

The white woman reached for him, offering him her assistance, but he ripped his arm away from her and glared.

"Leave me," he snarled.

The woman, neither appearing frightened nor upset, nodded her head in agreement.

"As you say, your grace." She nearly whispered.

"Don't call me that." He snapped.

"But that is what you are," she said.

"No, I'm not. I'm nobody."

"Viktor, please," Danon came to stand next to the woman. "Where is my sister? Where is Cecelia?"

Viktor stared at Danon, the shame he felt filling his face with heat. His throat tightened to the point that he couldn't respond, even if he knew what words to speak. Even if he knew how to explain to Danon the multitudes of ways he had failed.

"Ili, will you leave us?" Danon asked the woman.

She curtsied in obeisance and left out the door, nearly floating it seemed, though Viktor wondered if the sea water damaged his mind. She pulled up a silken hood, concealing her face completely before entering the sun-drenched deck of the ship.

"Is she a witch?" Viktor asked.

Danon snorted with laughter. "No, she's my wife. Princess Iliana of Sunstone."

"But she glows?"

"She was born with a strange skin tone, devoid of color. Dusting herself with mica prevents sun damage to an extent, though it does look quite beautiful." Danon stared at the door in longing.

"You're... married?"

"Yes," Danon turned his attention back to Viktor. He slumped in the chair Ili had previously occupied. "My father found an alliance with the Goldenones advantageous amidst this current turmoil."

"You mean the rebellion in Korith?" Viktor said.

"I mean my sister!" Danon stood so fast the chair shot out from behind him and tipped over. "My father would never forgive himself were he to let daughter and grandchild die amidst a kingdom so confused, no one knows their friend from their enemy."

He slammed his hand hard on the bedpost, wincing only slightly before gritting his teeth and staring down at Viktor.

Viktor felt the shudder of a headache with the impact of Danon's hand, but he forced himself to focus on the Panther prince's words. One word, in particular, kept repeating itself in his head. So much so, it forced his lips to speak it themselves.

"Grandchild?" He asked slowly.

Danon sneered and hit the bedpost again. He turned and stalked away from Viktor, only to turn and pace back.

"We intercepted a messenger ship attempting, and failing, to skirt the Sea of Storms for the Lagos. Mother Oora sent word that she too required my father's obedience, or his daughter—and first grandchild—would die." Danon attempted and failed to calm himself. "I sent word onward to my father while I turned towards Scree. For my sister. And your unborn child."

"*My* child," Viktor emphasized.

Danon glared at him, his chest heaving with the emotion he felt for his sister. But Viktor only felt cold. The weight of Cecelia's sacrifice was heavy within him, sure, and it threatened to suffocate him lest he push it away and allow the cold to enter.

"I left her," he finally said. "I... I went home. To see my brother."

"And you did not return," Danon said. "Ramiro was assassinated and his wife took hold of the kingdom with that Fair Folk freak at her side. And rumor has it now the queen is missing. Cecelia had no one to trust around her. A viper's nest would have been more hospitable than this damned continent."

"I didn't know," Viktor argued, "how was I to know? Rees said the Unis were under control. The Fair Folk were surrounded."

Danon hissed and rolled his eyes. "Rees. That slimy snake. No doubt he's doing the Prevailing Mother's bidding now. One monarch dies, one goes missing, and he just steps in and obeys another. Men like him survive because they know how to play the game." Danon stopped and stared down at his feet, his thumb tapping out a rhythm on his thigh. "But you," he said, "you're the one that betrayed her. You left her there. And for what? A cursed sword?"

He stalked to a beautiful armoire, bolted to the cabin floor, and ripped the door open. Inside was Ephram's sword, leaning against the corner. Danon grabbed it and flung it on the bed, where it landed heavily on Viktor's shins.

"You... you have it." Viktor reached for it, but stopped.

"I bought it off that crazy woman, Sally. We were docked there not long ago. Several of my men treated in her establishment, only to overhear a man rambling on about outsmarting an exceptionally large man, the king's guard marshal or whatever. Per their description, I knew it was you. I had to enter into negotiations with Sally myself to retrieve the sword. And you."

It appeared a foul taste erupted in Danon's mouth with this last bit. His face twisted in a frown, like he tasted something sour.

"How did you know I'd be there?" Viktor asked.

The sword sat dead in his lap, and he suddenly had the urge to fling it across the room.

"The sword is exquisite," Danon said matter-of-factly. "I figured a man like you would want it back. Wish I could say the same for my sister."

Viktor stared down at the worn gold of the sword's hilt. He imagined the many years his father wielded it, his large hands wearing the shape smooth. He imagined the time it spent in Ephram's hand, deftly fighting for something Viktor once thought noble. Would it ever fit in his hand?

"I was afraid," he muttered, his eyes tracing the last of the filigree that still held its form on the handle.

"Of what?"

Viktor stared a moment longer before answering. "After Ephram died, there was no one else for me to..." but he couldn't finish, for the words stuck heavy in his throat.

"Love?" Danon offered. And when Viktor scowled he added, "come now, we might be men but we all possess the ability to love. It is not merely a woman's power. You loved your brother. As I love mine. As I love my sister."

"Perhaps," Viktor nodded. "But without him, I was alone. And I liked it. I owed loyalty only to whoever paid for it."

"Like Ramiro."

"Yes," Viktor said. "But then you and your sister came. And I... I felt I could love her too. And I was afraid."

"I see," Danon said.

"I have to get her back." Viktor turned to Danon.

The boy seemed to have aged years since his absence from Korith. When Viktor last laid eyes on him, he barely seemed past childhood. But now, standing before him, Viktor saw a man that could command an army. That could command a kingdom.

"Danon, I was going to go back. I didn't know she was with child, I swear by it. But I needed the sword. When it was stolen, I knew I had to retrieve it and then go back for Cecelia."

Danon studied him long and hard. He chewed on the inside of his lip, his anger seeping red on his forehead. Finally, he sighed and his shoulders relaxed.

"Well," he said, "now you have the sword. Let's get her back, shall we?"

Beware the waif with her innocent face and pitiful demeanor, for she is not what she seems. She lurks in the dark woods and lonely paths, haunting those who wander too close, begging for help. But beware! The waif takes what she likes. Including your life. Stay by your mother's side and heed not the waif's strange tales, for they are but distractions. If you find yourself wrapped tightly in her web, fear not. Ask a question thrice. Three times and the waif must answer. Three times and the magic within must give itself up.

Didymus Hargrove
Walking Trees and Other Fables

Chapter Forty-Nine

Cecelia left Meira at the edge of the forest. The tall trees of Bruss stood sentinel behind her as she waved Cecelia onward. A great field erupted from the edge of the forest, crawling across the rolling hills before plunging back into another forest. Cecelia was amazed by how small the trees were. Her perspective had changed, she realized, and nothing would be the same.

She made her way through the new, smaller forest. The forest floor was lumpy with moss and ancient tree stumps that slowed her pace. She traversed game trails whenever she came upon one, knowing the animals always found the fastest way through.

Slowly, the terrain turned to stone. A few outcroppings poked their heads through the trees before submerging again, only to reappear later. More and more these rocks grew until she walked on granite and shale. Stone worn away by feet and wagons. Stone worn smooth by time.

The land sloped downward, telling her she finally made her descent on the other side of the mountain. She tried not to think of Viktor, but he was the only thing she could think of. Her body grew close to his. She could tell. She could always tell.

The sun reflected off the sea in the distance. She was so close. A light breeze picked up, bringing with it traces of salt. A love letter in the wind.

She sighed and slowed her pace. Meira had insisted on leaving her with a few extra pieces of bread and cheese. *To sustain you,* she had said. Cecelia sat on a rock with it, thankful she had met the woman. That she had met the entire family. She might not have found her mother, but she understood a bit more of the strange place her mother hailed from. A place responsible for shaping her mother. For making her the woman who would leave and venture the Sea of Storms and somehow, miraculously, survive to marry the prince of the Lagos.

She imagined the bleeding hearts on her father's desk, each flower someone her mother had had to leave behind.

The ring on her hand, Viktor's ring, caught the sun as she ate. She admired it for a moment. It had been kind of him. But then he had left. Her grip tightened around the ring, her hands balling into fists, but she forced her hand to lie flat again. She would find him and speak to him and sort it all out. Hearts as fragile as theirs needed careful tending. Was that not what she told him?

Her eyes fell across the valley, splaying itself before her, settling her gaze on Craigburna. But something else caught her attention. A speck moving slowly up the trail toward her.

Cecelia sat up straight, shoving her goods away. She knew better than to display her possessions freely when on the trail. Better for strangers to guess what you have than to know. She left her canteen out, stealing sips while she waited. Her gaze never left the moving speck.

The speck soon grew into a human, which soon shifted to a small girl. She wore a worn cloak and no shoes. Her hair was stringy and messy. But her eyes gleamed. Like she had been crying.

"Oh, miss," the girl spoke to her, finally looking up from her toiling walk up the mountain path.

"Hello," Cecelia said slowly. "Where could you be off to with no shoes and no supplies?"

"Oh, is that water, miss? I thirst awfully. You see, I've lost my way."

"I see you are alone, though you walk a well-marked path," Cecelia said. "What way were you heading?"

The girl pointed up the mountain. "There. My father is heading to Fearing and then on to Wilsden. I fell behind, playing knights in my head with sticks and trees. Have you seen him? A man large and broad with a braided beard?"

Cecelia hesitated. She did not wish to let this girl know she had not climbed the mountain road like most people, but circumvented it by taking the river and then the forest of Bruss. Something told her any association with the Fair Folk might mark her as an enemy. Instead, she shook her head no.

"I'm afraid I haven't," she said.

The girl eyed her suspiciously, perhaps wondering how a woman could miss seeing such a man.

"I have water to spare," Cecelia suggested, hoping to distract the girl. "Please, help yourself."

She handed the canteen over to the girl, who took it gingerly. She eyed Cecelia's hand, her eyes tracing the jewel of Viktor's ring.

"That's some ring," the girl spoke over a full mouth of water.

"Yes," Cecelia said.

"Must be a great lord with a ring like that," the girl added.

Cecelia tried not to smile, but couldn't stop herself. She found the girl's presence refreshing after walking by herself, sinking into her own thoughts and the sound of her own voice in her mind. What she once considered solitude, she now considered maddening. Besides, the girl was right. The ring *was* beautiful. Cecelia stared down into the facets, watching the sun shimmer beneath the surface.

"Perhaps," she looked up to find the girl was gone.

Cecelia frowned, her mind reeling, scrambling to make sense of the past few moments. The girl had been real. Cecelia knew that. Her canteen sat on the rock where the girl had been.

She felt it before she had time to stand. A cold, simmering pierce in her back that quickly turned to a raging fire. Fierce warmth flooded across her skin where blood poured out from the wound. Cecelia fell back, her body rigid with pain, unable to stay sitting. Her body revolted against her, giving up when she wanted to fight most.

Her head cracked against the rock. The connection sent brilliant light through her vision, blinding her. It reverberated through her head, bouncing off her skull. Cecelia pondered, momentarily, how it could be possible to hear one's head strike a rock from both the inside and the outside.

A dark shadow blocked out the sun. It took Cecelia's eyes a moment longer than normal to adjust. Everything she saw was still blurry, but she could make out the girl's face. Only it had morphed somewhat.

Her eyes glimmered, but not with tears. Magic. And while she still maintained a youthful visage, something about the girl seemed timeless. She was at the same time young and old. Cecelia cursed herself for not noticing sooner.

"Who are you?" Cecelia blurted out, the pain searing up her back and into her neck with each syllable.

"I've roamed this land far longer than you," the creature whispered, all semblance of a child's voice gone, "and I've no use for your kindnesses."

The thing reached for Cecelia's hand and she could not find the strength to fight it off. It ripped Viktor's ring from her fingers, raking it across the knuckles, sending a searing pain through Cecelia's hand.

"But this," it hissed, "I do have use for."

It bent down low and kissed Cecelia on the forehead with lips wet and sticky. Its breath smelled sulfuric but also sweet. Cecelia's head spun.

It was gone as soon as it appeared. The thing, not a girl, not really, vanished into the shadows of the trees, leaving the bright sun beating down on Cecelia.

With effort, she could move her head. She turned it slowly one way and then the other, realizing the creature had indeed left her to die. A tear rolled slowly out of the corner of her eye, past the slope of her nose, and into the corner of her mouth. The saltiness tasted sharp, keeping her awake a moment longer.

How badly it reminded her of the Lagos. How badly she had wanted to return there.

But she never would. Her father said as much.

Her finger felt naked without the ring. She wiggled it, feeling the lack of metal against her skin, earning herself the reward of a sharp burn up the wrist. It had been the one thing she'd chosen, she realized. He had been the one thing she chose.

Just for herself.

She did not remember being picked up. Her eyes had opened and closed several times while she lay dying on the rock. The sun seemed to move at a faster pace then, quickly setting, injecting the sky with a red eerily similar to the blood she seeped beneath her.

But the trees, dark like wraiths, moved above her. The sound of a wagon wheel jostling on stones matched with the movement she felt beneath her. She sighed and it hurt. She tried to adjust her body, but it, too, hurt.

"Easy," a soothing voice spoke from the darkness, "you are alive. But barely."

She wanted to speak, to offer her usual sarcastic comment that somehow sustained her, but found that this time she couldn't. This time, the pain was too much. This time, she believed this person who told her she was only just alive.

A hand reached from out of the darkness and rested on her forehead. The coolness of the skin on Cecelia's own calmed her. She slowed her breathing, feeling the magic before realizing she was being magicked.

"Nora?" The only name that seemed to come to Cecelia's mind, to her lips.

She thought she could hear a smile in the voice from the darkness when it spoke next.

"No," it said, "I am no one special. Just... a finder of things. And I've been looking for you for quite some time, Panther princess."

Some Fair Folk oral traditions date Gri'goru back to creation, though tales usually differ on Gri'goru's exact origins. Some state the creature was meant to be a tree—usually a Grey Oak—while some say it was destined to be a pinnacle of granite. Despite these differences, all tales agree Gri'goru wanted more. The creature wanted to be the TALLEST tree, the LARGEST pinnacle. Gri'goru would not be satisfied until it was the best. The Earth Mother, tired of Gri'goru's wasteful negativity, forced the creature out into the world and left it to fend for itself.

Priest Clarynce Craag
The Dark Bestiary

Shunning its once ambitious ideals, Gri'goru found humans soft and foolish.

Fair Folk Oral Story Excerpt

Chapter Fifty

Danon insisted he could not make landfall with Viktor to look for Cecelia. Having already done so when he entered Sally's Champagne Palace to broker a deal for Viktor's life, Danon felt he pressed his luck.

"The kingdom is at war," he had said, "a Panther prince's arrival would only stoke the fire. We will wait here. The rest of our fleet is not far, anchored just past the Spit of Scree in friendly waters. Should we need the manpower, we'll be ready."

Viktor was too tired to argue. Since Ulla's attack, he felt older than usual. Perhaps it was merely the wear on his body. Or perhaps it was the weight of his task. Cecelia was somewhere before him, hidden within the kingdom, carrying his child. He'd have to find her. It would not be an easy task, but he assured Danon he'd do it.

The walk through Craigburna took him past Sally's once again. Music trickled through the windows and laughter fluttered on the sea breeze. Viktor increased his speed, not wanting to spend any more time near the establishment than necessary.

Lara One-Eye leaned against the doorframe of a backdoor, puffing a pipe. She raised it to Viktor as he walked by, smirking.

"See you fared alright," she called to him.

He wanted to curse at her, but he was too tired even for that. He ignored her and kept walking even as she catcalled to his back. But soon the common gulls drowned her out and her voice became a distant echo of their shrill calls.

Outside the city gates, he started the climb up the valley. The road was dusty but would soon give way to stone. At the top of the first hill, he rested. Danon's ship, with its large black sails, loomed in the harbor below. Viktor watched the wind ripple through the dark fabric, a snarling panther painted on the side.

When he reached the top of the second hill, he pushed onward. The sun was rising fast and would soon beat down on his neck. He needed to make it to the forest for protection. His plan was to repeat his steps, hoping Cecelia was angry enough to follow him. Hoping she proved as good a tracker as she was a warrior.

The summit of the third and final hill grew beneath his feet, and at the top he met a wagon party. Two old men bickered back and forth about a wagon wheel that posed a threat of breaking. A small girl stirred a pot of water for the camp meal nearby, actively trying to ignore the men but failing miserably.

"Would you two shut it?" She yelled over her shoulder at them.

They quieted, but only for a moment. The girl looked up to see Viktor watching them and stood abruptly.

"Boys!" she called to the arguing pair. "You've done ignored your duty."

The men silenced themselves at her words. They turned their attention to the girl and then to Viktor, who stood at the hill's edge. Together, they leaped in front of the girl, separating Viktor from the wagon party.

"Who are you?" The first one asked.

"What do you want?" said the second.

Viktor realized they were twins, each a mirror of the other. They even braided their beards the same way. Stood the same. When one balled his hand into a fist, so did the other.

Viktor held his hands up to show his passivity. "I only want the trail," he said. "I'm heading up the mountain."

The men glared at him, not convinced.

"The trail runs both ways," Viktor continued, annoyed at the men's aggression. "It's mine to take as I please, just as it's yours."

The first man moved his mouth to speak, eyebrows still angrily turned downward, but the girl spoke over him.

"You're right," she said. "Forgive us, sir. Our mistress, whose got some control over these two, went on to Craigburna to see about a new wheel."

Viktor peered past the men and at the girl. She seemed barely older than ten and three. Not quite a woman, not quite a child. And yet she wielded authority over the men. They relaxed and stepped backward, giving Viktor more room.

Their wagon leaned heavily to one side, favoring the weakened wheel. It'd need an entire new one to finish the trek to Craigburna. The wagon itself was open roofed, though the party had draped a thin cloth across the top, protecting whatever was inside from the sun. There was a sudden movement within, and the wagon shifted slightly. The girl watched Viktor, gauging him, to see if he noticed. She caught the eyes of the twins and suggested with her head toward the wagon. The men stepped closer, blocking Viktor's view of the wagon.

"As you said, good sir," the girl said, "the trail is yours as much as it's ours. We'll not stop you from availing yourself of it."

It was her way of telling him to move on. Viktor knew when he wasn't wanted. He glanced at the wagon one more time, wondering, before giving up and moving onward. He could see the trail ensconced by trees just over the ridge. The sun's heat would give way to the coolness of the shade. The anticipation of it made Viktor's feet antsy. Whatever had been in that wagon, they didn't want anyone to know about it. What did Viktor care, then? He had a Panther princess to find.

The sun was setting when he reached a small creek. The Daughter, a thin waxing crescent, whispered from the sky while the Mother twinkled in the rippling water in her waning crescent. He watched its shape move and dance on the surface while he filled his canteen. A sudden crack within the bushes brought Viktor to his feet, his sword halfway withdrawn before he realized it was a child.

Another girl, though this one seemed younger. Her hair was a mess and her feet shoeless. She smiled weakly at him and pointed to his pack.

"I'm so hungry, sir," she said, "could you spare some vittles?"

Viktor shoved his sword back into its sheath. He could barely make out her face. She was shrouded in the shadows. Her dark hair fell across her eyes, making it impossible to make out their color. Noticing he stared at her, she brushed away a stray piece of hair from her face, a gem glittering on her finger.

Viktor's heart skipped a beat. His stomach sank to his knees.

His mother's ring.

"That's a mighty fine stone for a dirty orphan," he said, suggesting to the ring she now hid behind her back.

"Oh?" the girl said.

"Perhaps not for a greedy phantom, though, is it?" He added.

The girl snarled at him, her teeth bared and sharp. "A stranger in these lands," the voice, or perhaps voices - Viktor was unsure - said, "she deserved what she got."

Viktor calmly withdrew his sword again, this time fully. The sensation of control that overcame him amazed him. The sense of order when he withdrew Ephram's sword felt like no other sword he'd ever wielded. It was as if all paths had led to that moment. All memories of his past life gave way to this one instant, facing the phantom. Facing the creature that stole his mother's ring from his wife.

The mother of his child.

"Where is she?" He asked her.

The creature crouched and bared its teeth, ignoring Viktor's request.

"I'll ask again, what did you do with her?"

The thing lunged, but Viktor was ready. He saw the attack before it even happened, anticipating the creature's movements. He kicked at it hard, sending it flying backward into a giant stone.

"Again creature. Where is my wife?"

Viktor held still, waiting. Shadow Children were fearsome things, seeking the lost, stealing from them. It was like a snare, an unavoidable attraction. Viktor had been scared into obedience with tales of them as a child. Stories meant to warn children of wandering off. Stories told by mothers to keep their children safe.

But Ephram embellished the stories, adding bits of knowledge he himself had heard. Three times a question asked, and the truth it must give. Three times was all a Shadow Child could take.

Viktor watched its body wrack with pain, fighting the words that clawed up its throat. Its eyes bulged from its head. But the thing's mouth obeyed its rules, rules of an ancient magic even the Fair Folk didn't understand.

"Silver in her back," it hissed, still struggling to stay its tongue. "Blood on a rock."

Viktor stepped toward the thing, pinning one frail arm with his boot. He shoved the tip of his sword to the phantom's throat. It looked up at him, its face attempting to recreate the image of a child. But it flickered, shuddered, and went dark again.

"Riddles," Viktor growled, "are not what I asked for."

The creature spat at him, but Viktor easily avoided the spray. Swallowing hard, the creature had nothing else to do but speak.

"On a wagon to Craigburna," it sputtered, black blood bubbling at the corner of its mouth.

"A wagon?" Viktor let up the tension on his sword only slightly, surprised by the realization that Cecelia had been the one in the wagon.

She had been so close, and he had let her go.

"In her brother's arms, she will die!" the phantom wailed, lunging once again at Viktor.

The sudden strength of the waif threw him off balance. A root beneath his boot tripped him further still. The creature clawed at his arm, winning itself an opening where it thrust its body at his chest. The creature was too close to fight with his sword and it pinned him too tightly to the forest floor to reach his dagger in the small of his back.

The child's face flickered once again, no longer youthful, but menacing. Teeth, sharp like knives, snapped at his face. Viktor used all of his strength to hold the waif away, encircling its throat with his hand.

And then he saw it. The ring of His Brilliance sat snug on his finger. Perhaps Viktor imagined the glimmer of the rays' edges. Perhaps he only pretended to know they were sharp. But the cut on his palm still stung from where he'd accidentally sliced his hand. The pointed ray had sliced clean and deep.

Viktor shifted his hand so that the ring bit into the waif's neck. The intense pain startled the creature, and for a moment she eased her assault. Viktor pushed harder. The creature writhed in pain. She pulled away from him and in that moment, Viktor removed his dagger. He plunged as hard as he could through the phantom's neck and watched in fascinated horror as black tendrils of blood ran from its white skin. It oozed past him, sinking into the moss covered earth, steaming.

"No," Viktor said to the quiet forest as the creature's screeching ceased. "No."

When healed by magic, people often feel a sense of enchantment that can be compared to a cooling sensation beneath the skin. Although not entirely unpleasant, many report feeling like something struggles for space inside their body where there is no space to be found. This sensation is referred to as Ic'icasha or The Cold Whisper by the Fair Folk.

Court Historian Alfred Peri
    The Scroll of Children: A Collected History of the Fair Folk

Chapter Fifty-One

Cecelia drifted in and out of consciousness. When she was awake, dull pain rose from beneath her. Yet with every jolt of the wagon, it simmered, causing her to inhale sharply. A hand would emerge from the darkness, warm and gentle, to rest on her forehead, to soothe the pain away. Her eyes would grow heavy, and she'd drift off to sleep.

She had time, before finally succumbing to slumber, to realize she was being bewitched. Someone, the owner of the gentle hand, was keeping her asleep. Keeping her comfortable. Cecelia was grateful, but also angry. She did not like feeling the pity of others aimed at her. She did not like asking for help. Or not asking but receiving it, anyway.

Her eyes fell on her hand, lying palm up, almost like a forgotten appendage. Where her ring should have been, the knuckle was purple and bruised.

She did not like feeling alone.

Slowly, she pulled her other hand to her stomach, cradling it. Where her baby should have been.

She did not like feeling like a failure.

When next she woke, the wagon jolted constantly. There was no stopping the movement, no soothing the pain.

"The cobbles cannot be avoided, princess," the calming voice Cecelia associated with the gentle hand said. "But we will be there soon. Rest."

The hand was placed on her forehead, but this time Cecelia did not feel the magic. There was no extra warmth, save for the normal heat from one's skin. She did not feel the drowsy effect, nor the lightheadedness that she had learned to associate with bewitchment.

"Where?" she muttered.

Her abdomen ached with every breath and attempting to utter syllables was nearly unbearable. She clamped her eyes shut, despite knowing she wouldn't sleep. Couldn't sleep. Instead, she focused on the heat of the palm on her forehead, not of an unnatural power, but of a person. A being. Someone caring for her.

"Craigburna, your grace." The voice said. "Your brother docks a ship here."

"Danon," Cecelia said, out of breath.

The pain of the wagon on cobbles was too much for her. The person, whoever they were, could not ease her discomfort any more. Her body, deciding it could not bear the pain any longer, used its own magic to deal with it. She passed out.

It was as if her words had summoned him. She lay in a bed and Danon sat on the edge, head in hands, muttering. She took him in as much as she could, every inch, before closing her eyes out of pain. Her head ached horribly. Her back, more so.

"Tell me you're praying," she managed to say. "Tell me you've asked the Mother to relieve me of this pain."

Danon sat up and reached for her hand. He squeezed it tight.

"She said you'd live, but I did not think it possible." He said.

Cecelia cracked her eyes open again. They watered with the effort, turning her brother's image into a watercolor mess.

"Who?" Her voice rumbled deep within her chest.

She felt sick. Like the time she was ten and four and came down with such a hacking cough, she was bedridden for two weeks. But there was also the pain in her back, where the waif had stabbed her. And the pain in her abdomen where the baby should be. But that pain wasn't real. Not really. Though it didn't make it go away any faster.

"Wilyna," Danon answered. "A sorceress, it would seem."

Cecelia stared up at the ceiling, admiring the foliage that reminded her so much of home.

"Her traveling mates nearly worship her. Perhaps they're bewitched, though she claims to be no one of importance. Merely..."

"A finder of missing things," Cecelia said over him. "Yes, she told me."

"I'm sending her back," Danon said, "to find Viktor. Her companions said they saw him, passed him on the trail, but they didn't know. Couldn't know."

Danon's voice trailed off as he studied Cecelia. She felt his eyes permeating her skin, attempting to wager whether or not Wilyna's words were true.

Would she live?

"You sent my husband away," Cecelia mused, "to find me?"

Cecelia could barely believe it. Viktor had run from her. She thought she hunted for him. But it seemed the predator had become the prey.

"I won't attempt to speak for him," Danon said, "I'll let him do that. But I will say he was eager to find you."

"Eager?" Cecelia tried to smile at the word.

Eager was not a word she would use to describe Viktor. Ever. Cecelia wanted to speak more to her brother, or at least attempt to speak. She wanted to convey to him the feelings she had of the Lagos. Of how lost she felt. How homeless. And how glad she was to see him. But a knock at the door bid the moment gone. A knock, and the passionate feelings she had carried with her were told to wait once again.

"Beg pardon, your grace," a voice, the voice from the wagon spoke at the door, "but we are ready to leave. I only wished to speak to the princess before I go."

"Of course," Danon opened the door more, allowing sunlight to fall across the room, blinding Cecelia.

She hissed and covered her eyes with her arm, immediately regretting the movement. Her side groaned and her back seared with pain.

"I'd avoid sudden movements, your grace," the voice said.

Cecelia lowered her arm incrementally, allowing her eyes to adjust to the light. Before her stood a woman, gray of hair though her face was youthful. Cecelia tilted her head, hoping a shift in the light would clarify the woman's features. No, not gray. Her hair was the lightest shade of purple. A shade found in the Trailing Mosswood in the mountains of her home, sun-bleached and thirsty.

"Wilyna," Cecelia's voice was still grumbly and sore. It caught in her throat and she had to force each syllable out. "A sorceress, I am told."

"Yes, your grace," Wilyna kneeled beside the bed. "It is an honor to be at your service."

The corner of Cecelia's lips ticked up to form the start of a smirk. "Marvelous," she said. "A Korithian witch is honored to serve a foreign princess."

Wilyna shook her head. "No. A roaming sorceress, sensing a grown man's brokenness, finds what would make him whole."

Cecelia stared at the woman. She swallowed hard her next words, preferring not to speak them. The romanticizing of her husband tasted poorly in her mouth.

"I met Viktor in Wilsden. He arrived on horse and I...," Wilyna trailed off.

"What?" Cecelia said. "You what?"

Wilyna tried to smile, but it was apparent her thoughts were not happy ones. "I saw his aura. I'd never seen one so dark. I knew I had to follow him. I had to know why it was that way."

Cecelia went pale. "Are you sure?"

Wilyna shook her head. "I could never forget it. It was like twilight. Like when I would hunt through the underbrush for my dinner and used the darkness to keep myself hidden."

G'rig's words filled Cecelia's thoughts. And then her father's.

A darkness.

"I tried to keep him safe until I knew what it was he wanted. What he was searching for."

"Which was what?" Cecelia asked.

Wilyna's breath caught, leaving her momentarily speechless. Cecelia's question surprised her, as if she should already know the answer. Cecelia watched Wilyna through narrowed eyes.

"Well, you," Wilyna smiled.

Cecelia had no response. She stared at the floor, attempting to piece back together the aged and faded designs on the rug. She felt lightheaded. Her hands shook but she shoved them beneath her back.

"Are you alright Cecelia?" Danon asked.

She rolled over and away, facing the distant wall.

"I'll go," Wilyna said. "She needs rest, your grace."

Footsteps faded and the door gently shut. For a moment, Cecelia thought she was alone. But Danon's shadow fell over her.

"What's wrong with you?" He said. "She saved you and you act like a ... like a sullen child?"

Cecelia sighed. She followed a grain of wood along the wall, hoping Danon would go away.

"Cecelia?" Danon demanded.

She rolled over to face him, the tears hot on her cheeks. They traced crooked pathways to her lips, leaving their bitter, salty taste reminding her of her weakness.

"I was with G'rig. He brought me across Korith. Well, most of the way. He mentioned Viktor. He mentioned his dark aura. Wilyna saw the same thing."

Danon frowned. "And? Don't tell me you believe in fortunes now, do you? You've been in this kingdom barely two turns of the Daughter, Cecelia. You couldn't have fallen victim to the Fair Folk's tricks already?"

Cecelia shook her head, wiping angrily at her face. "You don't understand, Danon. Father saw a darkness too. Like a creature in the bush. Like Wilyna said."

Danon stared at her, biting his lip. Finally, he nodded in agreement. "Alright," he said, "what does it mean?"

"I don't know," she said.

Her father sent them to find the darkness. If the darkness was Viktor, then what? She wanted him. Truth be told, she loved him. And their fortunes were bound, like the moons, like the seasons, like the tarot cards G'rig used to read Viktor's fortune.

No matter how dark the path seemed.

She inhaled deeply, preparing herself for the speech she had practiced in her head. The one that expressed her fragility at the loss of her mother's identity and losing her baby. At the weakness she felt when she was alone. About the pain of Viktor's abandonment and the bewildering things she had seen on her journey to Craigburna. But again, fate would not allow it.

A woman knocked on the door and entered, barely waiting for Danon's reply.

"You must eat," the woman said to Danon, thrusting a plate of salted fish and rice at him.

"I'm not hungry," he began, but was quickly cut off.

"You are not a martyr, Danon," the woman said.

She glanced at Cecelia, perhaps just realizing she was awake, and pulled herself back. Her snarl became more a whisper and her ferocity transformed to passivity.

"You are worried. And busy with commanding this fleet. I understand. But you are useless to all if you do not eat and keep your strength."

Danon stared at her. Cecelia knew he was too proud to admit she was right, but something stayed him from arguing further.

"Wise words," Cecelia said between coughs, "who dares speak to the heir of the Panthers in such a way?"

The woman drifted closer to Cecelia and kneeled. It was there in the full light blazing in through the nearby window that Cecelia saw her fully.

Hair, like moonlight, fell down in long braids, framing her luminous face. Eyes the color of sweet apples stared kindly at her.

"You're the princess of Sunstone, Iliana." Cecelia said.

Rumors in the Dry Vineyard were that the Golden Lord whelped seven children on his Nubarian wife. But the last was not just any child. A child of the moon had been bestowed to the worshippers of His Brilliance. People could not decide if it was a bad omen or good. But looking at the woman, Cecelia found herself enamored by her beauty.

"My wife," Danon's words cut through Cecelia's thoughts. "We were married immediately on the island of Duwu, with His Brilliance's Righteous Servant as witness. He insisted. Father relented. Iliana's father brought a fleet to meet us, and once married we turned toward Korith, steering wide, attempting to find an easy way back on the continent."

Cecelia sat up a little taller and looked past the beautiful princess at her brother. "That's a lot to arrange so quickly."

Danon chewed his lips, nodding in agreement. He glanced at Iliana, who offered nothing to add.

"You knew," Cecelia finally said, "before Korith."

Danon cleared his throat. "Father told me I would marry Iliana, yes. He told me there'd be a need to take her dowry—a portion of the Golden Lord's fleet—back to Korith. To help you."

She looked back at Iliana. "Did you not have a say in this? Just follow your husband on a mission with no real purpose? Father told me to stay, Danon, and stay I shall."

Danon scowled at Cecelia but offered no retort.

Iliana bowed her head. "I thought my husband's quest to save his sister a noble one."

Cecelia turned back to Danon. "I cannot leave, brother," she said. "You know this. You've come here for nothing."

"No," Danon said, "father is... sick, Cecelia. He will not last through the winter. He told me to find you. I need you to come back with me. I need you."

Cecelia wanted to laugh. She also wanted to cry. Didn't he see? Didn't he see the truth of it all? She wasn't meant to be there, in the Lagos, living amongst them.

Just like her mother.

"I won't go with you," she said. "I want Viktor, and nothing more."

Danon frowned. His hands balled into fists, but he attempted to relax them and smoothed out his pants instead. When he opened his mouth to speak, Cecelia cut him off.

"Nothing more," she growled.

Thoojun is a poison common in Vocan, used primarily by thieves to deal with witnesses of their crimes and mitigate any damage of being caught. Mountain Wormwood makes up a hefty part of this poison, though the distinct soil smell comes from the addition of dirt dug from around the base of the highly poisonous Lily of the Moons. Dried vanilla is traditionally added as a jest, meant to lighten the scent of the wormwood and bring a comforting smell to the - albeit dangerous - situation. While an antidote does exist, the knowledge to produce it is limited to the Minor Continent and Inush.

Ka'asi ult Polath Vroot
  Lybrum Vene'orum

Chapter Fifty-Two

Viktor practically ran down the mountain. Or, at least he tried, until he grew too tired. It wouldn't do to pass out from exertion on the trail. He didn't know what else might befall him should he pass out. Rumor had it that there were many Shadow Children in Korith. Or that it was unkillable. Though the inky black ooze that seeped from the creature's wounds said otherwise.

The walls of Craigburna grew within the darkness before him. He picked up the pace again. Lights from inside the walls tossed their soft glow to the skies, softening the shadows. But nothing compared to the light of the Mother, even while she waned.

Viktor didn't know if the feeling in his stomach was due to lack of food or the hopeful proximity of his wife. Either way, he knew it was from a form of hunger.

Sally's Champagne Palace loomed ahead. Light spilled out from every window, offering sounds from inside. The place was full by the sound of it. Laughter and yelling mixed with an odd music played on strings. Bodies, their features indiscernible amidst the shadows of the building, leaned against banisters on the upper floor. They peered out at the night like Starry Owls. They puffed on long pipes and whistled at him.

He ignored them, only chancing a look at the doorway where Lara One-Eye had cat called him earlier. She was gone, of course, replaced by two guests enjoying each other's company a bit too brazenly.

Only when his feet pounded on the boardwalk did he slow. His heart beat so hard he could feel it emanating from his bones. Danon's ship floated peacefully in the black waters of the harbor ahead, calling to him. The sounds of the waves lapping gently at its side soothed him further. Cecelia was there. He could feel it. He'd explain himself. Perhaps she'd forgive him. Perhaps not. Either way, this weight he felt on his chest would finally dissipate and he could finally breathe again.

His were not the only footsteps on the boardwalk. A sudden thudding accompanied his steps, which turned faster and faster. Viktor turned to see what followed and met with a toss of powder on his face. He inhaled sharply and sneezed. He choked. It smelled intensely of wormwood and garden soil. Vanilla too. He felt his knees meet the wood grain of the boardwalk and the searing pain as it bit into his skin, and then he felt nothing.

When he awoke, his head screamed, but he quickly got over the pain to focus on his surroundings. He hated that he was growing accustomed to being knocked out. It wasn't something anyone expected to have happen more than once.

If at all.

This time, he wasn't lying in a cushy bed. Instead, he sat tied to a chair. The floor before him was scrubbed wood, left shining by a recent cleaning. Further away sat a wooden desk, and behind it sat Sally.

"Sally," he said, tipping his head in a greeting.

Sally sighed. "Sorry Viktor," she said, "truly. You must believe me when I say I had nothing to do with this."

"I'm in your office, Sally, so excuse me while I find that hard to believe."

"It wasn't my idea." She replied.

He wanted to ask her whose idea it had been, but the person of interest interrupted.

"It was mine," Danica said, emerging from the windowed alcove. "I paid her for the use of her office. She speaks the truth."

Sally, for the first time, looked scared. She took a glass and poured some cognac and sipped at it quietly.

"Your grace," Viktor said, "I thought you were missing or..."

"Dead?" Danica sneered. "You hoped I was dead, didn't you?"

Viktor knew better than to answer that question, though he desperately wanted to. Instead, he studied the queen, noticing how tired she looked. Her clothes were worn and stained. Her boots, not meant for riding, cracked at the seams.

"Rumors were you were dead, though I knew that couldn't be. Insects like you don't die."

Danica's nose flared and the blush that filled her face turned her once delicate skin a violent shade of red. She slapped Viktor across the face, yelping as she did so. She cradled her hand to her chest and glared at him.

"I should've killed you when I had the chance. I should've let Rees kill you when he wanted to. But I stayed his hand."

"Why?" Viktor asked, his face tingling with the contact of Danica's hand. He could still feel it, every inch of her palm, on the side of his face.

"For her," Danica growled, "I did it for her."

The anger fell away for only a moment, and the sting of his face disappeared. He should have noticed. The constant attention given to Cecelia. The closeness. Danica was a vapid and cold woman, but transformed into something resembling a human when in Cecelia's presence.

"You fool," he finally said, "you senseless fool."

This angered Danica more. The red of her cheeks extended to her ears. She started to sweat. Sally excused herself, whispering a goodbye, before leaving the room. Danica watched her go before turning back to Viktor.

She creeped toward him, removing a small glass bottle from a pocket hidden in the seam of her dress.

"You'll take me to her," she said. "I'll redeem myself by bringing you back to her."

"Not even for the Mother, I won't." He replied.

She gripped his face, twisting his hair in her hand, forcing him to tilt his head backward. He gritted his teeth, seeing her untwist the cork from the bottle with her free hand.

"You'll do it," she said, spittle landing on his cheeks, "because as soon as you drink this, you'll start to die."

"Then I'll die in this chair," he said.

Danica smirked. "And leave her with questions? Women like Cecelia demand answers, Viktor. You don't have long now."

She shoved the bottle into his mouth, glass clashing with teeth. The liquid was ice cold and slightly sweet, though it turned bitter in the back of his throat. He tried to spit it out, but she dropped the bottle and pinched his nose shut, forcing his body to take over for his brain.

After he had swallowed, she shoved him away. The chair tipped. He crashed onto his side, hitting his head on the wooden floor. His headache returned and his vision blurred. The fire, roaring in the hearth not far away, filled his vision with reds and oranges. From above, he heard Danica's voice.

"The Moons rise, Victor," she said, "you haven't long. Let us meet our love together."

Cool water on his face woke him. He had passed out again. He hadn't been out for long, though. The fire still roared and the darkness of night still seemed the same saturated black as before.

"Get up," it was Sally, kneeling next to him with her cognac glass. "She's left, though I don't know where. You must get to the ship. It's docked in the harbor, not far away. Surely you can make it?"

"Is that a question or an order?" He muttered.

Realizing Sally had untied his hands, Viktor pushed himself into a sitting position. The headache was gone, miraculously, and his vision cleared. Water dripped down his face, down his neck, and into his tunic. He looked at Sally.

"You could have used cognac," he told her.

"I never waste the good stuff," she smiled. "Now, come. The poison she used is uncommon in Korith, but in Vocan it is as common as beer. The white woman on Danon's ship, the Golden Lord's get, will surely know how to treat it."

"Because she's a witch?" Viktor grunted with the effort of standing, aided by Sally's help.

"No," Sally scoffed, "because she's smart."

And the seventh child, the child of prophecy Princess Iliana, would marry the Prince of the Archipelago of the Moons, marking the beginning of what the archipelago called The Era of the Benevolent Moons.

Logician Mykel Meralko
   Islands of Fortune: An Examination of Island Nations

A woman with lavender eyes,
And skin that shimmered with moonlit grace,
Bathed in midnight's mystic dyes.

Robyn Sweet-tongue
Personal Bard of His Brilliance's Righteous Servant
Bride of Prophesy

Chapter Fifty-Three

"The love of your brother is admirable, your grace," Iliana said to Cecelia while she dabbed a moist cloth to her forehead.

Cecelia felt fine. Her back, though sore, ceased to vex her. The pain in her head subsided considerably, and only kept a fuzzy taint in the corner of her vision, nothing more. Iliana informed her that Wilyna seemed a well-practiced healer, not leaving Cecelia's side until she had administered her treatment. Not leaving the ship until she was certain Cecelia would live.

And perhaps she would, Cecelia considered.

"Have you not several siblings yourself?" Cecelia asked.

Iliana briefly frowned before transforming the look into a smile. It was beautiful. The broad planes of her face glittered with mica, creating the most divine of images. If the girl herself claimed to be the Daughter manifested, Cecelia might believe her.

Might.

"The children of Sunstone are spread far and wide as soon as they can walk. Sent to study. Sent to learn a discipline. We are each assigned a duty, according to our aptitude. I would not know my siblings from a stranger, your grace."

"I see."

Cecelia noticed a hint of sadness in the girl's voice, hidden at the edge. She put on a fantastic show, remaining stalwart and strong. Cecelia wondered how hard she'd have to push to make her crumble. How easy would it be to break her?

Not that she wanted to. But her father married Danon off to the princess quickly. He had kept this from her, sending her to Korith not knowing her brother was already pledged. She hoped her father thought the situation through. The Goldenones were worshippers of His Brilliance. The Sun god. The Pretender. And while Iliana seemed blessed by moonlight itself, she worried the girl would have a negative influence on her brother.

"What type of duties?" Cecelia asked, probing.

It wasn't her place to arrange her sibling's marriages, but she still felt obligated to form her own opinion.

Iliana sighed. "One brother was sent off to the temple to be reborn as a priest. Though, thanks to his connection to the throne, I'm sure he'll spend his days eating and drinking and getting fat."

Cecelia choked on a laugh.

"And a sister was sent to Nubaria, to my grandfather's court, where she plays at being my grandmother's lady-in-waiting while siphoning secrets to my father."

Cecelia admired Iliana's possession of brutal honesty.

"And you?" Cecelia asked, "What would *they* say of you and your duties?"

Iliana twisted her lips beautifully, thinking. She tossed the cloth to the side table and leaned back in her chair. It was an unladylike posture, but Iliana remained the picture of grace even while doing so.

"My father's favorite," she concluded. "His most precious, raised to be an ornament on his already illustrious crown."

"And what do you say?"

Iliana looked dumbfounded, as if no one had asked her that question before. As if it were the first time anyone asked her what she felt her duties were.

"I trained as a healer," she said. "Which I enjoy. I studied the tenets of your religion, of the Mother and Daughter, and consider myself a convert. I studied diplomacy. I studied your family history. I was raised as a pawn to further my father's scheme of peace between our kingdoms. But I have worked tirelessly to not be just a pawn."

Cecelia offered Iliana a genuine smile, though it pained her temples so and brought back a sting of the headache.

"And you," Iliana asked, "what of your duties? I learned long ago of a girl that would be queen, though many complained she did not deserve it. That she wasn't really a Panther. And when I married your brother, I learned it was I who would one day wear the crown meant for her. So, your grace, what do you say your duties are?"

Cecelia felt her throat tighten. She wished she could blame it on her injuries, but that was beyond the truth. Deep down, she knew it was what really ailed her. The lack of identity. The lack of duty. She trailed her gaze out the window, watching the setting sun cast its dying rays across the water.

"I don't know," she finally said, her voice wavering though she pushed through. "Once, I thought it was to serve the Lagos, to be the best ruler I could. But then I slowly realized it would never come to that. When my father sent me here, to Korith, I knew I wouldn't return. So I killed those dreams."

Cecelia looked at Iliana, still sitting so relaxed in her presence, though thoroughly engaged in Cecelia's words. There was a kindness in her eyes that brought forth a memory Cecelia had long since buried. A memory of her mother, sitting on the grand steps of the harbor, allowing Cecelia to dawdle after the gulls. People walked by, glaring at her mother, confused as to why she was given a place of privilege by their king. They looked more kindly on Cecelia, only a child, but even then, their eyes judged her.

But not her mother's. Her eyes gazed down on Cecelia like she raised the moons themselves. Her eyes told Cecelia she was precious. She was special. She was loved.

A tear threatened to fall down the corner of Cecelia's eyes. She hid her movements to wipe it away, pretending something itched her ear.

"In Korith, I thought I could find the truth of my mother. Where she came from. Who she was. How, by the Mother, she crossed the Sea of Storms. And then I... I thought I would be a mother. But it wasn't to be so."

Cecelia could not hide the tears then. And truthfully, she didn't want to. She let them fall, hot and wet, down her cheeks. But she did not cry out. She refused to give voice to the feelings of hopelessness. Better to unleash them through tears, let them fall where they may, and move on.

Tears are not useless, her father told her once, *let them water the soldier within.*

Iliana grasped Cecelia's hand, but said nothing. She waited patiently while Cecelia released the pent-up feelings she held, feelings she could never give words to. Feelings she never would. Because sometimes pain required silence and tears. Sometimes pain had to run its course before withering away.

Iliana sighed, but only because she seemed to feel Cecelia's pain with her. She squeezed Cecelia's hand.

"The Mother gives and takes, your grace, but may the Daughter save us from the worst of it."

Cecelia silently shook her head that she understood, though she didn't. Not really. Not any of it.

"Perhaps you looked for your mother in the wrong place," Iliana whispered, not wanting to upset the soothing silent balance the room had come too, "perhaps it is here you should look."

She extended her other hand and gently touched her fingertips to Cecelia's chest, to her heart.

"Who she was to you is just as valid and real as who she was to your father. To the people she left behind. She is a part of you. And that is no mystery, your grace."

Cecelia swallowed hard, shaking her head in agreement. Iliana was wise beyond her young years. As intelligent as she was beautiful.

"You're right," Cecelia said. "You certainly are astute. A gem worthy of adorning her father's crown."

She winked at Iliana. Iliana shoved Cecelia's hand away playfully but smiled all the same.

"And what about Viktor?" Iliana asked. "Is he not a worthy consolation?"

Cecelia picked at her nails. They peeled and tore from the weeks of parading across Korith with its different climate. With its strange people.

"Viktor... was a distraction. At first." Cecelia admitted. "In time... I learned to fix my position from him, like a sailor using stars."

She stared out the window again, watching the sky turn from red to orange. Clouds floated past in the most delicate shades of pink. Gulls cried out on the evening breeze. Everything seemed as it should be. But to Cecelia, it wasn't.

Wilyna promised to bring what she desired back, but she found herself keeping time with the rocking of the boat. Each shift of the hull in the waves meant time had passed. Each back and forth added up, measuring minutes to hours.

Her heart ached physically, and her breathing confused itself. She didn't know if she was inhaling or exhaling. The world spun around while she tried her best to steady herself. But even Iliana, her kind hand outstretched in order to calm Cecelia, was strange. A strange girl meant to be her sister. It was too much for Cecelia.

She wanted Viktor and all that it entailed. His surliness. The irrevocable pain they had caused each other. His skin on hers. But more than anything, she wanted to hear him call her *Champion* one more time.

And then she heard it. It snapped her from her dizzy spell, infusing the moment with steadiness. Her eyes widened when she heard it again. She looked at Iliana, who also cocked her head to one side, attempting to hear the voice over the waves lapping at the wooden hull.

"Champion!" the voice called from outside.

Sally, the Golden Lord sends his youngest away just like the rest. To lands unknown but not to worry, I will unearth where she's going. He continues to buy up golden salt pearls to adorn another violently lavish piece of jewelry for the queen. She enjoys wearing as much as she can. He also spends quite a bit of time in his newly dug out garden, inspecting and tending—with great care, I add—Nubarian Bloomfire. I needn't remind you the oil of such flowers burns wicked hot, and can even burn in water.

Rangar Bruno Vylvan
Letter to Salmora Li'Adamou

Chapter Fifty-Four

VIKTOR MADE HIS WAY through the Champagne Palace, thanks to Sally. She allowed him to lean on her shoulder while she guided him through the maze-like hallways. At one point, he thought he heard splashing, but he allowed Sally to pull him out a side-door into the darkness.

The night was cool. A sea breeze blew strongly off the harbor, bringing with it a taste of salt. Viktor also tasted a bitterness that he chalked up to the poison. It possessed a disgusting aftertaste, one he never remembered experiencing before. Like bile, but worse. Like he had eaten pickled cabbage and fell asleep immediately after. Or dared to try the vinegary fish the Fair Folk favored.

But the night air revived him, and he could hold himself up. Sally filled the silence of the night with her voice, a silence Viktor desperately felt he wanted to experience. He didn't dare tell the woman to shut up, though. If it weren't for her, he might still lay in her office, dying slowly, not knowing his salvation may be on Danon's ship.

He could only hope she was right.

"The white woman should know what to do," she said to him, picking up her dress so it did not soak in a puddle of unassuming liquid. "The Golden Lord is said to have sent her to the Minor Continent, to Vocan and Rystra, to study healing. The Golden Dome is also ripe with healers, all educated at the Akademia of Healing in Phocan. No doubt she's had access to their teachings as well."

"Do you hope, or do you know?" Viktor said.

His stomach lurched slightly, and he stopped his movement. If he stood still and let the breeze ruffle through his hair, he could balance himself. He could feel, momentarily, like death was not waiting for him.

"I pay enough to know all the going-ons of the so-called royalty of this world. Something I learned a long time ago, as a street rat, is that knowing what those with power do with their time is useful."

Sally grabbed Viktor by the arm, sensing his loss of balance. He righted himself and tore his arm from her.

"I feel fine," he lied.

"You won't for long," she said. "This is the False Recovery, something Thoojun is well known for. You are doused with the poison and pass out. You awaken to feel slightly sick, but then fine. And then it strikes. You shut down quickly. It won't take long then."

"Great." Viktor said. "Perhaps less talking and more walking?"

"I was doused with it once when I was younger," Sally continued, ignoring Viktor's request. "But if Thoojun is common in Vocan, the antidote is more common. Found in nearly every household. Some people even use the poison as a drug, experiencing some sort of rush by rendezvousing with death before cheating it."

Viktor wasn't sure when Sally stopped talking. He stared ahead at the rocking boat, watching the black mass of it shift in the last of the sun's light. Orange plunged across the sky, swiftly followed by the most saturated of reds. It made Viktor thirsty. Lights within the ship softly glowed through the portholes. Somewhere inside, he'd find Cecelia. But his chest tightened, and he had to stop walking again. He had to wait for the dance with death to pause itself before continuing.

He realized then that the hands that held him were now on his right arm and not his left. And they did not feel as Sally's did, soft and enveloping, but cold and rigid.

Like claws.

He looked over his shoulder to see Sally standing in the shadows, a forlorn look on her face. Slightly terrified, slightly sad. He then looked to his right to see who now bore him toward Cecelia. Though he knew who it was.

Danica pulled him toward the ship, blood now splattered on her forehead and in her hair.

"What happened to you?" Viktor asked, finding it hard to catch his breath.

"I thought it prudent to look more the part," Danica said.

"The part of what?" Viktor said between breaths. "No need to stretch yourself to look sunstruck."

Danica glared at him and yanked hard on his arm. The force itself did not hurt him. His arms were nearly as big as the woman herself. But it sent a dizzying spell through his head. He needed to stop again, feeling like he might vomit, but Danica continued to pull him forward. Unrelenting. Unyielding.

"I will tell her you tried to hurt me," she said, a hideous smile teasing at her lips, "that you came upon me on the road and realized that dragging me back to the Prevailing Mother would redeem you, would allow you to live freely. But a stranger came by us at night and poisoned you. Beat me. We were left with no supplies and you with no wits. So I decided to bring us back to her. To bring you back for one more farewell."

"And why would you do that?" Viktor wanted to laugh but found he couldn't. His body revolted and refused to do as he told it.

"Because I'm gracious," Danica replied sharply. "Because I am kind."

"And worthy of her love?" Viktor said. "You will never be worthy, Danica, because you are a swine. You want pretty things and power. Something Cecelia is, and you are not."

He used all his power to control his body and turn towards her. With the last of his strength, he grabbed her by the throat and brought her close. His voice was giving way and he didn't know how much longer it would last, but he needed to tell Danica one last thing.

"And she is mine," he growled at her. "She will never be yours."

Danica looked as if she were about to cry. Her face contorted, convulsed, but she remained in control of it. She forced it to sneer, to go from ugly sad to ugly angry, and she shoved him away.

He stumbled, caught himself, and kept walking with his feet feeling heavy. It took great focus to pick them up, move them forward, and set them back down. He soon forgot what to do with his hands. His body was out of sync, out of motion, and he felt dizzy once again.

"Champion!" He called as loud as he could toward the ship.

It was not far now. Surely someone would hear him. Surely.

"Champion!" He called again, hoping Cecelia would hear it and know. She would know.

Danica's claws reached for him as his vision flipped. He felt himself tipping, top heavy, like his head weighed ten stone. Danica righted him, but barely.

"Champion!" He called one last time, knowing he wouldn't have enough to yell it again.

She appeared on the deck from the forecastle, arm around a lady in a translucent tarragon shroud. Iliana, Viktor realized, and Cecelia. His salvation.

He tried to speak, but his lips grew numb. Danica dragged him along again, pulling at his arm, though this time he was thankful. He did not know if his feet would obey his own will. Danica's seemed more than enough for the both of them.

"Your grace," Danica called sweetly to Cecelia, "your grace."

Cecelia yelled loudly at her brother, her words indiscernible from the breeze, who appeared from the Captain's Quarters. A commotion on deck told him the gangplank was being lowered and Danon himself jumped down to greet them. He took Viktor from Danica's arms and for one moment Viktor allowed himself to feel relief. Though Danon smelled of sweat and fish, it was better than Danica's stench of hatred.

Danica raced to Cecelia and wrapped her in her arms. Viktor felt his relief leave him and instead felt the icy fear of death approaching. He reached madly for Danon, afraid he'd fall despite Danon's sure grip on him.

"Iliana!" Danon yelled back to the white woman, "Iliana, quickly. Something is wrong."

"I fear he is poisoned," Danica's voice, now falsely scared, spoke out.

Viktor could no longer see her, or anything, as his vision was splotchy. He kept blinking, hoping it would clear itself, but it was useless.

"I know not of what," she said. "a stranger in the night robbed us and left us for dead. I'm afraid it may be too late. I tried to get us here as soon as I could."

"Your knowledge is little," Iliana's voice, soft like the sound of rain, said beside his ear.

A small hand grabbed his elbow and ran another through his hair, feeling his forehead.

"But I know what this is. We must get him inside now, Danon."

"As you say," Danon's voice came, and then the gentle tug on Viktor's arm.

He was half dragged and half carried up the plank. More hands wrapped around him, from who he didn't know. He heard the cadence of Danica's voice over and over again, followed by the annoyed sound of Iliana's. He didn't know what they spoke of, but he could tell Iliana wasn't pleased.

Once inside the forecastle, they eased him down into the same bed he had occupied before. The blankets were in disarray. Someone had recently occupied it. It smelled like Cecelia and Viktor inhaled deeply, only to cough.

"Blood," he heard Iliana say, "there's blood."

When Queen Jana the First Queen learned of the means of her mother's death, she grew enraged. Some say it was this rage that fueled her desire to seek the throne of Korith, and start the war that would eventually lead to the Age of Queens.

Court Historian Jepsuth Jeffrees
Age of Queens: A Complete Discussion

Chapter Fifty-Five

Danica stood between Cecelia and the forecastle. Cecelia had watched her brother and several sailors drag her husband into the room. Iliana offered her a nod of her head before shutting the door, leaving Cecelia in a state of unknown. Would he live?

"I am relieved to see you," Danica said, her arms still wrapped around Cecelia.

"I must admit," Cecelia said when she finally dragged her eyes from the door and momentarily pushed her fears away, "I worried something ill had befallen you after Mother Oora seized Kasier."

Danica pushed herself away from Cecelia, finally, and set her face serious.

"So you know?" she said. "You know what that witch did? She betrayed me!"

"I warned you," Cecelia said. "I did."

Danica dropped her eyes demurely, her hand reaching for Cecelia's own. "I know."

"Where did Viktor find you?" Cecelia then asked, not wishing to waste any more time.

"Oh, in the mountains," Danica said, suggesting vaguely with her head in the direction of the reaching peaks. "When he saw me, he beat me, and said he'd take me to Oora."

"To Oora?"

"Yes. That he'd redeem himself by presenting me to her like a prize. Only when we were robbed, and Viktor poisoned, did I think I had a chance. I knew I needed to find you, had heard there was a Panther ship in the harbor of Craigburna."

"But you brought Viktor, even after he hurt you?" Cecelia tried to piece together the puzzle Danica presented, but it wasn't fitting properly.

"Of course," Danica reached for her again, but Cecelia dodged her hand. "For you. I brought him."

Cecelia stepped back and studied the queen. Danica seemed desperate. There was a crazed look in her eye, like a dog about to attack. It unsettled Cecelia.

"Viktor searched for me," she said. "He would not have wasted time returning you to Mother Oora. He could not care less about the Fair Folk and their plight. Less so about remaining in their good graces."

Danica started to roll her eyes but thought better of it. Instead, she shifted her shoulders, transforming into a visage of empathy. She held her head high.

"Viktor is a liar, dear Cece. I hate to tell you. He always has been. I should have warned you sooner."

The way Danica shortened her name to emphasize their closeness grated on Cecelia's skin. It did not sound the same as when her brother said it. It felt heavy. And dangerous.

"Viktor has never lied to me," Cecelia said.

"He left you. Abandoned you at the palace."

"But he never lied," Cecelia spoke harshly.

Honesty, Cecelia decided, was much more important than Viktor's presence. She could love him wherever he was. She could not, however, love something that wasn't real.

Danica wilted a little, but perked herself back up almost immediately.

"I'm sorry," she said. "I shouldn't have supported the match. But my husband lied to me, too. We are both better off without them. You'll see. It is good they are dead."

"Viktor isn't dead," Cecelia said.

"He will be soon," Danica said, reaching once more for Cecelia, "but at least we have each other."

Cecelia leaned against the ship's banister, letting moonlight fall onto the crown of her head. The moons rose high in the sky. Their beams cast a cool, eerie glow across the ship's deck. It illuminated Danica and her clothes. They were ripped apart. and caked in dirt. Blood had trickled and dried from a wound on her forehead. Her hair was a wild mess, tangled in all directions.

But no other wounds. No other injuries.

They stood together in silence, letting the harbor noise fill the void for them. Cecelia felt no need to speak. Her husband was nearby. Her friend was no longer missing. But something still felt strange. The way Danica looked at her bothered Cecelia. It made her heart rise in her throat and her skin want to recoil. She kept reaching for Cecelia like a clingy child.

And Cecelia never favored children. Not really.

Time seemed to carry on forever. Like it no longer mattered. But then the forecastle door ripped open. Iliana, her face a dark shade of red, stomped across the deck toward them. Danica stepped closer to Cecelia, hand wrapped in hers.

"What is it?" Danica whispered. "A sorceress?"

Cecelia chuckled, but cut it short upon Iliana's arrival. "Danica, this is Iliana of Sunstone, wife of Prince Danon, heir apparent to the Panther throne. One day, she will be my queen."

Iliana had forgotten, or perhaps chose to forget, to pull her veil up over her hair. Her face, uncovered, twinkled in the moonlight where it bounced off the many flecks of mica. She squinted in the rays, though it did nothing to hide the fact that her eyes, once a sweet pink, now shone red.

"You." She pointed to Danica.

"What?" Danica leaned closer to Cecelia, trying to blend their bodies into one.

Iliana waited for nothing more. Two sailors stood nearby, and she suggested to Danica with her head, her motions full of queenly authority. The men pinned Danica to the banister. She couldn't move. Her hand was ripped from Cecelia's as Cecelia was jostled out of the way.

"What's going on?" Cecelia demanded.

Iliana reached into Danica's skirt, searching roughly for something. Her hand disappeared into a hidden pocket, only to emerge with an empty glass bottle.

"Ebu," Iliana spat at Danica.

"I'm afraid I don't speak barbarian," Danica replied.

"Translated, it would mean stupid fool. Idiot, if you like." Iliana replied. She offered the bottle to Cecelia, still staring at Danica.

"Smell it, your grace," she said. "And tell me what you sense."

Cecelia glanced at Danica, who appeared wide eyed and afraid. She gingerly took the bottle from Iliana and sniffed the mouth of the bottle. It smelled woodsy, somewhat, or like disturbed garden soil.

"Like a garden after it rains," Cecelia said. "A garden of the Lagos. Or of Inush. Not of Korith."

Iliana shook her head. "Like wormwood. And soil. And perhaps... vanilla?"

Cecelia slowly shook her head, amazed that Iliana could so easily name the scents that she herself could not.

"Thoojun," Iliana said then. "Poison."

They both slowly turned their heads to look at Danica. She did not fight her captors any longer. Instead, she bristled, her chest heaving, her face serious.

"It isn't mine," she said.

"Oh?"

"Perhaps the robbers on the trail put it there after attacking us?"

"Perhaps," Iliana agreed.

She took the bottle back from Cecelia and stared down at it. She rotated the smooth glass in her hands, thinking.

"It was potent. Very strongly made. He did not stand a chance."

Cecelia held her breath. For a moment, the rushing of blood filled her ears and she lost all other noise to the sound of her heartbreak. Danica wrenched herself free of the men and grabbed Cecelia around the shoulders.

"Oh dearest Cece," she whispered in her ear. "We have each other. At least we have each other."

Iliana still stood next to them, admiring the bottle. She twirled it and twirled it, throwing light off the surface onto the nearby mast and sails.

"If it weren't for me, he'd surely be dead." Iliana finally said. "Regardless..." her voice trailed away.

Cecelia tensed beneath Danica's arms. The quiet that grew felt like grave soil piling heavier and heavier upon them. The gulls called, but they suddenly seemed to be laughing. Danica refused to let go. Instead, she squeezed tighter, whispering hotly in Cecelia's ear.

"It's a lie. All lies."

Cecelia allowed her thoughts to linger for just a moment on her father. What he would say to her when it was all over. But she pulled back from these thoughts, knowing it didn't matter. She'd never face him. Never answer to him again.

The dagger kept in the small of her back slipped into her hands flawlessly. It slipped even smoother into the soft recesses of Danica's body. The warmth that ensconced Cecelia's hand told her she had struck true. Danica's body tensed and her breath hitched sharply. She leaned back, staring wildly at Cecelia, her eyes asking what she was unable to make her mouth say: why?

"You took too much," Cecelia whispered, lowering Danica to the ground.

Together, they sat in Danica's blood. Tears fell down both their faces, though Cecelia couldn't place where hers came from. From sadness. From fear. From angry attrition. She looked up at her brother's wife, wanting more comforting words to fall from Iliana's mouth. But they never came.

When Danica stopped moving, Cecelia gently laid her on the deck, smoothing her hair around her face. She stood and wiped the bloody blade on her dress. Crimson slashes decorated the grayed cotton.

"Viktor will be glad to know the lying beast has been dispatched." Iliana sighed. "Doubly pleased it was by your hand."

Cecelia froze halfway through returning the dagger to its hiding place. She looked at Iliana. "He will be alright?"

"I apologize, your grace," Iliana smiled. "Once I administered the antidote, Viktor was lucid and more than willing to tell me everything that happened."

"I must speak to him," Cecelia said.

Iliana nodded. "Of course, your grace. He is most eager to see you, too."

Empty is the crib,
Empty are the arms,
Of a mother whose child
disappeared with the night.

Tova Whispers, Korithian Bard
Gone, Child

You were right, of course. I should have remained with you. But you also underestimate me. As do they. And I will make them pay for it. With or without you.

Queen Jana the First Queen
Letter to Unknown Recipient

Chapter Fifty-Six

When Cecelia entered the room, she ran to Viktor and kissed him. Her dress was covered in blood and it impressed itself upon the blankets, like kisses.

"What's this?" he asked. "Are you hurt?"

She shook her head and kissed him again.

"It's Danica's," Danon's voice broke through their peace. "She bleeds out on my deck. Do they only teach you to kill in the Dry Vineyards, not dispose of the bodies?"

Cecelia frowned. "Don't be crass. She must be buried, as befits a queen."

Viktor watched his wife. Each muscle on her face moved meticulously to conceal how upset she was. Each one masked her sadness while giving way to her apparent joy at reaching him.

"You killed her?" He asked.

Cecelia swallowed hard and then shook her head. "I could not stop myself. It was instinctual. I've lost so much, Viktor."

She looked down at her hand, held palm up between them. Blood dyed it like body paint found amongst some of the more frivolous Fair Folk. It trembled slightly. She looked at him for assurance.

"It was either you or me," he offered her, "and I wouldn't have been as kind to grant her a swift death."

"She was my friend," Cecelia breathed.

"She was *my* queen," Viktor countered, "and I was meant to protect her. And Ramiro. A muddy job I did of that."

Cecelia nodded her head. "Perhaps the darkness father spoke of was me?" Cecelia tossed in Danon's direction.

The prince had made himself comfortable in a velvet lined chair. He poured a glass of water for himself, offering one to Cecelia, who declined it.

"Doubtful," he said, sipping at his drink.

"Agreed," Viktor threw in. "You might have strongly influenced the queen, but the Unis were already trouble long before you arrived at court. Ramiro was distracted by you, aye, but a better king would have known to keep his focus on his enemies."

"The Prevailing Mother, when she realized Danica's infatuation with you, used it to distract her." Danon said. "You were a pawn, dear sister."

"It's over," Viktor petted Cecelia's arm, his body insisting on finding any way to touch her.

"I know that it should be, but I feel that it's not," Cecelia said.

Viktor's stomach sank with his wife's words. He wanted to find some way, any way, to help her see that everything would be fine. It had taken him an entire journey across Korith to realize how much he needed her, and he didn't plan on spending any more time not showing it.

He dug in his pocket to produce his mother's ring, tucked safely within after retrieving it from the Shadow Child. He gently opened her hand and dropped the ring within, closing her fingers around it.

"You lost this," he said.

She stared at it and smiled. "I thought I'd never see it again."

"We can go anywhere, Champion," he told her. "Let's leave this all behind us."

Cecelia sighed and leaned against the headboard of the bed. She followed the shape of the gemstone with her fingertips. Viktor noted how bruised they were. How bloody and dirty they had become on her journey. And even though she had walked herself into the room, he noticed how badly she limped. She, too, had taken her fair share of beatings to find him.

She, too, deserved a rest.

"We will need a safe place to raise the baby," he whispered. "Where would you have us go?"

Her face seized then, crumbling from relaxed smoothness to broken panes of stored up hurt. The tears ran hot down her cheeks as she struggled to inhale. There was anger there, and fear. Many emotions wound their way down her face in the path left behind by her tears.

"There isn't a baby, Viktor," she said between shaky exhales, "I lost it. When the Unis attacked and I fell into the river."

"Oh," he said, but didn't mean to say. The word leaped from his mouth without forethought. He accepted the scowl he received from her, squeezing her hand tightly within his own. "I'm sorry I wasn't there, Champion. I'm sorry I left."

After several deep breaths, she gained control of her feelings and face once more. She shook her head. It was the only acceptance of his apology he would ever get. She turned to her brother.

"Father said I wouldn't return home," she said. "Perhaps it is best if I don't."

Danon wanted to argue, but Cecelia continued, staying his tongue.

"I do not belong there, Danon. I never have. I was tolerated because of father. But, as you say, father is dying. I will have little protection."

"*I* will protect you!" Danon said.

Cecelia offered him a sisterly smile. "Perhaps from detractors. From those wishing to slander me out of boredom. But from your own mother? From Elyeanor?"

Danon said nothing.

"I wouldn't ask it of you anyway, brother." Cecelia continued. "I have *my* champion. What more do I need?" She squeezed Viktor's hand with her own.

The forecastle door flew open. Wilyna entered, followed closely by Iliana. Within her arms was a bundle wrapped in blue damask.

"Wilyna," Danon stood. "A fine finder you turned out to be. Viktor arrived here already. Poisoned by the queen."

"As it was known," Wilyna said cryptically. "I was not looking for Viktor."

"But," Cecelia stuttered. "You said you would find him?"

Wilyna sighed, offering Cecelia her kindest smile. "I said I would find what you desire. I knew Viktor would return. I knew it would be so by Danica's hands. Instead, I set my search for a different prize."

She gestured with her hand for Iliana to step forward. The princess stooped before Cecelia and Viktor, displaying the sleeping face of a baby.

"Princess Jana," Viktor whispered.

"Oora will kill her if she remains in Korith," Wilyna said. She stared down at the baby, though her eyes weren't seeing Jana. They were seeing options. Possibilities. "Most certainly the Unis would make her disappear."

"What should we do?" Cecelia asked.

Wilyna frowned. "Perhaps she deserves to rule, to follow her father," she said, but then shrugged, "perhaps she doesn't."

"She's just a baby," Iliana said. "She deserves to grow!"

"I agree," Wilyna said seriously. "But who will take her?"

Iliana looked to Danon, who looked to Cecelia, who looked to Viktor. Viktor ran his hands through his hair and sighed. Cecelia masked her feelings too well and he could not gauge what it was she truly wanted. He looked at Jana, sleeping soundly, sweetly, and looked back at Cecelia.

"Would you trade a crown for a baby, champion?"

History
OF
THE KORITHIAN THRONE

Below lists the names of the monarchs of Korith, beginning with the conquering of the Great Continent by Thrash'gar.

THRASH'GAR THE DESTROYER — Conquered the Great Continent. Ruled 27 Years.

Ruled 18 Years. — **VRASH'GAR**, SON OF THRASH'GAR

NEIL'GAR, SON OF VRASH'GAR — Ruled 31 Years.

Ruled 11 Years. — **AN'TULL**, SON OF NEIL'GAR

OTIO'TULL, BROTHER OF AN'TULL — Ruled 22 Years.

Unified the warring people of Korith. Ruled 25 Years. — **MARGRESH THE BOLD**, SON OF OTIO'TULL

MARGOT THE WISE, SON OF MARGRESH — Established agreed boundaries between Kortih, Vrokar, Vrethage, and Stratsogar. Ruled 37 Years.

Ruled 13 Years. — **ALDER**, SON OF MARGOT

BERRON I, BROTHER OF ALDER — The War of Expatriation Begins. Fair Folk are forced from their homes and lands. Ruled 18 Years.

Ruled 29 Years. — **BERRON II**, SON OF BERRON I

BERRON III, SON OF BERRON II — The Treaty of the Lands is signed, ending the War of Expatriation. Ruled 31 Years.

Ruled 3 Years. — **VERMO**, SON OF BERRON III

AROS THE BLESSED, BROTHER OF VERMO — Survived the First Great Burning of the Palace by the Fair Folk. Ruled 42 Years.

Introduced Divine Kingship to the realm. Ruled 16 Years. — **BERRON THE SERENE**, SON OF AROS

PORCHI I, SON OF BERREN THE SERENE — Ruled 32 Years.

Ruled 22 Years. — **MORTI**, SON OF PORCHI I

CRONI, SON OF MORTI — Died in the Second Great Burning of the Palace. Ruled 8 Years.

Ruled 14 Years. — **PORCHI II**, BROTHER OF CRONI

HALLMAN, SON OF PORCHI II — Ruled 25 Years.

Ruled 18 Years.. — **KLARONCE**, SON OF HALLMAN

WYLDA, DAUGHTER OF KLARONCE — Maintained sole rule until forced to marry. Ruled 10 Years.

Timeline of Rulers

- **PERSIUM** — HUSBAND TO WYLDA. Ruled 19 Years.
- **VYCTORIA VARGA** — HUSBAND TO PERSIUM'S SON. Ruled 13 Years.
- **RYEN** — NEPHEW TO PERSIUM. Ruled 19 Years.
- **MARKOS** — SON OF RYEN. Ruled 19 Years.
- **LYANA** — NEICE OF MARKOS. Ruled 7 Years.
- **GARRIT** — COUSIN OF LYANA. Ruled 12 Years.
- **BORJIT** — SON OF GARRIT. Ruled 14 Years.
- **VONNAN** — SON OF BORJIT. Ruled 19 Years.
- **HALLYN** — SON OF VONNAN. Last of the sun worshippers. Overthrown by the rebellion of Maurkam I. Ruled 22 Years.
- **MAURKAM I** — COUSIN OF HALLYN. Accepted the worship of the Mother and Daughter for his victory over Hallyn. Ruled 30 Years.
- **JEPSUTH I** — SON OF MAURKAM I. Ruled 25 Years.
- **JEPSUTH II** — SON OF JEPSUTH I. Ruled 19 Years.
- **MAURKAM II** — SON OF JEPSUTH II. Ruled 23 Years.
- **BRESSA** — DAUGHTER OF MAURKAM II. Ruled 12 Years.
- **VROSHUN** — BROTHER OF BRESSA. Ruled 9 Years.
- **LEESUM** — SON OF VROSHUN. Ruled 17 Years.
- **LARIC I** — GRANDSON OF BRESSA. Ruled 16 Years.
- **LARIC THE LESSER** — SON OF LARIC I. Squandered his own purse. Allowing the palace to fall to near ruin. Ruled 18 Years.
- **LARIC THE GREATER** — BROTHER OF LARIC THE LESSER. Rebuilt the palace. Ruled 20 Years.
- **FREDRYC** — SON OF OF LARIC THE GREATER. Ruled 22 Years.
- **TALLON** — SON OF FREDRYC. The Start of the 13 Year Curse. Ruled 13 Years.
- **ORYIAN** — SON OF TALLON. Ruled 13 Years.
- **DORIAN** — SON OF ORYIAN. Ruled 13 Years.
- **MARIAN** — SON OF DORIAN. End of the 13 Years Curse. Ruled 22 Years.
- **NORIAN** — SON OF MARIAN. Overthrown by the rebellion of Romo. Ruled 10 Years.
- **ROMO** — DESCENDANT OF LARIC I. Ruled 22 Years.
- **RAMIRO** — SON OF ROMO. Present King.

Please enjoy an excerpt from
M.T. Solomon's next novel:

*WHISPERS
IN THE
DARK*

Book Two of the Dual Moons Duology.
Available October 2024
Copyright © 2023-24 M.T. Solomon

Chapter One

THE ARROW PIERCED THROUGH her mother like she were made of paper. The bolt, shot from an ordinary crossbow, was nothing special. Bits of steel and wood, both worked by the hands of man to form them into a weapon. A weapon that ripped the life from her mother so easily.

And why?

Lisi only watched her mother fall into her sister's arms for a second. It was long enough to see the way her face crumpled. To see how much blood she lost. How little life she had left. Her sister caught her gaze and only offered her a tight, curt nod. Nora did not like the way Lisi preferred to do things. But Nora couldn't do what Lisi could.

Lisi extended her hands and begged the earth to fuel her. No, not beg. She needn't beg anymore. Instead she commanded it to, and it happily obliged, offering her all it held within the roots of the great black pines and ancient shoulders of shale jutting from the surface of the forest floor. The nearby great stags, their hearts shivering in their chests as they wondered what man cold want with these hermits, gave what they could. Even the tiny tubers, still growing in the ground and not ready for pulling until first frost, offered up their power.

Lisi never wondered why the men of Korith did things. Not when she held such power.

She unleashed the pooled up energy, sending fire shooting across the clearing. It licked at the three soldiers on their horses, sending the animals into a chaotic fit. The men were thrown from their rides and struggled to stand in their heavy armor. Lisi jerked her head, and the nearby tree roots wrapped round them, pulling tighter the harder they struggled. One man was nearly blue when Lisi arrived to observe her work. She tutted at him.

"The Forest of Bruss is neutral," she said.

"Not...anymore," the man struggled to fight a root that cinched his throat closed. "Glynrok wants the high ground...to strike...that fake," but he couldn't continue, the roots wrapping around his mouth.

Lisi glanced back at her mother and Nora. Her sister held her mother in her lap, like their mother once held them when they were babies. Nora stroked her mother's hair and sang to her. Soothing her. Softening the pain that her mother surely felt. Easing her gently into the eternal darkness of the earth.

That was Nora's power. As potent as Lisi's, and certainly just as valuable.

"Pity," Lisi said, turning back to the men. "Your Glynrok thought he could have whatever he wants, including my mother's life."

She stepped on the writhing man's hand, tearing a silver messenger tube from his grip. It was thin and delicate silver. Craftsmanship that only came from the Fair Folk. Her father's people.

"And why would you Unis scum have this, I wonder?" She mused.

The soldier bared his teeth at the pain, his eyes dilating, his chest heaving. "To keep it safe." He barked between ragged breaths.

"From what?" Lisi asked.

"The wrong hands."

"Hmmm," she twirled the silver chain with her fingertips, the small messenger tube spinning like a medallion. It flickered in the burning light of the fire Lisi cast, still consumer the underbrush nearby. "It's in my hands now."

The roots slowly squeezed. She watched the life leave the soldiers. Quietly. Nora hated when Lisi made a show of it. Life is sacred, she always said, *all* life.

Lisi returned to her sister and mother. The pair folded over one another, a flower yet in bloom.

"How is she?" Lisi asked, though she already knew the answer.

"She's gone, Lis."

Nora stared at their mother's face, her thumb tracing the lines of her cheekbones. Nora's forehead was already coated in sweat. Her hand shook slightly while she held her mother tightly for just a little longer. It was another difference in their powers, the fatigue. For Lisi pulled from around her, but Nora had to pull from within.

A sacrifice Lisi was happy she didn't have to make. Power in the earth was eternal. It was ceaseless and—if used properly—powerful. But Nora needed strength of a different sort to perform her works. Her body was the source. And everyone knows how frail a body can be.

How weak.

How human.

ABOUT THE AUTHOR

M.T. Solomon is an Alaskan free-lance writer. She wrote her first book at the age of six. At eleven, she wrote and hand bound several children's books, most of which were riffs of Calvin & Hobbes with a female protagonist. She graduated from Portland State University in 2012. Besides writing, she also coaches high school volleyball and is a passionate supporter of equal opportunity for female athletes. She lives in Alaska with her husband, three sons, a poodle, and her beloved labradoodle Drogon-Francis.

https://www.themtsolomon.com

Join my newsletter to find out what I'm working on next, freebies, and an inside look at what a freelance writer does. Follow the link at my website to sign up!

Printed in the USA
CPSIA information can be obtained
at www.ICGtesting.com
LVHW041037300923
759629LV00005B/31

9 798987 942017